# A FLOOD OF BONES

## AN ALICIA FRIEND INVESTIGATION

### A. D, DAVIES

CRATER OF THE NORTH PUBLISHING

www.addavies.com

ISBN: 978-1-9999781-4-3

**Cover by Perie Wolford**

## NOVELS BY A. D. DAVIES

**Adam Park Thrillers:**

*The Dead and the Missing*

*A Desperate Paradise*

*The Shadows of Empty men*

*Night at the George Washington Diner*

*Master the Flame*

*Under the Long White Cloud*

**Alicia Friend Investigations:**

*His First His Second*

*In Black In White*

*With Courage With Fear*

*A Friend in Spirit*

*To Hide To Seek*

*A Flood of Bones*

**Standalone:**

*Three Years Dead*

*Rite to Justice*

*The Sublime Freedom*

**Lost Origins Novels (as Antony Davies):**

*Tomb of Aradia*

*The Reaper Seal*

**Co-Authored:**

*Project Return Fire* – with Joe Dinicola

*For all those who are hated without reason*

# PROLOGUE

THE FLOODS CAME at the end of summer, and the land gave up its secrets.

It is ancient land, rent from eons of change, of long-dead plates shifting atop molten rock during the planet's infancy. Through meteor strikes, the rise of mammals, and the extinction of millions of species—mammal and bird and plant—this ground has endured multiple ages of ice. Over millions of years, glaciers carved valleys and ripped open ancient caverns, and storm after storm lashed the rock and soil, closing many routes into the earth. Here, hidden from the eyes of all species who rose and fell throughout the ages, water and pressure birthed a spiderweb-like network of caves and underground rivers, seemingly endless to any creature unfortunate enough to venture inside. In the modern epoch, even with human technology, no one has been able to map them in their entirety.

All this violence and carnage—the wrath of nature and the ravage of time and space—shaped the land known to its current prime inhabitants as "God's Own Country," a term adopted even by those who do not believe in a creationist deity.

This is *Yorkshire*.

This is the English county where Emily Brontë penned *Wuthering Heights*, presenting Yorkshire's beauty and harshness to a hungry world; where it is said the limestone ravine of Gordale Scar served as inspiration for Tolkien's description of Helms Deep in *The Lord of the Rings*; the county where Bram Stoker once holidayed and found the ruins of an abbey in the coastal town of Whitby so eerie and foreboding that just seven years later, *Dracula* took the literary world by the throat and launched a thousand imitations.

Such a land has many tales to tell, tales of literature and of nature. But the hand of man dictates how much beauty is allowed to remain. From farming to mining, quarries to windmills, the carving of this land is no longer the preserve of ice sheets, of tectonic devastation, or rocks falling from the sky. And sometimes, this uneasy pairing—man and nature—will combine to bring about the unsealing of one of its stories.

When a farmer harvests his crops, leaving the ground flat and hard from a long, hot summer, it is difficult for rain to find anywhere to go. Water has no will of its own, always seeking the lowest point, obeying gravity and the angle of the surface on which it settles.

The land shall, of course, absorb some small measure. But now those who tend the land are no longer required to plough disused fields. They choose to leave those hard slabs alone, and in some cases are even incentivised to remove trees and bushes whose roots might otherwise aid in the absorption.

The water must go somewhere. That somewhere is always down.

Downstream.

Downriver.

Downtown.

Because wherever man springs up, wherever he mines or ploughs, towns and cities are built. And when the land can no longer contain the water, it is the industrial and domestic dwellings and roadways that swell and bear the brunt of the sheets of driving rain. As it comes up against walls and dead ends, hills of tarmac and more hardened land, it rises, driving people from their homes, proprietors from their businesses, and tourists to the closest route away from here.

Further up in the hills, the effects can be even more pronounced. Old cave systems, once inaccessible to humans, fill with rainwater. The rivers and streams deep beneath being unable to cope with the additional flow, their once-simple egress points act as dams. This pressure—for water is a heavy substance—pushes open the millennia-old rock and mud, and exposes the earth's wound for all to see.

In one instance, it is a wound filled with flesh and bone.

As those old remains spill into view, their secrets draw more eyes, more violence, and more wrath—and write another chapter in the haunting landscape of God's Own Country.

# PART I

# CHAPTER ONE

THE PRESS SCRIMMAGE at the field's boundary was subdued. Hardly a "scrimmage" at all, not like it had been when Detective Constable Knowles first hosted the gaggle of reporters on the edge of Basil Warner's farm.

When the initial scattering was identified as human bones, thought to have been from official graves disturbed by the subsiding floodwater, the press had acted like feral cats sniffing food for the first time in weeks. They'd been bored, Knowles supposed, covering the clean-up of one of several towns in the region, Moleford Bridge or Todmorden. Since they'd run out of angry debates over the responsibility of the government to "do something" about the increased flooding in recent years, they were eager to move on to something fresh. And human bones surfacing unexpectedly was as fresh as it got.

Figuratively speaking, of course.

Knowles kept quiet for the moment, preferring to let his boss, Detective Chief Inspector Watson, do the lion's share of talking to the dozen journalists. Watson clearly preferred it that way too.

"Right, right. More have been exposed, but we're keeping an open mind, just like when we started this." Watson was fifty-something and lean, sporting a thick but trim ginger moustache and a voice so deep and inflected with his native Scottish it made the ground shake when he let loose. Today was more of a ripple. "When we know more, we'll let you know."

"Is that your assessment alone, or does your detective constable concur?" someone asked—a lady from a regional paper whom Knowles recognised as a fair and balanced journalist, but whose name escaped him. "Apologies for asking a junior officer over his boss, but ... DC Knowles has been on this from the beginning."

Watson stood aside for Knowles to answer.

Knowles stepped forward. His walking boots and socks looked comical tucked into his suit trouser leg, but it was a necessity, as he had learned early on in this scut-work investigation. He was more concerned with how Watson would view his performance in front of the cameras than any result concerning the bones. "What DCI Watson says is correct. We don't know anything conclusive yet."

The same journalist followed up. "We've heard the new bones might be even older than last week's, but are well preserved. Is it likely they met the same fate as the earlier ones?"

"We don't know the fate of the earlier ones either." Knowles kept in mind the advice dished out to all detectives when dealing with the press—namely, keep it factual and simple. Don't lie, but don't offer more than you have to. "We need to spend the appropriate amount of time confirming they are human, dating when they went into the ground, and identifying them. Then we can ascertain where they came from."

"DC Knowles," said a new journalist, a man from a national newspaper, "are you now running this investigation?"

"Detective Inspector Beatrice Cross is still in charge," Watson said. "DC Knowles is a capable lad who solved a murder earlier this year, despite his relative inexperience. He answers directly to DI Cross, but I have every faith in him taking a more active role."

"Is his appointment to lead detective a sop to the liberals in the area?"

Knowles realised who this man was now: Philip Brent, journalist for *The Sentinal,* a far-right newspaper that made the *Daily Mail* and *The Sun* look positively centrist. His mention of a "sop to liberals" was because Knowles was a young black man, a face the West Yorkshire Police liked to get out there as often as possible. Knowles assumed if *The Sentinel* weren't having a go at his race, they'd be harassing Watson over Cross's gender.

"Do I strike you as the sort of berk who goes in for 'sops'?" Watson replied. "No, y'little shitweasel. DC Knowles is a capable officer, and he isn't in charge. He's spearheading it under the beady eyes of DI Cross. If there's evidence of a homicide, Knowles, Cross, and our fine forensics team will find it. If it's a disturbed graveyard, we'll return the remains to their hallowed ground. If it's a caving expedition gone wrong we'll be able to inform the families and give them a proper burial. *Et* bloody *cetera*. Now, if you'll excuse us—"

"One more please?" came a female voice from the back of the not-quite-a-scrimmage.

Watson sighed and pointed to the older lady who politely shouldered between Philip Brent and a cameraman from the BBC. With her grey hair loose and blowing in the light breeze and wearing a knitted blue cardigan, she did not call to mind a typical journalist. Her slightly narrow eyes and tan skin suggested a mix of Caucasian and southeast Asian heritage. If Watson noticed her lack of press credentials, he didn't let it show. "I don't think we've met."

"Maisie Jackson." The woman's kind tone came across as almost American, slightly inflected with a Yorkshire twang. "I've been doing a little research, and—"

"Have y'now?" Watson gave a small chuckle. "And y've chosen this moment to share your, eh, 'research' with a senior officer, his constable, and the press corps?"

"Your sarcasm is much appreciated, DCI Watson. But you might like to note that if the new bones are much older than the first ones, you may have found the burial ground for the Lainworth Ripper. Or even the Priest on the Hill murders."

Both Knowles and Watson stared. Watson risked a sideways glance at Knowles, and the young detective constable understood this moment could set the tone for the rest of his day. Screw up, and he'd be on Watson's shit-list, despite Watson being the one who prodded the woman to explain.

Knowles said, "We haven't discounted anything, Ms Jackson. If there are links to any unsolved crimes, you can be sure we'll exhaust every avenue. Thank you."

That signalled a close to proceedings and both detectives turned their backs.

Out of earshot, Watson asked, "Who or what is this Lainworth Ripper knob?"

Knowles opened his palms in a muted shrug. "I have no idea, sir."

Watson slapped him on the back. "Nicely handled, lad. Now let's get a look-see at these bones."


The original scattered bones surfaced a week ago. They were thought to have belonged to animals at first, until the farmer found a jawbone which was unmistakably human. Watson had immediately scrambled his top detectives and SOCOs—scene of crime officers—from Halifax, the closest town with a fully manned police station, and assigned DI Beatrice Cross as senior investigating officer. She brought Knowles in to give him a little more forensic experience, which he welcomed. But as soon as it became apparent the bones were at least fifty years old, one possibly upward of a hundred, the manpower was scaled right back. They retained the mobile lab which was parked at a local beauty spot, the only flat land around here that was high enough to be safe from a flash flood, and one SOCO in the form of Madeline Lawrence. Both Bea Cross and Madeline were local to the area. Cross actually lived in Moleford Bridge, fifteen minutes from Basil Warner's farm—the land on which the latest discovery was made. There had been rumours of a relationship between Cross and Madeline, although Knowles had no clue if they were true. And he didn't care.

He had been given the case to clean up. Ostensibly, it was an exercise in the type of work at which all coppers needed to excel if they were to advance—meticulous attention to detail, to cataloguing, to forensics, and drawing conclusions.

Madeline was testing the bones and what little preserved flesh remained, attempting to officially age them, but based on her years of experience she had already stated she was 99% certain that they had been interred for forty to sixty years. The only way they'd be older was if their original resting place had remained air-tight all this time.

"Y'didn't have t'deal with this knob before, did you?" Watson asked as they approached the scene.

Basil Warner, the elderly farmer, stood aside from the operation, watching.

"I haven't met Mr Warner in person," Knowles said. He had shadowed the SOCOs more than the DI.

"Mad." Watson paused in his step, the soggy ground creeping up over his black leather shoes, and waved to DI Cross and Madeline Lawrence.

The pair were fully suited in their white paper forensic suits to examine the remains, and an older constable named Vickers kept the rangy old farmer company. No one noticed Watson waving.

"Mad as in angry?" Knowles asked.

"Mad as in mad as a box of badgers." Watson advanced again, trying to catch Cross's eye. "Try not to speak to him unless y'have to. *Bea*."

They'd reached the opposite side of the makeshift boundary, wooden stakes with *Police Aware* tape strung between them in a twenty-foot-wide octagon. Bea Cross acknowledged her boss with a raise of the chin. She was wearing Wellington boots with her paper suit, which made it simple to tramp over to Watson and Knowles. "Guv. Malcolm."

"What's it look like?" Watson asked. "More graveyard debris?"

Cross shook her head. "We haven't established the first batch was from a graveyard."

"No, but that's what we think, isn't it?"

"I'll tell you what *we* think when there's some conclusive evidence." When Cross said "we" she looked pointedly at Knowles. "Detective Constable, would you care to join us?"

Knowles glanced at Watson, then up and down at Cross's outfit.

Cross lifted the tape. "Don't worry about the suit; there's no evidence to disturb. Just don't touch anything without gloves."

In truth, Knowles was more concerned about soiling his clothes than contaminating evidence, but he signed in and stepped into the cordon, snapping on his disposable gloves. He didn't want to stray too far from Watson before the DCI had a chance to formally dismiss him, but he viewed the new bones—femurs, ribs, and part of a skull—that Madeline was bagging up. This collection was only the first section uncovered. They'd get more people out to comb the freshly-revealed land now the river had pulled back to its banks.

"*Are* they older?" Watson asked.

"Yes," Cross said. "We think so. Could date back to the early twentieth century, possibly late nineteenth."

"What's the story, then? We going t'be turning up skeletons for the next couple o' months?"

Cross was as tall as Knowles, which gave her a couple of

inches on Watson. Her glance between the two took a downward turn. "DC Knowles can fill you in on the geography."

Knowles pointed up to the limestone-crusted hills a couple of miles north, a steep crop of land that Basil Warner counted as his own. "The river is a tributary for the Calder. Comes down from the Dales." He traced the thin line from the hills and along the fields at ground level, its bank skirting a hundred feet from the spot on which they stood. "It's usually thirty feet wide, but swamped this field and the next. The additional water started a couple of miles upriver, and surged down. It's this backlog into the River Calder that caused Moleford Bridge to flood."

"Aye," Watson said. "Fascinating. What's it got t'do with these?"

If he'd read Knowles's reports, he'd know this already, but Watson wanted to be seen as a hands-on guy in case the investigation turned up something major.

Which left Knowles reciting his report verbally. "Sir, we have bones from at least four bodies dating back approximately fifty years. We now have a collection of much older ones too, bringing it to six. The water is important because it gives us two possible sources: either the bodies were disturbed from a burial site nearby, on what is now Mr Warner's property, or they were placed in the ground further up in the Dales, and flowed down."

"So it *could* be cavers who disappeared," Watson said.

"We're looking into missing persons," Cross answered. "But we're having to requisition manual records from the 1960s to the 1980s."

Watson rolled his eyes. "Okay, whatever. Age 'em, bag 'em, and get the poor buggers back in the ground ASAP. If there's DNA on file, great; if not, stick it on the back burner and pick up your cases in Halifax. Keep me informed."

The DCI trod carefully back the way he had come, and Knowles made the mistake of making eye contact with Basil Warner. The farmer was about seventy years old, and from what

Knowles had seen, sported a near-permanent grey stubble on his sagging cheeks. His hair was a mystery, since he'd never taken off his flat cap in the company of the police officers.

"You!" the man called. "You in charge?"

"We've been over this," Cross replied loud enough for him to hear. "*I'm* in charge."

"When are you gonna be finished with all this? I got to get sorting things here."

Knowles felt mischievous taking a back seat here, but his DCI had all but instructed him to steer clear of the man. So while Basil Warner issued threats to start charging rent, Knowles busied himself by gazing back up to where the scrimmage had been held.

Most of the journalists were making their way back to the road, with only the BBC and Sky TV cameras and reporters remaining to sum up all the things they hadn't learned. But one person wasn't moving back to the road.

One person was disobeying the instructions given to all press.

And now DCI Watson was gone from the scene, this person clearly thought the rules didn't apply.

"Excuse me, ma'am," Knowles said. "I need to speak with that lady."

He told Cross where he was going, signed out of the scene, and intercepted the grey-haired lady with the faint Yorkshire-American accent. "Ms Jackson, you need to stay back, where the press were instructed."

Meeting him head-on, Maisie Jackson smiled. "Oh, I'm not press, young man. I'm just a local historian. And you might have fooled your boss and the newspaper folk, but you didn't fool me. You've never heard of the Lainworth Ripper or the Priest on the Hill, have you?"

# CHAPTER TWO

"FIVE MINUTES, Ms Jackson. Tell me what you think happened."

Maisie liked the handsome young detective far more than the Scottish grump who'd led the press briefing. Although not affiliated with any national or even regional publication, Maisie had recently started up a newsletter which she titled "The Moleford Bridge Journal" (available for free online or in limited ten-page prints, which she distributed via the library and a handful of friendly coffee shops) and ordered some business cards over the internet listing her profession as a journalist. She covered items of interest regarding both current and historical matters. And the bones revealed by the receding floodwaters last week were most certainly of interest.

Under the shade of Basil Warner's fading sycamore tree, Detective Constable Knowles spoke slowly and a little loudly. "We are of course interested in local knowledge, ma'am, and I'm happy to listen to what you have to say."

Maisie stiffened and squared her shoulders. "Detective Constable Knowles, I am fifty-two years young, I hold two degrees and a masters, and I live off a passive income generated by my textbooks which are still used in universities and higher education the world over. I am no amateur. Nor am I hard of hearing. Or were you under the impression I'm some sort of senile granny with a low IQ?"

His mouth opened slightly and his whole demeanour suggested he'd like to fold himself into his shoe. "Ma'am, I'm sorry, I—"

"I know I appear a tad older, but my brain is top notch. I take care to research my subjects thoroughly. And if the rumours about the age of these bones are correct, I may be able to help."

Knowles swallowed, glanced back at the two ladies in their forensic suits cataloguing the discovery and trampling all over the scene with the sort of confidence only possible when someone has made up their mind about the evidence already. Maisie waited patiently for him to come back to her.

He said, "Yes, ma'am, what is it you would like to pass on?"

"You need to start looking seriously at the possibility of these being related to a series of disappearances that occurred in the 1970s. For the older ones you found today, we had our own Jack the Ripper imitator, the Lainworth Ripper."

"Lainworth." Knowles frowned. "Is that anything to do with the Lainworth estate?"

"Lainworth was once a small village west of Moleford Bridge. Back in the 1920s, it was still seen as separate, but Moleford absorbed it as it grew. And yes, it's where the estate is now. One particular gentleman back then took offence to the number of Jews settling locally, and used a bayonet to slice up some of the more vulnerable members of that community. It was, in a way, awfully similar to a devil worshipper who was active in the 1800s."

"I never heard of this."

"You're young. And many of these stories are legends based

on vague facts. Plus, they don't tend to tout anti-Semitic murders in the tourist brochures." She smiled at Knowles's nod, glad he was listening. "The Lainworth Ripper was never caught, but the investigators at the time were torn between the notion of a shell-shocked war veteran unable to control his actions, and a homosexual."

Knowles looked confused. "A homosexual?"

"It was a different time, Detective. Anything 'different' was seen as suspicious, especially in the post-war years. They only found six bodies, but he could have murdered up to ten more. Those who were found were ... *displayed*, one might say. Much like the older satanist killings."

"The Priest on the Hill?" Knowles said.

"Oh, you've heard of him?"

"You mentioned it earlier."

"Ah." Maisie bit back her disappointment. "Yes, a member of the clergy in the 1800s went a bit loopy. Father Henry Pickersgill. Murdered in the name of Satan, hoping to bring about an end-of-days scenario or some such. I haven't conducted as much research into that chap as I'd like."

Knowles again gazed toward the women and the bones. "So you think these bones, the ones dating back a hundred years or so, might be the missing victims from the Lainworth Ripper?" Back to Maisie. "But the more recent bones…"

"Fifty, sixty years ago," Maisie said, "a lot of people went missing. All over the country, but there were occasional spikes in specific areas. They were largely seen as undesirables—prostitutes, migrants of colour, that sort of thing—so not much was done."

"That was local? To Moleford Bridge?"

"Moleford lost a few, yes, but it was mostly the surrounding larger towns. Halifax, Huddersfield, Todmorden. Maybe wider. There were voices asking questions, but none loudly enough to reach the people who needed to hear."

This time, Knowles faced Maisie. "Names?"

"I haven't been able to find names yet. You might have more success on that front. Right now, I'm only putting it to you as part of the cycle."

"What cycle?"

This was the aspect of her theory she didn't want to voice. The part she expected to relegate her back to senile-granny status. "If last week's discovery is not the result of a ruptured graveyard, but the uncovering of a killer's dumping ground from the 1970s, that's around fifty years ago."

"Right."

"The 1920s was another fifty years back."

"Yes." Knowles's frown returned.

"Guess when the Priest on the Hill killings ceased."

Knowles held still, thinking. "You're going to say the 1870s, aren't you?"

Maisie nodded slowly, keeping her lips a straight line rather than a grin.

Knowles stood there in silence for a long moment, watching her, appraising her. Then, keeping his expression and tone neutral, he said, "Thank you, Ms Jackson. We'll certainly look into it."

His outstretched arm directed her back the way they came, and Maisie let her mouth twist into a lemon-sour pout. In response, Knowles's face adopted a deeper neutrality, if such a thing were possible.

"Ma'am?"

"Fine. If you don't want my help, you're on your own." Maisie pulled her chunky cardigan tighter, hitched up her long flowing skirt, and tramped back out to the road.


DC Knowles returned to the octagon of bones, satisfied he'd handled the woman perfectly well. He would have to log her musings, as they did all tip-offs, but that could wait. Now it was time to get his hands dirty, learn from Madeline Lawrence the best cataloguing techniques, hopefully locate the origin of these lost souls, and return to normal as soon as possible.

Evading the watching farmer, he ducked under the tape to find DI Cross holding what looked like a skull, with Madeline matching several smaller bones to its base. He recognised the brown-stained lumps as vertebrae.

Knowles bent to view their work. "Ma'am?"

"Madeline thinks she's identified a few bones from the same body," Cross said.

"That bag." Madeline pointed with her foot at a swatch of coarse material inside an evidence bag on the trestle. "This skull was wrapped in it, and these little piggies..." She showed Knowles the two thumb-sized bones. "They were attached to the cloth. Bits of thread snagged them." She went back to angling them into the skull. "They're about the same age as the others we've located nearby, and the same colour as this poor sod."

She positioned the first vertebra and showed Cross, who agreed with a nod. Knowles followed Cross's eye and saw Madeline had fitted the bone snugly in the small depression at the base of the deceased's cranium. Then she placed the second vertebra end to end on the first. They appeared to match.

"We'll need to do more tests to be sure." Madeline took them away and started bagging and logging the two bones separately. "But I can say with some certainty that *these* vertebrae belong to *that* head. And the person was murdered."

"How can you be sure?" Knowles asked.

Madeline held up the second vertebra, stumpier than the first. "A clean cut through here. Meaning?"

Knowles gazed around at the other body parts, the remnants of several human beings dead long before he was ever born. "Poor sod was beheaded at some point."

Cross handed him the skull. "Shadow Madeline. Do as she says. If you have any questions, you know where I am."

Cross began retreating toward the edge of the scene, but Knowles called her back. "Ma'am." When she gave him her attention, he said, "Have you ever heard of the Lainworth Ripper?"

# CHAPTER THREE

IT WASN'T a statement commonly heard in the early hours of a CID squad room, but then the person who spoke wasn't a common detective.

"Don't mess with me; I've just finished my kickboxing class."

Alicia Friend was responding to Detective Sergeant Ball, who had listed a witness as a "tart" in a statement instead of a "sex worker," and insisted he wouldn't change it because it was how she "self-identified." He used the air quotes in a sarcastic fashion, which was impressive because air quotes indicated sarcasm in and of themselves. It got Alicia's brain in such a muddle that she needed some breathing room.

"I'm not sure my DI should be threatening to knock me out." Ball leaned back in his chair, hands behind his head.

Since returning from a stint in uniform, having demonstrated an ability to act professionally, look smart, and demonstrate diligence and empathy, he'd regressed into the emotionally stunted teenager-in-a-middle-aged-man's-body that he'd always been. He had crumbs in his beard and it wasn't even nine a.m.

"I wasn't threatening to knock you out," Alicia said. "I

wouldn't *threaten* that. I'd just do it. If I wanted to." She frowned. "To be clear, this isn't a threat."

Ball smirked. "Takes more to knock someone out than a sucker punch from a little lady."

"You'd know all about getting knocked out," DI Cleaver said from his desk three over from Ball.

"At least I can take a bit of physical." Ball rubbed his head where, a few years ago, he had been literally knocked unconscious while following a lead to warn Alicia of danger she might be in. Since such a blow was a far more serious injury than TV and movies like to portray, he'd wrangled three weeks off, a compensation payment, and the eternal respect of his colleagues—eternal, that was, until they got sick of him bragging about it. Now it was a source of amusement, something they brought up to berate him. So not very eternal after all.

Alicia pointed to the manila folder on Ball's desk, where he had put the printed report. "Two things. First, change the damn statement so the wording won't get us eviscerated by a first-year lawyer if this ever goes to court. Second, call me a 'little lady' again, and maybe we'll test how tough an out-of-shape old school copper is against *moi*—the new generation."

Ball placed his hands on his desk and called to DI Cleaver, "Hey, I think my supervisor is bullying me over my weight and age. Can I put in a complaint?"

"Sure. File it right here." Without looking up from his keyboard, Cleaver fired Ball his middle finger.

DC Ndlove, at her desk across from Cleaver, giggled into her fist, her eyes also on the screen. She and Cleaver were prepping for court, so both were keen to avoid distraction.

"Fine." Ball's grin cracked. "I see I'm going to have to take it to the top."

As he gathered his jacket to head into DCI Murphy's office, ostensibly joking but more likely half-hoping the Sheerton station's CID chief would overturn Alicia's decision on the "tart" reference (he wouldn't), Donald Murphy himself appeared at the door.

"Alicia, I need a word," Murphy said. He noticed Ball. "Do you need something?"

"No, he doesn't." Alicia approached Murphy.

Ball raised a finger. "Actually—"

"When I get back from the boss's torture chamber, we'll arm wrestle for the tart, okay?"

"Tart?" Murphy said.

"Long story." Alicia made for the office.

"Not that way." Murphy hooked his thumb toward the squad room's exit. "Video conference. They require your expert input."

"*My* expert input?" Alicia fluttered her eyes at all those present. "Why, you'll make me blush, boss. Who's 'they'?"

Ball sat back down and opened his folder, and Alicia guessed she'd return to a clean statement, jury-fresh and judge-ready.

"Calderdale," Murphy answered, holding the door for her. "Chap you helped out in that Harris Manor murder—Knowles, is it? He requested a consult and his DCI approved it. Let's see what they've got."


The video conference room had cost tens of thousands of taxpayer money, a bill Murphy happily signed off on. Even the Home Office had encouraged as many forces as possible to accommodate such facilities due to the savings they might imbue through cutting down on the need to travel for meetings and conferences, mainly for detective chief inspectors like him—and above, of course. But the travel budget for management had only reduced by a few percent, and the room went unused most of the time.

The desks were laid out in a semi-circle facing a concave bank of four screens and four cameras. On the other end, a near-identical setup would project Alicia and Murphy onto the four screens, giving an uncanny impression of actually facing the people with whom they were meeting. At the moment, the trio visible on the screen conversed silently, pointing at boxes on their desks, which mirrored the boxes here.

Murphy pressed a button and the symbol of a mic with a red line through it flipped to a mic on its own, coloured green. "Hello, Halifax. Are we online?"

The ginger-haired DCI Watson, with whom Murphy had enjoyed several full-throated and opinionated debates over whisky at various conferences through the years, looked up and commenced speaking. No sound came out. Murphy cupped a hand to his ear and mouthed, "You're on mute," and pointed at the same box he'd pressed.

Murphy sat, stretching his long legs out to where the camera's field of vision wouldn't reach.

Alicia settled next to him. "Oh, hi, Malcolm, nice to see you."

The young black detective to the left of Watson raised a hand and mouthed a greeting. Still silent.

Murphy cupped his ear again, and this time lifted his box to show them the speaker setting. The woman on Watson's right appeared to get it, and pressed the button. A crackling sounded and the screen went blank.

"Christ," Murphy said.

"Can you hear us?" came the woman's voice. "We can hear you."

"Hear but not see," Alicia said. "Try hitting it with your shoe."

The screen flickered to life and everyone settled down.

"Wow," Alicia said. "The shoe thing almost never works."

"It wasn't the shoe," Watson said with typical bluntness. "Are we ready?"

"I think so, Gordon," Murphy said.

"Good, good. Hate these damn things." Watson waved his

hand, indicating the conference suite. "Time it takes to set up, we could've driven over."

"Thanks for hosting the call," DI Cross said. "I think we met a couple of years ago? You were a DI then."

Murphy racked his brain. He was only in his fifties but was already forgetting faces. Or perhaps he just didn't care to remember every irrelevant detail the way he used to. He gambled. "You were seconded to Leeds?"

Cross nodded and appeared satisfied.

"Introductions?" Murphy said.

They went briefly round the room, ending with Knowles, who indicated he knew Alicia from earlier in the year.

"Good to see you again." Alicia composed herself in a way Murphy knew she found hard: subdued and professional. It only had a limited shelf life, though, so he hoped to make this quick.

"You know about the bodies we've been pulling out of the dirt up here?" Watson said.

Murphy nodded. "A couple of grave sites disturbed by the floods, wasn't it?"

"DI Cross, why don't you do the background?"

Cross placed her hands flat on the desk and faced Murphy. "Three weeks ago, Storm Carly arrived, and the Calder Valley and surrounding towns suffered their worst flooding in ten years."

Murphy wasn't keen on the current trend of the British meteorological officials naming every storm that happened to make landfall in the UK. He wasn't sure if it annoyed him that the UK population needed such theatre to make them take note of the dangers, or if it was because the next storm would be named Donald.

"Six months' worth of rain fell in less than forty-eight hours," Cross said. "Much of it soaked into the ground, and experts have hypothesised several underground rivers must have reached capacity. They broke through the soil and rock that served as dams for years, and we're springing leaks all over the Dales. That started a chain reaction, whereby the tributaries to the River Calder filled and broke their banks, which in turn sent the Calder into overflow. My town, Moleford Bridge, was badly affected, but the low-lying farms were fully submerged."

"You've tracked their path from up in the Dales?" Alicia asked.

"Approximately," Knowles said.

"Only approximately?" Murphy said.

DCI Watson rubbed his thumb and forefinger together. "Not much in the way of money. We'd need teams on top of teams, helicopters with ground-penetrating radar—all for a bunch of bones without a homicide we can prosecute."

Both Knowles and Cross turned their heads quickly to their boss, then back to the cameras. Murphy guessed some unspoken agreement had been broken. One of the reasons Watson would be unlikely to ascend higher than detective chief inspector was his inability to keep his thoughts within the confines of his head. When he had a strong opinion about something, he had little time for tact. Which was surprising given what Murphy knew about his preference for rough sex with rougher men—an activity Watson preferred to keep to himself.

"It's one reason we wanted an expert to take a quick look," Knowles said. "Someone with a track record in identifying serial killers and their motives."

Alicia sat forward, fingers interlinked, her feet crossed and tapping beneath the chair. "Why would you suspect a serial killer?"

Knowles paused, with a glance to Cross. The DI indicated for Knowles to run with it.

"We moved back up the first field, the one where we found the bones we think are around a hundred years old, and located more. Eight separate people, at least, but of course there are no complete skeletons. What we did find demonstrated trauma not found in nature. They were cut. Intentionally."

Watson folded his arms but clamped his mouth shut.

Knowles barely stuttered at the gesture. "The others, the ones we thought were fifty or sixty years old, came from the same direction. But, being less decayed, they were heavier so didn't scatter as far. They also retained some sinew and ligaments, so the arms and a couple of ribcages got caught on plants and rocks. Once we knew the direction, it was simple enough to stumble across them. We gathered enough to suggest a similar degree of trauma—cuts and blunt force—although we can't tell if any of it was post- or pre-mortem."

"Eating right into my SOCO budget, I can tell ya." Watson stared at Murphy as if hoping for moral support.

Murphy remained non-committal; he understood the financial problems, but with this many unclaimed bodies, they had a duty to investigate fully.

Knowles waited to be sure the pair were done, then continued. "We also located items we wouldn't normally expect to find in an unploughed farmer's field."

"But the field *was* ploughed nine months ago," Cross added.

"Meaning anything found there was deposited recently," Alicia said. "Sure, I'm following."

"These things," Knowles said, "included clothing, bits of manmade fibres, the metal of buttons and zips, items of jewellery. More small bones too, and some personal effects like wallets and purses—empty of cash but not photographs. They've helped ID a few of the bodies—or at least the IDs are assumed at this point."

"DNA," Watson said. No need to elaborate. DNA testing was costly and time-consuming.

"Malcolm, your storytelling skills are excellent," Alicia said sweetly. "But if you wouldn't mind ever so much getting to the juicy bit?" She clamped a hand over Murphy's forearm. "Because there's a juicy bit coming up, I can feel it."

Knowles smiled for the first time, but quickly suppressed it when both Cross and Watson glanced his way. "We were correct about the age of the older bones. Victims of a man who was never caught, operating from around 1920 through 1925. Several Jewish residents went missing or were found murdered, presumably by the same man, known locally as the Lainworth Ripper. The more recent ones, which we estimated to be from the 1970s, were correct too."

"Meaning little chance of the culprit being alive," Murphy said.

"Exactly." Watson stared out from the screen..

"But," Cross said, firmly but politely, "one of the victims we IDed was Shona Maynard. An eighteen-year-old sex worker reported missing in 1983."

Knowles read from an expensive-looking notebook, certainly not police issue. "Dana Reynolds, 1978; Valerie Msuba, 1975; Virgil Baines, 1974." He closed the book with a snap. "All black. First or second generation immigrants."

"There was a man in that list," Alicia said.

"Yes." Knowles threaded his fingers together, flat on the desk. "The ages appear to span a wider range than a typical serial killer would typically target."

Alicia adopted a more serious tone. "It's true, a serial killer will often hunt a specific 'type'—blondes or redheads or black women or white homosexual men under thirty. But that's too narrow an assessment, and profiling the victim rarely gets us anywhere. Your guy looks organised, no need to show off, none of that clichéd wants-to-be-caught nonsense. Concealed the bodies for a long, long time. The bones from the twenties are interesting, though. Any evidence linking them to the same ground as the more recent ones?"

"Water washed away most but we're comparing the samples, hoping they absorbed some of the same minerals or contaminants, or something that points to a location."

"Hmm." Alicia thought for a moment. "1920 through to 1983. That's sixty-three years. If a person was killing back in the twenties, aged, say, as young as sixteen, he'd be seventy-nine in 1983. It's conceivable, if he remained fit and had a quick method of subduing the victim."

"And he'd be a hundred and fourteen years old today," Watson said. "We did the sums."

"No one to prosecute," Murphy said. "I'm not sure how we can help."

The trio in Halifax remained silent so long, Murphy wondered if they'd frozen.

"It's tricky," Cross said.

"It's stupid." Watson looked at Knowles. "It's your show, kid. Come on, we're exhaustin' every avenue on behalf of the victims, aren't we?"

Knowles appeared unfazed. Perhaps he was used to Watson's acerbic nature, or maybe he just felt he deserved it. "In 1877, a priest named Henry Pickersgill was found to be the culprit in at least forty killings. From what we can tell, he spent over ten years snatching people and murdering them. He laid their bodies in a crypt beneath his church where his flock worshipped. It became known as the Priest on the Hill killings. Not sure why— his church was in the valley." Knowles spoke like he was in court.

Murphy thought the DC's tone was a benefit in situations like this, but time was pressing. "I hate to hurry you along, but Alicia is very busy. Why is her expert input required?"

"Theoretically…" Knowles swallowed and fired another of those tentative glances that Murphy thought signalled a conflict played out before they even requested this meeting.

Cross said, "DC Knowles has let a local crank get to him, and is buying into a theory that—"

"Ma'am, I'm sorry to interrupt," Knowles said. "I'm *not* buying into it. I just want to … eliminate the possibility."

"Fine." Cross looked directly at Alicia, a creepy effect of the shaped facility. "DI Friend, in your expert opinion, is it possible that a cult of devil worshippers dating back to the nineteenth century could be working in fifty-year cycles?"

"Fifty-year cycles?" Alicia's eyebrows bobbed. "Ah, now I understand."

"Understand what?" Murphy asked.

"1870s, 1920s, 1970s," Knowles said. "Every fifty years. And we're approaching 2020."

Watson opened his arms and grinned, spreading his ginger moustache. "So how about it, DI Friend? Are we needing t'go looking for a cult that might be about to start killing again? Or is DC Knowles as crackers as the weirdo who made up this shit?"

Alicia didn't have nearly enough information for an adequate analysis, but that didn't stop her scolding Watson for using such aggressive terminology. "People aren't mad—or crazy or insane—simply because a grouchy DCI disagrees with their far-out ideas," Alicia told him. "They're mad, crazy, or insane because their brains aren't wired correctly. A 'mental breakdown' is actually a psychotic break in which someone's mind switches to a reality alien from the normative perception. Such psychotic breaks take the form of suicide, depression, or outward aggression. Sometimes they take the form of believing a type of person needs removing from the planet for the good of the rest of us."

"Y'make the Priest on the Hill sound like a victim," Watson said.

"I doubt he was as insane as you're imagining. I have had personal contact with many of the people we term 'serial killers,' and most were as sane as you or I. A minor tweak of their brain wiring, a short circuit in the empathy department. The Century Killer, for example." Alicia had spent time in therapy herself in recent years, and managed to distance herself from the emotions she used to feel at just the mention of his name—his real one or the nickname by which most referred to him years after he was caught. "Richard Hague just lacked any sense of empathy. Every other emotion was completely intact, except when it came to his own needs. He was a narcissist, which means everything he wanted took precedence over everything else, including his victims' right to life."

Watson dead-eyed her and simply said, "Yawn."

Alicia half-smiled. She liked having someone to work her magic on. "Brainwashing. For some group to hide this well for this long, breeding killers to prey on the undesirables of the day, they'd need to be organised and precise."

"Can you back up a moment?" Cross said. "What do you mean by 'undesirables of the day'?"

"Black immigrants," Alicia said. "They were non-too-popular in the seventies and eighties. Jews in the pre-Hitler years were still widely hated. And I don't know the profiles of the Priest on the Hill killings, but I expect you will find they were poor, perhaps diseased, or just outsiders passing through."

"Meaning it's organised."

Watson sighed and put his face in his hands. "I thought we were doing this to rule out crackpot ideas."

"May I have a moment?" Murphy asked.

"Sure." Watson spread his hands. "We've got this room all day if needed."

Murphy hit the mute button and turned to Alicia. "We're a little pressed for time, so I need to be sure—are you serious?"

While Alicia enjoyed having a boss whom she also considered a friend, it had its drawbacks—such as how he could see through her when she was being insincere. And he was half-right now. "Donny, it's not a cult of people cycling round on some celestial calendar. It's not devil worshippers. The fifty-year cycle could be a coincidence, or it could be people copycatting earlier killings. If the Priest on the Hill and the Lainworth Ripper are public record, it's possible one inspired the other. Or a murderer happened across the gravesite of the Lainworth guy, and thought, *Ooh, I can get away with murder too.*"

"So you're just winding up a senior DCI and an accomplished DI in the Calderdale force for the fun of it?"

Alicia shrugged. "Pretty much. Plus the ginger guy is being really mean to my friend Malcolm, so—"

"Y'know, we can still hear you." Watson sat with his arms folded again, his head tilted.

Alicia checked; the mic symbol in the corner of the screen was still green. Cross's face remained stiff, her smile buried, while Knowles blinked.

"Murphy," Alicia said, "did you do that on purpose?"

Murphy's face glowed red. "Sorry, Gordon. Alicia is … she has a unique perspective on life as a police officer." This time he muted it properly. "Right…"

"Don't worry, he's only at the First Stage of Alicia. It takes five, remember? When I've worked on him—"

"You're not going to work on DCI Watson, or DI Cross."

"She likes me already." She reached for the unmute button, but Murphy held up a hand.

"Doesn't matter." Murphy took a breath and rubbed his moustache, a far trimmer style than Watson's. "You have a case-load here. You don't work for the SCA anymore. We can't be loaning you out willy-nilly."

"Donny, ignore the cult thing for a minute. If the bones from the seventies and eighties are all murder victims, concealed for decades, and the killer was never caught, then this is a bigger case than anything we've seen since Hindley and Brady. Probably worse than Peter Suttcliffe or Harold Shipman."

"You can't choose your investigations, Alicia. Just because this might be a glamorous cold case doesn't mean people here in Leeds can pick up the slack left by your absence."

"Don't you care about giving the families closure?"

"I care about the arson case on Methley Grove. I care about the four muggings that appear to be linked in—"

"We can hear you again," Knowles said.

Watson scowled. "Aw, you had to spoil it. I was enjoying that."

Murphy did a double take from the speaker box to Alicia and back again, his face reddening once more. "Damn it, Alicia."

Alicia grinned, displaying her dimples to full effect.

"DCI Murphy." Cross affected that confident, stilted posture again—hands flat, shoulders square. "I would have hoped since we're part of the same force, some more cooperation would be forthcoming. Your detective has a history of solving complex serial crimes, and if she is correct in thinking the seventies' killer or killers were inspired by the Lainworth Ripper, it'll be useful to have her on board."

"Her caseload here…" Murphy struggled to wade through the request without sounding either heartless or territorial.

"We can send over cover," Cross said.

"We can?" Another glare from Watson that lasted a second or so before he faced front. "Aye, okay. We'll do swapsies. DI Shah is competent, a quick leaner. He'll sub for your psychological analyst. Shall we say a week?"

"Two days," Murphy said.

"Three," Alicia said.

Murphy groaned. "I don't have much choice, do I?"

Alicia stood. "You most certainly do not. Gents. Lady. I have some personal things to organise first, but I'll see you first thing."

# CHAPTER FOUR

ALTHOUGH ALICIA'S mum loved having Stacey for the night, her heckles had started to rise whenever Alicia requested a sleepover due to work commitments. Dorothy, or "the Dot-Bot," as Alicia affectionately referred to her mum, knew nothing of Stacey's biological father, and the man's absence gave her a stick to wave at Alicia regarding childcare and the absence of romance in Alicia's life. So while the Dot-Bot objected to the arrangement on philosophical grounds, she never turned down the opportunity to spoil her granddaughter for a whole evening.

Having arranged for her mum to collect Stacey the next morning at seven to get her to and from the nursery, Alicia was able to pick up the girl from her granddad's this evening and head home to her two-bedroom terraced house in Chapel Allerton, one of the nicer suburbs of Leeds. It was just big enough for the pair of them, with a neat little garden that wasn't particularly neat at the moment.

Alicia's daughter had originally come as a surprise to her—a shock, if she was honest—and although the trouble that followed had abated, she remained on constant alert. Almost three years old, Stacey had a grownup half-sister, now calling herself *Kate*, not Kat*ie*, but the pair had never met in person.

Kate had spent time in a mental health facility, having checked herself in at Alicia's urging. Now released under the care of Dr Rasmus, she communicated with Alicia via letter. Not email; Alicia had insisted on that. Email was too immediate, and could create the illusion of a conversation. Initially, Kate had been keen to meet Stacey, but Alicia wanted to wait until Kate was well enough to live on her own. Then, oddly, when Alicia was ready to take that step, with Kate holding down a barista job, it was Kate who said no.

She'd told Alicia they should wait until she was discharged from Dr Rasmus's care. Or at least until she had the courage to switch off the machines keeping her father alive.

Kate's father, and Stacey's: the Century Killer.

Alicia shuddered as she removed her clothes in front of the mirror. Of late, she'd grown somewhat vain. A fitness kick she commenced a year earlier and maintained through various sports had left her with less body fat than pre-baby, and she felt much better—lighter on her feet, stronger in general. All part of a raft of measures to be the best mum she could. No point being a cool detective if you have diabetes or can't run faster than the bad guys.

Stacey giggled on the bed, holding a Paw Patrol toy in the air and whizzing it around with sound effects combining an engine and the yipping of a pup. Her favourite character was one of only two girl dogs in the cadre of canines that appeared to serve some high-tech master in the assuaging of disasters in a very accident-prone small town, but she was currently playing with the small orange vehicle belonging to the dog that talked with a faintly Yorkshire accent—in the British-dubbed version, anyway, as opposed to the original Canadian.

"What do you think?" Alicia held a small black dress to her chest. "Too much?"

Stacey looked at her and frowned. "See your bum, Mummy."

Alicia checked her panties and pulled them straight. "Better?"

"Wear the pink one."

"I don't have a pink dress."

"Pink pants." With those two words, Stacey caved in on herself with laughter, lost to the comedic image of pink undergarments.

"Thanks, you're a big help." Alicia returned the dress to the hanger and selected a sparkly top and low-slung jeans instead. "Less formal. Much better."

"Eethor coming?" Stacey asked between hiccups of laughter.

"Yes, he'll be here at six." Alicia lay the jeans and top on her bed next to clean underwear—*not* the pink ones—and socks. "Grandpops says you had a long nap."

Stacey nodded enthusiastically. "Long sleep."

"Where shall we take Iothor, then?"

Alicia's phone made a croaking noise to say a text had arrived from her best friend Roberta. She checked it, not hearing Stacey's reply.

---

Third date. Hope you shaved your legs ;-)

---

Iothor—whose name was difficult for most adults to pronounce, and even more so for a nursery-age child—was a schoolteacher Alicia had met earlier this year. At the same time she'd met DC Knowles, actually. Iothor worked with Robbie at a Leeds high school. His Icelandic charm and rugged looks had given Alicia all sorts of flutters at the time, but she had resisted Roberta's offer to set them up for weeks. Between establishing a routine with Stacey, settling into her new house, and the pressure of her senior role at work, it hadn't seemed like the right time. Finally, a fortnight ago, Robbie had persuaded her to make time, and Alicia ventured out with the big Viking—then again the following week. Both dates had been adults only. Tonight he'd be hanging out with Stacey in more than passing for the first time.

Alicia texted back:

It's the 21st century. No social pressure. Get with the times.

Robbie replied immediately:

Meaning your legs are a prickly mess?

Alicia glanced at Stacey, who was gazing up at her expectantly. Plainly, the girl had made up her mind about dinner, although it'd be way past her usual bedtime.

Feeling a bit naughty, Alicia texted:

Forget my legs, you should see my lady garden.

She giggled, and Stacey imitated her.

"So what did we decide?" Alicia asked.

"Pink."

"I meant dinner."

"Oh. Pizza."

"Right." Alicia didn't object. They had a far healthier home life than most people she knew, and pizza was the only junk food Stacey went for. She rejected burgers and hot dogs outright; she wasn't keen on meat at all, so the house was largely a vegetarian zone, if only by default rather than intent. "Pizza it is."

Alicia's phone croaked again, Robbie's reply to Alicia's lady garden imagery being a green face vomiting.

"About right." Alicia tossed the phone on her bed and carried Stacey to her room.

She surrounded her daughter with Paw Patrol pups and told her one of the girls from Frozen was stuck in the desert (her bed), then retreated outside and closed the toddler gate on both Stacey's door and the top of the stairs. As she listened to Stacey mounting a rescue operation, Alicia pondered if taking her on the date was a good idea.

The *third* date.

Stacey's regular bedtime was at seven p.m., which meant she would be a true pain in the arse by half-past eight, probably throwing a spectacular tantrum wrought by exhaustion and frustration. But it meant Alicia would have an excuse not to bend to the socially anticipated third-date behaviour of shagging her boyfriend for the first time.

*Was* Iothor Maksson her boyfriend?

Robbie's texts had set her mind wandering.

No, she had no intention of sleeping with Iothor tonight. If he was going to be the guy to rejuvenate her ailing love life, he'd understand why she wouldn't be sleeping with him, without her spelling it out.

And yet.

Alicia was nothing if not impulsive, and while that had gotten her in trouble in the past—in more ways than getting knocked up by a man she had completely misread—she still prepared for every eventuality. So, despite having zero intention of exposing her legs to Iothor this evening, she lined up her shaving foam and barely-used razor on the bath shelf next to her gel and shampoo, then climbed in the shower to prepare.

Alicia was proven correct about her daughter's sleep-deprived behaviour, but the majority of the evening went well. Iothor had only met Stacey twice, both times leaving her in Robbie's capable hands as he took her mother away (Alicia hadn't said anything to her own mother about the dates yet), so they were familiar with one another if not quite comfortable. A large man with a blond beard and broad shoulders, Iothor cut an intimidating figure for most, but to Stacey he seemed to be a large toy. She sat on his lap while they waited for a table at the Pizza Hut restaurant, poking and prodding him as if she expected him to beep or emit light from his eyes. Once they were seated she chattered inanely about the plot of some TV show she'd watched—probably *Paw Patrol*—in a way that suggested Iothor was equally enamoured with it. He played along.

The grownups spoke in code about Alicia's work, replacing "bodies" with "potatoes" that had surfaced after the flood, and how they were seeking to inform the owners where they could be collected so the spuds could be buried correctly. She could not conceal the fact that it was going to take her away for a few days —which she needed to tell Stacey about anyway—but she hoped to get back to Leeds every evening to put Stacey down. And if she did things right, it wouldn't take long to determine the bones' origins and to alleviate any concerns of a cult resurfacing.

After they ate, Stacey threw a pizza crust on the floor. Iothor picked it up. "Ah, oops." Stacey grinned and dropped a second.

"Stacey," Alicia said sternly.

Stacey met her mum's eye, a third crust held aloft. Iothor froze, uncertain what to do. And Stacey flung the crust at him. It hit him in the face, and he gasped, held one hand to his face.

"Ow, ow, ow," he said, hamming it up.

Stacey's eyes bulged and her mouth dropped open. "Oh, oh, sorry, sorry!"

Iothor sat on the floor, rubbing his eye and pretending to be seriously hurt. Alicia let him carry on, since it seemed to be piquing a sense of fear in Stacey. She'd hurt someone, and she felt bad about it.

*Oh, thank God for that.*

Nurture was winning over nature.

Empathy.

But as Alicia sat congratulating herself on her parenting skills, the fear overwhelmed Stacey and escalated to tears. Iothor ceased his play-acting and looked to Alicia for his cue, but Alicia just shook her head and sat closer to Stacey, putting an arm around her.

"Did you say sorry to Iothor?" she asked.

Stacey nodded, leaning into Alicia. Her eyes turned to Iothor and reiterated her apology. "Sorry."

"It's okay." Iothor pointed at his eye. "See? All better?"

But Stacey's tears were flowing now, and although her petulance had eased, Alicia expected it was just the start. Sure enough, the girl reached for a fourth crust and threw it at Iothor.

Alicia pushed the plate away. "No!"

And that was the last they heard of it, because Stacey exploded into full-on monster mode. She shouted, she screamed, she cried. She didn't know what to do with herself.

"I shouldn't have kept her up this late." Alicia juggled Stacey and her bag as she hurried toward the server station, searching for her purse.

Alicia declined the waitress's offer to bring the bill to their table and while the payment was authorising, Stacey tried to push away from Alicia. Iothor reached, offering to take her. Alicia relinquished the girl, and for a moment it worked. But Stacey must have spotted the switcheroo trick, and increased her volume.

With the card back, Alicia retrieved her daughter and walked shamefacedly through the restaurant, apologising to diners as she went.

Outside, as she located her car on the street, she found her phone was ringing, but it could wait until she got Stacey settled. Iothor waited too, awkwardly shifting foot to foot, and when Alicia closed the door on the wailing infant, he said, "Thank you for a nice evening. It was good to meet her properly."

"Yeah, I'm sorry about that." Alicia looked up at Iothor, a foot taller than her. "Thanks for trying."

"Hey, if I'm going to keep trying to impress you, I have a lot to learn."

"Not put off by tonight?"

Iothor ducked slightly to view the interior of the car; Stacey's muted crying was still audible. "I teach high school students about history. I can get used to this."

"Did you park nearby?"

"Taxi."

"Ah." Alicia guessed he was hedging his bets. To his credit, he hadn't raised the prospect of going home with her, and she was grateful when her phone rang again. "Do you mind?"

"Go ahead."

Alicia checked the screen. It was Kate Hague, Stacey's half-sister. "Crap."

"Bad news?"

"I'm sorry. I—" Alicia retreated a few feet, and answered the call. "Hi."

"Hi, Alicia?" Kate said. "Is this a bad time?"

"No, it's … I have a couple of minutes." She felt bad listening to Stacey, but the girl had gotten quieter since being strapped into her car seat.

"It's my dad."

Alicia's hands went numb. Her knees literally weakened, and she felt the blood drain from her face. It must have shown, because Iothor quickly approached, holding out his hand in an offer of support. She gathered herself and waved him off. Then she thought better of it, reached out a hand, and let him hold it. She smiled her thanks.

"What about your dad?" Alicia asked, hoping, so dearly hoping, that he'd finally passed away.

"I'm going to do it," Kate said.

"Do what?"

"Switch him off. It's what I need to do. He's never going to wake up, never going to be able to answer my questions. I need to close that chapter on my life."

The words stuck in Alicia's throat, but she forced them out. "Good. That's really good. I'm—"

"Will you be there?"

Alicia grew dizzy and gripped Iothor's hand tighter. "Me?"

"He's had a big impact on you too. And you helped me so much, I … it's okay if you say no."

"No. I mean … yes. Of course I'll be there. Do you know when?"

"I'll have to make an appointment with the doctors there, but … I'll let you know. Is that okay?"

"Yes, absolutely!" Alicia heard her voice turn high-pitched and consciously altered it. "Just call me when you know a date."

Kate thanked her and hung up, and Alicia faced Iothor. They would definitely not be sleeping together tonight, but she owed him the truth. He'd never even asked about Stacey's dad, but if he was prepared to put up with the monster he'd met over dinner tonight—to put up with and get to know her—he should know that her father, a man who'd murdered over one hundred people, was going to die in matter of days.

# PART II

# CHAPTER FIVE

THE MOBILE LAB had been borrowed from Lancashire, which Alicia was sure would be a sore point with many of the locals. The county's rivalry with Yorkshire made the interplay in George R. R. Martin's *A Game of Thrones* novels resemble a playground spat.

The workspace was housed in the back of an HGV trailer, currently stationed on one of the few flat spots of land in the area which was both hard tarmac and at a high enough elevation to ward off worry of more water damage. According to Wiki, which Alicia reviewed on her phone before setting off, the car park served as either the starting point for one of two walks in the area, or the halfway mark for the longer route encompassing both windswept trails that took people in a large circle—or half-moon, depending on the choice. But that confused Alicia—if it were a circle, surely the car park could be the end point *and* the starting point. She knew from her father that ramblers had their own ways, and their ways usually involved definitive and widely accepted starting and finish lines, usually located near a pub.

With an emergency overnight bag in the boot, Alicia parked her Toyota Auris in one of the remaining spaces and stepped out to be greeted by DC Knowles and DI Cross. Cross was taller than Alicia had expected, matching Knowles for height but somewhat shorter than DCI Murphy, who must have inherited beanstalk DNA somewhere down his parental line. Knowles attempted to greet Alicia with a formal-looking handshake, but she slipped aside and pulled him into a hug, which he returned awkwardly.

Alicia disengaged. "I see my mentoring paid off."

"Umm…" Knowles was not the most verbally astute fellow, even when he mellowed out. He was more than likely worried about Cross, his unofficial mentor in Halifax, and didn't want to rub her the wrong way. "This is DI Cross."

"We met." Alicia offered her both arms outstretched, really hoping she'd take up the hug, but the DI simply reached for Alicia's hand and shook it.

"Glad you could make it, DI Friend," Cross said. "Thank you for taking the time. I know it must be a big imposition."

It was an additional forty-five minutes of travel, not a huge issue, but Alicia accepted the thank-you.

"Shall we?" Cross indicated the steps up to the lab.

Knowles led the way, followed by Alicia, with Cross bringing up the rear. The detective constable entered a code, which he revealed to Alicia—050689. "My birthday," he said.

Alicia fired up a stink-eye especially for Knowles. "Are you actively trying to make me feel old?"

"He does that a lot," Cross said.

Knowles gave a near-smile as he entered and held the door for the pair of DIs.

Alicia had expected a full-on spaceship bridge full of screens, computers, maybe a hermetically-sealed cubicle for analysing DNA and bullet fragments. She was disappointed. The walls on either side of her bore banks of five metal drawers, each a foot high, five feet long, and two feet deep.

"We would normally use this to bring equipment out to us, not store evidence," Cross said. "I wanted something nearby rather than using police resources to transport bodies to the morgue every time we dug up a new one, and this lab gives the anthropologists a decent base."

"Anthropologists?" Alicia said.

"A few professors, and some of their brighter students." Knowles gestured toward the east. "Universities from Leeds, Huddersfield, and Manchester. They're treating it as a learning experience, but they're better placed as experts to match bones together, trying to identify how many actual bodies we have."

Cross opened a long drawer which had been sectioned off into several compartments, marked with letters and numbers that would be matched back to evidence logs should an inquest or trial be forthcoming. Within each thirty-inch partition lay a collection of bones, all bagged and labelled with unique numbers.

"We haven't found a complete skeleton yet," Cross said. "Virgil Baines is the closest we have, with hips, thighs, one and a half arms, a skull, and a number of vertebrae."

"I assume he isn't here," Alicia said.

"No." Knowles moved to a position beside Cross. "We're treating him as we would a body uncovered yesterday."

"All the bodies we've IDed could potentially be homicides," Cross said, "and given the timeframe, there's an outside chance the perpetrator could still be alive."

Alicia continued to scrutinise the meagre collection of bones. "How do you know these belong together?"

"There was some connective tissue, and when the size of one ulna matches another almost exactly, it's a safe bet. And then there are the coloration matches." Cross's hand hovered over the bag, a curiously reverent gesture for a senior detective. "We're doing DNA to confirm matches, of course, but the anthropologists have done a lot more with much older finds. Usually it's archaeological in nature, but apparently there's a way of analysing the porous structure of preserved bone matter."

"They dated a peat bog corpse to ten thousand years before the last ice age," Knowles said.

Alicia nodded and turned from the remains. "And Shona, Dana, Valerie, and Virgil to 1974 onward."

Cross closed the drawer softly. "We have tentative IDs on others."

Alicia faced both detectives. "The IDs are new."

"Youth gives a person youthful energy. *Some* people can work all night."

Knowles strode over past the second bank of drawers to a door, which he opened. Again, there were no high-tech gubbins to be found, just more storage, although this section seemed newer, cleaner, more ... *lab-like*. Not a complete laboratory, but the evidence boxes here were translucent Perspex, ranging in size from shoeboxes to suitcases, all sealed with plastic snap ties and categorised much like the remains. Many were labelled with two number sequences—a unique one, and those corresponding numbers on the bones.

"Items found attached to the bodies," Alicia said.

"Those with two numbers, yes." Knowles hovered his hand over one of the boxes then withdrew it. "Where there's only one number, the items were found on the ground. But we're fairly certain most, if not all, belonged to the people in those drawers at some point."

"You've matched some items to known missing persons?"

"Not completely." Knowles picked up a thick binder. "I raided the archives last night. Back in the seventies and into the eighties, it was all manual, so I couldn't just pop in a bunch of keywords like I can now."

"Poor you."

"By eleven, I decided to document them all unofficially." He opened the binder to show the papers—at least two hundred—containing photographs of belongings. It was plain Knowles had taken the pictures on his cellphone—his finger was in many of the shots—then amassed them via a collage app and written the evidence number on the jpeg itself. "There were old photos of people who vanished during that time. We'd enlarged a few distinctive possessions like necklaces and watches, rings and bracelets. To save time, I photographed the photos."

"Signing out the files too much trouble?" Cross asked.

"As I explained earlier, ma'am, if we match one of these to an item in these boxes, we can formally sign out all the relevant case files."

Cross smiled at Alicia.

"She's winding you up," Alicia said.

"Right." Knowles didn't seem put out as he held the binder open and located the box he was looking for. "Pamela Dixon, 1974." It was a shoebox-sized container. He pulled on gloves, wrote the time and date then signed his name on the evidence log, and used snips to cut away the ties. He opened it to pull out a heart-shaped pendant, which he dangled from his fingers. "A gift from her mother. She gave Pamela's twin sister an identical one."

Alicia moved her face close enough to make out the tarnished metal and what might have been mud on the chain; she recognised it as decaying human remains. "Enough for analysis?"

"We've sent it to the lab with a rush order," Cross said. "When I showed up this morning, Knowles was already here. In the same suit as yesterday. Looking very pleased with himself."

"How many?"

"So far?"

*So far…*

The words sent a chill through Alicia, one that overwhelmed yesterday's morbid excitement of being involved in what could turn out to be a famous case. She always enjoyed that charge, the sensation of anticipation at taking on something far from the mundane, but when faced with the true cost of that crime, she retreated. Those words, *so far*, held the promise that they had not yet identified all the articles recovered. The number they had matched to real, honest-to-God people was depressing enough to warrant such a pause.

"Yes," Alicia said. "How many official missing persons are no longer missing?"

"Fifteen," Knowles said. "And there's more you need to know."

Knowles didn't enjoy showing off, but Cross had spent a lot of time with him recently, and advised him to shout about his accomplishments more often. He'd been embarrassed to boast about catching the murderer of a schoolteacher earlier in the year, mere hours after the act, because he didn't believe he would have managed it so quickly if it hadn't been for Alicia Friend's coaching. Heck, she'd figured it out long before he did, but wanted him to take the credit. It could also have been because Alicia didn't want the paperwork, but he thought it was more that she understood he'd benefit.

So having come up with this shortcut to IDing the victims through their possessions, he had decided to ride the momentum. He'd stayed up all night with the camera and app, logging everything meticulously, and then come back out here with a four-pack of Monster energy drinks and got to work.

A *little* credit wouldn't go amiss.

*Maybe it'll come later*, he reasoned.

"Full tests are some way out but preliminary results returned markers for African descent," he said. "Including the matter on this necklace. And Pamela Dixon was black. Most of the fifty-year-old ones show similar markers, but it isn't conclusive."

"Jesus..." Alicia's upbeat tone had died, and her shoulders were slumped as she leafed through the pages Knowles had marked with sticky notes on which he'd scribbled the evidence box numbers. "All these ... from around here?"

"No, not all," Cross said.

Knowles jumped back in quickly. "Shona Maynard was from Leeds. One of the items of jewellery I found also matched a disappeared girl from 1978 in Manchester. Found dental records which tentatively match Derek Reynolds, a white British man from Leeds. Julia Peacock is a sex worker from Todmorden."

Alicia stared into the box with the heart-shaped necklace. "And the killer or killers might still be alive."

Cross nodded. "Unless it's the Lainworth Ripper from the twenties who took up again in the seventies."

"No."

"No?" Knowles said.

"You know what he's doing, don't you?" Alicia asked.

"What he's doing?"

"How this killer is hunting." Alicia faced Knowles. "Think about it. What links Manchester and Leeds with Halifax in between? What was here in the seventies but not the twenties?"

Knowles put all the evidence out of his mind. All thoughts of a future court case vanished. He took a step back, flew up high, looking down, visualising all he could see—a technique he had developed after the murder case went his way. He added Alicia's question to his mental image and came to what he assumed was the same conclusion.

"It's the M62," he said. "The motorway opened in 1960-something. He was using the Leeds-Manchester-Liverpool corridor. In the twenties, combined with the problems of motoring technology, it would have been impossible."

"Not impossible," Alicia said. "But very hard. And even if the Lainworth Ripper was very young—say in his twenties—he'd have been well into his eighties by the time Shona Maynard was taken."

"So it's settled," Cross said. "We have a live case?"

"Maybe." Alicia mulled it over, trying to summarise it for herself as much as the others. "The killer of these fifteen people was active in the seventies and eighties. Strong enough and organised enough, *and* sane enough, to transport people here to murder—or to murder them and *then* transport the bodies. He wasn't an eighty year-old. Most killers of this nature are in their thirties, but not exclusively. So yes, until we prove otherwise, we treat this as an active case."

# CHAPTER SIX

AN HOUR before Cross and Alicia departed to make further enquiries, Knowles was ordered to grab at least four hours of sleep before returning to duty, so Alicia spent the next few hours getting the lay of the land. There were worse ways to do this than as a passenger in DI Cross's Vauxhall Insignia, the two DIs heading for the former mill town of Moleford Bridge.

"My home is on the outskirts of town," Cross told her as she steered them down a winding road. "It's one reason I landed the case. I think DCI Watson expected me to hover over it rather than getting elbows-deep in it. More of an archaeological case than a police matter at first."

"He's going to regret bringing me in, isn't he?" Alicia said.

"You and I would have come to the same conclusion."

Alicia didn't doubt it. Probably not as quickly, but she knew Knowles was bright, and if Cross had reached the rank of DI she was no slouch either. "The problem is, now I have too many theories blowing around my noggin." She rapped on her head with her knuckles. "All branching off our initial brainstorming back at the lab."

Cross's forehead creased, eyes on the road.

Alicia elaborated. "My brain processes data much faster than a regular brain. I call it my computer. I feed it facts, and it spits out conclusions. Usually I have to work backward to compute the logic manually before it can be used in a statement or interview, or especially in court. And right now?" Alicia shrugged and attempted a dimple-heavy smile. "It's a bit overloaded."

"So the conclusion you steered Knowles toward back in the lab," Cross said, "that someone murdered these people independently of the Lainworth Ripper ... it was just the first hypothesis to emerge?"

"Yup. The 'best bet,' as the search engines call it."

After coming down one hill, they'd driven up another. The road was only wide enough for one and a half cars, and they had to pull into passing places three times.

"But there *are* other theories," Cross said. "No evidence, just scenarios that fit."

Alicia tapped her head again. "My takes on them just aren't ready yet." In fact, as she spoke, more scenarios turned and twisted. "What if the Lainworth Ripper was a twenty-year-old who stopped killing Jews in the twenties out of fear of getting caught? Then when transport links allowed him to go undetected, his urges overwhelmed him again?"

"Seventy-something in the 1970s. Not inconceivable."

"A nice old man luring prostitutes and the like into his car, hitting his victims with drugs before killing them. He could go on into his eighties before dying himself."

Cross nodded, steering around a tight bend. "Or ... there's someone he's passing on his knowledge to?"

"You mean, what if he had a son, trained as his accomplice?"

"I don't know. I'm just floating ideas." Cross smiled, eyes flitting sideways to Alicia. "What if there really is some satanic cult that resurfaces every fifty years?"

A serious moment held the air heavy inside the car, then both women smirked at once.

"I hate to lecture," Alicia said, "but Occam's Razor is usually right. The simplest solution normally bears out."

Cross appeared focused again. "But not always."

Alicia's far-fetched spit-balling merging with the notions of a local crank—or a "historian and citizen reporter" as Maisie Jackson apparently described herself—left her pushing those scenarios aside. "No. Not always."

Bodies of people, last seen in places on or around the M62 corridor, had turned up, slain by someone unknown. That was all the *evidence* so far.

"Where are we heading?" Alicia asked.

"Library," Cross said. "They'll have old maps of the region. Plus, Lauren and Costas—they're our librarians—they've been around since the eighties. Probably the seventies too."

As they crested the rise, a town came into view—a settlement of blocky grey and black buildings set into the surrounding hills as if carved there by a sculptor. Chimneys rose from its depths, dotted seemingly at random—typical of this part of the world, a legacy of its industrial past. Many of these factories and mills attained protected status, and although they no longer functioned, the occupants of these towns would sooner cut off the right arm of every resident than surrender their iconic buildings.

"You can see the shape of the landscape," Cross said as they descended. "Usually, water funnels through, but when the river farther down burst its banks, it caused a backlog that covered much of the lower town."

Alicia had seen the pictures—people in boats rescuing neighbours, business owners chest-deep attempting to save their wares while police and rescue services pleaded with them to leave. There were calls for formal enquiries, demands for someone to blame, be it the farmers for allowing their fields to turn into hard slabs rather than water-absorbent sponges, or the EU for over-regulating waterways and countryside, or the government for this or that, or climate change, or…

The list went on.

As they drove into the town itself, the buildings rose on either side, some dating back to the 1300s, but most only as far as the seventeenth century. The original builders had used larger bricks, hewn locally, which lent even the simplest of constructions a solid, near-immovable quality. Tidemarks remained on almost every wall. Even those on somewhat higher ground had not escaped unscathed, the flow having channelled into bottleneck streets.

Cross navigated the roads, waving occasionally to a familiar face. Traffic was heavy, winding around the dozens of maintenance vehicles and construction crews brought in to shore up places damaged three weeks ago.

"Moleford Bridge's library was one of the buildings that suffered the Boxing Day floods a few years ago," Cross said as they turned into a narrow street. "It got refurbished, shifting public meeting rooms and IT equipment from the ground floor up to the first. But there's only so much you can do. When more flooding was on its way, they shifted most of the books and what-have-you out of the way. Reopened fairly quickly this time."

She parked on Cheetham Street with a police sign on her dashboard, and led Alicia around the corner and inside the sand-coloured library. A boxy design, with a modern entrance neighbouring a hairdresser, it smelled the way libraries smell: clean, fresh, with a heady mix of paper and fabric.

Lauren sat behind the main desk in a wheelchair, a thin-haired lady in her late-sixties or early-seventies, while a tanned man with jet-black hair of around the same age pushed a cart of books around, placing volumes back on the shelves in the exact order on which they were stacked on his cart.

Organised.

Spry for his age.

*Stop it, Alicia. Stop suspecting people without evidence.*

Lauren beamed as DI Cross approached. "Bea, how lovely to see you."

Cross leaned over the counter to give Lauren a peck on the cheek, and when Costas joined them she embraced him in a hug that lasted longer than Alicia and Knowles's had earlier.

They broke, and Costas spoke with an accent Alicia couldn't place; she guessed at something Mediterranean. Like with Iothor's clash of Icelandic with Leeds, the librarian's Yorkshire accent took precedence. "They got you on them bones, eh? Bet ol' Basil ent too happy."

"He's as happy as you'd expect." Cross's whole demeanour had softened since meeting the couple. "This is Detective Inspector Friend."

The pair shook hands with Alicia in turn, and Alicia refrained from her usual introduction of "Call me Alicia," in favour of caution, allowing Cross to lead. "Nice to meet you."

"We're looking for two things," Cross said.

"Always happy to help." Lauren rolled around the side, pushing her wheelchair manually with an ease that indicated she'd gotten used to the process over many years. She lowered her voice conspiratorially. "Is it the bones?"

"I couldn't possibly say." Cross tapped her nose with her index finger and winked. "But one of the things we hope you can find is anything on the Lainworth Ripper."

It was an unexpected approach. Everything Alicia had seen so far suggested Cross was as uptight as her detective constable, but in the company of Lauren and Costas she resembled a favourite niece returning for a meal after months of absence.

Lauren looked sideways at Cross. "The Lainworth Ripper?"

"From the 1920s?" Cross said. "Apparently, he was a murderer of Jews and—"

"We know the episode," Costas said. "I'll see what I can do. What's the other thing?"

"Maps." Cross glanced at Alicia.

"The M62 corridor," Alicia said. "And what came before it—1950s onward, preferably."

"Oh, that'll be the A62," Costas said. "Yes, a pain in the arse, all that construction, but worth it."

"You remember the old road?"

"My parents settled here in 1965, so the M62 was already open, but folk here were still talking about it even then."

Lauren reached out a hand to hold one of her partner's. "Do you know much about Moleford Bridge?"

"Only that it used to be big in terms of mills and other industry," Alicia said.

"Yes, yes, that all died out long ago. It was '65 when the hippies discovered this place—hippies like my mum and dad. I was a little young, maybe eight or ten, but one of my earliest memories is dancing under the stars with a bonfire going, and flowers in my hair. The locals claimed to hate our parents' kind, but the influx brought art and food, and that meant money."

"Rejuvenated the town overnight," Costas said, his Mediterranean accent winning over the Yorkshire this time.

"You remember the old routes?" Alicia asked Lauren.

"Vaguely." Lauren waved a hand. "People spoke about the new road like it was either a gift from Satan delivering all these hippies in their camper vans, or a blessing from God that allowed faster travel to the big cities. Shops could import more cheaply—clothes, food, and the less official herbs." She mimed taking a drag on a spliff. "And sold it to residents new and old."

Alicia looked at Cross. She didn't need a history lesson, but was disinclined to be blunt about it with a pair who seemed so nice.

Cross took the hint. "Thank you, Lauren. That's useful, as always. But we could really do with the maps."

The elderly couple nodded understanding.

"I'll grab the books," Lauren said. "Costas, would you mind setting up the detectives in room 1A and digging out the maps?"

"Of course."

Within fifteen minutes, Costas had set them up in a near-sterile air-conditioned room that brought to mind a less cluttered version of inquiry rooms normally established in police stations. Costas plugged in a Nespresso machine and unlocked a cabinet with cups and pods—which he informed them guests usually had to pay for, but he'd make an exception—then went to find the maps.

As DI Cross made the first coffee, Alicia said, "Hey, this doesn't constitute a bribe, does it?"

"Only if we turn a blind eye to all Costas's and Lauren's crimes." Cross handed Alicia the first cup. "Do you have a problem with that?"

Alicia sipped. "No, this is good enough to get them a pass on anything up to grievous bodily harm."

"What do they need to offer to get away with murder?"

"Biscuits."

Cross checked the cabinet and produced a tin of assorted biscuits. She shook them.

"Doesn't count if we take them ourselves," Alicia said. "Sorry, but they're going down."

Cross smiled and finished making her coffee, and both sat at a desk just as Lauren entered.

The librarian had a serious face, a stark contrast from her earlier sunniness. "I'm sorry, but I have to report we don't have any books left on the Lainworth Ripper."

"None left?" Alicia said.

"We only had four to begin with. Well, three only on that subject, but a fourth one mentions him. A rather lowbrow volume about local monster legends, which also talks about—"

"Lauren," Cross interrupted softly. "Are they missing or were they checked out?"

"Checked out."

"And who has them?"

Lauren bit her lip. "I'm not sure I can say. Data protection and all that."

Alicia mirrored Cross's friendly tone. "Would you like us to obtain a warrant?"

Relief poured out of Lauren in a huge, long breath. "Thank you! Yes. Please, if you wouldn't mind."

Cross tapped the tabletop. "Of course, no problem. Although, unofficially, if it was Maisie Jackson who checked them out, might you be willing to contact her on our behalf and maybe have her call me? Voluntarily?"

Cross slid her business card across the table and Lauren plucked it up and grinned, nodding.

"Absolutely." Lauren winked. "*If* it was her."

Costas returned with four tubes three feet long. "These are all I can find. They cover areas around Calderdale." He placed them one at a time on the table. "1950. 1955. 1960. 1965. They are reproductions, but I can request the originals if you need them. We put them in storage after the last lot of floods. They go up to 1995, then is computerised."

"Thank you, this looks great." Alicia picked up the first, popping the top and turning it over to shake out the contents. Then her phone chimed to say she'd received a message.

And so did Cross's.

The two detectives locked eyes and their shoulders dropped as they read that more bones had been discovered farther up the valley. Cross's phone rang. She showed Alicia the caller ID before answering: DCI Watson was not going to be pleased.

# CHAPTER SEVEN

THE ROUTE out to the freshly unearthed remains took Alicia and Cross through the back end of town and an accumulation of old dark-brick buildings mingling with modern redbrick constructions like shopping centres and council offices. Then Cross sped them past a new estate of houses, a school, leisure centre, and a church called Church of the All Saints. This latter building, Cross told Alicia, was a welcome addition to the crumbling St. Mary's on the opposite side of the recently-built residential district. The Church of England backed the fresh construction on the condition it did not modernise its design in terms of the shape or add liberalised stained-glass art like single-gender unions, although it was happy to accept the advances of central heating, air conditioning, and wifi—with the wifi turned off during sermons. They merged the new church with the old, in spirit if not physically, and although some parishioners refused to accept the new house of God, Cross speculated they'd have no choice soon.

"You know a lot about the church," Alicia said.

"I live on this estate," Cross answered. "House is new-build so there's zero storage and the bedroom is the size of a kennel, but it comes with a twenty-year warranty so I'll be able to sell it on soon."

Alicia's house was built before the Second World War. She'd looked at a couple of new-build houses, but the shortcomings Cross mentioned had put her off more than the idea of a hundred-year-old building.

They rose out of Moleford Bridge and hit a main road, and drove past signposts to places like Todmorden, Mankinholes, and Lumbutts. They circled around the hills and at one point skirted a massive rise of land which, judging by the number of signs pointing to public footpaths, Alicia assumed made for good rambling. When a monolith resembling an Egyptian needle appeared in the distance, Alicia asked about it.

"You've not heard of Stoodley Pike?" Cross said.

"No. Is it famous?"

"Around here it is. Stoodley Pike is actually the hill, not the monument, but people tend to confuse the two. From the end of the Crimean War—1856, I think. Replaced an earlier monument from the Napoleonic wars."

"Wow," Alicia said. "This is like being chauffeured by an encyclopaedia."

"I can shut up and let you Google it if you prefer."

"Nah, I'm interested. Any cool stories about it?"

"Not really. Unless you count a huge coincidence."

"Coincidences can be cool."

Cross checked her sat-nav for the next turning, which would take them onto smaller roads. "It'll wait. We're nearly there."

"How many more bodies?"

"Hard to say, apparently."

All they knew was that a couple of geologists invited by one of the senior anthropology professors had analysed the scattered remains and the accumulation of other debris, and charted a path up the most likely fells. A small group had trekked for three miles and located the trail of bones, scattered through a tight crevasse, like litter after a festival. When Cross parked up on the side of the narrow road as directed by a constable decked out in all-weather gear, it was plain they would be heading on a ramble of their own.

Like Alicia, Cross carried Wellington boots in her car, but she was wearing walking shoes already so she offered Alicia the boots. Alicia accepted, although the footwear was two sizes too big. They climbed over a stile and schlepped over the field, which was not yet marked with police tape. Instead, there was another police constable at a second stile several hundred yards away, who waved.

"Still early days," Cross said. "Watson is sending SOCOs and someone to manage the scene."

The pair reached the next boundary and crossed over it, the constable directing them toward the rocky outcrop ahead. It was all marked footpaths until they found a third officer, again decked out as if a hurricane were due, who pointed directly over a hump in the rock-covered landscape.

"Don't go if you feel unsafe," he advised. "Professionals will be here in four hours to help facilitate access."

"Professionals?" Cross said.

"Oh, let's give it a go," Alicia said. "You only live once."

Alicia marched on ahead, the boots like flippers but offering great grip. Cross caught up, and as they moved over the top of the bank, they understood why they might need professional assistance.

The hillside fell away—not quite sheer, but angled so steeply as to appear close. Water flowed in narrow rivulets, some forming miniature waterfalls. People the size of action figures milled about halfway up, crabbing sideways and upward in a diagonal fashion.

"Is that the geologists?" Alicia asked.

"They're contaminating the scene," Cross said. She waved and called out, "*Hey!*"

Her voice echoed down to them, and one of them waved back.

"*Get away from the bodies!*" Cross hollered.

Alicia was of the opinion that there wasn't much that could be done to contaminate the scene further, seeing as the bodies had been buried for decades and ripped from their resting places by gallons of water and tons of mud. But they had to consider it live. A conviction was still a possibility, and any brief could point to the number of people who handled the evidence before it reached a clean lab.

The people below signalled they couldn't hear, so Cross waved frantically to get them to steer clear. Instead of going back down, one of the people started up toward the two detective inspectors, while the remaining pair held still.

"It's a start," Cross said.

"What's this place, then?" Alicia asked.

"I don't know. I'm not much of a rambler." Cross kept her hands on her hips, gazing around at the sun-dappled land. "If I have my bearings right, the Beacon is a few miles north."

"Beacon?"

"*The* Beacon. A hill. Used to be a, well, a beacon. People would light a series of them stretching out to the coast in the event of invaders."

*Iothor would be fascinated by that.*

Alicia shook thoughts of the Icelandic hunk from her brain and concentrated on the task at hand.

The footpath they were on snaked away from them and down, then up the opposite side, forming a valley—albeit a narrow one. The gash in the hillside gave the impression of another valley forming, although the process would be so long that no one alive today would live to see it.

"There's been some landslip." Cross pointed to an accumulation of brown sludge near the bottom, where water pooled before spilling into a stream that would eventually meet with the River Calder.

"Think it exposed the bones here?"

Cross shook her head. "This place would have looked like Niagara." She indicated the top of the rocky gash. "Hill carries on for a way yet; we just can't see the top."

Alicia was having trouble visualising all this. She thought she liked nature and rugged landscapes, but she realised she knew very little. Cross wasn't even an expert; she was just sharing local knowledge.

The figure approaching was a broad-shouldered woman in her sixties with binoculars hanging around her neck. She wore a bright blue hardhat, sturdy walking boots, black trousers, and a lightweight jacket that appeared waterproof. Cross made an "ah" which Alicia interpreted as recognition.

"What are you people doing down there?" Cross said.

"Sorry, Bea," the woman answered, stopping about six feet away. "I was being nosy. Hope you don't mind."

Cross narrowed her eyes. "Don't mind? Why would I mind you trampling all over the bodies of people killed fifty years ago and dumped—"

"We were praying."

Alicia peered around the side of the woman, down at the pair who remained. They hadn't moved.

"Duncan called me." The woman unzipped her coat a few inches. "The world's most handsome geology professor. Thought I might be interested. In the find, not ... you know."

The woman eased the binoculars aside and unzipped her jacket, revealing that her black trousers were part of more familiar ensemble, as the white Roman collar at her neck showed her to be a member of the clergy.

She extended her hand to Alicia. "Lucy Viera. I'm the minister up at St. Mary's."

Cross stepped aside, waving a hand as if apologising. "Right. I attend Lucy's church. St. Mary's."

"Not tempted by our big shiny rival just yet." Lucy smiled warmly and shook Alicia's hand too.

"Why did the professor call you?" Alicia asked.

"We go way back. And he thought it might be church-related."

"A graveyard disturbance?" Cross asked.

"No, no. Priest on the Hill. But it isn't related to Henry Pickersgill, apparently. Or the ruins of his church." Lucy angled her head closer and lowered her voice as if conveying a secret. "It's just over the next rise." Back to normal. "One of the other people down there is an anthropologist. He says the bones are more likely to be the Lainworth ones."

Alicia was growing more fascinated by the stories up here. "The Priest on the Hill. Church-related."

"One of my guilty pleasures. Someone came asking about it recently. Do you know Maisie Jackson?"

"We've met briefly," Cross said.

"She heard I owned some of Henry Pickersgill's original writings, so I let her have a read-through. Bit of a scandal, back in the day—a priest 'switching sides,' as it were."

"So it was definitely devil worship?" Alicia said.

"Yes, although in today's language you might say he was delusional. Spoke with the horned god himself, took instruction, and acted accordingly."

A man's voice came from behind. "Mind if I join you?"

They turned to see Knowles clambering up the rise to join them.

"We haven't been gone four hours," Alicia said.

"I'm fine." He looked as fresh as if he'd had a solid eight hours.

Cross checked her watch. "Are you disobeying orders?"

"Caught a good three in the back of one of the vans, ma'am.

A lot of shouting woke me up and I heard about the discovery." He came up beside them, nodded hello to the vicar, and raised a set of binoculars to his eyes. "Looks like the geology guys paid off."

"We'll call in search and rescue cavers," Cross said. "There's a complex system under a lot of this land.

Knowles lowered the binoculars. "The professor already found what might be an opening. He thinks it's probably a series of smaller holes in the cave network rather than one big one, although he can't rule that out."

"DCI Watson approved the spend?" Alicia asked.

"Not yet." Cross took the binoculars from Knowles and scanned along the trail where the remains were scattered. "But with the publicity this will generate, he won't have any choice."

Alicia smiled. "Good point. Perception has a powerful effect on the loosening of purse strings."

"Then let's not waste time." Cross handed the glasses back to Knowles. "I'll coordinate back at base. You okay bringing DI Friend back with you?"

"Sure."

With that, Cross turned to Lucy. "We'll pray this weekend? The congregation?"

"Of course." Lucy touched Cross's arm and squeezed.

Then Cross left them, with a parting comment for Alicia to return her boots when she could.

Alicia faced the minister. "Lucy." Big smile. "You mentioned the ruins of a church. Is that your Priest on the Hill church?"

Lucy beamed back. "Certainly is."

"And did he have anything to do with the Lainworth Ripper?"

"No, Henry Pickersgill was caught and hanged decades earlier."

"Was he well known? Locally? Like a big bad bogeyman story?"

"Not particularly. He's not *un*known. He ministered in Mole-ford Bridge, but a small parish who were more puritan than modernists, even by the standard of the day. He had his flock build a smaller church, as high up as possible, for quiet contemplation. To be nearer to God, he said."

"But...?"

"But he lured people there." A smile formed, then died, but a real enthusiasm entered Lucy's tone and manner. "Some from the town, but most from outside. Took them up there with a promise of absolution and prayer, murdered them, and sent them down a deep crevasse. *Really* gruesome."

"Directly to hell," Alicia said, unsure if a vicar should be quite so gleeful talking about this.

"What are you thinking?" Knowles asked.

"Lots of things." Alicia paced, her chin down. "The Priest on the Hill found this cave system, big enough to conceal his kills. Then if the Lainworth Ripper decided to take up the same hobby, he could simply have researched it himself and used the same grounds."

"Or stumbled across it by accident."

"Or that. And similarly, a killer in the seventies either stumbles across the same location, or finds a disturbed body, or whatever, and they have their dumping ground."

"Could have hidden it," Lucy said.

The two detectives looked her way.

Lucy shrugged. "Sorry. Just saying. If it had a hidden entrance, there's every possibility it could have been revealed in some text or map or whatever."

Knowles held himself still, but seemed to grow an inch in height. "You have something you wish to add, ma'am?"

"Oh, I'm no expert. I just came across the story one Halloween and it stuck. The church has some of his old diary pages, but they're nonsense."

"We've got four hours downtime." Alicia turned a full, slow

circle, taking in the view as she spoke. "How about we spend some time comparing the three incidents?"

"You can pop to the vicarage," Lucy said. "I'll put the kettle on, and—"

"Ma'am," Knowles said. "Thank you for your input, but we can't discuss an active case with a civilian. If you have anything to add, we'll listen, but if you're not a qualified expert in this, I'm sorry. We have to limit the people with access."

Lucy maintained her smile but her eyes weren't selling it. "Of course. No problem."

"Okay." Alicia tramped off toward the road. "So where are we headed?"

Knowles followed, with Lucy tentatively bringing up the rear. "I don't know. Library?"

"I thought you researched the disappearances. You had all the answers earlier this morning."

"That's not my research."

Alicia halted, facing the two following her. When they also came to a stop, she said, "Who gave you the research?"

"Maisie Jackson," Knowles said.

"Then let's go meet Maisie."

## CHAPTER EIGHT

THE HOUSE REMINDED Alicia of a fairy-tale cottage: higgledy-piggledy brickwork, small cross-framed windows, and a thatched roof. It was positioned at the top of a winding vegetable garden of beans, squashes, and sprouting food such as broccoli. A greenhouse occupied a quarter of the space, full of winding vines and red fruit. All the outdoor growing aids appeared crafted by hand, from bamboo poles strapped together for runner beans to climb, to raised borders made from 2x4 planks painted with bitumen to prevent rot. Wool pellets and gravel formed barriers between crops and around the perimeters of the beds, with gravel paths in between—products Alicia's friend and boss DCI Murphy had once grumbled to her about being "supposedly slug-proof" but which he lacked the time to maintain, so he resorted to chemical protection instead.

"Impressed?" Alicia asked Knowles as he gazed at the garden.

"This is not what I expected."

"What did you expect?"

"A grotty flat overflowing with bin liners full of crap hoarded over the years."

Alicia wound through the path, slowly making her way to the

front door, which she could tell was constructed of heavy wood even from fifty yards away.

After dropping Lucy Viera at St. Mary's they'd come straight here and parked on a narrow private lane, off the main road into Moleford Bridge. Maisie Jackson's house was one of a gathering of similar properties, spaced hundreds of yards apart, and from what Alicia could see, each house appeared unique. They were old, too—some thatched, some with more modern slate roofs; a tiny makeshift community sequestered in their own little corner of the region. The top-notch mountain bike with chunky tyres chained to the side of Maisie's house was the only item that appeared out of place.

At Maisie's door, Alicia gestured to the large steel knocker.

"You know you want to," Knowles said.

He was right. She really, really did. As she lifted the stiff metal lump on its hinge and brought it back down with a loud clunk, she got goosebumps. The second knock was even cooler.

*Amazing how little things from the past bring such pleasure.*

"Excuse me!" The woman's voice came from near the greenhouse.

Knowles waved that way but Alicia had to get on tiptoes to see over a fence of peas. The grey-haired woman stood at the greenhouse door, her gardening-gloved hands balled into fists on her hips.

"Police," Knowles called. "DC Knowles. We met a couple of days ago, ma'am. Can we have a word?"

"Are you going to make me come all the way over there?"

Alicia and Knowles navigated a path to the greenhouse, where Alicia got her first good look at Maisie Jackson and was hit with an overwhelming sense of déjà vu.

"Have we met?" she asked.

Maisie examined Alicia's warrant card up close, then looked her up and down. "I doubt it." She held out a hand as if to cup Alicia's chin but wasn't close enough to make contact with the gardening gloves. "No, I'd have remembered a pretty little thing like you."

Alicia wasn't sure what to make of the gesture. Even as Maisie turned and led them into the roasting-hot greenhouse, where the sweet fragrances of tomatoes, chillis, and fresh soil permeated Alicia's senses, she pondered the notion of knowing Maisie. It was more than déjà vu, she was certain.

The woman with the trace of an American accent moved easily, but dressed like someone thirty years older than the fifty-two Knowles had informed Alicia she was. She was clearly mixed race; Caucasian dominated, especially from a distance, but the narrowing of her eyes at the outer corners and flattening of her nose leant her a south-east Asian quality.

Alicia felt her brow furrow as her memory banks churned. "Ms Jackson, are you sure we haven't worked together before?"

Maisie touched her fingers to a chilli plant with yellow bulbs, one of several on the left side of the greenhouse dug into soil in a bed on the floor. "Quite sure, thank you."

Knowles pulled his jacket up his shoulders, wafting a little air around his torso. "Ma'am, you mentioned a lot of research you'd done recently surrounding the remains found on Basil Warner's property. I was hoping you might be willing to share a little of what you've found."

A wry smile played at Maisie's mouth as she crouched opposite the chillis, beside a bed of tomatoes supported by string. "Been a hot summer. Haven't seen such a good crop in a while. I'm still producing peas. And have you *seen* my marrows?"

"The vegetables are … very impressive, ma'am. As is that." Knowles tilted his head toward several tall plants at the rear of the greenhouse: marijuana. "Personal use, I assume?"

"I get the feeling you want to know something specific." Without turning her head, Maisie moved back to the first bed, attention on a second chilli plant, leaning closer to examine the thin red peppers. "A question, Detective Constable. Or one your boss might prompt you for."

"My boss?"

"You're asking the questions; she is observing."

Alicia was now more certain than ever that they'd met. "Ms Jackson, the gardens in this road look fantastic. How did you avoid the flooding?"

Maisie had at some point picked up a set of secateurs, and now pointed them at Alicia. "Very good, young lady. You almost had me there."

"I almost ... 'had you'?"

Maisie rose and placed the cutting tool in the pouch on the front of her flowing dress. "Buttering me up so I'm less hostile toward the upstart who dismissed me as an idiot a couple of days ago."

"I didn't—"

"Don't deny it. You thought I had little to offer beyond interference and wasting your time."

"Yeah, Malcolm," Alicia said. "Don't deny it." To Maisie, she said, "Am I buttering you up better by siding with you against my colleague, or would you rather be buttered up by explaining your garden's miraculous escape from the flood?"

Maisie's stern expression melted and her whole body relaxed. "I thought I'd like you the moment you arrived." She walked past them and out the door.

"*And...*" Alicia followed, bathing in the fresh air. "Did you see us approach and come into the steamy greenhouse just to make us uncomfortable?"

"My, my, you are a bright one."

"What?" Knowles said.

"Ms Jackson just looked at the plants in there without actually doing anything to them. Letting us talk while she pretended to be grouchy and got a read on us. Dresses and acts like an elderly lady for reasons known only to her, but is very sharp, and not even close to being physically hampered."

Maisie gave a little clap—not quite sarcastic, but neither was it serious. "Do go on."

"The bike is serious equipment, meaning you use it regularly." Alicia gestured to the mountain bike she spotted when they first arrived. "You don't have a car registered to you, and the position of this place is far enough from the town to enjoy the peace and quiet, but close enough to nip to the shops for a pint of milk on foot if need be."

"Oh dear—and you were doing so well." Maisie clasped her hands before her. "Care to guess what you got wrong, DI Friend?"

Alicia looked around again, taking in all she could, including stepping closer to the woman herself, positively ecstatic at being invited to analyse a subject who seemed not the least bit annoyed at her efforts. "Not milk. Maybe rice milk. Or almond."

"I prefer oat."

Alicia snapped her fingers. "Damn, I was close though."

Maisie smiled. "Come on in. I'll make you a cup of tea."

As they followed, Knowles was clearly about to ask what that was about, so Alicia enlightened him. "Vegan. There are no animal fibres on her clothing, no leather, and only minimal manmade material. The bike, the bitumen—but the bitumen on the raised beds extends the life of the wood, which is better in the long run."

Maisie opened her front door. "Gosh, you like to talk, don't you?"

Knowles offered a grin. "Girl needs a hobby."

Maisie paused, giving him the stink-eye. "Nobody likes a smartarse, DC Knowles."

Knowles paused, his face dropping in panic. "I'm sorry, I didn't mean to imply—"

Maisie's squint melted into a smile.

"Oh," Knowles said. "You were messing with me."

Maisie looked at Alicia from the doorway. "We're going to have some fun with this gentleman."

Inside was exactly what the exterior suggested. The walls were exposed brick, and to the right in her kitchen was a chunky wooden table and six chairs, an Aga stove, a deep ceramic sink, and stone worktops. Alicia expected the living room would sport rough carpets, a worn couch and a very comfy armchair for reading. Maybe a small television.

Maisie filled a kettle with a whistle cap and placed it on the stove to boil, then invited the detectives to sit. "Not there," she said when Knowles headed for a chair near the sink. "I have my oddities. Would you mind using those two chairs?" When they took the other seats as directed, she said, "Okay, my turn."

"Your turn?" Knowles said.

"Detective Inspector Alicia Friend. Quiet, but loves to talk, meaning she's definitely an observer, a thinker, someone who isn't used to *leading* an investigation, so she lets the young protégè do that. Normally, it's the DI doing most of the talking. Which makes me wonder if she isn't the same detective who brought in the Century Killer and the awful man kidnapping girls a couple of winters ago. She's a gunslinger type brought in for the trickiest cases."

Alicia placed her hand on her chest and gave a shallow bow. "At your service. Although I'm branching out into 'proper' police work now."

"Good for you. DC Knowles is a tricky one. A rising star, just lacking experience. Obviously thorough, clever, but he's held back by something. Fear, I think."

"Fear?" Knowles said.

"Yes. You're afraid of something. Screwing up, probably. That's why you're so precise, so hesitant, so scared when you thought you'd offended me a few moments ago."

Knowles said nothing.

"Yes, terrified of looking incompetent—or, heck, appearing to be anything but the consummate professional."

Knowles pulled his jacket straight, then looked down at himself and unbuttoned the jacket. "You were on the job, ma'am?"

"Almost." Maisie came and sat beside them.

"Maisie Fong," Alicia said.

For the first time, Maisie's face dropped into sincere concern. "I haven't gone by that name for a long time."

Knowles stayed silent, his turn to observe.

"You wrote some of my favourite text books," Alicia said, her processor having cut through the static. "You lectured at my university a couple of times."

Maisie swallowed. "Fong. My maiden name. Back then, it didn't do to change your surname when you were building a career. You were a student of my husband?"

"Criminal psychology. Cuthbert Jackson is your husband? Of course. Jackson." A common enough name to have foxed Alicia on where she knew Maisie from.

"*Was* my husband. We separated a few years ago. Never got divorced formally, so I kept his name. It made things easier. But that's all I took from him. Everything here is my own."

"No children?" Knowles asked.

"No children," Maisie said. The kettle whistled and Maisie rose to tend to it. "I live off the royalties of my books, some investments I made in the nineties that didn't burst with the rest of the bubble. A simple life, but fulfilling. When I'm frugal."

As Maisie poured water into a teapot, Alicia said, "It would be great to get your expert opinion on this."

"I think you're expert enough, dear." Maisie poured a measure of oat milk into a milk jug and added it to the tray with the teapot.

"You've got a head start on the research."

"The Lainworth Ripper? I hardly think you need to worry about him."

"You know who he was?" Knowles asked.

"Not exactly. But suspicion fell on the nephew of the Earl of Calder. Winston Wright." Maisie gathered three cups and saucers and added them to the tray. "He served in the trenches of the Great War in 1917 to 1918, and was considered a hero. Became quite outspoken about the awful planning of the armed forces' officer class and railed against the government of the day, against everything they did." She brought the teapot and accessories over to the table and placed them beside Knowles. "As part of that rebellion, he joined a fledgling political movement that demanded strong leadership, originating with the *people* of the country. He and his lackeys needed a focus, though. A simple bogeyman. Someone to blame for the ills of their lives."

"Jews," Alicia said.

Maisie placed a tea strainer on one of the cups, opened the ornate teapot lid, and gave the contents a stir. "Jews. So when the first disappearances happened, suspicion fell on the group. Without direct evidence, things eased up for a bit, until Winston was forced to leave them at the behest of his uncle, who was quite opposed to the movement. It might have … embarrassed the family, apparently."

"Who were they?" Alicia asked. "This group."

"Fascists," Knowles said, then added nervously, "Right?"

"Correct. Although I don't think that word was in common use." Maisie paused. "A belief that the common man elected idiots to office because they didn't have the guts to elect men who would do what was needed to prevent a repeat of the Great War. Simplistic minds come up with simplistic solutions. Jews ran the world, ran the global businesses that were largely responsible for the tension leading up to the war. They needed to be brought to heel. A core facet of the Jewish race—or religion, or whatever—was selfishness, according to Winston and company, a hoarding of wealth and knowledge. It would take serious change to break their grip. But the earl didn't share his nephew's view. Put pressure on the lad to distance himself from such activism. Certain inheritances might find their way to good causes instead of being passed down the line. Soon after Winston's resignation from the party, worse things started to happen."

"He progressed from disappearances to displaying the corpses," Knowles said.

Having left the tea to brew long enough, Maisie poured a little milk into a cup before adding tea, a few leaves gathering in the strainer. "The investigation into disappeared Jews was never a focused inquiry like we'd get today. I can only speculate that the authorities largely shared Winston's distaste for the Semite community, and lacked the resources to do much more than basic work."

Alicia accepted the cup and saucer. "And a killer who wants to enact change doesn't like to be ignored."

"So he ups the ante. Six dismembered bodies turn up within a few months of each other. Then suddenly it stops."

"Winston stopped killing?" Knowles said.

Maisie repeated the tea-pouring process with a second cup. "I'm only speculating about Winston. He is the only prominent person mentioned during that time. Local journals, history of veterans of the war, and what few suspects are mentioned in the Lainworth casebooks. The killer could have been a nobody."

"Any clue—if it was Winston—why he stopped?"

Maisie put the teapot down with a clunk. "He was found mysteriously hanged near the river. A spot where one of the bodies turned up."

"And the killings definitely stopped after his death?" Alicia said.

"As far as I can tell. But as I said, the records are sketchy."

Knowles took his tea and sipped. He pulled a face that

suggested he wasn't sure whether he liked the beverage or not. "That's good to know."

Maisie poured a final cup. "Good?"

"The more recent bones we turned up," Knowles said. "It means the culprit might still be alive."

"Ah." Maisie sat at the end of the table, hands around her cup, the chairs on either side of her empty. "The human need to punish wrongdoing. Tell me, Detective Constable Knowles, if you find the killer is alive, what age do you suppose he is?"

Knowles looked at Alicia.

"I think it's safe to share." Alicia tried to match Knowles's official demeanour. "Maisie Fong's work was some of the most useful for my education. Lots of my friends too. More than just the assigned texts—her memoir." Alicia addressed Maisie. "Sorry to sound like a fangirl. But your lecture was a high point of that year. Kept me going. If it wasn't so … inspirational, I don't think I'd have stuck it out."

"Well, I'm happy to have had a positive influence," Maisie said. "What would you like to share?"

"It's public knowledge that we found two sets of bones."

"From the 1920s and 1970s." Maisie sipped her tea. "You've uncovered some more."

"Yes," Knowles said. "South of the Beacon."

"Oh, yes, the Priest on the Hill. Have you found more of his legacy too?"

"Only a very small amount. The thing we haven't revealed to the press is…" He looked again to Alicia, his senior officer.

"We can rely on your discretion?" Alicia asked.

"Yes," Maisie said.

"We … well, Detective Constable Knowles has identified a number of the victims."

"Are they of a type?"

"Sort of."

"Sort of?"

"Mostly minorities, but not exclusively."

"Black, predominantly," Knowles said.

Alicia sipped her tea. She'd never tried oat milk before, although she'd sampled almond milk and hated it. Oat milk in tea was marginally less vile, but she sympathised with the face Knowles had pulled earlier, her own lips retracting tightly.

"It's an acquired taste," Maisie said. "When I made the decision to stop consuming goods that tortured animals, I found milk much harder to give up than leather."

Knowles hadn't touched his since the first sip, and appeared in no hurry to acquire that particular taste.

Alicia sipped a little more out of politeness. "It's not that bad."

"The 1970s, correct?" Maisie asked.

"And into the eighties," Knowles said.

"A bad time for people of colour."

Knowles laid one hand on the table and another over it, eyes on them. "Not that much has changed."

"Oh, my dear." Maisie placed one of her hands over Knowles's. "The tiki torch brigade are just pale shadows of the sort of hate we faced in the seventies. Minorities still suffer, of course, but racism was *mainstream* back then."

Knowles pulled away gently. "I'm sure that's the case."

Maisie almost smiled over the teacup as she brought it to her mouth again. "DC Knowles, I won't minimise any experiences you've had by trying to one-up you. And I certainly had it much easier than most black and Pakistani and Indian people. The police barely needed to conceal their prejudice. A white woman working as a prostitute was considered scum and barely worth their attention, as evidenced in their dealings with the Yorkshire Ripper. Can you imagine how much attention they would give a *black* prostitute disappearing?"

Alicia knew she'd get to the point eventually. "Manchester, Huddersfield, Halifax, Leeds."

"The M62 corridor. I suppose he thought he was being clever. Hiding his bodies where no one would find them."

Knowles took out his notebook, a swish moleskin number with the pages glued flush to the spine, meaning any torn out would leave an obvious gap for a defence lawyer to exploit. Which was helpful, providing Knowles didn't put too much in there. "Is it too early to speculate that the seventies killer came across the Lainworth Ripper's dumping ground, then decided to use it himself?"

"No, I think speculation is healthy," Maisie said. "Although stumbling across it by chance wouldn't turn him into a killer. A normal person would report it, not turn into a homicidal maniac."

"He could've been looking for somewhere to hide a body," Alicia said. "Planning."

"We're safe assuming his target is someone of colour," Knowles said, "since the majority of the bodies have fit that profile."

"I think so." Alicia ran with it, brain and mouth in sync for a change. "Wants to kill someone, needs a place to dump them. Doesn't need fame, so doesn't want it exposed. Digging a grave draws attention, and with Ian Brady and Myra Hindley fresh in the nation's memory, it may have felt wrong or just plain risky."

"Indeed," Maisie said. "But if they want to make a statement, why so desperate to conceal the body?"

Alicia's brain pinged and she grinned. "Malcolm? Are you there yet?"

Knowles nodded. "I think I was there before you for once."

Maisie placed her empty cup back on the tray. "Well?"

"He knew his first victim. Or was familiar with who they were."

Alicia clapped briefly. "Care to offer a profile?"

Knowles contained a bashful smile and shook his head. "Nah, I'll leave that to the expert."

"White male," Alicia said. "Local. Either unemployed or working a menial, low-skill job. Not wealthy. Miserable. Struggles with relationships, both sexual and platonic. Believes other people are the problem, not himself, and needs someone to blame for his crappy life. Stalks someone doing better than him, someone *unworthy* of doing better than him. Wants to kill them, but is afraid. He explores local ground, maybe local legends, and finally finds the stash of bodies in a cave out on the Dales, up over the hill known as the Beacon." Alicia's mind whirred smoothly. "It's his trigger. Killing his first, getting away with it. He likes it. And he does it again."

A heavy stillness settled over the kitchen.

"Or he murdered his wife for the insurance," Maisie said. "Murdering a loved one is traumatic. But continuing the compulsion … might have started to enjoy it to suppress the trauma."

Alicia nodded along, feeling like a student again. She'd made fanciful leaps of logic where no evidence existed.

"First murder often leads to another," Maisie went on. "It could be the trigger that set him killing others."

"Or he'd already killed someone by accident and needed to dump the body," Knowles said.

"Or he was a hired gun. Or he was a racist who experienced a psychotic break. Or a million other reasons."

Alicia picked up the thread, returning to the actual evidence, to the most logical explanations. "Without a motive, we have no starting point. So we look at two educated guesses: that the killer knew his first victim, which led to others; or that he targeted people of colour for his own reasons. Whichever, it's something more complex than a simple sadist."

"I concur," Maisie said.

Knowles armed himself with a pen again, hovering over his notebook. "Were there any groups like the English Defence League or the British National Party around at that time?"

"The BNP is mostly in decline now, but it was active back

then. The EDL is fairly new. Neither has a big presence here in Moleford, but I know there's always been a small element. There are clubs where I've seen a lot of Union Flags and St. George's crosses and the like."

"Flags don't mean racists," Knowles said.

"No, but an over-abundance of something can indicate over-compensation. Plus, I did some actual research."

"What sort of research?"

"White supremacist groups back then didn't have to be as careful as they do today." Maisie stood and wandered out of the room without an explanation.

Then, as Alicia rose to follow her—assuming that was the intent—the older woman returned. She handed Alicia a thin book called *The Last Vanguard of Britishness*. Contained within a plastic library sleeve and printed on cheap card, the black-and-white cover displayed a crowd of young men marching down a London street with a Union Flag at the front. Most appeared to be skinheads or punks, although from what Alicia knew of the era, true punks acted in the opposite way; they tended to veer away from such nationalism toward anarchy, where everyone lived their own lives independently. Nationalism would be counter to that movement, although protesting government institutions may have offered some common ground.

"Published 1972," Maisie said. "No attributed author, but the words on the flag here suggest it was written by a member of this group."

Alicia squinted to see the words on the flag, which were a little blurred due to the quality of the picture, the age of the book, and the sleeve preserving it.

"The Yorkshire Vanguard," Maisie said. "They went away for a while, but like many of these groups, they sparked back to life."

"What is it?" Alicia asked.

"A book made up of letters. Not an epistolary novel, but real letters. Written to publications and MPs, presumably designed to discern who was on their side. Some MPs replied with support, the communiqués of which are also printed. Some showed a distaste for their attitude; also printed. They note which letters to newspapers were published by editors and in which media publications. It's a … manifesto, of sorts."

"These clowns are still around?"

"Yes. Smaller now, but still ticking along. The Vanguard is active out of the Strangers' Club in town. It's run by someone called Bertie Bradshaw, aged seventy-two years, seven months, and three days."

Alicia stared at Knowles. "Meaning?"

"Meaning," Knowles said, scribbling frantically, "that he'd have been in his early twenties at the height of the killings. He might know something."


After the two detectives finally took the hint and departed, Maisie celebrated her relief by slowly and carefully wiping the china cups with a damp cloth before using an organic mix of bicarbonate of soda, essential oils, and soap nut residue to act as a washing agent in a sink of warm water. Maisie believed chemicals, even those in washing-up detergent, should be avoided wherever possible, but she didn't wish to explain all that to the detectives whom she now watched leaving her garden.

Although glad she'd been able to help with the investigation, she was a little disappointed that they'd needed her help at all. They were supposed to be professional law enforcement, and someone like Maisie—retired, eager to be left alone—shouldn't have to be the one to push them in the right direction. Heck, she'd only started her research in the first place because she saw how disinterested the police were in potentially making arrests. All the talk had been about the relatives finding closure and giving the bodies "proper burials."

That was back when only a handful of bones had been discovered, though. Now they were into double digits, originating from two different eras. It was probably why her stomach was giving her a little trouble; the conflict of annoyance that the police hadn't looked beyond Google for their research into the matter, and gratitude that someone as sharp as Detective Inspector Friend was pushing the youngster in the right direction.

"Are they gone?" a boy asked.

"Yes, Peter, they're gone." Maisie could no longer see the two detectives as the twelve-year-old boy stood on tiptoes by the sink to peer out.

A girl came and stood beside Maisie as she placed the last of the cups to drain and dunked the teapot. Two years older and slightly taller than Peter, she asked, "Will they be back?"

"I think they will, Joanne. I think so."

# CHAPTER NINE

ON THE WAY down the lane from Maisie Jackson's house, Knowles pointed out two things: first, they never did find out how Maisie's garden escaped the flooding unscathed; and second, him and Alicia barrelling into the Strangers' Club to have a word in the middle of the afternoon might not be the best idea. *Community policing at its finest.*

At the bottom of the lane, Alicia prodded him in the arm. "You're not frightened of a horde of racist thugs, one of whom might have killed a couple of dozen people thirty years ago, are you?"

He knew she was joking so replied with a quick shrug. "As long as we're armed with Glock 17s and no one minds me shooting them in the face, we should be fine."

Alicia pumped the air. "O-*kay*! Now it's a party."

Rather than tooling up and descending on a pub full of potentially drunk white supremacists, they headed to the library, where Alicia introduced Knowles to Lauren and Costas. In a private room up on the first floor, she used Knowles's laptop to log on to the West Yorkshire Police's intranet service.

"Researching the Vanguard?" Knowles asked.

"There must be something on them." Alicia accessed the criminal record check function, got a ping to her phone as part of the two-step authentication, then entered "Yorkshire Vanguard" in the advanced search box, seeking out affiliated individuals.

"Might be worth asking the local press about them," Knowles suggested, pulling out his plus-sized smartphone. "Moleford Bridge isn't exactly renowned for groups like this. It's a nice place."

"Couple of hits." Alicia scrolled through the results of convicted criminals who were known to associate with an organised nationalist association. "Old convictions. The worst incidents, major assaults, go back to the nineties, and some less detailed stuff in the eighties. Some football hooliganism since 2000, a few violent reactions to terror attacks and child trafficking rings. Most recently Michael Strickland away at Millwall last year, who is still inside for ABH. James Grantham, cautioned for criminal damage at an anti-Islam rally in London two years ago, along with Russel Davy, Mortimer Jones, Robert Bradshaw, and Sean Pryor."

With Alicia monopolising his computer, Knowles looked up the rally via a conventional internet search on his phone and found an article from the *London Evening Standard*. "A ton of these guys went down, not just Vanguard. I remember it now. Made the national news. Only a few incidents. Claimed provocation by anti-fascist counter-protests. Our boys are named in the press too, but a quote from the group leader—*Bertie* Bradshaw, not Robert here—says he never intended it to get violent. In fact, he apologises formally, says he was trying to break up a skirmish, but his actions just escalated the situation. He retired after this, apparently. Too much 'biased press intrusion'."

Alicia had accessed an intelligence report on the group; police forces around the country routinely monitored any club or organisation that might conceivably be considered "extreme." From Islamists professing sympathy, or in some cases outright support, for terrorist acts or wishing for the eradication of Israel, to Christian charities whose language bordered on the militant when it came to abortion or gay rights. The Yorkshire Vanguard fell far closer into the Islamist side of the spectrum than either group would ever admit.

"Chap called Glenn Bishop appears to be running things now," Alicia said. "Since the London protest, they've kept a low profile unless something specific crops up. They led a demonstration outside a mosque where a half-dozen paedophiles used to worship before being identified and arrested."

"Any violence?"

"No, things calmed down when the imam invited them all in for a cup of tea."

Knowles looked over her shoulder, unsure if she was joking again or not. She was, it seemed, perfectly serious. "A joint statement?"

Alicia nodded. "After chatting with the imam and a couple of prominent Muslims, Mr Bishop claimed to be satisfied that worshippers were not hiding child molesters within the community, and was surprised to learn that it was members of the Muslim community who had tipped police off to the six men's activities. That fact hadn't made the press because investigations were still ongoing. Glenny-Boy accepted their sincerity." Alicia sat back. "Well, that was big of him. What a peacemaker."

For some reason, that troubled Knowles more than if it had erupted into violence. "He appears reasonable."

"Appears."

"It was set up," Knowles said.

Alicia nodded agreement, smiling up at him from her chair. "Look who's getting his profiler hat on."

"More my *Art of War* hat. I forget the exact quote, but Sun Tzu says that to defeat your enemy you must know your enemy."

A knock sounded at the door, and Costas poked his head in. "Hi, Abhu Noon is here to see you? "

"Who?" Knowles asked.

"Abhu Noon. One of our councillors. He said you were expecting him."

"Not exactly," said a man striding in. His voice was clipped and formal without a discernible accent, neither posh nor Yorkshire. He was bearded, tall, and wore a sky-blue turban and a dark pinstripe suit, his shirt and tie so crisp he would have fit in with any executive boardroom in the country. "I never actually said they were expecting me. I said I was here to discuss matters with them."

Alicia was already on her feet, wagging her finger. "That was very naughty, not to mention rude."

Abhu Noon halted and looked at Knowles as if for clarification on something.

"Meet Detective *Inspector* Friend," Knowles said.

"Now, since you intentionally deceived Costas here," Alicia said, "what do you have to say to him?"

Mr Noon turned his head, frowning. "Sorry?"

"That's correct, you should be saying sorry. But tell Costas, not me. And I want to hear you mean it."

"I'll be outside," Costas said. "Or I can call for backup."

"Thank you, Costas, that's very sweet of you, but backup won't be necessary." Alicia bounced on her toes, her hands balled into fists. "I'll take care of him if he tries anything."

Abhu Noon simply stared. "Are you really a police officer?"

"Are you really a councillor?" Knowles asked.

Mr Noon squared his shoulders. "I want to know about any progress you are making on the bodies found, and what connection this might have to the Yorkshire Vanguard."

Knowles's heart thumped as he pictured Watson chewing him out over such a swift leak. They hadn't reported their line of inquiry to anyone yet, meaning... "Shit." He reached for the laptop and closed the lid, glimpsing the search results beforehand. "We cannot comment on an ongoing investigation. I assume I can rely on your discretion, councillor."

"Sneaky," Alicia said.

Mr Noon took a seat uninvited. "Officers, I—"

"Detectives," Knowles said.

Alicia had a curious expression that Knowles couldn't read, one that seemed to be saying *get a load of this guy*, and he hoped she wouldn't keep up the routine of speaking to the man like he was a toddler. Sure, he was being an arse, but they were the police; they served the public, including arses.

"Detectives," Abhu Noon said with a what sounded like great effort. "I have been elected by the people here to represent them in—"

"Bin collections," Alicia said.

She was smiling, but Knowles sensed there was more.

"I beg your pardon?" Mr Noon said.

Knowles stepped in. "I think what DI Friend is saying is that she wants to clarify your role here—"

"No." Alicia still radiated that pixie-like grin. "I'm saying he's a glorified bin-man. Bustling in here demanding a progress report on matters that are none of his business." Now the smile showed teeth, stretching her lips wide. "Mr Abhu Noon is a councillor, not an MP, and therefore responsible for getting people's bins emptied, cleaning the streets, maintaining the flower pots you see around town. The biggest of his responsibilities in the council offices should be facilitating the flooding clean-up operation in conjunction with government agencies. Not looking over our shoulders. In fact, even the MP himself wouldn't be entitled to a front row seat. So I'm confused, Mr Noon." The smile dropped into a dead stare. "What exactly do you think you are doing here?" Then the smile popped back into existence.

Mr Noon, to his credit, simply clasped his hands together. "I'm sorry to barge in like this, but I do have people asking me about it every day. I have to at least try to find answers."

Perhaps Alicia read his manner as being all bluster. Now that Knowles thought about it, Mr Noon's demands struck him as a bluff, since he really didn't have any leverage in this. Some people considered councillor and MP to be similar positions, but they really were not.

"Sir," Knowles said, "we are currently pursuing a number of leads. If we need help with local knowledge—business owners and the like—perhaps we can call on your expertise and experience?"

The councillor stared at his hands, his face neutral as he examined his fingers, before returning his gaze to Alicia with a slight smile to mirror hers. "The Vanguard aren't as bad as the press makes out. They supported me in my campaign, you know."

Alicia moved in front of Knowles before the DC could speak. "You know Bertie Bradshaw?"

"I know Glenn Bishop. A bunch of lads who want to defend British values. Some girls too, but mostly lads. I really think they're trying to see through the colour of people's skin and simply be sure those coming here are integrating. Not living separately with archaic traditions and prejudices."

Silence reigned now, and blood thumped up Knowles's spine. He couldn't quite believe what he was hearing from the Asian man. Knowles stepped to the side, catching a glimpse of Alicia's mouth, which was open in a slit. She was plainly as gobsmacked as him.

"You want to be an MP," she said.

Abhu Noon's chest puffed up and he squared his shoulders toward Alicia. "I don't know what—"

"You do." Knowles paced slowly, riding Alicia's coattails. "I see it now. There's talk of snap elections all the time these days, and you want to position yourself as looking out for voters by liaising with the police. You want to reach out to as many demographics as possible. By working with people like Bertie Bradshaw and Glenn Bishop, you get a handy two-for. You show people like *Sentinel* readers and general racists that you're able to work for them as a human rather than a Sikh man, *and* you show more liberal-minded folk you're able to negotiate peacefully with a right-wing element. Doesn't matter which party you represent."

Mr Noon stood and pulled his suit jacket over the faint bulge of a stomach. "I'm an independent."

Knowles held out an arm toward the door. "Then independently leave us to do our damn jobs. We'll be in touch if we need you. Sir."

Abhu Noon took a business card from his wallet, and with his eyes on Knowles he handed it to Alicia, faced the door, and departed.

"Now that was awesome." Alicia held up a flat hand for a high-five and Knowles slapped it. "Now let's go chat to Bertie Bradshaw before our future prime minister gives them a heads-up."

# CHAPTER TEN

THE STRANGERS' Club struck Alicia as a nice little drinking hole set into a long row of pubs on a hill heading into the town centre. She liked the possessive punctuation in the title, too, suggesting the establishment belonged to all strangers who happened by, not one single stranger. She guessed that made her part-owner. It was located on the outer part of a shallow bend near the bottom of a hill, an outcrop rounded in the large blocks ubiquitous to this region. A tidemark from the chest-deep water stained the wall and, like most other businesses nearby, they'd stocked up on sandbags that had given little in the way of protection. The sign was either retro or old—it was hard to tell—and in the middle of the afternoon, the place was doing brisk trade.

She and Knowles watched the place from across the street for a few minutes.

"You sure you want to go in?" Alicia asked.

Knowles rolled his eyes and set his jaw in the way men do when they want to dismiss another's concerns. "You heard the councillor. It's not about skin colour. Besides, if I played the health and safety card every time a tense situation cropped up, I'd never leave the office."

"Ooh, get you. Hope you know karate or something."

"I get by."

Another macho bit of posturing, but Alicia wouldn't call him on it yet. Maybe later. If she could bring it up in a funny way.

They crossed the street and entered, finding it more cramped than it appeared from outside. It was also brighter than Alicia had pictured it, more modern: light wooden floor, gleaming poles, four ultra-HD TVs large enough for sports coverage. Union Flags hung everywhere: one draped over the bar and bunting hung across the walls in waves. Even the towels bore the colours, and a portrait of Queen Elizabeth II took pride of place. The bar circled the centre, while booths dominated the perimeter and tables and chairs were dotted throughout.

A dozen male patrons and a couple of women milled around with pints of lager and ale, some in small groups, others alone or in pairs. Surprisingly few skinheads; most patrons dressed in jeans, some shorts, a few football shirts, only a smattering of leathers. An unusual couple looked up at Alicia and Knowles, their gaze lingering. Both were in their twenties; the man wore a white formal shirt, black trousers, and shoes, while the woman had cut-off denim shorts, a white vest top, and a denim waistcoat. Her hair was blond streaked with purple, while the guy sported a full head of thick, brown hair, expertly coiffed, and he looked sort of familiar.

The chap tapped a nearby fat man with a beard and a Leeds United shirt, and that guy's group of three pinpointed the detectives.

Alicia gave a little wave. "Hi, guys!"

Everyone clocked them now, nudges and pointed fingers spreading word of the intrusion.

Knowles held out his credentials. "Police. Carry on as you were. We're not looking to bring anyone in."

"Good," the Leeds United fan said. "'Cause we done nothing wrong here. Just having a drink."

"We'll be having a quick word with Bertie, then be on our way."

No reaction from the drinkers. They continued to stare.

"Okay, nice welcome." Alicia wandered to the bar. "Bertie! Hello, Bertie?"

A narrow channel off to the right extended along the bar, but beyond was in darkness. From here, a older man emerged, hobbling slightly though he used no cane. He could have been sixty or eighty, but since his image matched the one on his file, albeit with more lines, no one needed to guess.

"Bertie Bradshaw?" Knowles said.

"That's me." The two years since he announced his retirement had not softened the man's features. There was a cragginess to them that seemed to pull the loose skin tight but was unable to smooth it out entirely. He opened the lid of the bar and stood with the taps and trays between them. "Saw you on the cameras. Police. What do you want?"

"I need to ask something very important," Alicia said.

"What?"

"Is the reverse-Tardis effect intentional?"

"The what?"

"This place. It looks bigger on the outside than it is on the inside."

"Right. Yeah. We're not properly open yet." Bertie turned casually, opened a panel over the cash register, and flipped a bunch of switches. Behind him, along the bar's channel, lights came on and the darkness bloomed to life, revealing a much wider space with a stage and open floor. "Fully licensed, if you're asking."

"Could we impose on you for a few minutes?" Knowles asked. "We need to ask about some former members of the Vanguard."

Bertie shrugged. "Hey, someone watch the bar, yeah? Gotta grass up some mates to these guys."

A ripple of amusement ebbed around the place, and as the big man in the Leeds shirt waddled to the bar, cheers rose.

"Not you, Russ," Bertie said.

The man's shoulders slumped in an exaggerated mime, and he returned to his friends.

The chap with the good hair who'd first spotted Alicia lifted his pint. "I'll watch out, Bertie."

"Thanks." Bertie made his way into the narrow route toward the back room, calling back, "And Scarlett, you watch your fella."

The purple-streaked blonde grinned and threw Bertie a thumbs-up. "No worries!"

Alicia and Knowles followed Bertie past the loos to the larger space that had plainly borne the brunt of the water damage: boxes stacked in leaning towers, wood ripped up from the left side, the boards of the stage itself warped and dark.

"My office." Bertie held open a door and flicked on the light.

Alicia looked inside the plain space and was reminded of a used car dealership office, where a person might sit while a salesman pretended he was losing money if he let a vehicle go for the price being proposed. Although the desk and chairs were cheap, the bookcase was new.

"Saved the books," Bertie said. "Put 'em upstairs. Replaced everything in here, though. Rest of the place should be fixed this week."

Alicia perused the shelves, mostly non-fiction titles. Plenty by people she'd heard of, standouts being titles by Anne Coulter, Donald Trump's *The Art of the Deal*, and biographies of luminaries such as Adolf Hitler, Winston Churchill, Margaret Thatcher, and Nelson Mandela. Alicia wondered about the last one.

There were more, too—big figures in the modern world and the twentieth century, people like Sarah Palin, Nigel Farage, and Teresa May; and the odd sop to the left side of the spectrum, subject matter including Tony Blair and Jeremy Corbyn, though nothing written *by* the pair. Lower down, other titles by people she'd vaguely heard of and some she hadn't: Paul Goodman, Robert Halfon, Remington Duval, Megyn Kelly, Glenn Beck, Katie Hopkins, Milo Yiannopoulos—all political pieces, by the looks of them.

"You like to read," Alicia said.

"That's some of the best detective work I've ever seen," Bertie replied.

Alicia scanned the lower shelves. The volumes here were decidedly scruffier—cardboard backed, some in plastic sleeves, local history and obscure subjects like canals and railways. She turned curtly. "Could we perhaps do this out there?"

Alicia didn't want to be trapped in that office with no exit except a window. If even a handful of the guys drinking back there got the idea to attack them, they'd have no back door.

"If it makes you more comfortable." Bertie led them out to the larger space with the stage, a fire exit in one corner propped open illegally with a fire extinguisher.

Alicia chose to not see it. "About the reading material. Shoring up your prejudices?"

"Understanding fellow strugglers," Bertie said.

Knowles had his pen poised over his notebook. "Strugglers?"

Bertie raised a hand in the younger detective's direction, a placating gesture. "Ain't got a beef with you, Detective. Long time ago, blacks were a problem, but they've mostly integrated now. Problems in black areas, they're mostly the same as poor white areas—money. Or the lack of. We're in the same boat. Born poor, stay poor, that's the establishment keeping us down."

"You're doing okay." Malcolm glanced around. "I mean, you will be, when it's fixed up."

"So are you." Bertie gave Malcolm an appraising once-over. "But the media in my youth liked to hype up the black menace. 'Need a mugger, get a ni—' get a black kid in. Ignored that white estates were circling the same drain. Especially up north, with

Thatcher and her lot pinning us down. Now we face a proper threat."

Alicia struggled to keep the cheery persona front and centre, but it was the way she worked best. If she let the hate bother her, she'd fold into a ball and never come out. The nice Alicia, the chirpy Alicia, blocked out that darkness.

So she painted on a smile, paced a couple of steps with a skip to her gait, and pointed happily at Bertie and said, "Muslims!" and intoned a dramatic tune: "Duh-duh-duuuuuh!"

Bertie dead-eyed her. "Take the piss all you want, love. But the enemy is real and it's living among us. Refusing to integrate, refusing to call 'emselves British. Always British-Muslim. Never get British-Christian or British-Sikh, do you?"

Malcolm's lips had pressed together, meaning he wanted to speak but was worried about saying the wrong thing. Alicia was getting to know him better and better, though, and let the silence hang until Malcolm filled it. "The six million Muslims in this country might disagree, sir."

"They might *say* they disagree." Bertie stuffed his hands in his pockets. "Look, they wanna live in their enclaves, fine. They can have their neighbourhoods. I'm against exterminating them en masse, and you can't deport 'em all. Who'd have 'em?" He gave a weak chuckle. "So we're stuck with six million terrorists, child abusers, forcing marriage between cousins—"

"I think you might have a bit of spittle on your chin," Alicia said, bored now.

Bertie wiped his chin, the back of his hand mysteriously dry.

"I must say, I'm impressed you read at all," Alicia went on, forcing the spring back into her step.

Bertie held himself stock-still, his fists back in his trouser pockets. What had seemed a casual gesture before now struck Alicia as concealment, possibly hiding anger at having his attitude questioned, wanting to swing a fist but able to resist. *Just.*

He sighed, shoulders relaxing. "Heard it all before, love. Did you come here to question my politics and taste in literature? Or was it something specific?"

"This." Alicia whipped the Yorkshire Vanguard book she'd borrowed from Maisie Jackson. "The ISBN is 1972. I'd like to know who wrote it."

Bertie's eyes brightened at the sight. He reached for it and Alicia relinquished the item, which he opened carefully. "Haven't seen a copy of this for a while. Library?"

"It wasn't on public display. The person who found it had to ask specifically."

"Of course it wasn't on display. Leftie liberal idiots won't want their safe place contaminated." He turned the book over in his hands, flipped to a couple of the letters written to newspapers and MPs. "A campaign to see which MPs would listen. Which newspapers supported us."

"Some are labelled as published," Malcolm said. "Some rejected, some ignored."

Bertie nodded along. "Yeah, I remember this coming out. I wasn't part of it. In fact, I opposed this sort of thing."

"You did?" Alicia said.

Bertie handed it back to her and spoke softly. "If you're not a liberal when you're twenty, you have no heart. If you're not a conservative when you're forty, you have no brain."

"Churchill," Malcolm said.

"Paraphrased, of course." Bertie wafted a hand. "Can't remember shit these days. What do you *want* exactly?"

"We'd like to speak to any of these chaps who might still be around."

Bertie shook his head. "What about?"

"About police business," Malcolm said.

"Anyone old enough to have written a letter'll be long gone, or useless."

"You were old enough," Alicia said.

"I was twenty. I wasn't involved with them."

Alicia pointed to the book cover, the grainy photo of the march. "Most of these lads are young. Take another look." She held out the book for him. "There's a list of contributors in the front."

"Then you'll go?"

Malcolm emphasised his pen and notebook. "Names, any ideas on locating them. Then we'll go."

Bertie turned to the page near the front and ran a finger over the words. "James Grantham comes in sometimes. He's in one of them electric wheelchair scooter things, plus he's strapped to an oxygen tank most of the time. Must be ninety by now. Doubt he's up to much, unless he's wanted for running over someone's foot. Which he enjoys a bit too much."

He continued reading, pausing at certain names.

"Danny Pryor died three years ago, but his lad Sean is a regular. I keep an eye on him for his old man. Remington Duval—he liked to write, published a couple of longer pieces, but I think he went the same way as Danny. There's one of his books on my shelf if you're interested."

"Thanks," Alicia said. "I'll pass for now."

"Martin Bainbridge ... the name rings a bell, but I couldn't point him out. Terry Grantham, James's little brother, he was locked up in the eighties for murder, never came out that I know of. Dead or still inside." He snapped the book shut. "That's all I can give you."

Malcolm kept scribbling. "James Grantham is still around, you say?"

"Yeah, but if he can remember last Tuesday it'll be impressive. And ... if you do talk to him, it's probably best if..." He gestured to Alicia. "If you do the talking. Maybe take someone else with you, if you get my drift."

Malcolm rubbed the back of his hand. "He still doesn't take to folk like me?"

"For some people, it'll always be about skin colour. For

people with a brain…" Bertie tapped his head. "It'll be about character."

Alicia summoned another of her high-wattage smiles especially for Bertie. "And about holding the same blind nationalism that you do?"

He sighed again, and explained in a patient, reasonable-sounding manner. "If there was a massive Muslim takeover, like an ISIS or Al Qaeda invasion that succeeded, the vast majority of Muslims in this country would rejoice. The only reason they're mostly peaceful now is because they wouldn't stand a chance against the rest of us. Stick in a Muslim dictator, and then you'll know where their loyalties lie. Wanna know their true nature? Pick up Tariq Bashir. Local rabble rouser for the fundies. He'll burst your liberal bubble, quick-smart."

Alicia was about to reply when the chap in the formal shirt called from the edge of the bar, "Hey, Bertie, there's a queue, mate."

"Cheers, Glenn." Bertie ambled up toward the main area, calling back, "Look around. Check out the books. Give Remy Duval's a go if you're interested in opening your mind a bit; decent writer in his day before he went the same way as the rest of the older fellas. Then bugger off; you're lowering the class of my joint."

As Bertie disappeared, the smart-looking guy lingered a few seconds, his athletic build clear under his shirt. He nodded, and followed the landlord.

"Shall we take a look?" Malcolm asked.

Alicia considered it, dropping into inspector mode for a second. "No. He could deny inviting us to look around, which will make it inadmissible. If we need anything, we'll come back with a warrant. Let's have someone run these names and see what comes back."

"Hope you're ready for a long night. This could take some time."

Bertie didn't like to think of the police as pigs, but the cavalcade of oinks as the door shut behind them compelled him to smile. Glenn Bishop slapped the bar as he leaned on it, he and Scarlett consumed with the hilarity of the joke. Sean Pryor, who'd lost some weight and tried getting regular jobs since his dad died, was happy to offer a mime indicating masturbation, and his pal Russel in the Leeds shirt flashed his belly. Of course, the coppers were long gone by the time this occurred, but it made them feel better, so why not. They'd be laughing and drinking that bit longer.

Then Glenn ordered a Diet Coke.

"Pacing yourself?" Bertie asked as he handed over the drink alongside Scarlet's pint of lager.

"Got work in the morning," Glenn said. "I start necking bevvies like this lot, I'll be a bleeding zombie. What's the filth want?"

Bertie loved how Glenn slotted his real question into a line of casual schtick. The guy took leadership seriously.

Although Bertie had hoped to pass the flame to Russel Davy after stepping down, Glenn had been a newer, fresher member with newer fresher ideas. A few had whispered they thought maybe he was an undercover pair of eyes for the government, but Glenn's actions since then had put paid to those rumours. He still seemed a little flimsy to Bertie, though. An administrator, always spouting about "the long game." That said, it was a democratic group and it was Glenn they'd elected, so it was Glenn they were stuck with for another three years, or until he quit, whichever came first.

"Asking about the old boys." Bertie nodded toward James Grantham, who'd scooted in while Bertie had been chatting with the blonde detective and the dark lad.

"Grantham?" Glenn said, surprised.

James was mid-eighties, but looked a hundred—sallow skin, the emphysema robbing him of muscle definition, his scooter making him reliant on mechanics to get him out of the house. His only remotely functional limbs were the arms that lifted his beer, his hands gripping the glass like talons, probably because they were the only parts of him he exercised. The advances of technology and the NHS provisions that gave him a measure of independence—the electric wheelchair, the mobile oxygen—just seemed to make him angrier and more bitter, as if he *wanted* to be restricted to his home, reliant on social services for company.

"A bunch of activists," Bertie said. "I gave 'em what they wanted. Nothing old bill can do to any of 'em. James, Dan, Remy, Tez—dead or dying."

Glenn nodded. "Hopefully that'll satisfy them. Bloody coppers."

"Hopefully." Bertie left Glenn Bishop to his soft drink, and greeted Sean Pryor with a big "Hey, hey!" as the lad ordered six pints.

Yes, the presence of the two cops had wound them up. Bertie might just be able to afford a lick of paint in the music room after all.

## CHAPTER ELEVEN

LUMB FALLS HAD BEEN a destination for walkers for decades. Probably longer. Nate Barlow didn't know. Didn't care. What he cared about was the way the light caught the water just right at sunset, how the unusually warm summer kept the water less frigid than most years, and how the plaque set into a rock gave him a chance to show his emotional side to whatever girl he managed to persuade to accompany him.

*The late poet laureate wrote a poem called "Six Young Men," inspired by a photograph taken at this spot just before the First World War.*

He read the last part aloud. "They all fought for their king and country, and made the supreme sacrifice." Nathan bowed his head solemnly. "Lest we forget."

"That's nice," Megan said, "but didn't you say you had some weed?"

Nathan pointed his clasped hands toward the plaque. "Doesn't it get you right in the feelings?"

"Whatever."

Megan had her hands the pockets of her tight jeans, the phone in her back pocket drawing Nathan's eye to her fine rear. While he'd listened and—at the time—agreed with the lectures at school warning against the dangers of objectifying the opposite sex, he had stopped paying attention when the subject turned to rape and what constituted consent. His mum had hammered all that into him long before he lost his virginity at fifteen to a very willing girl his own age. That had been in his creaky bedroom, not an awesome place like this.

A stream passed under a footbridge fifty yards back, feeding the main pool down a six-foot waterfall. Except in times of drought, the pool saw a constant supply of runoff from the surrounding hills. In this post-flood time, several new channels flowed.

All summer long, Nathan had marvelled at the place, and quadrupled his conquest count just by raiding his contact list. He didn't make any promises of a repeat performance, though. He was heading for university in September and wanted to be a popular guy around campus, so he figured getting his fill of local girls and gaining valuable experience in the process would serve him well.

Oh, yes, he made sure he pleased his partners. It wasn't a one-way street for him. He was a modern guy, after all.

Not that he needed a beauty spot to impress the girls he brought here. He was the epitome of an idealised teenage boy: handsome, as tall as an adult, and, having worked out since the age of twelve, he had pecs, abs, and solid muscular arms and legs. And he treated girls well, too. Or as well as he felt he needed to avoid a reputation as a dickhead.

"So." Nathan took a pre-rolled joint from his jacket and licked a stray edge to firm it up. "What do you think?"

"Pretty." Megan leaned against one of the damp rocks. Her cotton top clung to the shape of her breasts, and Nathan hoped against hope that no one happened by. It was why he waited until almost ten at night to make the suggestions to come exploring. He wanted to see her in all her glory, nude as nature intended, and girls tended to be shy any earlier in the day. He would reciprocate, of course.

*A modern guy.*

He pictured the pair of them stepping naked into the chilly-but-bearable water, buzzed a little from the weed, embracing, her leg curling around him as he lifted her in his strong arms…

"Nathan Barlow," came a girl's voice.

Not Megan's.

Nathan froze as Megan focused on him, her arms folded. Then Pricilla Haynes—a beautiful redhead who played hockey for the school and the town—stepped out from the rock on which Megan was leaning. Following her, Julie Maxwell adopted the same posture; blond and statuesque, actually taller than Nathan, she had been a little gawky until the long summer holiday between fifth year and sixth form in which she blossomed into the sort of beauty Nathan could see gracing a catwalk in the future.

"Pricilla," Nathan said. "Julie. Hey, how are you?"

"How are *we*," Pricilla said. "*We*'ve been talking."

Nathan held out the joint to Megan. "You in on this?"

Megan put the joint between her lips, unlit. "You seemed nice, so I checked you out online. Then you didn't seem as nice."

"I never promised anything." Nathan instantly felt a slug of bile in his gut as he said this. Wasn't that what misogynistic dickheads said? "Oh, wait…"

"Wait, nothing." Julie walked forward.

"Okay, so look, I may have misled you through omission…"

"And me!" A fourth girl appeared up top, another hottie from

Nathan's year, balancing on the level between the bridge and where the main waterfall spilled.

"Hi, Becky," Nathan called, still trying to remain calm … to convey he'd done nothing wrong. Yet his dumb remark—*I never promised anything*—echoed in the hollow of his chest.

"You're a shit, Nathan. Clever. But a shit."

Becky had been the first he had brought up here, the first he'd made love with under the overhang just out of sight of the bridge. She had told him she was just so happy in that moment. He'd been with her a few times since, but constantly craved others. Didn't see the point in settling down if he was heading off to uni to study astronomy.

That was stars, not horoscopes, as Pricilla had thought.

"Okay, girls, you got me." Nathan still wasn't sure if he should retaliate verbally, grovel and beg forgiveness, or simply run like hell. He had no idea what they were planning.

"Time's up," Megan said. "Time to pay the price."

Nathan frowned as the ground-level girls scooted to the rock and returned with super-soaker water guns, pumping the stocks like shotguns.

Oh, sure, he'd let them get their revenge that way. If it made them feel better. And he'd feel better too, having been punished for his lack of candour.

The three advanced.

Becky called, "Wait for me! I hid mine just here…" She crabbed over some rocks, searching.

But they didn't wait. Pricilla fired first, a jet of water splattering into Nathan's Saltrock shirt.

Something wasn't right. He sniffed at the wetness and an almost physical tang hit the back of his throat and pawed at his epiglottis. "What…?"

"My granddad's septic tank was being emptied this morning," Julie said. "We skimmed a little of the looser matter. Cool, huh?"

Julie fired, and that torrent hit him in the face. Then Megan's impacted his crotch, and as he bent over another squirt from Pricilla sluiced down his back. He cried out, hacked, swallowed vomit back, then turned to run. Becky had cut him off and opened her own assault.

One option: the pool.

Nate toppled in and waded away from them, waist deep as the cackling foursome sprayed and sprayed. He concentrated on keeping his mouth shut, planning to maybe climb to the top through the waterfall, leech some of the stink off him, and run back to town.

He'd been there ten seconds when he remembered the mobile in his pocket. "You bitches broke my phone!"

Megan fake-gasped. "Oh, no, he used the B-word! However will we sleep tonight?"

Having flanked him so there were two behind him and one on either side, both clambering over the rocks as he tried to escape. They opened a torrent, all four streams hitting him at once from different angles, warm human waste coating him, the occasional drop leaking through his lips. He opened his mouth to plead one last time, and a sizeable offshoot hit his tongue.

Nathan retched, brought up a mouthful of the Red Bull energy drink he had downed earlier, but kept most of it, and his dinner, where it belonged. He was about to duck under to escape, when the soakers fired empty. The girls just laughed.

He felt no anger or resentment toward them. His phone had full insurance, so he'd have a new one in less than a day; he wasn't even that bothered about it. He'd been dishonest, let his wants overwhelm his good sense, and acted like the sort of guy he swore he'd never become. Now he'd been punished for it.

He also wondered where they'd set up the phone to film the whole thing.

That was the only thing he wouldn't let them get away with. As long as it wasn't a livestream, he could persuade them to leave things be.

Probably.

"Part two!" called Megan.

Nathan looked at his attackers. They were hefting water balloons—only they were plainly heavier than water, containing something thicker. He did not want to imagine what that was, and he sure as hell didn't want to find out first hand.

He dove under the water and swam toward the waterfall, sensing the objects impact the surface like depth charges. When he came up he was right under the drop, the cool water spattering his head harder than he expected. The girls were cooing and calling him, shouting his own love-making lines back at him, the "*Oh baby*"s, the "*You make me so hot*"s, the—

Nathan was not alone under here.

There was someone on the ledge behind him, nestled in a depression at head height. Eroded over the years, it wasn't quite a cave, but large enough to explore.

He said, "Hey, look, I don't know what this is, but…"

The person didn't move.

Nathan pulled himself up for a better look, to placate this final conspirator and hope she wasn't about to slap a pie full of turd in his face.

What he saw made him heave the rest of his Red Bull from his stomach. It made him empty his dinner right out into the churning water below. And once he was done, he screamed louder than at any time in his short life to date.

# CHAPTER TWELVE

ALICIA GOT HOME LATE from Moleford Bridge, but was happy to leave the loose ends to the locals. She'd return with fresh eyes in the morning and focus on what she was best at: reading situations, and people. It was annoying to miss her kickboxing lesson, but it was Stacey she felt the worst about.

Although it was heartwarming to picture her mother's phone now coated in toddler slobber after Stacey insisted on a kiss goodnight, FaceTiming was no substitute for a real hug.

When Alicia knew she was going to be late, Dot had offered to keep Stacey for the night. Normally, Alicia would have said no and taken her little girl home, but two things stopped her: First, she wanted to be back out to Moleford Bridge as early as possible and a rush in the morning would be a bigger upheaval for all concerned; second, she'd received a text from Kate Hague.

*It's tonight. Can you come?*

Feeling bad about the imposition, she asked Iothor if she

could meet him at a pub they both liked, and he was happy to come along. She waited in a corner with an orange juice for herself and a Guinness for him. He wore a white pullover that clung to his shoulders and black jeans tight on his thighs. When he bent to kiss her cheek he smelled like apples.

"Sorry for calling so late," she said.

"It's only ten." Iothor cocked an eyebrow. "But it is a school night. You mustn't keep me too long."

Alicia smiled, belying the swarm of dragonflies shooting around her gut. She swallowed. Played with her glass.

"Are you okay?" Iothor asked.

"I need to tell you something."

Iothor stared into space a moment, then looked at his pint. "Ah. I see. You need to work more things out?"

"What? No, that's not what I mean. I'm not breaking up with you. Don't be silly. You're way too yummy and polite and well-groomed."

"Okay, phew." He lifted the Guinness to his lips which left foam on his facial hair. He licked it off.

"No, Iothor, you've been so patient. Understanding. And I wanted to explain a bit of it. About Stacey's dad."

Iothor placed his hand on Alicia's. She gripped his strong fingers. He said, "Is okay. I have baggage too. Bad relationships, they take a toll."

Alicia ran through the fraction of truth she'd revealed to him. She had never lied, just declined to talk about it. She'd said Stacey's dad was a bad person, that she hadn't known it at the time or she wouldn't have slept with him. Now, the only thing haunting her was that Stacey might inherit some gene, some obscure facet of DNA that had made her father descend into the realms of the unfeeling, violent persona—a creature without empathy.

Iothor had reassured her that no one had ever proved that nature trumped nurture. Anecdotally, it was the opposite. He reminded her of his own Viking heritage, of the baby-killing, woman-raping machines that had swept the northern hemisphere for generations. He understood, he'd said, and seemed to mean it, as he had never pressured her to reveal more than she felt comfortable.

"Stacey's father," Alicia began, after checking that no one was lingering in earshot. "His name is Richard Hague."

Iothor held still a long moment, his head twisting sideways a fraction so he viewed her through narrow eyes at an angle. A subconscious gesture of revulsion, Alicia was sure.

"The Century Killer," Iothor said.

"One and the same."

"How...?"

"His daughter was taken by an obsessed man willing to kill to play out his fantasies. I was trying to get her back."

Iothor's calm exterior cracked momentarily, but he snatched back the serenity that made Alicia so relaxed. Most of the time. "But ... how? Wasn't he...?"

"Obstructing the police investigation by torturing and killing key witnesses, yes. He thought he was better placed to locate his daughter than people trained and with years of experience. And like most psychopaths, he was an accomplished liar and very, *very* charming."

After a beat in which he leaned his elbows on the table and lowered his voice, Iothor said, "I would hope it was his *charm* that swayed you."

Alicia accepted the mild barb, although after weeks dating the teddy bear of a man opposite, it was more like a missile strike. She didn't blame him for wanting to retort, though.

"Who else knows?" he asked softly.

"Robbie, of course. My boss Murphy, although it's an unspoken rule that we never discuss it. A private investigator from New York who'd also joined the hunt that winter." She was extemporising now and didn't want to garnish that part of her life with flowery language. "Alfie Rhee. Richard killed Alfie's wife during his killing spree in the United States." She paused, meeting Iothor's eyes. "Alfie's wife was named Stacey."

"Jesus," Iothor sat back. "Is that everything?"

"Richard's daughter had a right to know, too, that she has a half-sister."

"The fruitcake?"

"She's not a fruitcake," Alicia said. "She was suffering deep clinical depression over the revelations, and a couple of years of trying to power through that depression led to a psychotic break."

"Did she not kill someone?"

Alicia shook her head. "I don't think so. I mean, it's possible. The body was found in Wolverhampton, but we have footage of her entering Leeds days earlier. She could have snuck back to do it, but that would require a degree of planning that I don't think she possessed."

"And there are plenty of people who seem to worship your… baby daddy."

Alicia swallowed back the phrase, the sarcasm hitting her in the gut harder than anything he'd said so far.

"I am sorry," he said immediately. "But Richard Hague, this Century Killer, he has a following. I have read about it. People who wish to continue his example."

"I know." Alicia bowed her head as Iothor's fingers enveloped her hands again. "Clean simple kills to rid society of parasites. But that isn't the issue. It's not the reason I'm telling you tonight."

"Tonight? Is there a purpose to this? Beyond telling me the truth?"

"Yes." She took a breath and released it slowly, wishing she'd chanced a stronger drink than the orange juice. "It's tonight Richard Hague is going to die."

Iothor couldn't say he was in love with Alicia, but he had certainly never met anyone like her before. The murder of his on-and-off lover earlier in the year had brought them into each other's orbit, and there had been a connection. Initially a suspect, Iothor had faith that she would unearth the real killer, and while he and his friends mourned the loss, his mind kept coming back to the little detective inspector with the highly unusual approach to police work.

She wasn't quite the tornado of quirkiness he expected—she was subdued because he was her first time dating since the father of her child "made himself unavailable," as she put it. Iothor could not have guessed "making himself unavailable" involved getting shot in the throat in a bid to save both his captured daughter and Alicia Friend.

And now here Iothor was, holding Alicia's hand as they walked the hall of Langton Hospital, a private clinic paid for by the aristocratic family who felt partially responsible for Kate Hague's traumatic kidnapping. The place where Richard Hague was kept alive by machines that pumped air through his lungs, nurses to clean him and turn him, a bed that massaged his muscles to keep them from atrophying.

Outside room 237, a sparrow of a girl stood next to a man in a long white coat, presumably the doctor, and two women in nurses' scrubs. On the way over, Alicia told him of her interaction with Kate—not the clinical diagnoses, but the key aspects like her alcohol abuse and how she'd fallen out of her exercise habits despite being a keen sportsperson. Iothor had expected a gibbering wreck, shaking and jerking spasmodically at every noise, not the young woman in the smart pantsuit and blouse. She wore her hair in a tight ponytail and although she was in her mid-twenties, if she'd been presented as a new student in the high school at which Iothor taught, he would not have questioned her admission.

She smiled as Alicia approached, but her mouth was the only

part of her that moved. Her attention wandered to Iothor, and Alicia introduced him as "a friend."

"Thanks for coming," Kate said.

"I'd be a fool for leaving you to do it alone," Alicia replied.

The two women held hands briefly, almost a handshake but more of a supportive gesture.

"You know Dr Rasmus," Kate said.

The man in the white coat shook hands formally with Alicia and they exchanged good-to-see-you-agains, then Dr Rasmus shook Iothor's hand. "She always liked the bigger men."

Alicia let her hair fall over her face, presumably to hide a blush to her cheeks. "This'll be good for her?"

"I do not know," Rasmus said. "It may be good. It may be bad. I advised against it at this stage in Kate's recovery."

Kate stood as stiff as a plank of wood, but she seemed fragile, like she could fold in on herself any moment. "Alicia, you said psychotherapy isn't an exact science. I've read a lot of articles, a lot of papers, and Dr Rasmus has helped get me to the point where I can live alone, keep my life in order, and even hold down a job. I want a boost. I want to move on. This is how I'll do it."

One of the nurses squeezed Kate's shoulder.

"Perhaps you will reconsider," Dr Rasmus said. "A couple of weeks."

"No." Kate looked to Alicia, not Rasmus, which Iothor deemed odd, but he said nothing. "It's time."

The other nurse opened the door, and Iothor viewed the father of Alicia's daughter for the first time. He'd seen pictures, of course, Hague now as notorious a killer in Britain's folklore as Ian Brady or Harold Shipman, but the man in the bed before them bore no resemblance to the square-jawed charm-monster in the media.

Dr Rasmus led the way, followed by the nurses. Kate froze in the doorway, with Alicia and Iothor outside behind her.

As a teacher, Iothor had seen teenagers who seemed strong

and stable one moment, then crumble into boneless wrecks the next as the emotional armour they had erected dissolved under the onslaught of whatever tragedy had befallen them.

Looking at Kate, he recognised the signs.

Alicia said nothing, though, just watched as Kate teetered between breaking down and pushing strongly through. The woman Iothor had become so close with—who kept her secrets yet promised to reveal them eventually—gave Kate time. She appeared to know just what to do: when to touch Kate, when to give her space.

One of the secrets Alicia had revealed on the way over was how she'd banned Kate from meeting with Stacey until Kate could hold down a job, lived independently, and posed no danger of a breakdown. After Kate had achieved that, Alicia offered to hold up her end of the bargain, but Kate declined. She wasn't all the way better, she said. She wanted to be all the way better before more big changes hit her. A decision like that wasn't the product of a diseased mind, Alicia told Iothor, but she had accepted Kate's decision.

"It's okay," Alicia said. "The doctor will do the actual switch-off."

Kate's gaze glided to her father, and Iothor couldn't help but do the same.

It was like the man whose arms lay atop the covers was slowly being absorbed by the bed. Skin was hanging off him, tubes going into his mouth for feeding and breathing, and in areas no one could see to expel waste. Had he not killed over a hundred people, Iothor would have felt sorry for him. And even given his status as a man of evil, Iothor did not wish to see a human being kept this way.

*Let him die*, he urged silently.

"I can't," Kate said, as if answering Iothor's plea. The girl shook her head and her armour vaporised, and she collapsed into Alicia's arms in a deluge of tears. "I'm sorry, I'm so sorry…"

"Little help?" Alicia said.

Iothor eased Kate's shoulders toward him, leaving her sobbing on Alicia but taking her weight on his own arms, and the pair of them helped her to a couch in one of the communal areas.

Kate sobbed as Dr Rasmus sat beside her, shoulders heaving as the tears came in waves. Alicia moved away, letting the clinician tend to his patient. She looked up at Iothor with sad eyes.

"Too soon," she said.

"So I see." Iothor gave a shrug. He wasn't sure why. "What do we do next?"

Alicia turned her phone on. "After a day like today? Normally, I'd be itching to get home to Stacey. Watch her sleep for a while like a creepy witch in the shadows. But tonight... there has to be somewhere open that serves whisky."

"Sounds like a plan."

Her phone bonged several times, messages coming in that had stacked up while she was incommunicado.

"Work?" Iothor asked.

Alicia's face darkened, a frown pulling her closer to the phone. "They found a body. A murder. Committed recently."

"But you are dealing with older ones. This can have nothing to do with your case, can it?"

"I really hope not," she said. "Otherwise, we have a hell of a crazy theory to work through."

# PART III

# CHAPTER THIRTEEN

NORMALLY, a night without Stacey gave Alicia the chance of a lie-in, even on days when she had to go to work. Unfortunately, with the news of a body showing up in a beauty spot not far from Basil Warner's farm, Alicia had slept only fitfully.

As she drove to the new disposal site, she mainlined coffee in the hope she could be sharp enough to connect any dots without making wild leaps of fancy. She and the other detectives all had to be careful: someone had planted an idea in their heads. It was a possibility they had dismissed, but this incident threatened to dredge it up and make them overcompensate.

*A killing spree that occurs every fifty years.*

A stupid notion, but one that a person with a hair-trigger imagination might embrace.

Patterns. Simple answers. Simple solutions.

Correlation wasn't the same as corroboration. She had to keep that in mind.

Despite the press being blacked out for the time being, parking was at a premium on the lane toward the falls—normally not a place for vehicles, but an exception needed to be made here. Once she found a spot on a grass verge, Alicia changed into her walking shoes and trekked up to Lumb Falls, flashing her ID at anyone who cared to ask.

*It can't be connected. This isn't my case.*

She followed the taped-off channels, rising steeply, until she came out of the quiet approach into a scrum of police officers and SOCOs. She was shepherded over a footbridge which traversed the small stream feeding Lumb Falls itself, a picturesque gathering of pools into which water fell from the one above before trickling away to its next destination. DI Cross was on-scene in fisherman's waders, observing the SOCO operation over the side. They'd rigged up a sort of rope bridge to reach the body, and evidence boxes were being transported from the rocky ledge to the side via a pulley system. Some clever clogs had diverted the main part of the waterfall using a V-shaped metal dam so the SOCOs could work, but the forensic officers were still required to wear wetsuits instead of the usual white coveralls.

When Cross spotted her, Alicia waved. Cross pushed around and made her way back to the shore, where she had to climb— which Alicia was sure would be omitted from the site's health and safety assessment.

"What have we got?" Alicia asked when Cross approached.

"It's grim." Cross led her around to where a wetsuit-clad man in his fifties operated the rope and pulley system, logging evidence as it arrived. "We haven't moved the body yet. Just retrieving as many removable objects as possible."

Gathered in separate bags in a weatherproof box Alicia noted earrings, a woman's watch, gold bracelets, shoes...

"How old?" Alicia asked.

"We think early twenties, maybe late teens."

"Been here long?"

"No blowfly intrusion to the flesh, so less than a day, although Maddy couldn't say whether they'd make it behind the waterfall. If it was the usual flow, maybe, but it's a bit heavier at the moment." Cross shrugged. "I'd expect a fox or badger to have sniffed it out if it had been here a while. How much do you know?"

Alicia had read the scant reports on the way over. Details were still under wraps, need-to-know, but she'd learned the body was female, was located in a shallow depression behind a waterfall, and homicide was the presumptive cause of death.

"Murder is definite?" Alicia asked.

"Oh yes. Come this way, you can see it better here."

Cross led her around the outcrop serving as a base for the rope system and pointed to where the two SOCOs worked ten feet away. It wasn't what Alicia had expected by any means.

At least ten pieces of a human being lay butchered on the ledge. Each arm was segmented into two and detached from the shoulder, and both dismembered legs were also cut into two. She had been decapitated. The pieces were in the wrong places, with the head at the groin and the arms pointing down from there, and the legs outstretched from the shoulders as if searching for a final, macabre hug.

Alicia wished she could have given her one. "On display."

"Yet hidden behind a waterfall," Cross said.

"Her skin looks dark. Any ID?"

Cross nodded. "Amina Shah. College ID was in her pocket. No address, no birthday, but we're visiting the college to find next of kin. Photo matches the head."

"Hate crime?"

"Possibly. Or honour killing. They're not unheard of, but I haven't seen one like this before. The cuts are fairly clean but not surgical; probably single blows, according to Maddy. Axe, machete, possibly a sword."

Alicia didn't want to voice it, but she had to. "Has anyone brought up the fifty-year thing?"

"Knowles did. On a conference call at five this morning when I woke up DCI Watson to apprise him of the progress overnight. Watson called him a Hannibal Lecter wannabe, and when

Knowles pointed out that Hannibal was the killer and Clarice Starling the detective, Watson called him Clarice for the rest of the chat. There were other detectives on the call, so expect it to stick."

Throughout Cross's summary, Alicia kept her focus on the dismembered remains of Amina Shah. "We're treating it as an isolated incident, then. Unless firm evidence links this to the older crimes?"

"Yep. I've been pulled off the historical deaths to run point on this. Maddy too. Once she's done here, Knowles can have her back. But this will get ugly, no matter how it turns out."

"Uglier than this?"

"If it's a hate crime, the Muslims and anti-fascist brigade will be out in force. An honour killing, the far right will use it as a stick to beat their drum again. And either way, the girl died horribly."

Alicia's general rule was to remain upbeat, to fight off the darkness of her job and demand that her true personality remain dominant. When she let the bad things intrude, she could not follow the advice of Nietzsche regarding becoming a monster through chasing monsters, and she made poor decisions— became blind to reality while her judgment skewed more toward justice than the law. Some would call it denial, many would say it was unhealthy, but Alicia's track record was in the top ten percent of law enforcement across Europe, so she wasn't about to abandon that need to cling to who she truly was.

But sometimes, she just couldn't.

For now, as she gazed into the abyss of human depravity, she allowed the abyss to gaze back into her. *Get a good look, you bastard. Because this is what's coming for you.*

"Want me to stick around?" Alicia asked.

DCI Watson had arrived and was striding across the foot-bridge. He spotted DI Cross and headed her way.

"He'll want this to stay with us," Cross said. "Profile won't be needed just yet. We'll find this guy through Amina's movements, her associations."

"Proper police work," Alicia said.

"We'll find him. If we need a consult, we'll call."

Alicia nodded and turned to leave. This wasn't her region, not her case, but she couldn't shake off the coincidence in timing. And despite her words to the contrary, Cross couldn't seem to either.

Alicia paused, hoping to offer a little insight, but would not do so uninvited. "For what it's worth, you probably worked out the basics."

"You have about thirty seconds until Watson kicks you out. So no time for games. Tell us what we haven't spotted that you have."

"Aside from the obvious brutality, the thing that stands out is a high level of organisation. This took planning. Not a spur of the moment thing. If it's a sadistic, random snatch, he'll be hard to catch. If it's a family member or some offended religious nutcase, it'll be simple. Someone who's been up here a lot, maybe changed their behaviour, suddenly coming home with muddy shoes or boots. A change."

"You have a gut on this?"

"It's not a passionate murder."

"Not a passionate murder?" Watson said, barely slowing until he was right up to the women. "What the chuff is that supposed to mean?"

Alicia sensed he was angry, although that might have been the early hour at which he had been roused. "Clean cuts, precise arrangement. The position of the pieces might be a crucifix or could have some other meaning. But it's like a project, not a punishment." Alicia let her mind whirr, expelling the feelings of revulsion that flooded her moments ago. "I assume the smaller pieces were held in place?"

Cross mimed the positions as she replied. "Small rocks that

look like they came from the pool here. Lined up down each side to keep the limbs from rolling."

"That's all I can give you for now. If you want my input, just ask. I'll be with Knowles up at the van." She gave them each a goodbye nod and walked away, hoping they'd call her back. They didn't. Yet the sense of coincidence rose steadily.

The cold of Nietzsche's abyss bloomed with warmth, and the cogs of her mind ticked.

She halted. Turned back to Cross and Watson, who'd fallen into conversation.

"For crying out loud, is no one going to explore this?"

Both slowly faced her.

"Sorry?" Watson said. "Did you forget something?"

"I have so much expertise in this area, and you're just going to gloss over the notion that someone might be inspired by these killings? Some sick individual who'd been wanting to kill, just because? Someone emboldened by the notion of mass murder having gone undetected for decades?"

"We haven't even released that those older bodies *are* murder," Watson said. "Far as anyone knows, it's an old graveyard that got wrecked."

"And even if someone got wind that it was a mass murderer," Cross added, "it's still not a direct connection."

"There's another possibility." Knowles had ghosted onto the scene unnoticed.

"What're you doing here?" Watson said.

Knowles exhaled slowly as Alicia hiked over to him. "Alicia said she was running late because she was popping by here. I assumed that was her inviting me to join you all."

Watson and Cross angled toward Knowles, both simultane-ously placing their hands on their hips.

Noticing the almost-comic effect, Watson dropped his hands to the side, eerily calm. "Explain yer possibility. And then both of y' bugger off and do what you're supposed to be doing."

Alicia observed Knowles as he kneaded his hands together and opened his mouth soundlessly. She bowed shallowly, which appeared to give him the confidence to give voice to his idea.

"We know this person was active in the 1970s," Knowles said. "This is becoming a much bigger crime than we first thought. It's going to be a big story, and if we haven't covered every single possibility, we'll be crucified."

"Tasteless," Cross said.

"Pardon?"

"The body," Alicia said. "You haven't seen it yet. It's laid out in pieces as if it's been crucified."

"Oh, sorry. I didn't know." Knowles cast his attention to his shoes for a second, then resumed. "But you know I'm right. If Alicia's theory yesterday turns out to be correct—"

"A suggestion, not a theory." Alicia raised a finger his way. "Brainstorming. There's no evidence for any of those scenarios. But go on."

Knowles seemed undeterred. "If this was a young man killing and hiding bodies back then, and his site was uncovered by the flooding... what if he figured he should start up again? If he's going to get caught, he may as well go out on a high."

No one moved. The diverted water trickled loudly, and voices from down the lane carried on the air.

"He'd have to be eighty," Watson said.

"Or seventy," Alicia said. "And we're also assuming the seventies bodies were the work of one person. Why not a pair? Why not a gang?"

Watson sized up his DI and she returned the favour. Both appeared to nod at the same time, but it was Watson who answered. "Murphy'll only extend your secondment if I keep manpower over there to cover. Which I can't afford without a damn good reason."

Cross didn't seem impressed, but with the pressure that would surely follow a murder like this, they needed to throw more at it. Not that Alicia *wanted* to stare at body parts or blood, or put herself in the mind of a killer once again, but—as cheesy as it sounded—she had a duty to try.

"Knowles and Friend, keep working the historical angle," Cross said. "Use the IDs on the bodies to bring me a suspect, if there's one still alive. We'll do the footwork here and get a read on the victim, her movements. Then we compare notes. If there's a hint of a crossover, it's a task force. If not, you're the cold case, we're the active one. Agreed?"

"Thank you, ma'am," Knowles said.

"Sounds good to me." Alicia was itching to get going now, but a uniformed constable was jogging their way. He slowed as he reached them, passing her and Knowles before coming to a standstill.

"Sir!" he called to Watson, then acknowledged Cross. "Ma'am."

"Problem?" Watson asked.

"Local rabble rouser," the constable replied. "Tariq Bashir? He's at the crime scene boundary with who he claims is the victim's family."

"The family is here?" Alicia said.

Watson snorted a humourless smirk. "Oh, great. That leaked out nice and quick."

"Guess I'm up." Cross sighed and started hoofing her way up the trail, allowing the constable to lead. "Everyone get to work. It's gonna be a long day."

# CHAPTER FOURTEEN

DI CROSS HAD FIRST MET Tariq Bashir during an outreach event two years earlier, in the wake of a small but brutal bombing committed by two Somali students pledging loyalty to one of the major Islamic terror groups active on the African continent. Their target had been a marketplace, but intel from the pair's fellow students—also Muslims, a fact that most media glossed over in their reports—allowed MI5 to intercept the Somalis' electronic trail, confirm an attack was imminent, and send the nearest police team in to arrest them as they boarded the number 92 bus toward Huddersfield. Unfortunately, their attack was more imminent than anyone had guessed—the two young men blew themselves up using a pressure-cooker device, killing themselves, the bus driver, and a disabled social worker, and injuring a family of four. Social unrest followed, and many churches, synagogues, temples, and churches banded together in the aftermath to condemn terrorism, far-right hate groups, and government cuts to community policing, which was widely viewed as contributing to mistrust from all directions in law enforcement.

Cross had attended the street party in the town centre as a member of her church, not a police officer, but she was recognised as such by some Asian youths she'd questioned on drugs offences recently, and a small but vocal rabble had accused her of being an undercover agent sent to infiltrate the gathering. It was Tariq Bashir who had stepped in, the voice of reason, backing up the vicar and demanding the youths' parents join them all to discuss why exactly Cross had needed to question them in the first place. Under their parents' withering gazes, the youths' bombast waned, and Cross cited data protection rules; the kids were over sixteen at the time so she couldn't speak about such things, since no charges were ultimately brought. She offered the ringleader a wink that suggested she was lying. She wasn't, but it gave the appearance that Cross was concealing their wrongdoing from their parents and added weight to the notion that she was "all right for a copper."

Bashir had spotted the wink and inferred the same, and Cross suddenly had an ally in a mosque that skirted the line between hardline and extreme. She knew him to be highly conservative, preaching that men are the head of the household and that women must obey the man's instructions; if the father, husband, or brother deemed it unnecessary for a woman to conceal her face entirely, it was acceptable for her to cover only her hair, which was about as liberal as the man got. He denounced homosexuals and feminists in the same breath, called for all forms of criticism of Islam to be outlawed as a hate crime (but not the denunciation of Judaism, for some reason), and referred to US and European foreign policy as "an evil crusade against the purity of Islam." Basically, he was an arsehole of the highest order, but a useful arsehole to keep onside, since the only thing he hated more than whatever president occupied the US White House was terrorism.

"Terrorism feeds the crusaders' war machine," he once told a TV programme on which he was invited to speak in the wake of the Somali students' bombing. "In the same way the Israeli occupation of Palestine feeds terrorists like Al Qaeda and Daesh, every time a brother commits murder in the name of Allah, the infidels strengthen their grip on Muslim countries, bomb more Muslim children, and take more of our land to line their already heavy wallets and feed their greedy bellies…" It went on like that for a bit.

So Cross never engaged in debate with him. She prayed for him, that one day he might let go of his anger and spite, and she gave him time if he ever wanted to talk. It may have been the sight of her approaching from the hedgerows that made him lower his megaphone and gestured for quiet from the dozen people who'd accompanied him in the minibus that waited just yards away.

She'd heard the taunts of "Justice Now," and "Muslim Lives Matter Too," and occasional breaks in the dogwhistle phrases for Bashir to declare that the police must act quickly, or suffer the anger of God. The final thing she heard from him was that they must never rest, never allow the police to rest until justice was done for Amina.

As the photographers and TV cameras rolled, Cross shook Bashir's hand. His grip was limp, as always. He didn't look happy, as such, but he did raise his eyebrows and the hard set of his mouth under his beard softened, if only momentarily. Without letting others hear, he said, "At least we have someone competent on the case." A fat man who wore loose-fitting traditional Islamic robes, he could have arrived directly from the Middle East, but as a born-and-bred Yorkshireman his tone didn't match his look.

"Good to see you, Tariq," Cross said. "I'm sorry it isn't under better circumstances."

"And I." He placed a hand on his chest. "Is it true? Was her body desecrated?"

"You mean… prior to death?"

Tariq twisted his upper body to take in the people behind him gathered near the red minibus, souped up with huge tyres for rougher terrain and daubed with Arabic writing, the name of his mosque, and several moon-and-star symbols alongside Union

Flags. Across the bonnet, in Arabic script, the phrase *Allahu-Akbar* announced their faith.

The people obeyed his order for quiet. A woman with a full-face veil, just the slit for eyes—Cross could never remember if it was called a hijab, a burka, or something else—sobbed on the shoulder of a man with a grey goatee and similar fashion sense to his imam. He, too, was in tears, and a boy of around twelve clung to the man's waist. Other people nearby exhibited either grief or anger—young and old, all plainly of the same ethnicity as Amina Shah.

Looking back to Cross, Bashir said, "These are Amina's parents. Please tell us you have some idea who took their daughter from them."

Cross's deep breath gave her time to think. No one had officially identified the body, but the college ID had either leaked from someone on the scene, or the college had been contacted more quickly than anticipated. The kids who'd found the body hadn't searched it and they all claimed they didn't recognise her, not that any of them spent much time examining the corpse.

But the police knew who it was, and the chances of this not being the daughter of the two heartbroken parents was slim to none. Keeping them sweet was the only real call.

"Tariq," Cross said, "we need time to process the scene. We need to gather information on her movements, and identify who she was last seen with and where she went. That will lead to who might have done it. So if anyone here spoke with her or saw her yesterday, I'd appreciate your support in gaining cooperation."

"Of course." Tariq pointed to a female youth in a black head-scarf and grey dress that covered her arms and reached her shoes. "Pala." He beckoned and she glided over, eyes flitting between Cross and Bashir. "This detective will ask you questions. Please answer them."

"We'll need a formal statement," Cross said. "But for now, can you recall seeing Amina at all yesterday?"

The girl nodded.

"What time?"

"Three?" Pala said.

"Was she with anyone?"

Pala shook her head. "We finished college for the day." Her voice was small and timid. "She left alone."

"Any idea where she was headed?"

"Home." The answer came quickly. Too quickly.

"Are you sure?" Cross asked.

"Home," Bashir said. "You heard her."

"Thank you." Cross dismissed Pala with a hand placed on her shoulder, and the girl returned to her friends. To Bashir, Cross said, "You're not going to help matters by protecting her parents' feelings. If Amina was doing something they might not approve of, we need to know."

"Then I will ask Pala about that." Bashir took out his phone, attached to which was a fan of five or six sticky notes. "*I* will break Amina's confidence, not Pala."

Cross acquiesced for now, but if Pala's third-hand account via Tariq resulted in the arrest of some boy Amina was seeing, or some activity of which her parents would disapprove, they would still need Pala's direct statement—and obtaining that retrospectively might be problematic in court. Now wasn't the time for that conversation, though.

Cross accepted the sticky notes. "What's this?"

"The news is already out," Bashir answered.

Despite the news being "already out" was more than likely down to Bashir himself Tweeting and blogging the rumours and leaks from the case, Cross gave the notes serious perusal. The names were scribbled, some with an "@" prefix. Five small pages of Twitter or Instagram handles.

"Trolls," Bashir said. "Amina's murder is justice for all the victims of Muslim terrorists and pedophiles. Or it is God's punishment? Or the rallying cry for a crusade that will begin by driving the Moors from Britain? I must say, they are getting more creative these days, although the F-word is far more prevalent than my quotes. Out of respect for you, Detective."

Cross pocketed the note. "Thank you. Such a gent. I will pass them to our cybercrime division. But I hope you understand, the trolling will take a backseat to finding who did this to Amina."

"It is why we are here."

"It is?"

"And it is why will be watching your every move very closely. We cannot allow these people to win, or to feel empowered. Any hint of slacking off or allowing perpetrators to slip through your fingers, or trying in some way to blame the community, and we will make your life a living hell."

And DI Cross did not doubt the man for a second.

## CHAPTER FIFTEEN

"IT'S GETTING TOO BIG," Alicia said. "I need Cleaver. He's the best at organising information."

"Watson's lucky I'm letting you stay as long as I am," Murphy replied through the speaker phone as she drove. "I'm not handing over another detective."

"We've got to be sure. We've got the historical aspects of the Lainworth Ripper and the Priest on the Hill, which could have been inspiration for the murders in the seventies. That might mean we have a suspect who's still alive, or yet another copycat. It's wide open at the moment, Don. Too many threads. I need to pull on as many as possible and tie off those that go nowhere."

Murphy went quiet.

"Come on, Uncle Don, this is an emergency."

He took his time answering, unclear if it was him hating on the nickname or if he was giving the request due consideration. When he did answer it was in a low voice, a hint of regret there. "I can't. If DCI Watson wants to formally request additional manpower, he'll have to do it through the deputy chief constable, or through my chief superintendent."

Alicia's turn to go quiet. Then, "Maybe I could go to Graham Rhapshaw."

"Police and crime commissioner sets policy," Murphy said. "I know he tried to interfere in a couple of cases but the superintendents have put him straight. He isn't an active participant, and he cannot order me to give up resources. You want Cleaver's skills on board, do it the right way. Otherwise, I'm sorry, it's a no."

Alicia said she understood, informed him he was next in line for babysitting this weekend, then bade him goodbye. She voice-dialled Knowles, who was in the car behind her. When he answered, she waved backward. "Hi there, can you see me?"

"Yes," came the DC's voice.

"Good. Follow me."

"Aren't we going to the mobile lab?"

"Not on your Nelly." Alicia raised her hand again, this time in a fist with her thumb and pinkie sticking out in a heavy-metal devil-horn salute. "Need to track down this cult, and we'll need someone who can dig into the history of this place."

"Really? We're going to her place again?"

"Try and keep up."


Alicia parked at the bottom of Maisie's lane a full minute before Knowles. The hills here were great for cruising down and boosting the hybrid saloon car's battery power. She was leaning on the bonnet, grinning, when Knowles ambled over.

"I was sticking to the speed limit," Knowles said.

"Whatever."

"It's a police-issue vehicle. We're fitted with black boxes that monitor speed."

Alicia pushed off and hiked up the lane. "Like I said, *whatever.*"

He caught up with her and they wound through Maisie's

garden to her front door, which she opened without any hint of surprise.

"Good morning," she said. "My rates are a very reasonable three hundred pounds per day plus expenses, non-negotiable. I'll notify you in advance of any expenses exceeding fifty pounds; otherwise you'll pay it without question."

"Rates?" Knowles said.

"As a consultant. I assume that's why you're here."

"Yesterday was a sales pitch?"

"No, yesterday was me offering information as a recently-qualified expert in matters pertaining to an open investigation. You dismissed me more than once, and now you realise you need me. I heard about the body up at Lumb Falls. Something of a coincidence, no?"

"May we come in?" Alicia's head bowed slightly; just enough to appear supplicant.

Maisie raised her eyes to the sky. When they returned to the detectives, she held the door and let them through. Three chairs were disturbed at the table as if she'd been entertaining until recently. This time, Maisie stood rather than inviting them to sit.

"Amina Shah was murdered yesterday," Alicia said in her most neutral voice. She realised this was a business transaction, and would have to start out that way, then build from there. "College student. Twenty years old. Mother, father, younger brother."

Maisie folded her arms. "Personalising the victim, DI Friend?"

"She was found by some horny teenage boy in circumstances I'm not sure I quite understand. Circumstances I'm shocked to realise are only a few years away from me needing to worry about with my own little girl. I still can't believe she's nearly four."

"Now personalising you. Interesting approach."

"Is it working?"

"A bit."

"Good. But we can't tell you much more without getting you onboard as an official consultant."

"What exactly do you need from me?"

"Officially? To look deeper into the 1920s and 1870s killings to provide clues regarding those in the 1970s and 80s. I'm not buying into the guff about a cult that pops up every fifty years, but there may be something to the echoes they've left."

"Echoes?" Knowles said. "What do you—"

"The echoes of past horrors." Alicia faced Knowles, guessing Maisie didn't need the lecture. "A place retains a verbal history that often lasts generations, even if it isn't spoken about. A killer like Jack the Ripper will cause ripples that keep people returning to his legacy. We had the *Yorkshire* Ripper in Peter Suttlcliffe, who remained free long enough to earn a nickname. The *Lainworth* Ripper, never caught. There are people who honour men like the Zodiac Killer, and the Unabomber. Even if it isn't a conscious effort—a guy with books and paintings of the Priest on the Hill—it's possible there are local legends and stories he'd have stuck to."

"Consciously or unconsciously," Maisie said. "Like osmosis from the ether. History leeching into the collective memory of the human community."

Okay, she may have been a little high.

Knowles's brows had all but knitted together, plainly perceiving the same thing.

"Something I learned from one of Maisie's books." Alicia fluttered her eyelids at Maisie. "Not that I'm trying to butter up the professor. Again."

Maisie stared at one of the empty chairs. "I haven't gone by the title 'professor' in a while."

Alicia got the impression that the older woman needed some personal contact, but when Alicia stepped forward and reached to touch her arm, she pulled away. Alicia stepped back. "Sorry."

"No, it's fine." Maisie brushed herself down and took a

couple of quick breaths before looking at the pair with clear eyes, as if she'd reset herself from some sense of confusion. "I'll do it. And the girl?"

"We're working on the remains from the seventies and eighties," Knowles said. "If we make a connection to yesterday's murder, it becomes a bigger joint task force."

"My, a task force. And who do we like for the resurgence in murder?"

Alicia exchanged a glance with Knowles, who appeared concerned about something. Revealing too much to Maisie without a firm contract in place, perhaps. Alicia chose to take the chance. "There are still people around who were part of that hate group you mentioned. The Yorkshire Vanguard. Bertie Bradshaw ran it for a while, a chap called James Grantham in a wheelchair, and others not around anymore. Danny Pryor, Remington Duval; someone called Bainbridge got a mention."

Maisie just nodded along. "You've been taking this seriously."

"Yes, ma'am," Knowles said.

"You have a wealth of experience," Alicia said. "And I'm not just saying that to keep you sweet. If you can do this bookwork, find a thread that links to the 1970s... maybe you'll find whatever it is you're looking for, isolated out here, pretending to be a batty old woman."

The smile Maisie gave Alicia radiated several things a smile usually belied. Sadness, regret, something deeper than both those. "You're based out of Leeds."

"Yes."

"Must be a long trip."

"It is."

Maisie opened a drawer beside the Aga stove and rummaged, producing a mortice key on a ring beside a Yale. "My front door has two locks. If you find yourself working late and need somewhere to crash, my couch pulls out into a comfy bed. I'll keep some blankets and a pillow beside it just in case."

"Oh, really, thank you, but I can get a hotel—"

Maisie pressed the keys into Alicia's palm and folded her fingers around it. "If this explodes like it might do, there will be media interest. More officers taking up hotels, and you might not want to make that drive. Organised girl like you, your husband or partner will be fine. Or you'll have sorted childcare somehow. Am I right?"

"I… I have backup, yes, but—"

"Then I insist."

Alicia's chest fluttered, touched by the kind offer. She'd have to check regulations regarding staying with a civilian while on an active case, but it would probably be okay. A cost saving if nothing else. "Thank you."

"And we might need to brainstorm an approach if you go after Remy Duval," Maisie said.

"You mean Remington Duval?" Knowles asked.

"Yes." Maisie switched her attention to him. "Remy Duval. Keen writer, essayist, researcher, and a vocal cheerleader for the Yorkshire Vanguard."

"We thought he was dead," Alicia said.

"Oh, not yet. Resident at Daisyville Retirement Home. He might barely remember his own name, but he is still very much alive."

# CHAPTER SIXTEEN

WHENEVER ABHU NOON entered his office in the squalid council chambers, his thoughts always turned to the brighter future that he was sure awaited him. He got stuff done. He was ideal for government. That blonde bimbo of a copper might have nailed his ambitions, but he let it wash off him. What self-respecting public servant *didn't* want to be elected to higher office? If you were doing good work at the menial level—finding the money to fix potholes, rallying volunteers to clean rubbish out of the canal, and of course ensuring the bins were emptied—then why not turn one's attention to becoming a member of Parliament?

He liked his job. But, at times, the people around him struck him as lazy, incompetent freeloaders doing the bare minimum to stave off getting fired until they could claim their pensions. Abhu frequently went to the Examiner to speak publicly about plans the council were making directly after his fellow councillors had dismissed the work as "not necessary."

*Only doing what is necessary is the same as going backward.*

Those words came from Abhu's grandmother, and were now

framed in embroidery on his office wall, the one with the damp stain in one corner.

The old building needed some work, but anything beyond what the insurance paid out for the government's latest environmental failing would look bad to the residents who Abhu was supposed to be looking after. A number of the old-school councillor types, the ones who *only did what was necessary*, wanted to take a hundred grand of the five hundred earmarked for community regeneration and invest it in both the public and private areas of the council offices.

It'd be nice when people need to come here for business, they said.

Abhu used his powers of persuasion to get enough votes to block that, but there were worse offices than his, and people were wavering. No one wanted to come to work when the only room that didn't exude a grey-brown hue was the council chamber itself, where a handful had taken to using their laptops for the important work of correspondence, regulatory paperwork, and socialising online during council hours.

*Slackers.*

Abhu had invited Tariq Bashir to his office, but the imam had declined on the grounds he needed to be in his community today for a vigil to which "all" were invited, so Abhu turned up too. The college grounds were awash with students of all creeds, subdued and mourning the loss of Amina, but Abhu talked his way into the congregation on which all were focused: Tariq Bashir, his assistants from the mosque, and the girl's family.

Tariq was giving speeches, as was the occasional man, with only two women being willing—or *allowed*, as it might well be within this community—to speak in public. No matter what Abhu's misgivings might be toward the more fundamentalist religious faithful, he reminded himself they were all able to vote.

Eventually, Tariq deigned to speak with him, and Abhu suggested they go somewhere private. He persuaded the imam to leave his flock—or his followers or subjects; whatever he called the folk who hung on his every word—and they left the busy crowd and adjourned to what was labelled a "café-bar." Inside, even at the pre-lunchtime hour, the establishment leaned more heavily toward the *bar* side.

Tariq checked the table and chair before he sat—to avoid, Abhu presumed, any contact with alcohol. It wasn't just oppressing women and homosexuals that this extremist treated with absolutism.

Abhu paid for two coffees and was told they would be brought to the table. He joined Tariq without worrying about what may have been spilled by the previous customers.

Tariq came straight to the point, his voice loud in the quiet cafe-bar. "You said you can help."

"I can." Abhu hoped his more measured tone would encourage Tariq to drop a decibel or two. "I know the lead detectives on the case. Sharp. Committed. But they're cagey."

"What are you offering?"

Abhu opened his arms, presenting an image he'd spent years perfecting with his cousin, Dayapreet, a freelance photographer. He kept his beard trim enough to be sure his teeth and lips showed when he smiled; his suit was a couple of centimetres roomier under his arms so it didn't bunch when he made ebullient gestures like this one; and his turban remained muted but spotlessly clean. "Tariq, I can be your bridge."

"Bridge?"

"Between your community and the police. And the press if you need a friendly write-up. I have a great relationship with the local *Examiner*, and a couple of the national newspapers if we find the police are screwing up."

"Why would I need you?" The big man wafted a hand, as if Abhu were a used car salesman trying to flog paint protection for which Tariq didn't wish to pay. "I can talk to the police."

"Ah, but you tend to take a more… combative approach. My way has a little more finesse."

Tariq leaned on the table, staring at the polished wood. The coffees arrived and while Abhu thanked the young woman, Tariq did not move. When she was gone, he breathed four times, deep and loud. "Abhu. That's like the Simpsons, yeah?"

Abhu swallowed, summoning the much-practiced response, the words as well as the smile. "That's Apu, with a 'P.' And he's a Hindu." He pointed to his turban, his smile widening. "Different religion. Different name. Pretty much nothing like Apu from the Simpsons."

The smile waned a little, as it always did while he waited for the person making that over-used comparison to join him. It was supposed to ease the other's embarrassment at the mistake, or to show he wasn't offended if the person was making a slightly off-colour joke. Dayapreet said that making fun of Abhu's name was racist, but Abhu shrugged it off.

*Even racists get a vote.*

"We have different religions," Tariq said, eyes hooded, no smile to join Abhu's. "But it is the same fight."

Now Abhu's smile disappeared and he employed another much-practiced expression: earnestness. "To a point, yes, but can you elaborate?"

"Amina's death is a hate crime, of that I am certain."

"How can you be sure?"

"Because she is a Muslim and Muslims are reviled by the people of this country."

Abhu attempted a "relaxed" pose while continuing to project concern, showing Tariq he was taking the man seriously. "Not by everyone. A small, very vocal minority. Like Muslims: Only a tiny number are dangerous, but—"

"*But*, the people here, my fellow Britons, treat us all like murderers and rapists. What can you do about that?"

Abhu took a few seconds to think, but he had his answer lined up. "I can show them the reality. Your human side."

"And how will you do that? We have the same fight, but you consort with the enemy."

"The police are not our enemy."

"I mean your friends in the Vanguard."

"The—?" But Abhu knew what he meant. Photos in the *Examiner* of him shaking hands with a young man at a rally last year. "That event was not anti-Muslim. Just because that's what the national papers called it doesn't make it true. It was anti-paedophile. It was demanding the police do more to stop such gangs. The most recent group to be arrested happened to be Muslims, but the rally was nothing to do with—"

Tariq raised a finger, the rest of his hand clenched in a meaty fist. "No. Do not do that. Do not pretend you are anything but a whore looking for people to like you. Whether you are a councillor or an MP or a senior police officer, you are a *politician*, and like all of them you will say whatever is convenient at the time. Right now, solidarity with the Muslim community is the convenient thing. Tomorrow, you will go back to empowering your racist friends."

Tariq sipped his coffee and pulled a face that suggested he didn't particularly care for it.

"How am I empowering racists?" Abhu asked.

"By giving them a brown friend."

"I'm not their friend. They just leave me alone because I do a good job for the town."

"They leave you alone because they can be photographed with you. Because you deny your heritage as a man of colour, of a religion other than theirs. You pander to them, looking for votes, allow them to wheel you out to prove to everyone who'll listen, 'Hey, look, a brown man shaking our leader's hand. We can't be racist.' You are a coconut, Abhu. A traitor to every victim of racism across this country. Your pandering, your desperation for acceptance, makes it harder for real people like me to fight them."

Abhu clasped his hands together to prevent them from shaking, but the anger leeched into his back and along his shoulders. His jaw tightened and he struggled to keep from shouting. "Do not call me a coconut. I am trying to make a *difference*. By fighting head-on, you just make them push back harder. I can't effect change where I am, so yeah, I want votes. I don't much care which political party, either. I just want to do the best I can out there. My record on community cohesion, on persuading people to care about the environment—"

Tariq made a "pfft" sound and rolled his eyes. "Environment. You think God cares what you do here?"

"Yeah, I've heard your thoughts on that."

"And you are jealous?"

"Of what?"

Tariq's mouth curled in a childish grin, almost mocking. "That I have a national TV platform, and you do not. I tell the truth—that only God will decide the fate of the Earth, not men like you. Millions hear me. You have to shake the hands of Nazis to get even a side note in a newspaper with a circulation of less than ten thousand. You are a little man, trying to offer me something I do not need in exchange for something I have no intention of giving."

"You're a prick."

"A prick with an audience."

"*Abhu.*" The hissed word came from two tables away, a clean-shaven Asian man a couple of years younger than Abhu—Dayapreet, his photographer cousin and chief image consultant. His *only* image consultant. And he was patting the air in a gesture that meant *calm down.*

Tariq glared at him. At the smartphone in his hand—with the camera lens angled toward the pair. The imam frowned, then gazed around, seeming to take in several things: Abhu, the coffees, the large window overlooking the campus where Amina's friends and family had gathered.

"You wanted to send an anonymous photo of us chatting," Tariq said. "Cameraphone so it looked like one of the students, not your... pet."

"Hey." Dayapreet stood.

It was Abhu's turn to gesture for calm. As Tariq rose to meet Dayapreet's verbal challenge, Abhu shifted upright too, where he coughed to regain Tariq's attention. "Okay, I think we need to chill out a moment."

"I'm not a pet," Dayapreet said.

"No." Tariq stared down Abhu. "Just a pair of batty-boy coconuts shilling for infidels who would not piss on you even if you were on fire. Race traitors. You might as well bleach your skin and join their ranks—"

The first punch flew, Abhu's knuckles flaring against Tariq's cheekbone. Tariq shook it off and responded with several blows of his own, Dayapreet's hands and arms trying to separate the two. But Tariq took offence at the peacemaking. He struck Dayapreet with an elbow to the gut, which sent an uncontrollable rage thundering through Abhu, who stepped up his assault.

Then the doors opened, and three men loyal to Tariq joined the melee. Two male bar staff rushed in as peacemakers, while one of the two women shouted that the police had been called.

And as Abhu fought back against the shoving and jabs that got through the peacemakers, and as the police—already outside serving as crowd control—burst through the doors, as his nose ran with blood and his brow stung from one blow or another, the main thought in Abhu's mind was, *This will not look good to the voters.*

## CHAPTER SEVENTEEN

"WHY ARE YOU CHARGING FOR THIS?" Joanne asked, walking alongside her brother and Maisie as the trio approached St. Mary's church.

"Is that even a job?" Peter said. "Researcher?"

"Consultant," Maisie said. "It's what I used to do years ago. I was never much for the rough stuff, but I was always great at the brainwork."

Joanne gave her a wide-eyed, slack-jawed look. "Better than the *police*?"

"Sometimes the police need a new perspective. I had a way of … interrogating things."

The front door to the church was locked, so they headed around the side toward the vicarage.

"In what way?" Peter asked politely.

"I take the facts and the people," Maisie said. "The circumstances, too, the events leading up to the crime. Then I ask what all the possible scenarios might be, no matter how silly. I call this triumvirate: *the events, the participants, the milieu.* I then work backward and eliminate all those that are impossible. It brings a certain clarity that comes with distancing myself from the human side of the crime."

Joanne appeared thoughtful as they all stopped before a door. "Is there always only one possibility?"

Designed to look hundreds of years old, the newer fittings were betrayed by their lack of warping and the addition of weatherproofing. "No, not always. That's when you have to drill deeper, bounce things off people around you, get their perspective. And whittle away until you reach the truth."

"Sounds like detective work," Peter said.

"Yes, but I'm not required to gather evidence and make a case for court. I just have to solve the crime."

"Ahh," the children said together.

"Before I knock, I need to ask you both a favour."

"What is it?" Peter replied.

"I have to talk grownup stuff with the vicar. Can you please wait out here? Don't play on the gravestones or break anything. And stay in view of this window." Maisie pointed to the glass in the genuinely centuries-old brickwork.

"I'll keep an eye on him," Joanne said.

"Me?" The boy looked incredulous, as if he could never do anything remotely mischievous.

"Both of you. Now go play."

They ran toward a willow tree, far enough from the graves to be respectful, close enough to make Maisie worry about them disobeying her. But she was here for a reason—an important reason—and she didn't need her train of thought fogged by two children asking question after question. She checked on them once more, and knocked on the door.

Lucy Viera answered quickly. "Maisie, hello."

The older lady had aged well; at seventy-something she was easily able to pass for early sixties—the opposite of Maisie, who no longer took much care with her appearance and had long ceased worrying about how old others believed her to be.

"Vicar," Maisie said in greeting. "Wonder if I might grab a little of your time."

"For you? Of course. Right this way."

Maisie followed her inside, curious as Lucy took her from the hall to the living room. She'd never been inside a vicarage before, and had imagined it would be a replica of the set of *Father Ted*, a sitcom she'd found hilarious when it aired far too many years ago. It was not like that, of course. Aside from the portrait of a dark-skinned Jesus and a crucifix, it could have been any small, modern bungalow.

"Tea? Coffee?" Lucy offered.

"I'm fine, thank you. Some water would be nice though."

Lucy gave a tight smile, disappeared out toward the hall, and returned moments later with two glasses of water. She sat in an armchair and gestured for Maisie to sit too, and the pair sipped their drinks.

"Is everything okay?" Lucy asked. "Does this concern Peter and Joanne, perhaps?"

"No, no, they're fine." Maisie sat up straight and put the glass in her lap, holding it with both hands. "*I'm* fine. Really. This is about something else. The Priest on the Hill business we discussed last week."

Lucy waited.

"The police are investigating the remains up near the Beacon and farther down on Basil Warner's farm, and I think you might be able to provide something of an insight."

The vicar shifted her weight. "Me? How so?"

"You gave me a little background, but you never mentioned you wrote a *book* on the subject. The Priest on the Hill. It's missing from the library, or stolen or lost." Maisie had checked sources online and found only morbid legends and short fiction relating to the actions of Father Henry Pickersgill. Lucy's self-published book from 1994 was the only source Maisie could identify that might give her facts rather than flimsy conjecture. "I was wondering if you might have a copy to hand."

"No, those books are long gone. I can tell you what I remember."

"That would be helpful."

Lucy waited. When Maisie turned her palm to indicate Lucy should proceed, the vicar asked, "Don't you want to take notes?"

"There's little I forget." Maisie folded her hands back together, her back straight.

"Okay, then, it's a dark-and-stormy-night type of a tale." Lucy relaxed for the first time since Maisie had entered, leading Maisie to wonder if it was a personal issue or something deeper. She added the possibility—of the *seventy-something-year-old* vicar having something to hide—to the list of scenarios percolating within. As the story unfolded, Maisie added each facet to her repository to access when she needed it.

Father Henry Pickersgill came to the parish of Moleford Bridge in 1860, a time when persecution of Catholics lingered in the national memory, restrictions on the religion having been lifted a mere forty years earlier. Yet, as with all equality legislation through the ages, the progressive thinking was not welcomed by all. Henry had suffered for his religion, railed against by those who declared themselves loyal to the crown religion rather than this Roman interloper. Throughout his childhood, he saw his father marginalised, his mother abused, his sisters forced to marry into Church of England families just to garner a glimmer of hope that their children might be accepted into good schools. Society's treatment of him and his brethren pushed him toward the clergy, and then to many communities where it was said he did good work before a bishop moved him on to the next needy congregation.

He was thirty-eight when he came to Moleford. Here, and in

the neighbouring towns of Lainworth and Todmorden, he became a popular figure, modernising his way of preaching, a vast change from his blood-and-thunder predecessor, yet soaked in puritanical conservatism. He taught that Jesus's compassion should be tempered with strong non-violent resistance to the discrimination Henry and other Catholics suffered throughout his life. He even converted families, those he helped out of poverty, drawing suspicion and annoyance from Christ's other followers.

It was around 1861 that the first of Henry's most prominent critics disappeared: a vicar who had taken the name John-Paul, but whose real name was Wilbur. He was a frequent target of Henry's mockery, due to John-Paul's inability to string together a coherent argument during their impromptu debates in public houses. John-Paul did, however, have more success in dissuading the council's permission for a second church to accommodate Henry's growing flock.

On the surface, it was a friendly rivalry, but Henry Pickersgill's journals—found much later—revealed a seething fury at the man.

*Waning Wilbur, the fake John-Paul,* Henry wrote one winter's evening, *has the cunning of a mud brick and the wiles of a dead fish. Yet he dares maintain his innocence in the matter of carrying forth the olde ways of oppressing the True Faith, dressed up in language befitting respectability. This man has no right to preach the word of our Lord. He must be silenced.*

The police were a fledgling idea back then, so when someone cut John-Paul's throat while he took a bath, there was little in the way of an investigation. There weren't even any records—none official nor those penned by Henry—indicating that suspicion ever fell on the Catholic priest.

In the time between Waning Wilbur departing this world and

his successor being appointed, Henry commenced building a second Catholic church without opposition. This was a temporary structure, erected much like an Amish barn, but when it was in place, no one was able to tear it down. Not even the most ardent anti-Catholic would desecrate a place of God, no matter that it was built on a wild hillside, miles from the town.

Over the next fifteen years, Henry oversaw the slow, steady replacement of the wood, the building of strong foundations, and the swift construction of an actual, functioning brick church. It was much smaller than the exterior wooden structure, and would hold only twenty or thirty worshippers, but Henry declared it a success. A place for quiet contemplation, for being alone with God, closer to His glory.

And his journals grew bolder.

Instead of hinting at the murder of his rivals, his feeling of greatness swelled, morphing into a sense of omnipotence.

According to one Church of England vicar, Henry's sermons descended into maniacal rants, and in Henry's own writing he began detailing the methods with which he subdued people he deemed unworthy of continuing life on Earth, and how he disposed of them to make God proud.

Rivals disappeared. Travellers passing through on pilgrimages and business ventures—the mills were growing in the region at this time—were reported missing. But it seemed the murder of someone Henry labeled an "apostate," a woman last seen one Sunday in the rival St. Mary's, of all places, was what brought suspicion down upon Henry at last.

Dorkus Maloney's body was not concealed. She was found, displayed like a warning to all, and it fell to the vicar of St. Mary's to investigate properly. A chronicler at the time, publishing an early form of a regional newspaper, wrote a piece that was published in a later crime textbook:

*And it was he, Bartholomew, who saw with his own eyes that Henry*

*Pickersgill had passed over from the path of Christ to the bosom of the devil. Making it his mission to trail the Catholic wherever he went, especially on nights the so-called priest imbibed of alcohol and was seen to be angry. Having followed him more than once to his hillside church, but unable to pursue across open ground, Bartholomew chose this night to wait in hiding. Here, he witnessed Henry himself arrive on horseback with a young woman slung over its back like a rug.*

*Unsure if the woman was dead or alive, Bartholomew followed Henry and found him entering a hidden door in the building, and down stairs that appeared on no plans for his holy place. Here, Bartholomew caught the evil priest at work with the naked woman upon an altar, one decorated with parts of a goat. She was dead, her throat cut, but still Henry defiled her with carnal lust.*

And yet.

It was the word of a recent appointee to the Church of England against that of a Catholic priest, now a feature of the community for nigh on twenty years—a figure who drew an alibi within hours.

A fledgling police force was expanding by now, though, so demands for an investigation brought with it a detective who acted more neutrally than other establishment figures, one who seemed particularly interested in the apostate found in public. And this formed the thrust of his investigation.

Within one month, the detective agreed that they had a prime suspect in their sights, and assigned people to watch that premises on the hill, more out of hope than expectation—a Victorian era stakeout of sorts—and yet it gleaned results.

Henry Pickersgill, so crazed with homicidal urges, so unutterably convinced that he was protected by supernatural forces stronger than anything mortal man could summon, continued his mission. Not for the devil, though, but for God and Jesus Christ.

*I will force Jesus to return,* his journal later revealed when it was found secreted in the Church on the Hill. *God will punish me for the breaking of His commandment, of course, but perhaps He will show me mercy. Mercy for sacrificing the sinners in return for bringing about judgement on the world. Will He find me wanting? That is His choice. But I know I cannot stop. I cannot stop until all the sinners are destroyed, either by God's hand, should He choose to rain judgement upon us, or my own.*

"Not a devil worshipper, then," Maisie said.

"No." Lucy handed the laminated pages to Maisie, each browned with age before being preserved.

There were five in total: three pages of Henry's own journal, a leaf from the textbook that had been issued as part of police detective training for a few years in the early 1900s, and the sketch of a crime scene as rendered by the detective who finally caught the Priest on the Hill.

"He wanted to accelerate the End of Days," Lucy said. "The Catholic Church knew about the journal, but they wouldn't let something like that out in the open. They preferred the story Bartholomew told. Devil worship meant they could distance themselves."

Maisie agreed. "The narrative is that he switched sides from Jesus to the Devil rather than a warped fundamentalism. Which would damage the Church."

"That's about it. What do you think?"

Maisie had a lot to process, but it was a good start. "The bodies. Did they ever exhume them?"

Lucy tapped the laminated page with the drawing of the dead apostate left in the town square for all to see. "There was a cave beneath the second church, the one up on the hill. Not particularly well sealed, so the bodies decayed and animals got in. It was impossible to put a number on his victims. Upward of fifty, though; of that they were certain."

"Not the same hiding place as the Lainworth Ripper or our seventies chap?" Maisie said.

"Definitely murder, then?"

Maisie swore inwardly. "Gosh, I'm rusty at this. Shouldn't have revealed that. But yes. Although you must wait for the police to go public."

"Of course. And no, it wasn't the same hiding place. They sealed Henry's place with dynamite."

Maisie rose from her seat and handed Lucy her empty glass. "Thank you for your time. It's been very helpful."

Lucy walked Maisie to the door. Seeing Peter and Joanne playing happily in the grounds, Maisie hesitated in the doorway. "While we're tying off the subject, do you happen to know much about those Lainworth killings? 1920, or thereabouts?"

Lucy shook her head. "I read a little, but there isn't much beyond the bodies that were found back then. Similar method of killing. But not much to interest you, I'm sure."

"I'm sure. Thank you again."

Lucy shut the door and Maisie strolled out toward the children, rearranging the laminated sheets Lucy had agreed to loan out. One in particular Maisie didn't want the kids to see: the drawing of a dead woman, cut into pieces and laid out in a public place, her body parts in disarray, positioned in the approximation of a crucifix.

# CHAPTER EIGHTEEN

EVEN WITH ALICIA'S machine-gun charm offensive, it had been a struggle for her and Knowles to gain access to the Daisyville Retirement Home. Although they were police, they had arrived during non-visiting hours, which confused the big lug on reception, and he needed to call his supervisor—at home, on her day off—for approval. Then he needed to nip off in search of an orderly to abandon her cleaning duties and cover him at reception. While his back was turned, Alicia stole a quick glance at the visitor log, flipping pages and zeroing in on Remington Duval's name wherever it appeared on the list.

A few regular visitors, some new, some that'd cropped up already: Glenn Bishop, Russel Davy; Sean Pryor was the name that stood out as the most frequent.

The woman replacing the receptionist arrived and plopped down on his seat. She picked up a magazine, leaving the phone headset to one side; clearly, they didn't get a lot of phone calls.

"Why didn't *she* just take us through?" Knowles asked as they walked.

The reception dude's eyebrows knitted together and his mouth turned down in deep thought. "Dunno. Mrs Li told me on the phone to show you through. She's called ahead to Remy's nurse already, so ... hey, doesn't matter, right?"

"There is a shocking absence of daisies here," Alicia said.

"Huh?" Again, the brows came together.

"Daisyville. Bit of a con, isn't it? If there are no daisies to brighten the place up."

"We have strict cleanliness standards," the receptionist answered.

"We still don't know your name." Alicia pointed at the badge on the chest of his purple scrubs. "Unless your name is Receptionist. Is your name Receptionist?"

"Umm, no. We don't put our name on the badges. Data protection or something. Security. I don't know. My name's Dave."

"Okay, Dave, pleased to meet you at last."

As they walked past the residential rooms, Dave's scrubs rubbing together made for a poor soundtrack.

Alicia had to speak over it. "So, Dave, where is everyone?"

"Day room," Dave said.

"Sure. Hope you don't mind my asking. It's like you're about to pull off a rubber mask and reveal you're an alien who's eaten everyone." Alicia halted, her hands gripping both Knowles and Dave. "You're not an alien, are you?"

Instead of confusion, Dave looked to Knowles in panic.

"Answer the lady's question, Dave," Knowles said.

Dave continued to stare. "I... umm..."

Knowles gave him a stern reply: "Do I look like a lady?"

Dave snapped his attention back to Alicia. "I'm not an alien. The residents are in the day room. That's where I'm taking you."

"Oh good." Alicia set off again, exchanging a muted giggle with Knowles who strode alongside. Oddly, she swelled with pride at him falling into step with her. "If you take us anywhere near a basement or a barn that looks like a spaceship, I'm calling in backup."

The joke appeared to penetrate Dave's armour as he chuckled. "I'll try to keep you away from spaceships. Besides, the basement only just got dry."

"How come the basement was wet?"

Again, Dave didn't seem sure. "The flood?"

"Thanks, I guessed that."

Knowles stepped in. "DI Friend's question related more to structure than cause, Dave."

"Oh, we're on a hill," Dave said. "Whole cellar filled up, like everywhere else round here. When it got to the top, it... I dunno, it equalised or something, and kept going down the hill. The main house only got minor damage. They told us about why and all but I only really paid attention to the new plan to evac the residents if it happens again. Rescue squad or army or whatever. There's a barracks a few miles away."

Alicia peered into the day room. Not a spaceship, but an open-plan area with a nest of tables on the side and a kitchen and serving hatch, at which were stationed comfortable chairs with what looked like seatbelts. The other side was full of big armchairs and a couple of beds, most of which were occupied. Elderly men and women appeared unaware of their surroundings, while nurses assisted others with medication. Only two residents engaged in activities unaided, both reading in the natural light of a huge window which overlooked a garden close to the house. The manicured garden's angle steadily increased until it fit with the contours of the hill on which it stood, while in the rectangle surrounding the flatter section white flowers with yellow centres bloomed.

"Ooh, daisies," Alicia said.

"It's chamomile," Dave said. "And that's Remy Duval. His nurse is Audrey. Be nice."

"Thanks." Knowles offered his hand and Dave shook it, then headed back the way they had come. He nudged Alicia. "You *were* mean."

"I know." Alicia stepped into the day room, gliding over toward Remy and Audrey. "I'll behave from now on."

Audrey sat in an armchair beside Remy. An older lady herself—late seventies at least—she wore the same purple scrubs as the other staff; Remy, in his nineties, was decked out in a formal shirt and smart trousers, his orthopaedic shoes polished to a shine. His hair was wispy and sprouted from his scalp between liver spots, and he sat tall in the chair so his skin hung loose from his neck. A slight tremble in both his head and his hands disturbed his resting state. One of those hands lay beneath Audrey's as the pair watched something out the window.

Audrey extended her free hand, pointing. "A robin."

Remy's mouth opened a touch, but that was the only hint he'd heard her.

"Mrs Phillips?" Knowles said.

Audrey turned her head to them and gestured toward two plastic-backed chairs she'd prepared, pulled over from the spares in one corner. Alicia and Knowles thanked her and positioned themselves to either side of the pair, so the view remained unimpeded. Remy did not acknowledge them.

"I'm Audrey." The nurse didn't offer her hand, just sat up more stiffly. "I'm not sure what you hope to learn from Remy. Something to do with his friends from an old club?"

"He wrote a book," Knowles said. "*The Last Vanguard of Britishness.*"

"We couldn't get a copy from the library," Alicia added. "But we saw one on a private shelf recently. We wanted to get Remy's take on the material before we asked to borrow it."

"Because the owner is somewhat unsavoury?" Audrey said.

"Perhaps." Alicia kept glancing at Remy, unsettled by something she couldn't quite grasp.

"Mr Duval," Knowles said, addressing the old man directly.

Remy's eyes flickered, but he didn't move a muscle.

"Please don't do that," Audrey said. "You might agitate him."

"We do need to ask some questions." Alicia faced Audrey, adopting a firm, non-perky tone. "It might be difficult, but we won't do anything that might put his health at risk."

"Dredging up the past will get him worked up. That's detrimental." Audrey again took Remy's hand softly in hers. "The poor man will be gone soon. Let him have a bit of peace in his final months."

Knowles tightened his mouth, plainly wanting to say something. Probably along the lines of comparing Remy's final days to the years of hurt he had dished out.

Alicia combined her uneasiness at observing Remy with her curiosity about the hand-holding. "Is there more between you two?"

Audrey pulled her hand away as if noticing it for the first time. "I am his nurse, Detective Inspector Friend. I was more. A long time ago."

"Friends?"

"Lovers, if you must know. We never married. Remy's head was turned by younger women, but … we loved each other for a while. I qualified to do this job, and I am his private carer."

"Does that pay well?" Knowles asked.

Audrey turned her head and scowled. "I am required to be paid for my work. I take minimum wage, and nothing else. Am I clear?"

Knowles held up his hand in a half-apology.

"You care for your…" She almost said *husband.* "Your partner. All the time?"

"Our time together is precious, even if Remy isn't always aware of it." Audrey smiled directly at him, squeezing the man's hand. This time his head moved a fraction in her direction. "Hey there, Remy. It's almost lunchtime. You hungry?"

His eyelids twitched.

"Good. It's shepherd's pie." Back to Alicia. "He has good days and bad days. Today isn't a good one. He had a bit of an episode this morning."

"Did you know him when he was young?" Alicia asked.

"You mean back when he was writing his book?" She gave her former lover a kind appraisal, as if remembering tender moments shared. "There was a lot of silliness back then. He thought he could change the world, him and his friend James. So many of us were... *confused*, I suppose is the word."

"That would be James Grantham?" Knowles asked. "And you bought into it too?"

Again Audrey's features pinched when Knowles spoke, although it could have been because he was hinting at another accusation. "It's fear that drives that sort of thing. The stuff the boys used to talk about. Oh, it was a different time. You didn't question when someone cleverer than you told you something. Remington *Duval*." She said his name like a teen might utter the name of a pop star she met by chance in a bakery. "He was smart, a public speaker, a writer. He talked politics like a pro. And he was handsome, of course. I was just a teenager, lapping up his every word." Her manner sagged a little. "It wasn't until I actually lived among the people he said were making the country a bad place that I understood how wrong he was. I suppose that's why we grew apart."

"You still loved him, though?" Alicia said.

Remy made a noise. "Nnnn."

Audrey tilted her head curiously. "What was that?"

"Nnnnnnn." Remy's hooded eyes were fixed on the window, but then swivelled side to side. A finger raised, the hand and forearm pinned to the chair by his infirmity.

"Oh, dear." Audrey stroked the man's hair, the visible skin bunching under her touch. He tried to pull away and Audrey stood, addressing the detectives. "I think you should leave now. He doesn't hear much, but when he does, we're not sure how much he takes in."

"Mr Duval?" Alicia tried, five feet away, at his eye level. "My name is Alicia. Can you hear me?"

His eyeballs were clear, brown irises gleaming. "*Nnnn.*"

"I insist you leave," Audrey said.

"He's trying to say something." Alicia remained in Remy's line of sight. "Mr Duval, is there something you need to tell us?"

The reply came in the form of a hard swallow and the tiny, almost imperceptible lowering of the man's jaw. "Gggnnnnnnnnnn."

"Please…" Audrey pressed her palms together.

Other people nearby were watching now, the two readers particularly disgruntled, while the nurses who had been doing their rounds stood by awaiting the call for assistance.

"It's okay, folks," Knowles said. "Nothing to worry about. Mr Duval is helping us with—"

"Nnnigger!" The old man spat on the floor.

Audrey's hands covered her mouth.

Alicia straightened, fishing a tissue from her bag to wipe the fine spray of spittle from her face. "Well, that was unpleasant."

Remy sat at an angle, the effort having dislodged his carefully set position. His mouth hung open, a line of drool glooping from one corner. Audrey helped him up, but he was now angled so he could see Knowles clearly.

"*Nnnnn,*" he said.

Knowles stepped backward, out of Remy's vision. It seemed everyone was staring at the young black man, waiting for his approval to go back to what they were doing. His nod gave them the okay, and Alicia joined him, ready to leave; their presence was achieving nothing. Once Audrey deemed Remy suitably cared for, she approached, her head bowed.

After a moment, she addressed Knowles directly. "I'm sorry, he … he's confused. He still thinks it's a time when that sort of thing was okay."

"That sort of thing was never okay." Knowles spoke the words softly. "No matter how some people want to rewrite history."

"Even intelligent people need easy answers sometimes," Audrey said. "Life is hard? Blame the blacks, the Jews, the bankers, capitalism ... anything but a complex series of circumstances that combine to give us the current status quo." She took a deep breath. "As I mentioned, *I* bought into it because Remy gave me someone to blame for my hardships. I know now that it was nonsense, because I broadened my horizons, moved away, lived in the real world. Remy and James and Dan, Bertie and the others, they never did." She appeared exhausted, as if she needed to shore herself up. "He was misguided, detectives, that's all. He wanted a better life for himself and whatever family he might've had in an alternate future. He's a good man, really." She looked back at her now-calm former lover. "Or he could have been."

Alicia thanked her for her time, and she and Knowles exited the room, making their way back toward reception.

"What struck you most about what she said?" Alicia asked.

"Are you mentoring me again, ma'am?"

She let the *ma'am* slip, taking it as sarcasm. "Yes. Do you like it?"

"Love it. I'm not sure what I think. She was making excuses for behaviour that was bloody awful even in the golden-olden days."

"Excusing her own views as much as Remy's?"

"Right." Knowles exhaled a quick breath through his nose, eyes front. "People always say that, you know? 'It was different back then.' When it's just the scum of society who see my skin as a threat, it's a danger but it isn't endemic. In the seventies, the eighties, my parents were hooted at in the street like monkeys, and the police would laugh along with it, tell my dad to get a sense of humour. In the workplace, he learned to laugh at jokes about his hair, his lips, the size of his dick Now ... now it feels like it's coming back."

"And they 'don't mean anything by it.' The sticks-and-stones excuse."

"That's not what you meant, was it?"

Alicia and Knowles stopped at reception, waiting for Dave to notice them.

"No," Alicia said. "I meant what struck you most about the manner of her delivery? Not what was said, but the way she said it."

Knowles approached the counter, having caught Dave's eye, and handed the man his pass, signing out in the book as he did so. He handed the pen to Alicia. "It was like she'd said it all before. Like she'd rehearsed it."

"Exactly," Alicia said. "She was prepared for this."

As Alicia signed out, her phone rang. She checked the caller ID. It was Maisie.

# CHAPTER NINETEEN

TARIQ BASHIR WAS A FIRST-RATE COCK-WOMBLE. Watson had never liked the guy, and always assigned others to deal with him wherever possible. Not least because Bashir would hate Watson even more if he knew certain things about him, although Watson kept his personal life to himself.

But politics are politics.

The imam had been arrested at the college Amina Shah attended, at what had been billed as a peaceful vigil to allow the girl's friends to come together to mourn—*whatever their race or religion*, Tariq had said. But the video invite he'd put out there had a tinge of distaste to that part of his statement. Now, with Watson standing three feet away from him, he was making another statment, this one to a small gathering on the steps of Halifax's main station, where he'd been brought three hours earlier.

"My name is Tariq Bashir, and I am the imam of the Lainworth-Khalid Mosque. Today, I was beaten by an official from the Moleford Bridge council, for the crime of daring to ask whether a white supremacist might be responsible for the murder of a Muslim girl last night."

Bashir was now in more westernised attire, a short-sleeved shirt and jeans. His robes had been spattered with blood, both his own and Abhu Noon's, and he had called a member of his mosque to bring him a change of clothes. Watson couldn't tell whether it was to look less Islamic for the cameras—which had never bothered the man before—or to better display the bruising and scratches on his arms and neck.

"I was questioned by two officers," Bashir went on, the dozen or so reporters lapping it up. "Questioning *me*. Continuing the oppression felt by all Muslims in this country, as if we are automatically the criminal, no matter what the crime. I was questioned for over an hour. An *hour*. Over a *scuffle,* started by one of their own, when they should be out looking for whoever killed Amina Shah."

Twenty-odd people from his community, standing to one side, made grumbling noises of agreement, waving homemade signs suggesting the police were not doing much and that "crusaders" should be fearful of God's wrath. The big red minibus with the Arabic script was parked illegally, but it'd take a traffic warden with balls of solid gold to issue a ticket.

Watson had already debated with Bashir about the notion of Abhu Noon being "one of their own." The idiot councillor had indicated to Bashir he had an inside line to the police, but Watson put paid to that so quickly Noon's head all but popped off.

"I stand before you with these marks." Bashir held up his arms and spread his fingers toward his face. "I will accept this. I will not demand further action, because I refuse to take resources away from a far more important task." He eyed Watson, who'd rejected Cross's offer for her be the public face for this highly charged task.

After Alicia called with the new intel, Watson sent Cross back to Moleford, authorising her to break the bloody bank if it meant getting a result—pretty much the same words Watson had suffered from his chief superintendent.

"I call upon the senior officers here." Bashir lowered his arms, "to commit, now, to leaving no stone unturned, to pledge that no person will be above the law, and to promise Amina's family, her friends, that her killer *will* be brought to justice."

Watson crossed the three-foot buffer he'd given himself. He had hoped to stay out of the same photographic frame as the man, but that appeared impossible now. He'd counted three ridiculous clichés in Bashir's last sentence alone, and one impossibility.

Watson cleared his throat, the reporters' attention rapt upon him. "Mr Bashir has no need to call for such things. We treat every murder with the highest priority, and Amina Shah is no different." He had to enunciate well with reporters. If he spoke with his natural accent and contractions, they might misrepresent what he said. "This murder was particularly brutal, but we have several inquiries, which we are following up through our very best officers. I believe we will find whoever did this. But we need time to work. It is not a case of kicking down doors and demanding answers." He made a point of catching Bashir's gaze here, before returning to the journalists. "You can look at my track record, and that of my detectives. Justice is blind. And we give our all to every case."

"So no promises?" came one question.

"We never promise results." Watson again made a point of catching Bashir's attention, this time noting that he kept his hands behind his back, rocking on his heels as if happy about something. "We just promise to do the best we can."

"Like a boy scout!" Bashir suddenly said. When all turned back to him, his supporters growing animated to hear what he had to say, Bashir resumed centre stage and opened his arms. "And there you have it. The mealy-mouthed excuses are starting already." A terrible Scottish accent followed: "*We'll do our best.*

*We'll do what we can.*" His face curled horribly toward Watson, his own voice reinstated. "Until it becomes, *We're sorry, we have exhausted every avenue.*" To the people gathered beyond the reporters, he called, "If the police cannot deliver justice for Amina, we must seek out the perpetrators ourselves. Unlike these people, *we*—Amina's family, friends, her *community*—will not rest until she is avenged."

Bashir then stormed off, cameras clicking, reporters calling out for further comment, for clarification.

Watson slipped back inside and got straight on the phone to his boss. "Yes, guv, that fat ball-sack is *definitely* going t' give us a problem."

# CHAPTER TWENTY

ALICIA AND KNOWLES arrived back at the library and made for the office that someone at some point had dubbed "the situation room." It appeared to have stuck—even with the civilians, since Costas's first greeting was, "Hey, how are you? There's a visitor in the situation room."

"Don't you ever go home?" Alicia asked.

"Of course. Do you?"

"Touché. Who's the visitor? Not another councillor?"

"He had police ID." Lauren rolled out from an aisle with a lap full of hardback books. "Big fella. Beard."

"He ate all the Hob Nobs," Costas said.

"Ah, Detective Sergeant Ball," Alicia said. "I predicted Murphy would cave. Should've guessed he wouldn't give us Cleaver, though."

"Those titles you asked for," Lauren said, referring to the list Alicia had submitted over the phone after her chat with Maisie Jackson. "They're not here. *The Last Vanguard of Britishness*, *The Priest on the Hill: A Memoir*, *The Lainworth Ripper Investigation* … we do have records of them, but I'm afraid some were logged as having gone missing years ago. Possibly stolen or just not returned, or we've simply lost them. Other branches don't have them either. I'm sorry I couldn't help."

Alicia thanked her for her efforts and adjourned upstairs. In the situation room, they found the man Alicia thought of as nominative determinism personified. If being called Baker would help you become a baker later in life, him being called Ball … well, he wasn't quite a ball, but Alicia like the imagery. He was browsing an iPad with his feet on the table, but she doubted it was official business.

"Surprise," he said flatly.

"Great to have an experienced detective on board," Alicia said. "By the way, we found some Hob Nobs at the crime scene and were keeping them safe in here prior to DNA analysis. Have you seen them?"

Ball held very still for a moment, then looked at Knowles. "She's dicking with me, right?"

"How long have you known her?" Knowles asked.

"Long enough." He closed whatever window he was browsing and stood to shake the man's hand. "DS Ball."

Knowles took it. "DC Knowles. Good to meet you."

Alicia gave Knowles points for sounding convincing. Ball was the anti-Knowles: only as presentable as he needed to be, as polite as was necessary to avoid disciplinary action, and hygienic enough—barely—to keep his colleagues from starting a petition to seal him in his own plastic bubble.

"What happened?" Alicia asked. "Did someone knock you out again so you could wake up here?"

Ball tutted and said to Knowles, "You'd think she'd be more grateful. Got beaten unconscious trying to save her life, and look how she treats me."

Knowles smiled Alicia's way. "Remind me to be more careful around you."

"Work?" Alicia suggested.

"If we must." Ball folded his arms and leaned on the desk.

Knowles remained standing while Alicia fixed her phone to the laptop.

"You're up to speed?" Alicia asked Ball.

"Mostly."

"You know we have bones and other remains from approximately the 1920s, and from the 1970s and '80s?"

"Yep, got that."

"And we've identified victims from the seventies and eighties as being resident along the M62 corridor between Manchester and Leeds."

"Yep. Minorities, mostly, right?"

"Good. And Amina Shah?"

"Girl killed and left by a waterfall. No connection we know of."

"Ah." Alicia raised her finger, transferring her phone screen to the laptop. "That may be about to change. Maisie Jackson is a civilian doing a little research on the historical angle, going even further back to a mass murderer named Henry Pickersgill, otherwise known as the Priest on the Hill."

"Cute," Ball said.

"Here." Alicia brought up the photo Maisie had taken of the drawing. "The victim, who left Pickersgill's church in 1877, was found in pieces, her arms and legs cut into two sections each, then rearranged like a crucifix." She let them view the picture properly: the feet and legs outstretched from the torso, the arms positioned pointing down from the hips, with the woman's head lying at the hands. "I get the impression he was going for an inverted crucifix, to pretend devil worship was at work. Thoughts?"

"Yeah, I'd go for that," Ball said.

Knowles agreed too.

"Many of the bodies disturbed by the recent weather were cut in the same places, or very similar. Dismembered at the elbow, shoulder, knees, thighs, and head. We can't know their position when they were laid to rest, though." She let the imagery sink in. "We have also learned, in the interim, that the victims displayed in public by our presumably shell-shocked Lainworth Ripper chap were in an identical state." Another pause. More thoughtful grunts. "The body found at the waterfall, Mr Hairy-Pants-Ball—can you guess what detail we haven't released to the press?"

"Same position?" Ball said.

"Gold star!" Alicia mimed pressing a sticker on Ball's chest. "When I asked the DI in charge about that detail, she *freaked*."

"I did not freak." Cross entered the room as if she'd been waiting for that very line.

"Okay, Ms Pedantic." Alicia exaggerated an eyeroll. "But you *were* impressed." As Cross introduced herself to Ball, Alicia added, "*And* she got DCI Watson to combine our task forces, so now we're one big happy club."

"I'm the senior investigating officer," Cross said. "We're grateful for the input, but our priority is Amina. We have teams working the conventional angles—her movements, her contacts with people, electronic trail, CCTV—and we're based up at the mobile lab. You guys are to tackle the historical stuff in case it shines a light on motive, method, opportunity. Anything it can tell us."

"Lines of inquiry?" Ball asked.

They ran through a couple of theories already voiced, namely that the 1970s deaths were copycats of those from the 1920s.

"Why copy it?" Ball asked.

"Giggles," Alicia said. "Or he thought it looked cool. Or he wanted people to think it was some demon bogeyman operating through time. I don't know yet. The only thing I'm certain of is that he's big on shock value—a need to express his anger. Even if it's in private."

"Another why." Ball pulled away from the pictures. "Why not display them?"

"Fear of being caught? Maybe he planned to reveal himself

when he got close to death. Maybe he liked his cover life too much."

"Cover life…" Knowles sounded like he wanted to contribute, but the longer he paused, the more it sounded like a question.

"A true psychopath feels nothing that most of us do," Alicia said. "He will not feel empathy for others, for example. But if he's grown up in a family environment, around other people, he'll know he needs to act a particular way or he'll be ostracised. And if he's ostracised, he isn't the centre of attention, and cannot gain the validation he craves. He knows he needs to act like he is normal in order to be accepted."

"Which is what we're looking at," Knowles said. "Either four psychopaths in four periods of time, following a pattern, or possibly three."

"Assuming they're working alone," Ball pointed out.

"But we don't have evidence one way or another," Cross said.

"So that's theory one," Knowles said. "In the 1970s, a psychopath has a breakdown, needs to kill, and his outlet is minorities. He follows the pattern of the Lainworth Ripper—my theory being that the guy never got caught, so maybe he emulated that."

"Not a bad thought," Alicia said.

"Thanks. The thing is, how does it link to Amina Shah? Either the person who did the 1970s killing spree was very young at the time, and the discovery of the bodies led to him starting up again now, or it's someone new repeating the pattern."

"He'd be old now," Ball said.

"We are testing Amina for toxins," Cross said. "A man in his eighties, or even seventies, would struggle to physically subdue a college-age girl. If there are no toxins, it's safe to assume yesterday's killer is someone entirely new."

"Okay, a quick breakdown." Ball paced now, hand to his head. "The Priest on the Hill guy kills people, cuts them up.

Then in the 1920s, some guy goes nuts for Jews and kills a few in public with the body parts arranged the same way, but hides others in a place that preserves their bones for a hundred years. Then, in the seventies, along comes a guy wanting to kill immigrants, sees all this—what, by accident? And chooses the same method? But doesn't display any in public?"

Cross interjected with, "We've got civilian researchers looking into old murders nationwide for any possible connections. Similar murders in the seventies and eighties. Could be if there's a solved killing, the wrong person got convicted over it."

"Okay," Ball said. "But then we have the girl yesterday, the same way, left out for everyone to see."

"Not the most public place," Knowles said. "But yes, the body would have been found quickly."

"A succession of psychopaths," Alicia said. "In a small place like this. It's unlikely but not unheard of."

"The priest was from outside the region." Knowles checked his handwritten notes in the moleskin book. "If the Lainworth Ripper was the guy Maisie thinks, this Winston Wright, he was from Nottinghamshire, only settled here because of his rich uncle. We assume the seventies guy was local because he'd need to keep dropping bodies up there, and to discover the hiding place. And we think Amina's killer is local simply because of the timeframe."

"So there still might be no connection beyond the method of postmortem butchery," Cross said.

"Unless it's the cult thing." Knowles looked up from his notes as if surprised he'd said that aloud.

"What cult thing?" Ball asked.

"The idea that the Priest on the Hill was the start of a mysterious movement," Alicia said. "The killings occur roughly every fifty years, so someone put forward the notion that it's organised that way for a reason."

Ball shrugged. "Okay, sure. Why not."

"*Why not?*" Alicia flicked his forehead and he recoiled, more from annoyance than hurt. "Because it's stupid."

Cross stood, open-mouthed at her action, but Ball seemed nonplussed, so she said nothing.

He rubbed the spot, which was turning red. "You go with the convoluted theory of one being inspired by the other, but write off the simplest idea?"

"It's not the simplest idea." Alicia's brain still hurt. It was trying to tell her something. And that was making her grumpy. Probably the reason she had flicked Ball. It was out of reach, though. "It's the simplest one to say out loud, but not the simplest to put into practice. An organised group, brainwashing a new generation to kill every fifty years, is easy? Think about it. If I started right now with Stacey, I could, conceivably, teach her things that she'll believe. Until she has any sort of contact with the real world, at which point she'll hear different points of view. And unless I've conditioned her very carefully, she'll listen. By the time she's old enough to go on a killing spree, she might be willing to do it, *if* I've managed to convince her that I am right and *the whole rest of the world* is wrong. Then, when that's done, she has to do the exact same thing to *her* kids, timing it so their first murder is fifty years from hers. Do you really think there's a possibility that four generations could produce that same result?"

"I suppose not." Ball looked chastised, a pupil browbeaten by a teacher.

"Okay, so let's recap," Cross said. "We use the historical investigation to narrow down a suspect in the seventies murders. If they're alive, we prosecute. If not, we hand it to the coroner's office. If it links to Amina, we do them for all the killings."

"I've got it!" Alicia said.

"Got what?"

"The reason my brain was hurting."

They all looked confused, but Alicia forgave them; they didn't have access to her inner workings.

"Listen up. If the seventies killings were inspired by the twenties, and Amina's death was inspired by the seventies, how did her killer know about the arrangement of the body parts?"

Silence. Thinking.

"We've been moving so fast on this—the conventional police investigation and the research side—that no one has asked *how* the killer knew. It's fair to say the press can learn that some of the older remains were chopped up, even though we haven't released it officially, but some killer? Who wants to take advantage?"

"It's public knowledge," Knowles said. "The books are out there."

"It's not, though. The books are *missing*. Have been for years, according to Lauren. Whoever killed Amina may well have been triggered by the bones disturbed by the flood, but whoever it was *had* to know the cause of death before we did. They knew, because they were a part of it in the seventies."

They all processed it.

Cross said, "We find who has the books, they're our suspect."

Alicia clapped Knowles on the arm. "And we know someone who has at least one of those, don't we?"

# CHAPTER TWENTY-ONE

THE STRANGERS' Club had a band warming up, and the male-female mix was more balanced than it had been the previous afternoon, but the welcome Alicia, Ball, and Knowles received chilled Alicia just as much as before. Although Cross insisted they didn't need to go mob-handed as a threesome, Alicia made a point that swayed her: "If Knowles doesn't come, it'll give them the impression he was intimidated, and we don't want to empower them any more than they already are. DS Ball is new to the investigation and as much as he looks like a hobo squatting with a police ID—"

"Pardon?" Ball had said, looking himself up and down.

"Despite that, he is good at reading people. And me—well, I need to get a read on Bertie and his friends too. For different reasons."

Cross had relented, but emphasised any overtime would be repaid in lieu, which everyone knew was code for "no overtime" since very few detectives managed time off. Alicia phoned her mum to book Stacey into the "Dorothy Hotel." Momentum was starting to pick up, and she needed a clear head, not clock-watching to pick up Stacey.

The Strangers' Club's smaller bar area gave off a vibe of relaxed anticipation—people in smart-casual shirts and blouses, some tee-shirts, a lot of denim, and the sounds emanating from the back room were mostly vocal with the odd guitar twang. The police presence served to agitate a couple of people, and two or three "casually" exited toward the loo.

Alicia craned her neck to see down the side of the bar itself. She noticed even more Union Flags than before, and when the band struck up for a ten-second burst they didn't sound like the death metal crew she'd expected; more like soft rock, something approximating the big-hair bands of the eighties.

"Help you?" asked one of the guys they'd met briefly yesterday—the smart one with the purple-haired girlfriend.

"Glenn, isn't it?" Alicia said.

He was with the woman again, his hand around her as if she might bolt at any moment, but her simpering expression suggested a deep affection for the man. As Knowles came further in, Glenn's arm snaked tighter. Ball mooched along, hands in his pockets, arrowing straight into the crowd. He was watched all the way, but showing less concern than a fly making its way toward a peanut butter sandwich. He eased himself to the front, where Alicia could just about make out two women and Bertie serving, although Bertie was also checking the fridges and taps as he went.

"Thank you, Glenn," Alicia said, "but I think we're fine. Quick word with Bertie, then we'll skip on out." She stepped toward Ball, planning on taking he same path, but Glenn stepped in the way. She halted. "Looks like I get to ask the question now."

"What question?" the woman with Glenn asked, her words a little slurred.

"This one: *help you?*"

Glenn disconnected with the purple-haired woman, his hands in plain sight, although one of them was holding a bottle. Alicia felt Knowles tense, and caught Ball eyeing the situation instead of attracting the attention of someone who might serve him beer. He only looked away from them to observe a few lads returning from the toilet who'd paid a visit as soon as the detectives arrived.

"I'm only asking because Bertie's busy," Glenn said. "You were asking questions about the Vanguard, and I can help with that. Better coming from me than hassling the old boys."

A throaty "Ahhch" made Alicia jump. She turned to find that an elderly man in a scooter had sidled up to her, an oxygen pipe under his nose. "What've I told you about calling us names?"

"James Grantham." Alicia stuck out a hand. "I'm Detective Inspector Friend. Nice to meet you."

James left the handshake hanging, his scornful gaze passing from Alicia to Knowles, then to Ball, who'd now returned to the group. The old man spoke with a rattle in his throat. "You wanna be careful in here, piggies. Lots of boys don't have the sort of restraint I do."

"What you going to do?" Glenn said. "Hit 'em with your breathing tank?"

"Piss off." James swung an arm toward the door, his fingers gnarled into near-claws. Only his thumb and forefinger appeared to have full movement, the middle one halfway unfurled. To Ball, he said, "Bloody kids. Think they know best."

"You were friends with Remington Duval." Alicia kept up the cheeriness. "That's funny. We're here to see if Bertie will lend us one of Remy's books. Unless you have one you'd let us borrow."

James laughed for some reason, which triggered a coughing fit. Immediately, two larger lads came their way, but Glenn beat them to James's aid. He helped the old man press the mouth-and-nose mask to his face and take a big hit of oxygen. When James signalled he was fine and held out a hand, one of the other lads passed him a pint glass with half an inch of beer left. James hacked a cough, then a bigger one, and spat something large and viscous into the glass. "Cheers." When one of the guys took it back and left it on a table, James said, "Heh-heh, yeah, Remy. He was something else. Fancied himself a la-de-da type, even when he was teaching some other crew a lesson. We called him the warrior poet. But I didn't read any of his shit. Sorry."

"Why do you need to know about Remy?" Glenn asked.

"Why do you need know why we need to know?" Alicia replied.

Glenn's friendly veneer slipped for a second but he tried to re-establish it, unclenching his jaw and spreading his arms. "I was elected the leader of the Vanguard, and you're asking questions about members and former members. I'm trying to get this group focused on the future, not the past, so if anyone has done something that might reflect badly—"

Knowles let out a grunt which Alicia tagged as instinctive, but Glenn heard it and paused. The band struck up another ten-second sound test, then cut out.

Glenn's friendly veneer remained, though. "I want to focus on positive things for Britain. Not screwing people over by race. Patriotism doesn't have to mean hating someone based on their skin colour." A glance at Knowles. "Just on how they behave toward the country they call home."

James fell into another fit of coughs, and this time it was Scarlett who assisted with the oxygen. Knowles made himself useful by passing the spit-glass. James reached for it, but there was hesitation, a long appraisal of the man proffering the receptacle, before he accepted, spat in it, and handed it back. Knowles placed it down.

"Thanks," James said.

"You're welcome," Knowles replied.

Ball hooked a thumb back over his shoulder. "That's Bertie?"

Alicia confirmed the man returning to bar duty was Bertie, grateful for getting back on track.

"I'm eager to build bridges," Glenn said. "With the police. And anyone who calls themselves British. Anything you need." He handed a business card to Alicia. "You want a book from

Bertie, fine. But I can be more help, more willing to talk to the police."

"Yeah, real piggie friend." James repositioned his scooter for a run at the bar. "Friends with the piggie and the niggie." He winked at Knowles. "Gotta have a sense of humour, right?"

"You know what's really funny?" the detective constable asked.

"What's that?"

"How we found one racist prick this morning with his mind turned to mush but a body that worked okay, and here you are with your body rotting all around you, but you kept all your brainpower. I'm not sure what's worse."

James snorted and pressed together a set of teeth that were far too perfect to be his own. "Yeah, well I'm bloody sure, and it ain't bloody funny." He took off, bumping people who didn't seem to mind, a couple even apologising along the way.

"You shouldn't be rude," Glenn said.

"Why not?" Ball asked. "You've stalled us long enough. Pretty sure everyone who needs to flush something or wipe clean and stash a weapon in the gents has finished their business. Now I'm heading through the back. Any of you baby-Nazis want to get arrested, you just lay a hand on me and see what happens."

It was one of the reasons Alicia had wanted Ball along. Knowles wouldn't take any crap, as he'd shown with James, but he didn't have the gritty presence of DS Ball—a guy whose patience only went so far before he resorted to tactics that were the only thing a certain breed of thug responded to.

Alicia gave Glenn a little wave, said, "Toodles," and led them to the side passage, where Ball slapped the counter to get Bertie's attention.

"Five minutes of your time," Ball said.

Bertie exchanged a glance with Glenn, who just shrugged, and the bar owner did not resist.

The band watched in silence the trio entered their space,

which was even more Union-Flag-coated than Alicia had seen from the front. Bertie joined them.

Alicia rotated as she walked, eyes on the bunting. "You know, there's such a thing as trying too hard. Gives the impression you're overcompensating for something. It's what fear does to people—"

"You need something?" Bertie asked. "Or you just going to criticise my décor?"

"May we see your bookshelf again?" Alicia asked chirplily.

"You know the way."

Despite the words, Bertie led them to the office in the corner of the room. It wasn't exactly cramped, but Alicia wouldn't want to spend too much time in here with all four of them, especially since it was so hot. Ball wasn't sweating yet, but it wouldn't be long.

"*The Last Vanguard of Britishness*," Alicia said. "You had a copy, I think."

Bertie rubbed his chin in an obviously fake manner, scanning his shelves. "Probably. One of Remy's, isn't it?"

Alicia said nothing, observing the pantomime. *Now why pretend to be thinking about it?*

"This one." Bertie selected the slender volume and eased it out.

Much like the pamphlet Maisie had unearthed, the book featured a group of men holding a Union Flag the size of a bedsheet. The colour was faded but it plainly featured Remy himself alongside three others, their heads shaved and faces deadly serious. They seemed to be in mid-speech—or mid-chant, as seemed more likely for the scene—while they stared at something behind the camera. The city, blurred in the background, looked like Leeds, but she couldn't be sure.

"Why d'you want it?" Bertie asked.

"We're eliminating people from our inquiries," Knowles said.

"You don't think Remy did that Muslim girl, do you?"

"You said he was dead," Alicia said. "He isn't. You lied. It's suspicious."

"I honestly didn't know he was still alive 'til Jimmy Grantham mentioned it yesterday."

"In what context?" Ball asked.

Bertie crossed his arms and leaned on his bookshelf. Defensive posture. "In the context of me having a conversation with a punter about what the police wanted with me. James said, 'Poor old Remington Duval, he's hanging on by the last of his brain cells.'"

Alicia thumbed through the book, reading the chapter headings.

"Anyone visit with him?" Ball asked.

"Remy?"

"Santa Claus."

"I didn't ask. But I think some of the lads who knew him through their dads might've popped up. They didn't say it outright, but they seemed to agree Remy weren't all there." Bertie switched focus to Knowles. "You're British, right?"

"Yes." Knowles kept his tone even, seemingly ruffled by his burn of James Grantham earlier.

"Good. No hyphen?"

"Hyphen?"

"Yeah, like, British-Muslim. British-Nigerian. British-Jewish. British-Something-That-Isn't-Really-British."

"Just British," Knowles said.

Bertie nodded sagely, as if confirming something. "Parents?"

"British," Knowles said.

"Is this going somewhere?" Ball asked.

"Just making conversation. While she gets what she needs." He gestured to Alicia, flicking through the book. "So, British born, British parents. Grandparents?"

Knowles exhaled through his nose. "I'm not sure I'm

comfortable having a social chat, sir. Would you mind if we stuck to business?"

"Like you stuck to business with Jimmy in his wheelchair?"

Alicia looked up from the book to find Knowles fighting with something inside himself.

"Nigerian," he said calmly. "My father's parents were Nigerian. My mother's were from Jamaica."

Bertie laughed, and in a well-practiced Caribbean accent said, "*Jamaica maan!*" In his regular voice, hushed, he added, "I actually like a bit of reggae."

"This is neat," Alicia said. "Reaching across cultural divides like big, juicy Colossuses of tolerance. But *this* is even more interesting." She opened the book to a chapter called 'The Nazis and Modern Britain.' "Remington Duval has some lovely views on Nazism. Want to hear some?"

"I've read it," Bertie said.

Ball raised a hand. "I haven't. May I hear?"

Alicia read the passage. "'Although it was absolutely essential for the magnificent Winston Churchill and our heroic troops of the Second World War to repel all invaders to our shores, the more I read about the foundation of the National Socialist Party, the more I understand why they rose to power. Oppressed by outside forces, financially raped by foreigners and their offspring, with their institutions in the grip of a Semite cabal that allowed no other faith to share their wealth, what else could a county do but allow a strong leader to wrest back control? Who else but Mr Hitler could have broken the Jewish stranglehold on their lives, and restore prosperity to a dejected people? If they had not attempted to destroy us, I suspect the Nazis would have made fine allies in Britain's struggle against modern attempts to dilute our race with the dark pigments of Africa and Asia, and the filthy habits of the Irish. At least we, unlike our American cousins, do not have to bend the knee to Jewish overlords.'" She closed the book and tapped the cover. "He has a real turn of phrase. *If they had not attempted to destroy us, I suspect the Nazis would have made fine allies.* A bit like saying if the crocodile hadn't tried to eat me, it'd have made a great pet."

Bertie's expression had remained stone throughout her extract. "I said I read it, not that I agreed with it."

"*Do* you agree with it?" Knowles asked.

"Some. Some not."

No one spoke for a few seconds after that; it was Alicia who finally broke the silence. "Can I borrow this? We'll give you a receipt. It's just for research."

A knock sounded and the door opened. Glenn entered with two men they'd seen the previous day acting as his honour guard, both shaven-headed; one was short and thin, his eyes small and close together like a rat's, while the other was tall and fat, his flab jiggling as he walked, even through his untucked shirt.

"Why are you interested in Remington Duval?" Glenn asked.

Beyond the three men, Alicia saw two more, with Glenn's girlfriend coming up behind. The purple-haired woman put a hand on her fella's shoulder. "Come on, Glenn. It's not worth bothering them with. Let's—"

"Scarlett, I *told* you…" Glenn gripped her hand and removed it, letting it drop, his eyes on Alicia. "You need to explain exactly why you're asking about a man who many here see as a founding father to the Vanguard. Otherwise, I might not be able to stop one of them doing something very, *very* stupid."

# CHAPTER TWENTY-TWO

"OUT," Bertie said. "Or you're all barred."

Alicia didn't need a breath test to see Glenn had imbibed a lot more since they left him; his beer breath now carried the stench of liquor. His friends' chests had inflated with machismo, their guts sucked in. She'd heard names bandied about the previous day and took a chance. "Sean Pryor and Russel Davy, huh?"

Glenn's lips thinned. He stretched out his clenched fists, not in the direction of the detectives, but to warn the oddball pair to keep cool.

"Glenn," the girl said.

"It's okay, Scarlett," Alicia said. "Your fella here's just being a good leader. The foot soldiers were obviously on at him to 'do something' or 'stop letting them pigs push you around' or something like that. Am I right?"

Scarlett barely flinched, moving to her man's side. "Can't you just go?"

"If you're scared of him, we can help," Ball said.

"She's not scared of me." Glenn placed his arm around Scarlett, his demeanour now far closer to what most people expected from neo-Nazi types. "And these lads've got minds of their own. I just wanted to come back here, see if I can be of assistance. But you're there with Remington Duval's manifesto, and I'm wondering if Bertie or even Remy should be getting legal advice."

"No need for that," Knowles said.

"Shut up," the fatter of the foot soldiers said.

"*You* shut up, Russ." Bertie strode forward, unafraid. "This is my office. This is my place. That makes it my rules."

Glenn stepped between them, Scarlett stuck to his hip, his face in Bertie's. "My boys. You want to start from scratch with your clientele? 'Cos I can take the lads elsewhere if you like."

"Think I need a sellout like you propping me up?"

"I think if we all headed off to the Lion instead of here, you'd sell to a Wetherspoons in less than a month."

"Easy, lads," Ball said. "We got what we wanted." He was the furthest detective forward. Although he spoke to Glenn, he was looking at Scarlett. "We're leaving. But if there are any problems, if anyone wants to report a crime, we're in town for a while."

"Thank you all for your time." Alicia hoped her words implied no one was in trouble even though she was already mentally drafting a memo to suggest raiding the place on the next busy night. "We must be going." She held the book up to Bertie. "Did you say we could keep hold of this for a while?"

"Aye." Bertie turned to Glenn. "How about we just let 'em out?"

Glenn gave his "boys" some unspoken signal, and all moved aside, Scarlett now smiling at the police. As the detectives passed them, out into the strains of a tune Alicia recognised but couldn't name, Glenn said, "Scarlett and me are happy. I don't do nothing to her she doesn't ask for."

Alicia paused, which meant the men with her paused. She faced Glenn and Scarlett, ignoring the lumps behind them— Russel half-sucked-in his gut to puff up his chest again and Sean's beady rat-eyes watched on. "It's not necessary, you know."

"What isn't?"

"The control thing." Alicia pointed back and forth between Glenn and Scarlett. "She likes you. No need to be paranoid about her running off."

"I'm not paranoid. I just know Scarlett likes a real man." Glenn slapped Scarlett's backside.

She giggled. "None of that feminism crap here."

Alicia didn't want to get into a debate about feminism with these people. She didn't particularly enjoy debating feminism even with people who *weren't* delusional about the subject. No, she wouldn't get dragged into that.

Scarlett must have picked up Alicia's eyeroll and seemed determined to provoke her more. Giving a doe-eyed glance to Glenn, she said, "It's not that I think women need to suffer."

"Oh, she's allowed to talk," Ball said, which was not helpful.

Scarlett only stuttered a moment before continuing. "Women are not equal to men. We're superior. That's why I love Glenn. He understands that we should be worshipped." She stuck out her cheek and Glenn licked it. "Mmm. That's why we shouldn't have to buy our own drinks. Why we shouldn't have to work." She grabbed Glenn's crotch, cupping everything she found in there. "So don't judge me. I like *real* men. *This* is what I want. This is what I *deserve*. Okay?"

Glenn grinned and tightened his embrace. "Now we understand each other better, maybe we can all be friends."

Alicia passed the book to Knowles, and figured she could throw the drunk yob a bone. "You're born and bred local."

"Two generations in Moleford. I got relatives going all the way back to William the Conqueror."

"So you feel more British than most of us."

"I have the history of my country running through my veins."

"Oh, eww. But if it makes you happy, fine. Let me ask you something…" And this was her tipping point. Reel him in or set him at arm's length. Make him think he's a suspect, and that the police might go looking deeper. Yes, that sounded good. "You do know it was a Muslim girl who was murdered yesterday, right?"

"I heard."

"And I'm going to learn you and your friends here were tucked up in bed—*separate* beds, of course—or drinking here all night?"

Glenn stood side-on, arm still around Scarlett, keeping her back from Alicia. "Are you accusing me of something?"

"I'm asking where you were between five and ten p.m. yesterday."

A faint smile formed and Glenn almost smirked. "You know it was probably one of *them*, don't you? She probably spoke to an infidel or refused to marry her brother or some other breach of sharia law."

"I'm sorry," Ball said gruffly. "I didn't catch that. Lady asked where you were."

The little-and-large act with Glenn bristled and their chests puffed out again.

"He was with me," Scarlett said. "Being a real man."

All stared at one another, not much movement. Only the shuffle of feet. Then three huge bangs sounded and everyone jumped, calming as soon as they realised the drummer had sprung to life.

"We'll be off, then," Alicia said.

The detectives recommenced their bid for the exit.

"Leave the book," Glenn said.

Once again, all paused.

"It's my book," Bertie said.

"It's actually mine." Glenn released Scarlett, freeing up both his hands. "I lent it to you. Two, three years ago. *Remember?*"

Bertie watched the younger man carefully. Warily. "Thought it was a gift."

"No." Glenn addressed Alicia. "It wasn't. It's mine. I'd like it back." He held out an open hand.

Alicia took it back from Knowles and opened the front cover. "This is glue." She showed the first page to Glenn and ran her finger over a rough spot a quarter of the way down. "The library had a book just like this stolen a few years ago. They use a very special chemical, one we can easily identify in the lab we have parked up across from the Beacon. Do you think, Glenn, if we tested it, we'd find the same type of glue here, in this book? Meaning the owner of the book must have—*gasp*—stolen it."

Glenn sighed, and shook his head. "You're not going to do any sort of testing on a book."

"If it's pertinent to a murder inquiry I might. And if you're not willing to give it up voluntarily, we could try for a warrant. And as part of that warrant, we'd bring in a whole host of officers to start grilling every member of your Vanguard of Britishness about their whereabouts last night. *And* searching the loos."

Glenn was about to reply, but Knowles cut in. "Just inconveniencing you, *sir*, will make a certain Tariq Bashir very happy indeed."

"What'll your acolytes think of that?" Ball asked. "Instead of lending the piggies a book, you piss the piggies off and they come blow the wolves' house in. Good leadership?"

Glenn took another moment, then pulled out his phone, aimed it at the book in Alicia's hand and snapped a photo. "If that doesn't come back to me in perfect condition, I'll be suing. It's a valuable first edition by someone we hold in high esteem. Clear?"

"Crystal," Alicia said.

"Let's go." Glenn tapped the two lads' shoulders, and they and Scarlett all moseyed on back round the front, as if they'd achieved some victory.

"Better going out back," Bertie said.

"Agreed." Alicia led them all to the fire exit, watched again by the band.

Outside, descending the metal staircase to the back car park, they all exhaled, none of them ashamed to show how frightened they'd been back there.

"From now on, we tread carefully with these guys." She waved the book. "And as soon as we get an *ounce* of evidence against any one of them, I want a warrant, and I want every one of Bertie's books confiscated."

"Why's that?" Ball asked.

Alicia knocked Knowles's arm. "Did you see?"

"Yeah," Knowles said. "Couldn't ask for that too, or it'd look suspicious."

"Ask for what?" Ball said

Knowles didn't reply right away, waiting to see if Alicia wanted the honour of telling him, but she left it to Knowles. "There was another book in there we should check out. He's been reading about the Lainworth Ripper."

# CHAPTER TWENTY-THREE

AFTER LEAVING Lucy's vicarage and calling Alicia, Maisie sent Joanne and Peter home, cycled straight to the train station, and hopped on the next service into Leeds, where their library would be far better stocked with the material she needed. Not to say Lauren and Costas, and all the others who worked in Moleford Bridge's library, didn't do a wonderful job, because they did, but Maisie expected she'd need a little extra oomph in the reference section.

Once inside Leeds City Library, she set about researching other legends, spanning wider than Moleford while keeping her home as the central focus. She piled the books she needed on the long table in the study room, where she learned far more about the violent proclivities of the people of the day than she cared to. It wasn't *news* to her, strictly speaking, but to read about it in such detail made her thankful to be living in such enlightened times. And yes, she included some of the worst places on Earth in that assessment.

*At least those places aren't anywhere near here.*

"Eww, that's disgusting." Joanne peered over Maisie's shoulder.

"I thought I sent you home," Maisie whispered.

"We came anyway."

Maisie checked on the other people present. No one seemed put out. Mostly younger folk—students at one of the city's universities, no doubt—with only one older gentleman who'd appraised her for somewhat longer than she'd been comfortable with, but Maisie paid him no mind. The study "room" was more like a study *hall*, a deliciously musty space with three long tables, computer terminals, and easy access to the reference sections.

Maisie ignored the girl and turned the page from the diagram and description of a hanged, drawn, and quartered highwayman. She landed on a page with a close-up sketch of a woman's upper body with her intestines spewing onto the ground before a cheering crowd.

"Oh, that's even worse," Peter said at Maisie's other shoulder.

"Would you *please* be *quiet*," Maisie hissed.

This drew the attention of two students and the older man, whom Maisie pegged, for some reason, as a birdwatching enthusiast. He just had that look about him. Maisie raised a hand in apology and picked a different book, this one a more up-to-date true-crime tome, covering 1970-1975.

*Unsolved in Lancashire.*

Funny—she'd used the phrases "unsolved murders 1970 Lancashire" and "unsolved murders 1970 Yorkshire" in her internet searches, but this book hadn't shown up. Must have been either out of stock or so far back on the page results it would have taken her days to find it.

She ran a finger down the contents.

"What you looking for?" Peter asked.

"Murders," Maisie replied in a whisper. No one looked up.

Joanne put her head in the way. "Why?"

"To see if there are any killings that look like the Lainworth Ripper or Priest on the Hill."

"Wouldn't the police be checking that?" Peter said.

"Probably."

"So why are you looking here?" The twelve-year-old boy pointed at a heading titled *Murdered by the Butcher?* "It'll be slower. There's no telling how up to date their digital searches are, or if every unsolved or solved murder will have been digitised—"

"Or if they'll allocate sufficient funds to resource a manual records search," Joanne pointed out.

Peter nodded. "You know how they go to the computers first and make conclusions without fully examining the milieu."

"Big word for a twelve-year-old," Maisie said, just as quietly as before, but generating a passive-aggressive glance from the birdwatcher.

"Which word?"

"Milieu."

"Six letters," Joanne said. "It's not that big. And you used it earlier."

"Complex, then. You should use the word 'setting' or 'situation'."

"Those words are all bigger than milieu," Peter said.

"I *know*." Maisie let her whisper become a hiss again, this time drawing a frown from someone who'd been listening on headphones before. She kept her voice as low as possible and moved her mouth as little as she could, turning into a bad ventriloquist. "I need the pair of you to leave me to work. Please."

"I thought you liked having us around," Joanne said.

"Yeah." Peter seemed close to tears.

Maisie buried her head in her hands. To herself, she said, "I really wish I didn't need to keep you near. If I could stay sane any other way…"

"You're not sane?" Joanne asked. "You seem sane to me."

"I am." Again, Maisie said it as quietly as breathing. "But I wouldn't be if I lost you. I need to concentrate, though. So can you please sit quietly?"

Peter smiled sweetly. "Okay, mommy, I'll be good."

Satisfied, Maisie turned to the page of the Butcher killings, learning that in 1972, a black girl called Fiona—Fifi to her friends— was found by a dog walker in a stream, her head cut off, her arms and legs missing. A subsequent search found a humerus—the upper part of her arm—stripped of flesh by animals; the remaining tendons appeared to have been sliced through rather than chewed, although it took a second autopsy, ordered four years later, to determine this. Sniffer dogs tracked down other parts at the time, but these were smaller bones ripped from the main parts by scavenging carnivores.

"It's possible," Joanne said.

"What is?" Maisie asked, again the whispering ventriloquist.

"That they're the same," Peter said.

"You shouldn't be looking at this sort of thing."

"Come on, mum," Joanne said. "You talk to us all the time about problems. We help."

Maisie sighed, not wanting to involve them in this. But she didn't think she'd work it out on her own. "Okay. There's no reason a police officer would be given this crime and think to check back to the 1870s and 1920s."

"Right." Peter started pacing, putting a finger to his lips the way his father used to when pondering a conundrum. "But *we* know about them, so we have them in our consciousness, front and centre."

"Meaning…" Joanne perched her bum on the table. "We *could* be inserting patterns because we're overly conscious of the potential for a pattern."

Still pacing back and forth, Peter wagged his finger. "Good point. Which means we have to factor in the *present-day* milieu as well as that of the 1972 killing of Fifi. Our thinking could be compromised."

"I wish you wouldn't talk like a grownup," Maisie said.

"I don't believe that's my fault, is it?" The boy peered at her as if peeking over spectacles. Again, just like his dad.

"Okay." Maisie rubbed her face. "Is our research into the past affecting our objectivity?"

"Let's blue-sky-think this." Joanne hopped down and joined her brother in pacing. They now crisscrossed each other. "You can easily imagine that Fifi was cut up in the same way. The beheading, plus the one injury that they can ascertain shows a blade was used to dismember her. At least one arm was cut up the exact same way as Lainworth and the Priest on the Hill, *and* those bodies found after the flood."

"It's a solid lead," Maisie said. "But one similar killing doesn't make a pattern."

Peter tramped off toward the main body of the library. "Okay, Jacksons. Forwaaaarrrdd march!"

The little boy had resurfaced and Maisie smiled. She stood to follow him and Joanne extended a hand to hold, although how much longer that would last she couldn't say. A teenager already, she'd soon be rebelling.

But wasn't rebellion a result of friendship? Of peer pressure? And if Joanne wasn't physically capable of making friends her own age, maybe Maisie would be able to hang onto this bond a little longer than most.

"Excuse me." The birdwatcher chap was now standing beside her, his voice hushed. "May I kindly request that if you must talk to yourself, you do it in an area where people are not concentrating on important work?"

Under his arm he held a book on steam trains.

*A train-spotter, not a birdwatcher.*

*Same species, different breed.*

"I'm sorry," she said. "Bouncing ideas around my head. Figuring things out."

"Thank you." He bowed shallowly. "But may I also say that if you feel the need for a human to... bounce ideas off, I will be in the café on the ground floor for the next hour."

"I'll… if I get finished, I'll bear that in mind. But we—I have a train at seven."

The man smiled. "Another time, then."

He departed, good-natured enough, but Maisie was not used to being hit on. It was one of the reasons she dressed down and kept her hair natural—she didn't like attention.

Then Peter and Joanne were pulling at her hands.

"Come on!" Joanne urged.

"Yeah," Peter said. "There must be tons of those cool murder books. Let's find some more for that nice Alicia lady. She'll be *so* pleased."


After another hour of research stretching from Liverpool's western docks, to Whitby's east coast cliffs and beaches, Maisie, Peter, and Joanne wandered out of the library into a cool late-summer evening and found a bench to make a private phone call. Detective Inspector Alicia Friend picked up straight away.

"Hiya," she said. "Anything else juicy for me?"

"You know how we talked about cults?" Maisie said.

"Oh, let's not get into that again."

"No, no, what I've found… it doesn't matter."

"Doesn't matter?"

Maisie didn't want to come across as crazy, the way she sort-of had in the library. She held Peter's hand, hoping the touch would calm her. "It doesn't matter, DI Friend."

"Alicia."

"Names don't matter either."

"What is it?" The detective now sounded concerned. "Are you okay?"

"The girl they found this morning," Maisie said. "She was cut up, wasn't she?" They hadn't released any of those details yet. Wouldn't be allowed to share it with a civilian researcher. "Her head, her arms, her legs. And the arms and legs were split in two as well. Like that apostate from the Priest on the Hill. Like the six Lainworth killings he left outdoors."

DI Friend just breathed for a second, plainly thinking through the confidentiality of her case. "Yes. Amina Shah was cut up and positioned the same way. You found evidence of others?"

"Between 1970 and 1985, in true crime books covering that era, there are exactly six similar killings. They were never flagged as being possibly linked because four of them were considered solved."

"Crap, that means—"

"It means false convictions and a distinct pattern." Maisie smiled in turn at the pair who'd helped work this out. "Doesn't matter if it's a devil cult, coincidental inspiration springing up every fifty years, or some psychic hangover tainting the land. Amina is just the first. There *will* be more."

# CHAPTER TWENTY-FOUR

FOLLOWING Maisie's rather grasping revelation, Alicia thanked her for her kind offer of accommodation, but said someone from the West Yorkshire Police had found her a bed in a simple but clean chain hotel on the outskirts of town. She told Maisie it was better to stay there to maintain the integrity of the evidence; if Maisie turned up something that proved valuable, they didn't want a defence counsel suggesting it had been concocted between an ambitious DI and an impressionable civilian.

Maisie said the last time she had been called "impressionable" was when her mother was trying to deter her from marrying Cuthbert, her husband. "Hmm, my *ex*-husband, I suppose," she said, but accepted Alicia's reasoning good-naturedly.

Given how Alicia's mind worked, she probably should have paid Maisie more attention, especially considering that Maisie's technique was one that helped unlock her own analytic abilities. What had once required a force of will to absorb every facet, weed out every impossibility, and see only what was physically possible now came naturally, in no small part due to the exercises in Maisie's textbooks. Although Alicia could not recall the exact wording, it boiled down to "seeing the whole picture at once;"

there were some more bits and pieces about speaking to the evidence, having it relate all the reasons it might be there.

Alicia had discarded that last technique years ago.

What Maisie had emphasised, in one lively talk to a large class, was encouragement for students to find their own ways of working, of shaping their own brains to approach the puzzles in the most open way they could. As she worked through her doubts, Alicia was close to calling Maisie back, and decided to do exactly that after signing *The Last Vanguard of Britishness* into evidence at the mobile lab on top of the hill.

That was when, as she exited the police unit, someone surprised her.

"DCI Murphy told me where to find you." Iothor placed his hands in his pockets, casual as you like. "Well, he told Robbie, and Robbie told me. He's a nice man, I think. Said you might need some good dinner after a long day. Or Robbie did. He concurred."

She skipped down the steps, ready to kiss the man, but there were other officers around and it was only seven p.m. Hard to resist, though; Iothor was wearing jeans and a loose collarless shirt, and he smelled fresh. She noted, too, that he'd trimmed his beard and used product in his hair. If Knowles and Ball were still working, though, she should be too.

As if reading her concern, Knowles stepped out, along with Ball. "Quitting time." Ball rubbed his face. "Long drive."

"You're not stopping over?" Alicia said.

"Nah, just got back in the house with the missus. Gonna bring her a Moleford newspaper."

"Why?"

Ball shrugged. "Something we used to do before we got married. Whenever one of us went somewhere new, we'd bring back a newspaper. Had a scrapbook full of front pages. Figured it'd be romantic or something. See ya."

He ambled over to his car, and Knowles stood there looking

tired. Cross was liaising with intelligence officers, tracing Amina's electronic trail, had but left a standing order for all to clock out as soon as they could, get some sleep, and hit the case back up fresh first thing.

"Cross said go home," Alicia told him.

"I know," the detective constable said. "But … there's work to do. We could ID more of them."

Alicia placed a hand on his arm and waited for his attention to fall on her, then softened her cheeks without smiling. This was her *stern-but-caring* expression. "Part of being an effective copper is knowing when to recharge."

Knowles relaxed, as if he'd been waiting to hear those very words. "Okay."

"Now, this big hunk of meat is taking me out for a curry." Alicia swung her arms toward Iothor. "Want to join us?"

Knowles smiled, shook his head. "I think I'll turn in. Thanks for the offer."

He wandered away, and Alicia hooked her arm into Iothor's, and they headed for their cars. "Right, then. Let's find some food. I just have a quick stop to make first."

Alicia needed to check in to the hotel or she'd lose the booking, so she brought in her overnight bag containing toiletries, underwear, pyjamas, and work clothes. Rather than the shower she craved, she satisfied herself with a quick wash and a refreshing spray of deodorant, then texted DI Cross to get a recommendation for an Indian restaurant. Finally, she FaceTimed and exchanged screen-kisses with Stacey, then returned quickly to drop into Iothor's compact Ford Fiesta and travel into the town.

"Hope we can have a more conventional date this time," she said.

"I don't know," he replied with a sardonic smile. "Attempting to turn off the life support of a serial killer is an original evening."

Alicia had worried it might have been the last she saw of the man. "Sorry I didn't get myself done up."

"It was a last-minute decision. I did not expect a cocktail dress. You look as lovely as ever."

They parked and followed Alicia's app to the restaurant Cross suggested, where they were seated straight away. It was a quiet night—only four couples were dining, tended to by six waiters. After their personal waiter brought out a plate of popadoms and a pickle tray, they got down to the serious business of small talk.

"Robbie set this up?" Alicia said.

"Yes. You asked her to help out your mom with Stacey. She suggested I pop over."

Alicia knew exactly what Robbie was suggesting, and maybe Iothor had his hopes up too. But she expected she'd disappoint him, given that she hadn't had time to sort out her muddled brain. She had pushed aside all thoughts of her personal life to concentrate on a multi-pronged investigation, where each prong served only to muddy the view of the others.

*Weird analogy.*

"How is school?" Just call her Alicia Friend, the small talk queen.

"School is just getting going again. New intake children are much smarter than most give them credit for. Talk politics when they should talk history."

"It all comes back around, doesn't it?"

"Often, yes." He snapped a popadom in half and spooned a sample of each pickle onto his little plate. It was a hesitation tactic. He wanted to say something, but prompting him didn't seem right. Alicia had learned he spoke his mind, even when he didn't necessarily want to; he just needed to build up to it. "Robbie mentioned the people you might be dealing with up here."

Alicia hadn't gone into detail, just said they were treating the Vanguard as witnesses at the moment. She told Iothor about The

Strangers' Club and the people who gravitated toward it, without giving specifics, pausing as the waiter delivered two Cobra Beers. Once they placed their main meal orders, they held a brief conversation about Alicia being careful, and how Iothor was pleased it was her leading the case.

"I'm not technically leading," Alicia said. "I'm leading my section, but the Scottish DCI is in charge."

They munched on the popadoms for a full minute. Alicia wanted to open up more, but too much was confidential.

"Racism is a natural human state," Iothor said.

Alicia wasn't sure she liked where that was heading. "Pardon?"

"The repel-or-die attitude." Iothor put his crispy food down and threaded his fingers on the table, a habit Alicia now wondered about, if it was an instinct or if he'd learned it kept people attentive, ready for one of his stories. "It is human nature, in a way. Where tribes of old have not repelled outsiders, they have been either absorbed or wiped out. Those with a fear of 'the Other'—who wiped them out before being wiped out themselves —they are the ones who survived. They had to dehumanise other tribes, to the point that even babies were nothing more than fodder."

"What about those who peacefully assimilated into other civilisations?"

"They did not 'survive.' The *people* did, but you rarely have one culture merging with another and seeing both their strongest traits continue. You see acceptance of another's superiority, as with much of the Roman Empire. Or you see clashes, as with my own Viking ancestors." His mouth turned up and his eyes dropped only for a moment; Alicia had ribbed him a couple of times about how often he boasted about his Viking heritage. "I think racism, fear of 'the Other,' is bred into the DNA. With our advanced brains, though, we can train ourselves to repel this feeling. We see logic, complex arguments, and complex problems, and realise it is not the race of a person that is the threat, but the actions of people as individuals. Most of us see this. But those incapable of critical thinking, or unwilling to try, are stuck listening to the fear passed down in their ancestors' genes."

Alicia was about to change the subject to something lighter when the food arrived, and all talk of racism and violence turned to just how damn good the food was. They swapped a couple of spoonfuls of each other's curry, and agreed Alicia was much tougher than Iothor, given the spiciness of her dish relative to his. Alicia drank a second beer, and they chatted a bit more about Robbie and exchanged funny stories until they finished their meal and paid the bill, too stuffed for dessert.

In a pub around the corner, Iothor switched to soft drinks —"I have to drive home, and I have work in the morning"—and Alicia queued at the bar, considering all Iothor had said about ancient memories in the blood, in the DNA, causing harmful thoughts and actions in the present. It was similar to the pitch Maisie had made—one Alicia had dismissed but would have to take seriously if she was going to encompass all the hypothetical scenarios. That was, after all, the purpose of looking into the cold case this way. And it would not be long before they had to reveal all to the world, speak to the press about more than twenty murders committed between 1972 and 1985.

*Ancient history infecting the present.*

Yes, she had allowed that to persist for way too long.

Instead of the soft drink, she ordered two double whiskeys and took them over to Iothor. She placed them firmly on the table and pushed one toward him.

He picked it up gingerly, as if the contents frightened him. "What…?"

"You're leaving the car and getting a cab." Alicia clinked her glass against his without sitting down. "Down in one, Viking-Boy. You're coming with me."

He was strong, yet treated her like a porcelain doll at first. As they rushed into her hotel room, kissing, he supported her back with his hands rather than hefting her up, and it was up to Alicia to set the level. It had been so long for her that she had no interest in pissing around with too much foreplay, so she gripped his backside and pressed his hardening length against her. She made up for the difference in height with tippie-toes at first, but he soon got the message. The kisses intensified and he untucked her blouse, letting her undo only enough buttons to allow him to pull it over her head. She couldn't remember which bra she'd worn and for a moment she was terrified it was her dull tee-shirt bra, but whistled silently in relief as she found a nice-but-functional brand—not quite lingerie, but it was no man-repellent.

She treated him marginally more roughly, yanking his top over his head the same way he had hers, and pawing at his belt. He reached behind her and unhooked the bra, and she was less worried about removing the garment than revealing it. One thing Stacey's birth had done was increase her cup size, and the appreciative sigh from Iothor meant their form came as a pleasant surprise. She dropped the rest of her clothes and stood naked before a man for the first time in over four years.

Unleashing him from his own jeans and underwear, she held his hardness in one hand. He was larger than she remembered the average size to be, or maybe it was Viking genetics rearing its head again. She traced the shape of it from base to tip, and felt him shudder under her touch. They fell onto the bed, lips hungry for each other. His fingers probed her and a dam broke within. She moaned with the release.

It was all coming back to her, muscle memory and instinct dishing out pleasure and seeking it in return.

"Condom," she breathed, only marginally worried about breaking the mood.

He froze in place and pulled away an inch or so. "Crap."

Alicia gave a massive disappointed sigh, sensing herself sinking into the mattress.

"I did not plan on…" He looked her naked body over. "Sorry, I *did* think it was just dinner."

For some reason, that truth about him made her want him even more. "Wait right here."

She rolled off the bed, opened her overnight bag, and emptied it on the floor, pulling out every side pocket. She located a toiletry bag she hadn't opened since loading it with just-in-case items like toothpaste and toothbrush, dry shampoo and travel soap, and—

"Yes!" She produced a box of three condoms, holding them aloft like a trophy. Then she said, "Wait," and took them to the lamp, switched it on, and checked the use-by date. "*Yes!*"

Even in the dark room, Iothor's grin was wide as Alicia unwrapped the box, bounding toward the bed as she emptied the three wrapped units.

"Okay." She ripped one open using her teeth. "You are going to be very tired at school tomorrow."

At one-thirty a.m., with two condoms tied off and disposed of, Alicia lay awake, watching Iothor sleep. Both were still naked; she saw no reason to don pyjamas if he didn't. Plus, it might squeeze an extra day out of her overnight bag.

His chest rose and fell. That rhythm, the simple intimacy of their nakedness, felt like a part of her past slipping away, a phase of her life story that had caused her such anguish dissolving around her. It also scared her to her core.

Now they'd taken this step, it meant she had a full on, bonafide *boyfriend*. He wanted to be with her even after learning of Stacey's dad, and hadn't rushed the sex side of things, willing to wait longer than most men. Although she was judging that gender by the younger members of the species. Younger even than Iothor, who was six years her junior.

*Am I a cougar?*

No, that was an outdated notion. She could be with whoever she wanted, as could Iothor. And this beautiful, tender, strong man had chosen to be with *her*, baggage and all.

She touched his rising chest just to be certain he was real and wouldn't disappear in a puff of smoke.

*Such a cliché. Simpering over a man like that.*

The fear resurfaced. Of explaining to Stacey why Iothor was sleeping over, of tempering her expectations for the relationship, how Iothor would not automatically be her new daddy just because he was spending more and more time with them. Not that Stacey indicated serious concern at the absence of a father in their lives yet; just the occasional curious mention, which Alicia feared could escalate once she started school.

Perhaps, *in time*, the question of Iothor's status in Stacey's life might go that far.

But with him being Alicia's first since Richard, she wondered if it was wise to settle down like that. To pour everything into this while she still dealt with the anxiety over what had happened, her complicated friendship with Richard's other daughter, and her job. Her mother would understand, and even be pleased—

"Oh, god, you have to meet my mum," Alicia said aloud.

Iothor stirred but didn't wake.

Alicia needed to drop off, but there was too much swirling right now. She flicked on the telly, catching the end of the BBC's international World Service news bulletin. A peaceful protest against a government crackdown on an ethnic group in Nigeria whose name she didn't catch had turned nasty, and America was changing its approach to climate change again. Then it was the weather.

More rain was on its way, a storm expected to make landfall

heavily in the south in a couple of days, with flood warnings in place for much of Cornwall and Devon. The pregnant presenter said there was a chance it would move slowly north, but it was unlikely to cause as many problems as the previous deluge.

The storm was called Donald.

Alicia couldn't resist a giggle and sent DCI Murphy a text message—

---

*Donald is on its way and it's looking like a wet one*

---

—which he'd receive in the morning. With that, she turned off the telly and lay there, imagining the horror of introducing her dreamy boyfriend to her mum.

For now, though, she'd not only slammed a door on part of her past; Iothor had given her a few ideas on the case, too. One in particular that was still too fragmented, too wild, had too many prongs. One she needed to get a grip on and try to decide if more death was on its way, and cut it off before more patterns emerged.

Because it was only a matter of time before things got worse.

# CHAPTER TWENTY-FIVE

RYAN NAJAFI WASN'T PARTICULARLY BOTHERED by the rumours surrounding the girl who had been taken. His parents were apoplectic, his younger sister even angrier. While his parents had spent the first years of their marriage rebelling against their culture, they'd embraced it much more in recent years, something his sister had picked up on.

Both his mum and dad were born to Iranian parents, immigrants to the UK in the 1950s, who tried to force them into marriage. Both had resisted strongly. In fact, it was getting their heads together to work out a way to combat the strict edict that had caused them to get to know each other—consequently fell in love.

The newlyweds soon bore a son, and gave him a western name with only an Islamic middle name—Mohammad. And when his sister came along six years later, they named her Sarah.

Ryan's mum never even wore a headscarf as he was growing up. She spent time in the hairdresser's with her friends, and working out at the gym when she hit her forties, and promised Ryan and Sarah they would never suffer the indignity of an arranged marriage.

But now as Ryan commenced the final year of his engineering degree, "never" had become "unless you want us to," and his mother's head was now covered—always a fashionable garment—whenever she ventured out in public. She'd inspired Sarah to do the same, with Sarah reasoning she should embrace her roots rather than run from them.

Ryan suspected it was the rise in publicity surrounding Islamic terror groups, and thus a rise in hatred toward Muslims, that had made Sarah regress to that ancient tradition. It was her choice, though, and nothing approaching oppression by Ryan's dad.

For his part, Ryan's dad had started attending mosque a few years ago, for the first time Ryan could remember. Ryan hadn't been inside one since middle school, and that was for an educational outreach trip.

He had no interest in fairy tales beyond a brief adherence to festivals like Ramadan and the subsequent Eid celebrations, which he thought of the same way many British celebrated Christmas and Easter: a tradition rather than a religious event.

This rediscovery of Islam had hardened Sarah's attitude, though. She'd embraced it more than her parents, and since she started wearing the niqab she'd endured taunts, looks, and even one woman trying to physically rip the garment off her. As a result, she began sharing militant-lite blogs and making a point to stand up to every bigoted arsehole she happened across, either online or in real life.

Ryan hoped she'd grow out of it at university.

After all, he was happily stepping out of a bar at midnight, having started drinking at six. He'd met two ex-girlfriends, and promised to call one of them to "catch up" and maybe just do a little Netflix and chill. He couldn't quite remember which one, but he'd figure it out.

For now, though, he was on his way to meet a girl who'd been dogging him for the past week.

*Lyra.*

What a name. At first, he had assumed it was some bot scamming him—a gorgeous girl liking a public Instagram post, then following him—but their conversations were either human-to-human, or someone had an AI that passed the Turing Test with flying colours.

It had started slowly. Ryan peppered his Instagram and Snapchat feeds with workout videos as well as regular business like feats of robotic engineering, but his favourites—and his most-liked posts—were of his own abs and thighs, and whatever other muscles popped up and looked good with a splash of olive oil.

This girl, Lyra, had told him she didn't believe his pics were him, and light flirtation followed. She gave up a few bits of her own body, fully clothed, and longer chats were the norm later at night.

It came across as classic, if clumsy, catfishing. And he wasn't an idiot. He found her pics on a stock image site, but never called her on it, preferring instead for the people on the other end to get their hopes up for an easy mark.

How pissed off were they going to be when they learned he'd been onto them from the outset?

Thinking it a variation on the Nigerian prince scam, he was amused, but it was going on far too long. She'd intensified her flirting the past couple of days, and even offered to meet twice. The third time was tonight, and in his drunken state he figured he should put an end to it.

So he had accepted the invite ten minutes ago, and made his way across Huddersfield town centre to a late-night club that had a reputation as a place where older wealthy men could pick up girls looking for a few weeks of luxury in their "relationships."

That was the fact that made his patience snap.

Whoever it was thought he had money, probably because his

dad was a big hitter in the music industry. Shame he never let Ryan mooch off the money he made. An allowance, just enough that Ryan didn't need a part-time job, and his university fees paid.

Genuinely, that was all Ryan wanted. It was more than most kids got.

So it was with a hot head and a thumping heart that he approached the club. His arms were pumped, his gait tense, ready for anything. But when he arrived, the doors were closed up tight. Locked.

Right. Old dudes really only go out on the weekends. They have work during the week.

He spun around, searching the empty street for someone, anyone, who might be watching, laughing, from another establishment—a takeaway, a pub, whatever. Yet it was all done up tight.

A bug bit his neck.

He slapped it, finding something much bigger than a squished insect. Checking his hand, the object appeared plastic: four fins with a metal point, like a small dart.

No, not *like* a small dart. It *was* a small dart.

And with that realisation, Ryan's vision spun sideways. Unable to move his arms or legs, he dropped. The ground came up to meet his face, and the world turned black.


Ryan awoke to stars and cold. *Freezing* cold, like he was in a meat locker. He still couldn't move his limbs, and his stomach swirled as if he were about to vomit. It took him a full minute to assess himself.

He detected only one semi-serious injury, which was his throbbing cheekbone, presumably where he hit the pavement. The longer he appraised himself, the more intense the throbbing grew. As whatever drug he'd been hit with dropped away, he found the injury agonising. Instinctively, he attempted to move his hand to the source of pain, but it was stuck.

Not paralysed, but *stuck*.

He was tied up.

He managed to move his head and blink away the fuzziness.

First, he established that he was lying on his back.

Second, looking down, he saw his chest hair, the skin of his stomach, and own dick lolling there between his legs.

Finally, he discovered his wrists and ankles were bound with what felt like leather.

"Very funny, Jacky," he said, although his throat hurt.

The dual assault of alcohol and the drug that had knocked him out made him taste the impending vomit.

"I thought you people didn't drink," said a man whom Ryan could not see.

"Me-people?" Ryan lay his head back. "Humans?"

"You know what I mean. Muslims."

Ryan had explained the limits imposed on him by his cultural upbringing plenty of times before, and grown tired of it years ago. But it was a necessary evil sometimes.

Right now, Ryan's heart thrummed in his chest and ears. This wasn't the sort of prank a uni mate would play, so his mind leapt straight to his sister's latest cause: Amina Shah. Taken and killed by thugs because of who she was.

"I drink." Ryan hoped it might endear him to the man now prowling at the edge of his eyeline. "I eat pork, man. Bacon sandwiches. Damn, I love those things."

"Oh really?"

"Yeah. Weird thing. I prefer tomato ketchup on bacon butties, but brown sauce on a sausage sandwich. How about you? What do you like?"

"I like people to shut up."

The man came fully around now, draped in some sort of robe. A massive hood concealed his head in shadow, part of a black cloak dotted with gold embroidered crucifixes. From one the oversized sleeves, a long blade protruded, glinting in the light.

*What light?*

Ryan looked frantically around, searching for anything that might tell him where he was. He saw nothing but the stars.

*Were* they stars?

No, just crystallised fragments in the rock ceiling.

Old bricks surrounded him, great chunky blocks of granite or limestone. Fires burned from sticks on the wall.

Perhaps that was what made the metal shine.

He was lying on something hard, fashioned around four feet high within a circular manmade structure. Flagstones on the floor. Another flaming torch burned next to a crisscross lattice-work door in one corner.

*Someone will see.*

*Someone will come.*

The man now stood over Ryan. "I know what you people are like. You get to lie if it means you can hide yourself in a country without detection. Eating pork, drinking…"

"Nah, man, I'm an atheist here." He tried to keep calm, but the high pitch of his voice revealed the rising panic. "For real. Just check my Insta. Please, man, just *look*."

"Even if you really don't go for the God stuff, it doesn't matter." He clanked the blade off the stone surface on which Ryan was tied. "It's only a case of waiting long enough before your natural state kicks in and you start killing us infidels or raping our children."

Ryan's nose filled with snot. His hands shook in their bindings. Tears breached his eyes.

It may have been a product of the sheer terror swamping him, or an act of petulance, or perhaps simply a subconscious gesture to honour his parents and sister as the final thoughts of his young life swam clearly into being; whatever the reason, he didn't care. He just yelled the words as loud as he could, into the night: "*Allahu-akbar*, you Nazi prick!"

"That's better," the man said.

And then the cutting began.

# PART IV

# CHAPTER TWENTY-SIX

ALICIA NEEDED COFFEE. She hadn't slept well, and after Iothor roused her before departing and the final condom went bye-bye, she couldn't think of a better way to blow the cobwebs from her sleepy head.

With him setting out so early to reach Leeds, Alicia had a little time before hitting the situation room to divvy up the day's tasks, so she took a chance that Maisie Jackson was an early riser. She was not disappointed.

Maisie seemed delighted to see Alicia, but an absence of cow's milk prompted an invite to a coffee shop in the town.

They didn't talk much in the car, just chit-chatted about the merits of various nut and other dairy alternatives, how oat milk was better for baking but Maisie preferred cashew in her rooibos tea and coconut in coffee, back to oat again for breakfast tea. "Lots of trial and error, but now I can't even remember what animals taste like."

"So when someone describes the taste of something as being like chicken, you're lost?"

"Apparently it's fairly similar to Quorn pieces."

They had the coffee shop—an independent establishment

serving every type of milk or substitute Alicia could imagine—all to themselves and settled onto metal seats outside. Their table overlooked a pedestrian square—a small thoroughfare where morning commuters either trudged or skipped by, depending on their attitudes toward their jobs. The parasols gave no shelter from the low morning sun, forcing them to squint.

The air was fresh, and the flow of the River Calder nearby provided a pleasant soundtrack. A hundred yards away, Alicia spotted small arch-shaped bridge spanned this narrow stretch of water—the Bridge that gave Moleford its name—and noted the town's coat of arms had recently been replaced.

"I'm sorry." Alicia adjusted her position away from the sun's glare. "If I sounded dismissive last night when you called."

"It's fine, Alicia. I know this is just background. But she *was* cut up, like the Lainworth Six."

"The Lainworth Six?"

"That's what I'm calling the six victims Winston laid out for people to see. Then there was the apostate Father Pickersgill left out—"

"Coincidence?" Alicia said. "Or intentional?"

"The bodies you've found from the seventies, are they dismembered the same way?"

"Yes."

"Then we have to ask, is the Lainworth Ripper actually Father Pickersgill's legacy? An acolyte who helped him, passing on his ideology to a new follower? Or just a man finding inspiration in gruesome lore? I know it doesn't ultimately matter, but it's a question that hangs there, just out of reach."

Alicia knew what she meant. Loose ends, even in historical events, were a source of frustration for anyone delving into them. "Intentional or not, there would have been people alive in 1920 who lived around here during the peak of the Priest on the Hill killings."

Maisie nodded along, as if that was the point she was trying to make. "Stories pervade, especially verbally. Now, not so much. But can we write off the coincidence of, in 1972, a murder committed in a field five miles away?"

"Which murder?"

"I should have brought the books, but there were too many to carry on the train. I made a note of the titles, though." She pointed to her head as she raised her cup to her lips. "A young woman of what they called Afro-descent, which is what passed for PC language in the eighties, was attacked by a man in a long rain coat. It all took place in a cornfield."

"Witness?"

"Disturbed by a farmer. He didn't see the man clearly, just that he was white. The girl had been beaten and, sadly, raped. Very horrible. The farmer chased the man off, but the girl was dead when he got there. The official story is that the perpetrator brought the girl—"probably a prostitute," as the text said—out here and carried out the assault in a car or van, then dragged her out to kill her. The girl's throat was cut, but the book goes into some gory details that make me think this was part of our pattern."

"What details?"

Maisie was only halfway done with her coffee. She looked to the side and spoke in a whisper. "I know. It's *not* nice. But it's important."

Alicia reminded herself this was a civilian researcher, not a detective, no matter how much she'd seen in the past. "I can look it up if you'd rather not talk about it."

Maisie gave her a look of resolve, pushed the unfinished coffee aside, and planted her hands firmly in her lap. "The girl's feet had been cut off with a small axe. Detectives reasoned that, with her being black, it was a slavery-type punishment. Similar to when plantation owners used to hobble slaves who tried to escape, smashing the foot so they wouldn't try it again, but when it healed they could still work." Maisie gave herself a moment before returning to the research. "When the farmer discovered them, he said the man was cutting her head off. He was only halfway through the neck."

Alicia imagined the scene, detaching herself so she viewed it as simply as other people thought about what to wear for the day. She hated doing this, finding it dehumanised the victim, but sometimes it was necessary. "It's harder than people think to chop off a head. Loads of little bones and tendons."

"An inexperienced fledgling killer learning his trade?" Apparently thinking better of wasting her drink, Maisie retrieved the cup.

"Unsolved?"

"Actually, no. They had someone for it. Colin Bakewell. He'd been accused of several GBH episodes involving rival football teams. Was involved in a fight in which one person was kicked to death but no one flipped on the others. And he was a member of a notorious white supremacist group."

"The Vanguard?"

"No, they were very low-key back then. This was some group with the number eighty-eight in their name. Based in Manchester."

"Eighty-eight. Eighth letter of the alphabet being H, so H-H, or Heil Hitler."

"You know your hate groups."

"Did Colin go down for it?"

Maisie raised her cup. "Died in prison, 1992. Colon cancer. Denied his guilt until the last day of his life."

Alicia sipped her coffee.

"What do you think?" Maisie asked.

"Opposing emotions," Alicia said. "A potentially innocent man dying in prison versus my experience of thugs like that."

"Meaning he probably got away with a great number of crimes that would likely have added up to his sentence, had he been convicted."

Alicia appreciated her words. "One of those non-convictions saw a person killed by a pack of feral young men. That'll help push any worries I have aside."

"If he was innocent, though, he'll be pardoned retroactively. If we use it and prove it."

Alicia pondered that. "An irrelevancy. The point is the here and now. If your event is what it appears to be—an early failure to cement the fantasy—then we're on the right track."

"To IDing the seventies killer, and possibly the person who murdered Amina? They might be the same person."

Maisie couldn't know that the detectives had gone over that several times already. Alicia didn't commit one way or the other.

"We haven't written off the possibility of an apprentice—"

Maisie's look of concern, her gaze finding something far over Alicia's shoulder, cut off the sentence. Alicia twisted in her seat to find two men from the Strangers' Club standing on the pedestrianised precinct, staring at the pair of women.

Both had their heads shaved, and the smaller one, whom Alicia remembered was called Sean something, looked odd in a suit and tie, the trousers baggy on his narrow frame, while the bigger one—the outright *fat* one, Russel something—was decked out in a fast food uniform, hands in his trouser pockets.

"Morning, boys," Alicia called.

The pair ambled forward, stopping six feet away—shoulders back, heads angled as if examining a distasteful looking slab of meat that smelled a bit off.

As soon as the pair began their approach, Alicia had flicked her phone to a voice-record app. She painted a smile on her face, discreetly removing her police ID to remind them who she was as she stood to greet them. Her memory shook their names loose, and made sure to speak loudly enough for the mic to pick up her voice. "Russel *Davy*, that's the name. And Sean *Pryor*."

"Got our names," Russel said. "What you gonna do with them?"

"Just speaking them aloud gives me goosebumps. Being in the presence of people who are delivering me from the evil clutches of unpatriotic scum ... it's humbling. How are you?"

"Stop bothering people who don't want trouble," Sean said.

"Why?"

The pair frowned and each looked to the other as if he might have an answer.

"Because it's not right," Russel said.

"Yeah." Sean laid a hand on his friend's back, a congratulatory gesture. "Why're you hanging with the vegan bitch? She a part of this?"

Alicia feigned surprise, a hand fluttering to her chest, and turned to Maisie. "Hang on, you never told me you were an evil vegan! These gentlemen just saved me from a fate worse than death." Back to the pair. "Thank you so much. I'll never speak to her again. Once I've finished my coffee."

Maisie was uncharacteristically quiet. Alicia didn't have her down as someone who'd be intimidated in public by men like this. They'd probably had exchanges before, meaning...

"So you've met?" Alicia said. "That's how you know she's a vegan. Did she oppose you on a demonstration or something?"

"More than one," Maisie said, without meeting their gaze.

"And..." Alicia ran it through her computer and came out with one of those conclusions that don't really need evidence because they'd never manage a conviction. "You've been to her house. Smashed up the garden maybe?"

Russel laughed and Sean gave a bit of a yucking chuckle.

"Bertie ain't got nothing to do with anything," Russel said.

"And a great man like Remy Duval ain't either," Sean added, his chin up as he stepped back, ready to depart. "You and this ching-chong-China-bitch better watch your step. I don't know who might've paid her a visit, but you better know someone might do it again."

Russel went the same way as his friend, stepping away,

preparing to leave but needing a parting shot. "And if it's her sending you our way, that explains why you're barking up the wrong tree."

Then they were gone and Alicia sat back down.

"Are you okay?" Maisie whispered without looking at Alicia.

"Fine, thanks," Alicia said. "Are you? I got that on a recording. The ching-chong thing would qualify as a racially aggravated—"

"No, let's just move on. If we file a small complaint, it might count as bias if we go after them for the bigger crimes."

Alicia ignored the "we" in Maisie's reply, and shut off the phone's sudden incoming call through her jacket. "What happened between you and them?"

"Nothing worth discussing here. You have a call."

Alicia had no intention of letting it drop. She'd pick right back up after the call, which she saw was from Knowles. She answered with a sarcastic, "Hello, DI Alicia Friend speaking. How may I help you?"

"Stoodley Pike," the DC said. "You need to get up there ASAP."

# CHAPTER TWENTY-SEVEN

SEAN WAS BUZZING from his encounter with the copper, and more so from his *ching-chong-China-bitch* line. He had made up on the spot and was proud of himself. So proud, in fact, that he relayed it to Glenn Bishop as the Vanguard's leader munched on a full English breakfast at their favourite greasy spoon. Scarlett dined on an identical meal, and Sean waited for an invitation to join them.

"Ching-chong-China-bitch?" Glenn said through a mouthful of black pudding and bacon. "Yeah, good one."

Sean wasn't positive, but he thought he detected derision in Glenn's tone.

Russel didn't seem to pick up on it. "Yeah. It was funny. Should've seen the slanty-eyed—"

Glenn held up a knife to shut Russel up, holding it there while he chewed and swallowed. "Look around."

"Pardon?"

Glenn had used his quiet, angry voice, which Sean recognised but struggled to understand. He was pretty sure Russel was in the same place—heard Glenn but didn't get it.

"He said look around," Scarlett said.

Glenn scowled her way. "They heard."

Both Sean and Russel obeyed, glancing about the half-full café. When an older man snagged Sean's eye, Sean just said, "What?" and the old guy went back to his breakfast roll.

Glenn said, "Sit."

Sean pulled up a chair and plonked himself in it beside Russel. When he reached for one of the laminated menus, Glenn jabbed his hand with the fork. "Oww. What's that for?"

Glenn placed his cutlery on his plate and rested his elbows on the table. He wiped his mouth and exhaled through his nose, as if restraining anger. Sean still didn't know why he was mad.

"It's simple," Glenn said. "We are out in a public space, not the Strangers' Club. And you're using racial slurs."

Sean frowned, still confused. "But she *is* slanty-eyed."

"And she is a bitch," Russel said.

"Doesn't matter about facts." Glenn maintained his icy tone. "You know this. We've been through it numerous times. If you want to fight this infection, we have to be subtle."

Russel matched Glenn's volume and attitude, speaking through his teeth. "We should be *fighting back*."

"We are. Recruitment is up, money is up—"

"Money." Russel dismissed this as if Glenn were reciting a fairy story. "We're not about money. You might like all that outreach shit, but we need action. And we took action today."

"By 'racially abusing' a mixed-race woman in front of a liberal police detective." Glenn dead-eyed him. "Well done. Who do you think won that bout?"

Russel readjusted his position; these chairs were not designed for his hefty backside. "Doesn't matter. We did our bit."

"Knobhead." Scarlett gave Sean and Russel the same dead-eye.

But Glenn didn't appreciate her input. "I'm in charge of these two. *I* will deal with them."

Scarlett held up her knife and fork like appeasing hands. "Go for it, love of my life."

"So the police are already harassing us," Glenn said. "Already going after our pensioners—Jimmy Grantham, Remy Duval, even Bertie—"

"Bertie'd be pleased with us."

"But *he* ran a bunch of thugs who don't like brown people. I'm running a *movement*. We will be a political party one day. But we can't do that if you're out in public using regular language in a world of political correctness. We need to be smart."

Russel placed a fist on the tabletop. "We need to be *strong*."

Glenn shook his head despairingly. Landed his gaze on Sean. "What about you?"

Sean didn't want to be caught between his mate and his boss, whom he also thought of as a mate. Russel had been Bertie's pick to take over the Vanguard, not Glenn, but Glenn made a good case for expansion and the boys had voted for him. He monetised the group in small ways, with cheap products featuring hardline memes that didn't quite break hate-speech laws, and there was a podcast he did every month that attracted some sponsors. He wasn't quite up there with the far right patriots in the US, but he was clever. He'd even got Sean a job in an office, and coached him on what to say and how to behave in a workplace full of cucks and political correctness—how he should never disagree with people when they used PC terms or if they slagged off a politician that most people despised.

*Just nod along to get along. We will rise, but we must be patient.*

So far, it had worked. Sean had kept his junior clerk's job longer than any other, and he put that down to Glenn's tactics and advice.

"I'm okay with that," Sean said. "I can go apologise. Say I got carried away."

Glenn considered it. "Only if you run into them again. Don't go seeking them out. It'll look staged."

Russel sucked his teeth like one of those black gangsta types who frightened the crap out of Sean whenever he went to a big city. Almost as much as the hairy terrorists the cucks called Muslims.

"Okay," Sean said.

Russel took back his hand with a shake of the head. "Grow a pair."

Glenn stared at Russel. "There's a reason he has an easy job shuffling paper around, while you flip greasy meat for minimum wage. You're now on your final warning."

"I'm on what?"

"Final warning, Russel. Screw up again, go against the simple rules I've laid out, and you're done. Out of the Vanguard."

Russel stood so fast his chair tipped over, banging to the floor. He didn't care about everyone watching. "We'll see what Bertie has to say."

"Bertie has no say." Glenn stood too, a good six inches shorter than Russel, but Sean had seen him destroy much bigger men bare-handed. "I'm in charge, I make the rules. You—and Bertie—follow them. Clear?"

Russel's top lip turned up, then he stormed out, leaving the chair where it was.

"Well handled," Scarlett said.

Glenn gave her a pissed-off look, then sat and stared at Sean. "What are you still doing here?"

"Sorry." Sean moved toward the door, but Glenn called him back. "Yes?" he said, expecting to be invited to join them for at least a cup of tea.

"Pick up the damn chair."

Sean righted Russel's chair and raised an apologetic hand to all those still observing the proceedings, then walked outside.

He agreed with Scarlett—Glenn had handled that absolutely right. Sean and Russel screwed up. And he privately vowed to fix it as soon as the opportunity arose.

# CHAPTER TWENTY-EIGHT

IN SHARP CONTRAST to the hair-raising speed Alicia had achieved in her Auris, the remaining trek up the top of Stoodley Pike—closer to Todmorden and Hebden Bridge than Moleford Bridge—was ridiculously slow. With no vehicular access possible, the only way to get there was on foot, unless you had access to the moors via mountain bike, approaching along the Pennine way's technical trail.

Even though Alicia was in the best physical shape of her life, and Maisie was no slouch in the hiking department, the direct route up the 1,300-foot hill proved to be a lung-buster. Not for the first time, Alicia was thankful for her walking boots.

Cross had already explained a couple of days earlier that Stoodley Pike was the name of the hill, but people often confused it with the needle-like monument at the summit. The construction, a hundred and twenty-one feet tall, had been erected at the end of the Crimean War in 1856, which made it almost as old as Maisie's native country. The monument replaced an earlier structure from 1814, commemorating the defeat of Napoleon and the surrender of Paris, which had collapsed thanks to decades of weathering and a lightning strike.

The higher they got, the more the wind picked up, and even on a sunny day like today it cooled the skin more than Alicia expected. She buttoned her suit jacket but Maisie barely seemed to notice the chill.

Soon, a helicopter came into view, parked a hundred feet from the monument, along with the fluttering police tape and two ancient-looking Land Rovers.

At the summit, the needle towered over Alicia. Police and forensics were already on scene, including DS Ball, who'd either volunteered or been ordered to serve as a crime scene manager, responsible for recording everyone's comings and goings and noting any evidence that left the scene. And what a scene.

It spanned at least thirty square metres with the monument at the centre and several grids set up throughout, spotted with the light splotches of footprint moulds. There was a strange calm about the place despite the number of people involved.

"Wow, you didn't walk up, did you?" Ball asked.

Alicia squinted at the chopper. "My ticket must've got lost in the post."

He pointed his stylus at the Land Rovers. "There's a staging area near the old church-on-the-hill thing that we're supposed to be looking into. They had vehicles. Call came in about another body, so we made our way here."

"And somehow you arrived before me."

"Yeah. Brutal murder, Nazis, devil cults—what's not to get up for? Seen the body yet?"

"No." Alicia scanned the ground of the taped-off area. "Where is it?"

"Round the side."

They'd come up on the south side, so the body must've been lying to the north. Alicia tried to remember which way Amina had been facing, but didn't think she had made note of that piece of the puzzle; she'd ask later, see if it was relevant.

"What's the story?" Alicia asked. "Who found it?"

"Dog walker again," Ball said. "It's always a dog walker. You ask me, we find everyone with a dog and keep their DNA on file, it'll eliminate a shit-ton of cases."

"Same dog walker as found Amina?"

"Nope. New one. They're all sick."

"It's natural," Maisie said. "People dispose of bodies in secluded areas at night. Dog walkers are often the first awake. And they're out there with animals with a keen sense of smell who'll investigate something out of the ordinary."

Ball levelled his officious stare at Maisie. Everyone had an officious stare occasionally, taking a jobsworth task too seriously. Now Ball exercised his jobsworth muscles. "Who's this?"

"Maisie Jackson." Alicia lifted Maisie's hand toward Ball. "Where are your manners, DS Ball?"

The pair shook hands.

"Civilian contractor." Maisie plainly read the same officious zeal Alicia had.

"The researcher." Ball tapped a few sections of his iPad screen. "She can't come in."

"Okay, then let *me* in." Alicia bounced, reaching for the stylus.

"No one gets in without full kit." Ball again indicated the Land Rovers, where a hard plastic box alongside a folding chair contained full white SOCO body suits with hoods. "You get dressed and stick to the paths."

Someone had laid out wooden planks on which a trio of officers—two men and a woman, judging by the body shapes—now stood, close to the north side. From their heights, it appeared to be DI Cross, DC Knowles, and DCI Watson. The four SOCOs did their thing on the ground, using plastic domes like portable stepping stones to get around without adding their footprints to the surface, while their assistants made notes and checked on the plaster cast moulds. In all, there were twelve people inside the cordon.

"DI Cross was very specific," Ball said. "And I quote, 'Even Alicia.' She's getting to know you well."

Alicia touched her cheeks. "Well, I'm blushing. I'm also not putting those on unless I really need to. I'll stay outside the tape for now."

"Still sign in, love." Ball handed her the stylus to scribble her signature on the iPad's electronic form. "Whole area's a crime scene for now. Only reason the tape ends here is 'cos we ran out of tape."

Alicia did as instructed, and Ball insisted on getting Maisie's details. She filled them in for him, and was left in Alicia's care.

They trekked with long strides, the ground underfoot soft but not soggy. Alicia really wished she'd brought a jacket now, the elevation and wind making her shiver. She'd need to get warm soon. Maybe the all-in-one forensic body suit would at least have kept out the breeze.

She checked the surrounding landscape too, thinking she could spy the hill known as the Beacon where the slew of older remains had emerged a couple of days ago. "Is that Beacon Hill?"

"Beacon *Hill* is in Halifax." Maisie had also developed a tremble to her speech, her cardigan pulled tight, greying hair fluttering wildly. "Although you can see Stoodley Pike from there. The hill you're talking about is *the* Beacon, where there used to be—"

"A beacon, I know." Alicia hoped she didn't come across as testy. "*God,* it's cold." Alicia was now past the three detectives—whose identity she'd guessed correctly—and looked over the area. "So where's this body?"

"Oh, my." Maisie covered her mouth.

She was looking up.

Alicia followed her eye line and suddenly understood the urgency, the scramble of the helicopter, the Land Rovers, the exuberant sealing off of the area.

The 121-foot monument had a boxy part at the base where

people could enter, then the needle section extended to the lightning conductor at the top. It was halfway up this slender shaft where a man's body hung.

No, not *hung*.

It had been stuck on. In pieces. The legs and arms were chopped in half, the feet and legs splayed at the top, with the arms extending down from the hips; the torso was upright and the head was left at the bottom. The victim had dark skin, and several smears of blood were daubed down the grey bricks.

"He was killed elsewhere," Alicia said.

"How is it held on?" Maisie asked.

"Malcolm!"

One of the white-clad figures turned, then the other two. The second two waved briefly then returned to their conversation. Knowles borrowed a cone of stepping stones and checked where he was placing them as he made his way to Alicia. "You coming in?"

"I don't think my presence there is required," Alicia said. "I see nails. Why is it still up there for everyong with a set of binoculars or a telephoto lens to see?"

"Can't drive a cherry picker up here, so the army's going to lift us one in by chopper." Knowles pointed to the sky as if Alicia didn't know what a chopper was.

"They don't have ladders?" Maisie asked.

"Ehh, yeah, but they don't think they can safely dislodge the body while balancing up here. And it'll take forever. We need to get him down before the elements remove all the evidence."

"How's it held up?" Alicia asked again.

"Oh, a couple of methods. The smaller parts are a nail straight through the soft bits into the stone. We're assuming a nail gun."

"The thighs and torso. That'd rip through a nail under the weight. Something extra?"

"Larger bits are resting on wooden blocks like a shelf, which takes the weight. A second or third nail through the flesh holds them in place."

"Why?" Maisie asked. "After the girl…"

"He wants attention," Alicia said. "The girl was supposed to do that, but we didn't release the details, so it just looked like someone snatched her off the street. A common murder. He displayed this one big time to be sure we couldn't hold it back. I assume the news is all over the place."

Knowles nodded. "The only reason the sky isn't swarming with press helicopters is because the army restricted the airspace until they finish their mission."

"So it's out there. Is Watson ready for the press scrimmage?"

"And for the imam. Apparently, a Muslim boy went missing last night— Ryan Najafi. They think this might be him, but we won't have confirmation for a few hours."

Despite the horror of the view, the sinking sensation of imagining the young man's parents receiving the news, and the coming storm of the press morbidly glamorising the death to sell more advertising, Alicia clicked to several conclusions. "He's made a big mistake."

"He has?" Knowles said.

Maisie agreed. "Mm-hm. He has."

"I assume there's no massive pool of blood," Alicia said.

"So far, we haven't found one."

"Big deep tyre tracks?"

"A few about half a mile away; might be ATVs. We're taking casts and expanding the search zone to examine the ground for all routes. You're thinking access?"

"I'm thinking access." Alicia was suddenly energised, spinning and pointing as she spoke. "And if there's nothing indicating a 4x4 in the immediate area, then we know something for a fact. There's no way a single person did this. Ladders, nail gun, body. You don't do that alone. You *can't* do that alone. And at least one of them has to be strong. It's a pair, at least. Possibly more."

Maisie had turned from the body, a hardness to her eyes. "*Possibly more.*"

"It's a starting point. Our first firm break." Alicia nodded to Knowles, and the younger detective backed off, returning to his superiors.

Alicia expected him to relay her conclusions, if they hadn't already drawn their own. She was about to suggest they return to the warmth of the road and her car when her phone bonged. The other detectives also received messages, but the handsets were inside their body suits, so Alicia managed to read hers first.

"It's the geologists," she called to them.

Knowles, Cross, and Watson all faced her.

"They found the cavern," she went on. "More bodies from the olden days. I'll take this one!"

# CHAPTER TWENTY-NINE

ABHU NOON and Dayapreet Virk asked to meet with Tariq Bashir again, a truce extended by the councillor in which he offered his condolences and assurance that he would not politicise his involvement in any way.

Yesterday, Tariq would have agreed to meet only to shove the coconut arsehole into the canal while one of the faithful filmed it. Today, though, Tariq did not feel he could turn down an offer like that. If the body found up Stoodley Pike was indeed Ryan Mohammad, Tariq would need all the help he could get.

For all his posturing, for all the things said about him online, in the press, and even whispered around the Muslim Council of Great Britain, he was committed to his people. He considered himself their guide through the murky realm of mortality, preparing them for the true life in God's world.

And he had failed Ryan. He felt responsible for the young man's soul being lost, and seeking justice was the only effort his own mortal self could achieve. The rest lay in God's hands.

Did Ryan's immersion in the decadent culture of music and sex, his lax attitude toward what he fed his body, and his seeming rejection of the faith condemn him to eternal damnation? He was a good lad, after all. He had helped his community, respected his parents, looked after his sister.

But Tariq suspected Ryan was doomed, and the imam bore that failure himself. If Tariq had just been stricter, commanded Ryan's parents to restrain the lad, organised a robust group to suggest far more strongly that he return to the fold, it was possible he'd still be here. Even if not his mortal body, then certainly Tariq and the family could have taken heart knowing he was at God's side, as Amina surely was.

Abhu and his little assistant, or whatever function Dayapreet served, were waiting by the lock, which offered a shady spot in which to stand. Like Tariq, they'd dressed down for the chat, although Abhu's turban was as tight and new-looking as ever. Tariq would never admit it, but he far preferred the fashions of this country than the traditional dress of his ancestral home of Pakistan and the other Islamic nations. But it was what people expected from him. He could hardly stand at the head of his mosque in blue jeans and a cotton shirt and expect to be taken seriously when condemning the US and British governments, Islamic-inspired terrorism, and loose morals all in one breath, as he was renowned for doing.

He stopped beside the pair. "Good morning."

"Morning." Abhu extended a hand. "Yesterday never happened."

"Indeed." Tariq shook the hand. "Emotions were high. Let's move forward."

They literally did just that, strolling in a line across the towpath.

"You believe another young person from your mosque has been killed?" Abhu said. "I'm so sorry. This must be a difficult time."

"I need answers for my people." Tariq kept his hands behind his back, his spine straight, as his physiotherapist advised to keep the intermittent pangs away. "Two killed in three days. You have police contacts?"

"Not quite police."

Tariq withheld an annoyed look, along with several annoyed words. For a second he thought he might be here under false pretences, but he remained open-minded. "Then who?"

"It's going to be hard to talk to this person, but please give it a chance."

Tariq committed to nothing. Just walked.

Birds sang and a light breeze rustled the trees. Their footfalls were light.

The only other person on the path was a fisherman sat in a folding chair as big as any armchair, concentrating on the water.

Dayapreet opened his mouth as if to speak but seemed to think better of it.

"What?" Tariq asked in the most pleasant way he could. It didn't sound very pleasant, so he added, "I apologise for my 'pet' comment yesterday. You are a part of this conversation. Please, if you have something on your mind, speak."

It was about as magnanimous as Tariq had ever been in his life.

"This might not be a great idea," Dayapreet said.

Tariq focused on Abhu. "Why not?"

The councillor now watched the floor as he walked. "Because … this is who I wanted you to meet." He meant the fisherman in the big chair, whose back was to them. "I promise, this will be productive. Don't go with your first instinct."

Tariq didn't like the sound of that, but steeled himself, threw up a prayer for God to guide him, and waited as the fisherman set his rod on a Y-frame, removed his hat, and stood to greet them.

"Bertie Bradshaw," the man said. "Pleased to meet you, Mr Bashir."

At first, it took every ounce of willpower, imbued by God or generated from deep within himself over the guilt of failing Ryan, not to punch this Bradshaw guy and send him tumbling into the canal.

While the Koran forbids the murder of innocents, it allows killing in the defence of Islam or one's own life. But only in *genuine* circumstances, against *direct* threats. Not flimsy excuses doled out by ridiculous ideologies like those espoused by ISIS or Al Qaeda.

*A child here is born to British democracy; it will grow up to vote for governments who defile Muslim lands. It is therefore a legitimate target, a threat to Islam, and its death will please God.*

Those words, which had been spoken by a member of his mosque, chilled Tariq to the bone. How someone could fall so far from the true path was beyond him. A young man, miserable in life, who found righteousness too hard without the modern trappings of wealth. He'd blamed others, blamed racism, blamed the British government. He slipped from the faith, forgot his true commitment to God, which made him easy pickings for cowards who called themselves generals; his mind was poisoned by the promise of a better life. It had broken Tariq's heart to pick up the phone and pass the boy's details on to DI Cross, but she was one of the few police officers he trusted to keep her word. Within six weeks, the boy had been picked up and, thanks to the employment of electronic surveillance, was now serving ten years. Such an experience, Tariq worried, might only serve to harden the boy, but for now he would not be committing acts that fuelled the hatred of people like the fisherman before him.

Tariq left the hand hanging, and Bertie Bradshaw soon got the message.

"Okay," the white supremacist said. "We have similar feelings for one another." A glance to Abhu. "I thought this was going to be friendly."

Abhu moved to the side. "Let's just say truce for now?"

"For now," Tariq said. "Why is he here?"

"We have the same problem," Bertie said.

Tariq took a pace backward, hoping physical distance would ease the revulsion churning in him. "What problem? No one is killing Nazis."

"We're not Nazis. But—" Bertie held up a hand. "Not the time for discussing that. The problem we both have is that someone is killing Muslims."

"How is that your problem?"

"Because we shine a light on your religion—" Bertie cut himself off. Obviously he was experiencing ill feelings similar to Tariq's. When he spoke, Tariq recognised the sentiments, although they had been reworded to seem less harsh. "We see your religion as a problem in Britain. We both know people like me can't stand how you treat women, how you kill animals in the most painful way possible, and blow up any shit that offends you."

*Be the bigger man here.*

Tariq's default state was combat. Verbally, especially. He never backed down from an accusation like this, never took it lying down. Sometimes it was inviting the offender into the mosque for friendly chats, for tea and cake, to see Islam's true face. But Bertie Bradshaw had experienced all that and it had no effect on him. He still saw only what he chose: the worst of the religion represented all of it.

"We differ in our opinions." Tariq's neck ached, tense from keeping all his anger contained.

"It's a problem because everyone knows we don't enjoy having people like you around." Bertie stayed where he was, shifting his weight foot-to-foot. "So we're the first port of call for coppers when one of you gets dinged. Or ... worse. Sorry, I don't mean to be insensitive."

"You'll be happy there's two less to worry about taking over your precious country."

Bertie shrugged. "No tears, admittedly. But you're wrong about being happy. People are people. If the rumours the press are putting out today are true, the older bodies they found date back to before my time in the Vanguard. So if there's anything going on that happened back then, if there's something linking it to the present, which seems likely—"

"Why is it likely?" Tariq asked. "Why would one be linked to the other?"

"Because it's the same coppers on both cases. Because the Vanguard was just forming back then. Full of idiots. People extreme even by that day's standards. And since we're pretty strong right now, with a lot more support than we've ever had, they want to push these murders on us."

"And you wish to deny any involvement?"

Bertie wet his lips. "Honestly? I wish I could be certain of that." Again with the little gesture of his tongue touching his lips, like this was some delectable confession. "I want to help. If there *is* something in this mass grave coming from the seventies, if it somehow caused the ... *losses* to your people ... then it goes deeper and further than the Yorkshire Vanguard could ever hope to reach. It's pure evil."

*If white supremacy is not evil, then what is it?* Tariq thought. He somehow kept the words inside.

As if reading Tariq's mind, Bertie said, "YV was never meant to do evil shit. We just wanted to keep incompatible races separate and happy. That's all I want now. You go your way, we'll go ours. Is there really anything wrong with that?" Bertie eased from one foot to the other, the same way Tariq did when his back was playing him up, redistributing the weight. "But nutters do get drawn to groups like ours. People who want to go full-on terrorist toward you guys. If there's some extremist sub-group infiltrating the YV, I want it gone. If some of our founders were a part of the seventies killings, I'll throw them under the bus in a heartbeat." Then Bertie adopted a more solid frame and tightened his jaw. "What's happened back then, what's happening to your people, it's *wrong*. Pure and simple. Civilised folk don't do that. Let the police do their job. If *we're* cooperating, I'm sure you can too."

"If not you, then who?" Tariq said.

"Have you ever heard of the Lainworth Ripper?"

"There is no killer in my community."

"It's from the twenties, before Lainworth went downhill and all the Muslims—" Again, Bertie cut himself off.

Tariq finished the sentence. "Before the Muslims moved in?"

"Place goes to the dogs, minorities always snap up the properties. I always thought it's 'cos you're used to it. Coming from places that are so much worse. That's not racist, right? Just fact."

"It is not fact, no." Tariq didn't want to get into the socio-economic factors surrounding the high poverty rates in districts with large ethnic minority populations; it made them sound like victims, and Tariq hated sounding like a victim. "But let's focus. You think this Lainworth Ripper could be relevant."

"Oh, yeah." Bertie crouched and came back up with a folded deck chair. Flipped it out. "Abhu, you guys know all about this. Why don't you take a walk? I'll fill in our cleric friend here." He patted the chair. "Take a seat, Mr Bashir. It's story time."

# CHAPTER THIRTY

THE FORENSIC ANTHROPOLOGIST was named George, and Alicia liked him immediately. He was all tweed and fur, like the teddy bear Stacey once created at a make-your-own shop. In his late sixties, George was a professor at the University of Manchester and brought with him a dozen students in fields as varied as anthropology, archaeology, and geology. They were "eager to gain valuable field experience," according to him. But Alicia read a curiosity in the young people, a zeal to impress and to not look astounded at the discovery.

The academic—a little older than Duncan, the anthropology professor whom Lucy Viera knew—had identified three sites as the potential source for the bodies, and they got lucky with the second. He was out with a couple of giggly followers taking more readings, and attempting to gain permission to map what might be a new series of interconnecting caves.

The cavern Alicia was interested in was located in a high valley between the Beacon and the hill on which Henry Pickersgill had built his second church. It was lit up with arc lights, making the interior as bright as it was outside. A different type of brightness, but bright nonetheless.

As a bonus, Alicia looked *totally* cute in hardhats and hi-vis vests, which George had demanded she wear. "I spent quite some time on that health and safety risk assessment, young lady, so you can do me the honour of following it. You too, Mrs..."

"Jackson." Maisie accepted the equipment without further comment.

Alicia had given her the chance to go home—would have dropped her off before coming here—but the former lecturer and author had insisted she wanted to see it through. If Alicia were in Maisie's place, she'd want to see, too. This was what she was researching, after all.

"We blasted through the main bedrock yesterday," George told them as Alicia marvelled at the huge space. "Then when we got echoes a few feet away, we dug manually this morning. Quite the find."

He explained that they'd accessed the cavern vertically at first, then found a horizontal entry point accessed along the slope of the valley floor, which took minimal blasting and a couple of hours of shovel work.

Now that she was able to enter without ducking, Alicia's excitement built. This was it—the place the bodies originated, the dumping ground-come-burial site of a phenomenally prolific serial killer. Possibly more than one.

She estimated the cavern was fifty feet wide and thirty high. It was strewn with boulders, rising and falling like a miniature reconstruction of the moors' landscape above. There was plenty of room for the students, also in safety gear but none as adorable as Alicia (she assumed), to go about their formal business of sketching, checking angles, and all the work that gaining extra credit entailed.

"They'll all get their names on any paper I publish," George assured Alicia and Maisie. "I won't hog the credit. Even though I technically could. I do know people who'd exclude them, categorise them as assistants—"

"Are there other ways in?" Maisie asked.

"Oh, yes, several. But none have been used for many, many years. Except one, maybe, but we'll get to that. See here." He showed them to a gaping hole at one end which, if Alicia was assessing correctly from her entry angle, came from the north. A significant number of rocks and a slurry of smaller stones and sludge gathered here. "This isn't my specialty. You'll have to ask Professor Handsome out there for the science."

Professor Handsome was the George Clooney look-alike geology professor whom Alicia knew only as Duncan.

"Basically," George continued, "there are miles of tunnels linking caves under the surface of almost every natural landscape on Earth. In archaeology, they find mummified remains all the time—some ancient race having interred their dead, or explorers getting trapped by disturbed land. And then that's where I come in. I determine age, and where possible I give them genetic background. If there's no DNA, we go to the historical record. It's quite an art when you get down to it." He splayed his hand toward the debris. "This is basically a large plug."

"A plug that got pushed out." Maisie peered into the sludge tunnel.

"As I understand it, this whole cavern would have been cut off from the rest of the cave network by an old landslip, possibly thousands of years old. The other caves and spaces filled up over many years, but the latest rainfall tipped it over the edge. Gravity did the rest, dislodging the plug and ... *splurging* into this space. Over there…" He pointed, then traversed the ground, bounding like a goat.

Alicia followed, with Maisie picking her own path. When they caught up, George showed them a horizontal tear in the rock, into which he shone a light. It found no end, just gobbled up by the dark.

"It's an exit point," George said. "There's a technical name for it, but I can't keep up. Like a very wide, but squat passage."

"So when this cavern filled with water," Alicia said, "it disturbed the bodies and sent them out there. Which leads farther down the Calder Valley, where the water punched out. Because the waterways were already flooded, everything flowed randomly."

"It drained out there like a bath." Maisie seemed almost as excited as George, and in the moment of her zeal for solving the question of "how," it struck Alicia that she rarely smiled. Now she was smiling, open-mouthed. "Carrying the bodies to Basil Warner's farm along the natural streams because they follow the contours of the land."

"We thought it wise to start categorising them," George said.

Alicia took in what he said but didn't quite understand. "What do you mean by that?"

"Over here."

It had been hidden from them at first, a lip of jagged limestone stretching across one corner. Over this line, George presented two arrangements of bones and several not-quite-skeletal human remains.

"The older artefacts are your Lainworth Ripper victims, approximately twelve people. Ligament has survived to show the bodies were not dismembered post- or perimortem, and you even have a little flesh and hair. It was very dry down here until..." He gestured to the plug of rock and muck across the cavern. "There are signs, in my initial examination, of cutting damage to the ribs, indicating a knife, or sword perhaps, was used to kill many, and there is evidence of not-insignificant blunt force trauma on all. Whether that was the fatal blow or used to render them unconscious, or even the disposal method, I'll need more time to offer a theory. This other section holds between fifteen and eighteen souls." George clasped his hands together low down before him. Not quite a conventional prayer, but certainly a moment of recognition for the dead. "Cut up. Like our older bodies, a number of them have flesh and hair, but it's far ... fresher, for want of a better word. More complete. A couple still have fingernails."

The second group was laid out in rows like the victims of a disaster, lacking only body bags. They appeared almost mummified, chopped up and bloodless, leathery and taut. Some were nearly whole, but many nothing more than random limbs.

"We made an effort with them," George said with a sense of regret. "Where the spread was minimal, we matched a few pieces to form a whole human, but the water intrusion must have scattered them. A lot. And others…"

"Others were carried partially away." Alicia pressed back against the weight in her chest. These were not some random corpses washed up in a field. They never had been, not to her. But now, in this place, the reality enveloped her fully—something to touch, feel, *fight*. "Not sealed off completely, but as good as. Preserved them from all but the smallest of bacteria."

"It was also very warm down here," George pointed out. "Not quite geo-thermal, but without moisture it's certainly enough to leech the body of its chemicals, leaving what fluids remain to react with natural human salts to serve as … brine, I suppose."

"That's right," Maisie said in schoolteacher fashion, glancing to the side rather than at Alicia or George. "A natural preservative."

"Nothing dating to one hundred years, though? No Priest on the Hill victims?"

"Potentially a couple of limbs," George said. "They're included in the older section, but I need to date them properly in a lab. Not many, I have to say."

Alicia took in the roof now, wondering. "You mentioned blunt force trauma when disposing. Do you think they came from up there?"

"Yes, that seems logical." George pointed out holes in the roof. "There are seven as far as we can tell. The vicar was here half an hour before you. She was particularly interested in those too."

"Vicar?" Alicia said. "Lucy? Was that her name?"

"I'm afraid I didn't catch it. Dusky-looking. Pally with Professor Handsome. Can I say 'dusky'?" He rubbed his neck, as if afraid the Language Police might rappel from above to correct him.

"Where did she go?" Alicia asked.

"She said she was going to church."

# CHAPTER THIRTY-ONE

ALICIA'S LEGS ACHED NOW. A *good* ache, from too much exercise. She hadn't visited the gym or attended a kickboxing or yoga class in three days, but at least she was making her cardio quota. Tramping directly up the hill her own way, off the paths that wound a route that'd be easier on the legs, meant she'd get there ahead of Maisie, who opted to take the sensible trail to Henry Pickersgill's former bolthole.

When she summited, Alicia was sweating lightly, and spent a few moments catching her breath, taking in the view of the Beacon rising out of the dip from which she'd just emerged.

The contours of the land, as explained by Maisie, twisted ever downward into the Calder Valley where any runoff would eventually either drain away or flow into the River Calder, or dump old bodies on private farms and public land. Water didn't respect boundaries or deposit its debris in convenient spots. And now that they had a clearer picture of the situation, it did nothing to help with the present.

*Who killed Amina?*

*Who killed Ryan?*

Lucy Viera was only the first member of the public to get

wind of a discovery up here. People had gathered on the Beacon and other surrounding hills. Some must have spotted the activity, others drawn by the blasting or signalled by friends who'd scouted and found something of interest. At least twenty observed from the higher peak, and a smaller number on the lower one where Alicia had met Lucy the day before last.

*Why was the vicar so interested in the discovery?*

The church that Father Henry Pickersgill built in the 1870s was largely a ruin now. The walls stood to a maximum height of six feet, while at their lowest spot it reached less than two. Sixty feet long and half as wide, it would not have held much of a congregation. Nature had reclaimed much of the floor, but it was still clearly laid out in chunks, and mostly intact. Even the rise of the altar at the front remained, and it was here that the kneeling figure of Lucy Viera prayed to a God shared between her own branch of Christianity and Father Pickersgill's. At least, in theory. Here, on the Calder moorland, the old bricks cut a gothic image, not representative of either church.

"Quiet contemplation," Alicia said, disappointed when her words did not echo back at her in a spooky timbre.

Lucy looked up from her prayer. She stood slowly and turned, her face sombre but pleasant, not angry at the intrusion. She wore the same thick jacket as when Alicia had first met her, the same binoculars hanging around her neck, the Roman collar still visible. The knees of her black trousers had dirt on them. "Hello, Detective ... Friend, isn't it? I do love that name."

"Thanks. I'm quite partial to it myself." Alicia approached, halting more than an arm's length away. The vicar's age put her firmly in the suspect pool for the 1970s and '80s murders. "How long have you been here?"

"Not long." Lucy looked around. "Hard to imagine all the death experienced in this place."

"Not that hard when you've been down below."

Lucy rocked on her heels. "You want to know why I'm so interested."

"That'd be nice."

"Henry Pickersgill. He fascinates me. It's a dark part of local history, one not many people know about. Do you know why?"

"Enlighten me."

"A cover-up. By the Catholic church. They suppressed the crime, called it devil worship. Plenty of Catholic resurgence in Britain at the time, and with the church being so powerful across Europe, no one wanted to annoy them. So newspapers only ran it once or twice, then it dropped out of the national consciousness. They moved on. Only ... I suppose an oral history is harder to censor."

"Where are the bodies? Pickersgill's victims."

"Taken."

Alicia strolled now, keeping a little distance between them. "Taken? Where?"

Lucy shrugged. "From what I can tell, the Church found out what he was doing, removed the bodies, and sealed it up tight. They were holy men, despite their political worries."

Alicia traced the perimeter, arriving at what she assumed was an altar, the raised part of land on which Lucy had prayed. "You think the PR experts in the Church also wanted to give the dead a proper burial? Last rites and all that?"

"It makes sense." Lucy pivoted as Alicia moved. "Their fanaticism was drawn from faith."

Alicia tried to summon an image of what the original building would have looked like. Here, the most solid part of the structure, where the walls were thickest and still stood higher than the rest, indicated a place of reverence. "Did Henry Pickersgill draw *his* fanaticism from faith?"

"I gave copies of the journal to Maisie Jackson. She's working as your researcher, isn't she?" Again, Lucy appeared open and cooperative. "You know as much as I do."

"You wrote a book."

"A short book. Which I spent a lot of money on. Publishers weren't interested so I went to a vanity press. Spent a good £2,000." She took her eyes off Alicia for the first time, finding the floor, a tad ashamed at her mistake. "They promised I'd get into book shops and they'd take care of any TV or movie deals. I thought they were serious. But they were…" Back to Alicia. "Well, they took my money and did the bare minimum to fulfil their end of the contract. Which was very little."

Alicia ran her hand over the bricks, which had seen some modern pointing, a bit of upkeep. "Who maintains this place?"

"The council. It's on their land, and people visit occasionally. I hear teenagers like to smoke weed up here."

"And booze a bit?"

"Not so much. Teens don't go for alcohol as much as they used to."

Alicia had heard the same from Robbie, and seen it in post-teen adults, how going out and getting drunk was seen as not-very-cool. She'd posited an aspect of rebellion in there, of seeing parents using alcohol in various ways, and therefore rejecting those activities the way Alicia would have turned up her nose at going for a nice long walk or hitting a museum.

"So where does the access tunnel start?" she asked.

Lucy strode over to the corner nearest Alicia where three big steps descended to an arched doorway, sealed off by a wrought iron lattice. "This way." Lucy veered from the door and sat on a hip-high section of wall, then swung her legs over. "Come on."

Alicia followed, using the same technique, wondering where Maisie had gotten to.

Down the same slope covered by the three steps, Lucy stopped and crouched at a circle of stones as wide as a manhole cover. The inside of the circle appeared identical to the outside: dirt and grass.

"This was his disposal point," Lucy said. "When he was

stopped, people were sent to explore the ins and outs, and they found this. Exploring down below, they discovered a chamber of horrors. The Catholics said Henry believed it to be a literal gateway to hell."

Alicia eyed it but didn't get down with Lucy. "Any other access points?"

"Yes, but all sealed up, as far as I know." Lucy returned to her feet as creakily as she'd risen from her prayers. "They took the bodies, sent them to God with Catholic blessings, and cut off the caves using dynamite."

"I guess the Lainworth Ripper just happened across another way in."

"Must have." Lucy turned a full circle, as if expecting to spot a hole opening up that no one in a hundred years had found. "Lots of people interested."

She meant the people gathered on the Beacon and the lesser hill opposite, the name of which Alicia had either forgotten or never learned.

"Hello?" It was Maisie's voice.

"Round back!" Alicia called.

Alicia hiked the same path back to the ruin, Lucy following, and greeted Maisie, who wandered the church floor.

"Have you seen who's up there?" she asked. "I thought I was mistaken at first, but I pretended to be resting while I gave them a good look over."

"You can see that far?" Alicia said.

"Not properly, no. But I'm sure I'm right."

Alicia didn't have to ask. Lucy just handed her the binoculars. "Thanks." Alicia then went with Maisie to a four-foot section of wall with a good view of the smaller rise where the lookie-loos had swelled to more than twenty. She raised the glasses to her eyes. "Where? Who am I looking for?"

"The pair furthest forward," Maisie said. "The purple hair."

Alicia adjusted the focus, and panned left. Too fast; it all blurred, so she adjusted her movement and landed on the pair Maisie referenced. No doubt. It was them.

"Glenn and Scarlett." Alicia lowered the binoculars. "Our Aryan lovebirds." She pulled out her phone to call DI Cross, but there was no service.

"What now?" Maisie asked.

Alicia passed the binoculars back to Lucy and thanked her, stepping out of earshot. "It's time to thin the herd. I don't care if it means we can't arrest them immediately. I want to look at them under pressure. I want to see how they react. And I need to do it quickly."

# CHAPTER THIRTY-TWO

BY MID-AFTERNOON, Alicia had dropped Maisie back at her house. The anthropologists had confirmed that eighteen people's remains were scattered about the cavern, dating from the late twentieth century, making it up to thirty-one bodies in total, although they couldn't tell how many of them were partial finds duplicated in the mobile lab. The near-complete bodies from the twenties suggested the Lainworth Ripper had not entirely mimicked the Priest on the Hill—only with those he left out in public.

This, to Alicia, indicated the Ripper was playing his own tune, until it came to making a public statement, at which point he resorted to the devil worship of the town's bogeyman.

Then the 1970s guy or guys took the public Lainworth slayings and Pickersgill's satanic violence, and built on it.

"The intact bodies from Lainworth tell me definitively there's no interlinked cult," Alicia told DI Cross once she got back to civilisation and her phone coverage kicked back in. "So that's the stupidest theory eliminated."

"DCI Watson is keeping the focus on this week's murders,"

Cross told her. "But you have, and I'm quoting him directly here, carte blanche to cover the historical ones."

Although she didn't say it aloud, Alicia was certain there'd be some link, some simple thread joining the past and present, but she hadn't yet found the correct web, let alone the strand that would reveal the spider.

Cross allocated Alicia two uniformed constables and reluctantly relinquished DS Ball back to her authority. She held on to Knowles, though, his conflicting priorities now out of his hands.

The absence of a police station was problematic, and interviewing people on their home turf wasn't that simple; it gave them an advantage, psychologically arming them with a confidence that relaxed the deception indicators. Something about the familiar allowed people to lie better.

"Right, let's make this place look like a cop shop," Alicia said as she and Ball returned to the situation room in the upstairs of the library.

"Nice." Ball seemed to relish the challenge, and literally rolled up his sleeves to set about it.

They moved out all but the most essential items, and hid things like coffee machines and files in cupboards, piled their own paperwork neatly and placed it on the floor behind a chipboard screen. Everything except a table and three chairs was stacked to one side. Alicia resisted the chance to make a handwritten sign saying *Police Station* but only because Ball hid the pens.

In the end, they had a plain room with no distractions. The single table was positioned in a corner opposite the window, which would allow daylight to illuminate the subjects' features and give Alicia a better read.

"Right." Ball rubbed his hands. "Who's first?"

## GLEN BISHOP, 13:00

Ball took the lead on the chats, explaining they weren't under arrest but were to be interviewed in an official capacity. Lawyers were allowed, but there were no accusations being brought, just establishing facts. It was the first stage toward a full interrogation. Ball preferred the more aggressive strategy of accusing people outright, dropping the evidence on them, then making like it was all a misunderstanding and getting them to open up, as if being honest would mitigate the sentencing. It was very hit and miss, though, and this other method—the establishing of stories, comparing them to facts known, and coming back to clear up inconsistencies—gleaned results in situations where the accused was combative by nature.

The shitty little fella in front of him was proudly combative.

Glenn Bishop carefully outlined his recent movements, his alibi being his girlfriend Scarlett Austin. Banging away, like young 'uns do.

Ball remembered those days, and he missed them. When he thought of this weaselly prick getting lots of quality sex, he disliked the white supremacist even more.

"You know anyone who might've expressed a desire to hurt a Muslim?" Ball asked.

"Why are you so certain this was a hate crime?" The younger man was in clothes more commonly associated with his type—white tee-shirt, jeans, blocky black shoes—not the suit he'd been wearing previously. "You lot always chalk it up to race. When a white person's attacked, it's never a hate crime. Even if it's a gang of blacks giving the victim a kicking."

"Oh, you're *so* right." Alicia espoused mock affection. Then she chirped even further into oddness with that perky bollocks she did so often. "Oh, wait, hang on." She strained, as if taking a really big dump, then the chirpiness bounced back. "Sorry, *facts* always bung me right up. Here." She mimed taking something from her backside and lay it on the table. "When it's demonstrated that race is a motive in crimes against white British people, anyone charged *always* get the same bonuses on top of the regular crime. It can't always be proved, but then nor can white-on-black or white-on-Asian crimes. Now." She pointed at the imaginary fact-turd. "Why don't you gobble that up and answer the question."

Glenn stared as if he were actually missing something on the table's surface, then shook it off and focused back on the detectives. Ball didn't say anything because he'd burst out laughing.

Despite how he acted toward Alicia, and his annoyance at her climbing the ladder while he languished in uniform, the place would be far duller without her.

"Whatever," Glenn said. "Point is, you jump to the conclusion before you've got the *facts*. Muslim gets hurt, it's someone like me. A hate crime. When, actually, it's statistically more likely to be someone from their own community."

"How so?" Ball asked.

"If you're attacked as Muslim, your attacker is twenty times more likely to be another Muslim than a white person. *Fact*." He slapped the exact spot where Alicia's fact-turd lay.

"Hmm." Alicia placed a finger on her chin. "Is that true, Detective Sergeant Ball?"

"I'm not fully up to date on my crime stats, ma'am," Ball answered, deadpan. "But I'm fairly certain that can't be true, unless you're talking stats in Pakistan or Saudi Arabia."

Alicia frowned. "Are we in Pakistan?"

"Nope."

Glenn scoffed, slouching back in the chair the way thugs do when they're trying to show how not-bothered they were. "Not yet. But given the rate they're taking over, my grandkids'll be paying money to the caliphate of the United Kingdom of Islamistan." He sat up and evened his tone. His accent lightened, as if this were a business meeting or round-table discussion. "Look, I don't have *anything* against them. I don't want them hurt, or dead, or even deported. I just want them to integrate into our society, to obey our laws, and just stop treating white people like they're nothing. They rape our kids because they don't see it as a crime, and their communities shield them. Either integrate, or leave voluntarily for a country that tolerates that shit. Is that so evil of me?"

"So you think a Muslim did it?" Ball asked.

"Possibly," Glenn replied. "They call it a false flag operation."

"They?" Alicia said.

"People-they, not Muslims-they." Glenn firmed his position by leaning both arms on the desk. "Governments do it all the time. You see it in conspiracy theories—nutters mostly, but sometimes it's true. They want to do something bad, so they make it look like something else. Like, 9/11 was the US government hitting themselves to justify war in the Middle East. I mean, I don't believe that, I know it was the Muslims, but that's the big example of our time. The 'weapons of mass destruction' lie to justify pulling Iraq into the wars is another. No reasons the Muslims here can't do the same. The girl and the guy getting it on outside of wedlock. Without their parents' permission? If they'd lined up some fat cousin back in their homeland for the girl to marry and she refuses in favour of some guy ... what do you *think* will happen?"

"Hey, I've got a question," Alicia said, almost out of the blue. "How well do you know Remy Duval?"

## SCARLETT AUSTIN, 14:00

"Yep, with me all night every night." Scarlett leaned over the desk so her tits spilled over her vest top a little, and whispered, "And there wasn't much time for him to sneak out and do bad things."

"Does he hit you?" Ball asked.

"Please." She twisted her mouth suggesting Ball was full of crap.

Despite the red-and-purple streaked hair, she was a pretty thing, but trashy with it, which made it better in a way. Great bod, with no wobble except where it counted. If she weren't so trashy Ball could imagine her on horseback in jodhpurs and a tight polo shirt. He tried not to imagine that, because it was all sexist and stuff, so he just accepted her trashiness, and that turned him on even more.

"He wouldn't dare," she said. "You know he hates people who treat women that way."

Ball tried to stop thinking of her as a sex object, but it wasn't easy. "What people?"

She opened her full mouth to speak, but stopped herself. Looked coy. *Coquettish?* "Oh, you're not going to entrap me like that."

"You have an opinion?" Alicia said. "Voice it. We can all be friends here."

"I know your tricks. Glenn warned me. Like at those protests. Don't let the lefties or the Muslims or whatever wind you up. Let *them* do the anger thing."

"He means a lot to you, doesn't he?" Alicia mirrored her body language, despite not wearing such skimpy gear. She might get away with it, though, if she were trash-fashion-inclined. "Glenn, he's a strong leader."

"Better believe it."

"And you'd support him no matter what."

"Of course."

"Loyal," Ball said.

She sat upright, a soldier on duty. "Of course, I—" Again with the coquettish expression. "Oh, nice one. No, not *anything*. I wouldn't lie if I thought he was a murderer. We all draw the line there."

## TARIQ BASHIR, 15:00

"This is harassment." Bashir clasped his hands, his big flouncy robes falling around the chair.

"Nah," Alicia said. "It was an invite."

"You read my rights. Feels like I'm under suspicion."

"Just clearing up a few things," Ball said. "You had a fight with Abhu Noon?"

"We're friends now. Check my Facebook page. I just friended him, and we took selfies this morning."

"What was the occasion?" Alicia asked. "Birthday?"

"Peace." Bashir didn't pull off coquettish as well as Scarlett, but he was welcome to try. "It's what we all want."

"Amina's family," Ball said. "Had they arranged a marriage for her?"

Bashir's eyes darted from Ball to Alicia and back again. "It is not my business."

"You know everything, though," Alicia said. "Come on, you can tell us. We'll find out eventually."

"Then yes. They were planning on taking her to Pakistan when she finished her studies."

"Did Amina know about it?" Ball asked.

"Of course. It has been planned for many years. Amina was devout. A good daughter."

Ball knew not to push the forced-marriage card. Big difference between *forced* and *arranged*.

He'd learned late in life that many people accepted arranged marriages, and only a fraction of them were entered into unwillingly. Those were crimes in the UK, even if the marriage itself happened abroad. Convictions were on the increase now that victims were more willing to speak out, not just with Muslims but all who ascribed to the practice. Ball didn't get the impression Bashir was lying, but it'd be hard to tell.

"What if she said no?" Ball asked.

Bashir stared a moment before answering. "Then her parents would have found someone else for her."

Alicia adopted her dangerous cherubic smile, the one she saved for the big questions. "Are they superstitious people?"

"In what way? You mean religious? Yes, they are religious."

"Do they believe in demons? Ghosts? Ghoulies?"

"Only those sent by God to punish man. Or by the devil to tempt the faithful."

"Could Amina have been led astray by a demon?"

"No. She was too sensible."

Alicia brightened even more now, and Ball knew what was coming next. "Or could her parents have murdered her and her secret lover and blamed it on a fifty-year cycle of violence perpetrated by a supernatural entity sent by God?"

Bashir didn't seem to know where to look. "Excuse me?"

"If she disobeyed them," Ball said, "there'd be consequences, wouldn't there?"

Bashir levelled his stare at the pair, hands flat on the table. "Listen very carefully. If you so much as *suggest* this to Amina's parents, I will destroy you. Legally. In the courts. This crime, and the murder of Ryan Mohammad, were the work of outsiders. People who hate us. And maybe you should add yourselves to that list. Racists need to be held to account."

"You're so right," Alicia said.


## SEAN PRYOR, 15:30

Alicia was *so* glad to have Sean in front of her again. "I witnessed you racially abuse a friend of mine."

"I'm sorry about that." Sean was slumped in the uncomfortable chair, arms extended, fiddling with his fingernails. They'd pulled him from his place of work to help with enquiries, assuring his manager that the lad wasn't in trouble and the West

Yorkshire Police would really appreciate him being released for the afternoon. According to the bobbies who brought him in, Sean had jumped at the chance. Now he had some difficult questions to answer. "I got carried away. She's always hassling us, that mad one. Maisie Fong, or something."

"Jackson," Ball said.

"Fong was her maiden name." Alicia remembered the woman's vitality during a university lecture many years earlier, gliding around the stage as she presented a guest talk on the importance of setting, of all the surrounding factors that impact on a person's life leading up to their death.

Sean shrugged. "Well, yeah, and that ching-chong line, I … I just wanted to hurt her. Figured it was her who sent you to pick on Glenn and Bertie. I just … I wanted to say something I knew would be insulting. I'm sorry. If she's around, I'd like to apologise in person."

That last sentence…

"How many times did you rehearse that?" Alicia asked. "The apology line?"

"I didn't." Sean sat up and his eyes widened, like the most honest rabbit in headlights she ever did see. "I mean it. I regret my actions."

*Coached.*

"Do you know," Ball said, "the police don't have to get a victim to press charges? We gather evidence and decide whether to charge someone or not based on the likelihood of a conviction. The wishes of the victim are sometimes taken into account, but not always. If they're scared of retaliation, for example, we can make it clear they didn't cooperate with the investigation. But we have other witnesses. Like a detective inspector. And it becomes her word against yours, or this interview in which you confessed to the crime."

"But I—" Sean held an open palm toward Alicia. "I need a lawyer."

"You don't," Alicia said. "I just want to chat. And not about your racially-aggravated language. Glenn and Bertie. They don't get on?"

"They get on." Sean relaxed a little. "But Glenn has a better approach. Long-term. Bertie and his lads——"

"Lads like Russel?" Ball said. "Your mate?"

"Yeah, like him. Russel was supposed to take over when Bertie retired, but Glenn promised a better way. We elected him, and he's done well by us."

"Like feeding you lines to appease the police if you let a racist slur leak out?"

"Yeah, like—oh, right, yeah. But he makes us see that sort of thing is wrong. Bertie never did. He didn't like Glenn supporting that Paki bloke—I mean, that Pakistani chap in the elections, but we did it."

"Which Pakistani chap?" Alicia said.

"The one Glenn was all friendly with. Who Bertie said was using us for votes. What was his name?" He snapped his fingers. "Apu. That's it. Like from *The Simpsons*."


## ABHU NOON, 16:15

"I'm friends with Tariq Bashir, sure. And I have a relationship with the Vanguard. Everyone's voices should be heard, detectives."

Abhu Noon was more than happy to come in, and chatted openly. Ball didn't like him. Despite the man's pristine exterior, there was something … *greasy* about him.

"You met this morning," Ball said. "Why?"

"We had a discussion about the police investigation and where it was going."

"He could have asked us."

"We have a third party who thinks you're barking up the wrong tree. He persuaded Tariq that he's correct. And I agree."

## BERTIE BRADSHAW, 17:00

"Piss off," Bertie said. "I didn't kill anyone in the seventies. I didn't kill anyone now either."

"You don't like Glenn," Alicia said.

Ball had gotten the same impression in the Strangers' Club. "At all."

"I don't agree with him monetising the movement," Bertie said. "But I stood down. They elected him. He's modelling himself on one of them Yankee DJ types on the net. Far right entertainers make a ton of money when they tap the right vein."

"You have a more pure vision for your hate-filled racism club?" Ball said.

"It's called freedom. It's called patriotism. It's called loving your country."

"You don't love your country," Alicia said.

That raised the balding man's eyebrows. "I don't? And what would you know?"

"I *know* Britain. We're a nation of immigrants. And descended from them." Alicia ducked down low, fingers gripping the table, looking up into Bertie's steel-jawed face. "You don't love that. You hate it. You just love your vision of what you *wish* your country was. And it's never going to be that. You *hate* your country, Bertie. *I'm* the one who loves it."

Bertie's gritted teeth came apart as he sneered, unable to find his voice. He likely wanted to raise it, to shout, to point, maybe smash something. He settled for, "I'm done here."

"One more question," Alicia said. "Please. How well did you know Remy Duval?"

## AUDREY PHILLIPS, 17:45

Remington Duval's nurse was less than pleased at having to travel all this way, but she spoke pleasantly when addressed.

"I didn't know him particularly well," she said. "Not before 1975, anyway. That's when we started courting. Or *dating*, as you young ones might say."

"And after?" Ball said.

Older ladies loved to imply that they'd put it about in their youth, but never said so outright. Alicia had said to probe that side of her.

"I got to know him very well." Another one going for coquettish.

What was it about that this afternoon? Ball wondered if he had a problem, seeing coquettishness where it wasn't actually present. He should ask his wife to try for that look. Might help things.

"He had other girls, of course," Audrey said. "Younger ones. Lots of loose panties and easily-spread knees thanks to the sexual liberation fad. But he *always* came back to me."

"And his friends?" Ball checked the notes Alicia had given him. "Dan Pryor. Jimmy Grantham. Bertie Bradshaw."

Audrey thought for a long moment. "I recall some of those names. Jimmy was James back then. Danny, I think I knew him. Or *of* him. They had this idea that they were doing something big. A great movement, saving Britain. I believed them, I think I mentioned that. But I grew out of it when I expanded my horizons."

"You broke free of them?" Alicia asked.

"Not 'broke free,' no. I loved him. I was virtually his wife for a long time. But other interests came along. I moved away. Came back years later, and we reconnected. That was at the start of his illness."

"You never had children? Either of you?"

"No, we didn't. Out of all that group, I think we were the only ones. Strange, considering how much practice we did."

And there it was. Saucy more than coquettish. But she liked people to know she was young once.

"Okay, so listen, I have a big question." Alicia displayed her dangerous-cherub look again. "Is there any chance, *any chance at all*, no matter how small ... that Remington Duval killed and butchered thirty-one people in a twenty-year murder spree?"

## GLENN BISHOP, 13:00

Alicia thought Ball had done a decent job of firing the agreed questions, and had improvised well when she'd butted in with a jab here and there. She got back to the rehearsed questions: "How well do you know Remy Duval?"

It was only momentary, but it was there. A tiny, near-imperceptible darting of Glenn's tongue, wetting his lips either to reveal something he did not want known, or to cover that fact with a lie.

"Just by reputation," Glenn said. "A great man with a pure vision. A little outdated for today's politics, but he wrote the core of our philosophy."

"Never been to see him?" Alicia asked.

"Ages ago, to pay my respects. Audrey said he was fading fast. We thought he was going to die. But it was a mild stroke. His mind was gone then. Sad to see, but she'll do right by him."

"Could he have killed upward of thirty people over a twenty-year spree?"

Again, the little tongue probe. "All he ever wanted was peace."

## BERTIE BRADSHAW, 17:00

"How well did you know Remy Duval?" Alicia asked.

"Hardly at all." Bertie's reply came across as matter-of-fact, no obvious deception. "Before my time. I read some stuff he wrote. He could write a sentence or two, that guy."

"Clever."

"Had to be."

"Why?"

Bertie shook his head like the police were the dumbest animals he'd ever encountered. "He tied you pigs up in knots. He read tons. Law. Old cases. Knew your techniques inside out. He also read old gangster bios. Worked out witness intimidation, and I'm talking before court is even a twinkle in the Crown's eye. Intimidate enough witnesses at the *scene* of the events you're talking about, and you don't have to worry about them saying shit to you lot. Better still, keep out of sight."

"So he wasn't a good man, then?" Ball said.

"Him and his crew went looking for trouble. It was a laugh to them. I stayed out of it. Not my crowd back then. I was never really into football, and that's where they let it all out. The anger, the violence. *At* the football, before or after. They'd be on the terraces with blood on their shirts, cheering on the Terriers. The folks around 'em would shake their hands and laugh at the stories of hammers and screwdrivers being the cause. Some of the time, they had wounds of their own, but no one cared about it. Not really. Just so long as the crews met up in places that didn't spill over into the public."

"Their wives, girlfriends, mothers," Alicia said. "They didn't care about their husbands and sons coming home, wounded, or with someone else's blood to wash out of their shirts?"

Bertie's grin turned sour. "They *loved* it. Certain type of woman is attracted to a certain type of guy. If they didn't have birds egging 'em on, no way they'd have the balls to come home at night with bruised knuckles and missing teeth."

## AUDREY PHILLIPS, 17:45

"*Killed* thirty-one people?" The elderly woman sat aghast at the notion. "Of course not. And why would you be asking this now? You've seen him."

"I'm asking about the possibility, Audrey." Alicia kept it pleasant. "Come on, you can tell me. Back then, did he go off for days at a time without telling anyone? Cagy responses when you asked his whereabouts?"

"I never asked his whereabouts. I trusted him."

"Because you were shagging him or because he threatened you into silence?"

Audrey's eyes were damp, and she didn't present the firm-jaw thing as well as the boys did. In fact, her conscious desire to exude sincerity made her tremble minutely. "If he did *anything,* and I do not believe he killed a single person, it was what he believed was best for his country. For the good of those he loved."

"Like you?"

"Yes, like me." A tear now rolled down her cheek. "He knew better, later in life. He even had a district nurse, an *Indian* girl, who came to his home regularly. Priti, her name was. Lovely name for a lovely girl. Five years she looked after him. *Five years.* He didn't want her at first, of course, but she was warned about him ahead of time. She persevered. And in the end, when Remy had to go into the home, they were both sad to part ways. In the winter years of his life, he saw the light." More tears, rolling freely; genuine regret, Alicia thought, for the man she saw as her soul mate, her husband in spirit if not in law. "Priti wasn't allowed to keep coming to him. She had other patients. So I took over. He loved her terribly, you see. He'd changed."

Alicia absorbed all that and processed what she knew so far. "He called my friend a nigger."

While the word shocked Audrey anew, it actually *tasted* horrible. Alicia couldn't remember the last time she'd said it out loud, and the bitterness made her question if she should have. But it needed to be out there, to have the effect it plainly did.

"His old brain is still there," Audrey said. "Percolating away."

"So if he had been a serial murderer in his youth," Ball said, "it might leak out one day during an episode?"

Audrey's tremble grew worse, to the point that Alicia guessed there was a palsy attached to it, accentuating its physical form when stressed. "Yes." She swallowed back what Alicia read as fear. "I suppose it might."

# CHAPTER THIRTY-THREE

ALICIA WAS FRIED. She needed her own bed. She considered inviting Iothor into it, but really, the yearning was beaten only by her need to hug Stacey and spend half an hour, if she was lucky, reading and playing with her. But first, she needed to see progress with *something.*

All the long sessions of the afternoon told her was that Remington Duval was *probably* responsible in some way for the historical murders, either alone or more likely as one of a pair. The only shred of proof driving her instincts on this was that people were covering up for Remy, trying to distract from him. While the dead men and the dying James Grantham were strong candidates, Alicia's money was on Remy leading others along, maybe Bertie himself, an apprentice of sorts. It was more than feasible that Bertie could have committed this week's crimes. That was conjecture, though. Fifty-fifty at best.

Remy, she was about ninety percent sure of.

He had the right personality type, consistent with fantasies of violence and an obsession with greatness. The man had immersed himself in police procedure and the methodology of other criminals who'd lived a long, mostly-free life; he had a following, brains, loyal family and friends, and his legacy had lasted years—all signs of a narcissistic personality that fit with almost every serial killer ever studied. The big difference? That Remy had achieved all those things, while most of his ilk were caught trying to rise to those lofty heights.

Plus, there was the big stumbling block of absolutely no evidence. It was one thing to *know* people were lying and to fill in the blanks; it was another thing to prove it.

Whatever their reasons, serial killers usually wanted to be remembered, to be revered. They wanted attention and respect, to show the world how great they truly were. It was partially where the misleading cliché of *they want to be caught* came from. Sure, some couldn't stop and wanted someone to help them, but a part of their brain wouldn't allow voluntary incarceration; however, mostly, it was so people at large knew who did the deeds.

*Recognition.*

Killers like Richard Hague—the Century Killer—were rare. He murdered simply to prove to *himself* that he could kill one hundred people without being caught. A personal challenge. When he achieved his target, he ceased killing and settled down. Started a family. After that, he only murdered during times of great stress or sadness: once when his wife died of cancer, and then he started up again when his daughter was taken by someone on the crazier end of the serial killer spectrum.

The big question was what to do about Remington Duval.

He was already in a prison of sorts, and no court in the land would try him. Alicia could think of two reasons to push it: first, the dead needed a reckoning, someone to point at and blame, even if that person could not pay a price greater than being left alive; and two, if the past was echoing in the present, it might finger whoever was haunting the modern targets.

Bertie, the apprentice?

James Grantham, faking how ill he was?

Glenn, the young pretender?

Sean or Russel—acolytes trying to impress?

Tariq, or someone close to him? An extremist hiding his motives in the white supremacy movement?

Or a random psychopath, with years of pent-up desire to take a life, flushed out by the inspiration of killers past?

Alicia really needed that hug.

Seven p.m. was usually the latest she put Stacey to bed but at five, shortly before interviewing Audrey, she'd phoned her mum, Dot, who informed Alicia that Stacey hadn't had an afternoon nap and was looking tired. Alicia selfishly asked the Dot-Bot, or "mum" as she preferred to be called, to put Stacey down for thirty minutes of power-napping, which was met with a pregnant pause that ended with, "Of course, whatever you think is best."

So when Alicia collected her daughter at seven thirty, the girl was grumpy and groggy, but brightened straight away.

"Mummy!" The beaming face Stacey pulled was enough to yank Alicia out of the fog of the day's business. She could have worked long into the evening, but sometimes, recharging the batteries is what's needed.

The happiness lasted only a few minutes, though, which was all it took to get into the car. Then Stacey appeared unwilling to talk. Even when Alicia asked about supper—usually Stacey's favourite subject—she just gave one-word answers.

After a journey marked by this stilted dialogue, Alicia parked a few doors down from her house—parking was always a lottery in this street—and took Stacey out of her car seat. The girl's animosity didn't show in the form of tantrums or sobbing, but in the silences between Alicia's questions and the forced replies, as if speaking to her mother took some superhuman effort. This always happened when Alicia spent a night or two away. The girl knew how to hold a grudge.

They approached the house as usual, the living room window and front door flush to the street. But there was a young woman leaning on the wall beside Alicia's front door.

"I want you to meet someone," Alicia said.

Stacey clocked the newcomer who waited nervously, her manner suggesting she was cold. "Who is it?"

"It's a surprise." As they reached the woman, Alicia offered a sympathetic smile. "Sorry I'm a bit late. This is Stacey."

Stacey gave a little wave. "Hi."

The waiting woman took her hands out of her pockets, nerves showing in her every move. "Hello. I'm Kate. It's very nice to meet you."

It was a simple trick to fool her own brain, and again Alicia recognised the selfishness inherent in enacting it: if a person is feeling overwhelmed at work, or in the home, doing something easy is a way of staving off the gloom. An "easy win."

Okay, not necessarily *easy*, because this was anything but easy. But something with a one-hundred-percent chance of success. Perhaps *uncomplicated* was a better word. Take all the things holding a person back, and select one thing they know is achievable.

Alicia might not have been able to solve a fifty-year-old mass murder, nor a double homicide, nor conclude what to do about Iothor and his excellent bedroom skills, and she was even worried about her absence from Murphy's team—but she was more than capable of setting up a meeting between Kate and Stacey. Even if it meant keeping the latter up past her bedtime.

Her call to Kate on the way home from Moleford Bridge had been brief, but went better than expected. If Kate wasn't yet ready to turn off her father's artificial respirator, that was fine. She'd made so much progress, and was much better than she'd been for years. She had to take heart from that.

At first, Kate refused. They'd agreed that meeting Stacey should wait until they'd left the spectre of the Century Killer far behind them, but that might not happen for a long time.

Alicia understood how hard it must be. The thing that drove Kate so hard toward mental instability was the lack of answers, and shutting her father down would cement the fact that those answers would die with him. A vicious circle with no end.

*I want answers.*

*He'll never be able to give them to you.*

*Then we should switch off his machine.*

*Yes.*

*But I want answers…*

It was far too soon to start confusing Stacey with the concept of a half-sister—the girl was only just starting to query why she had no dad—but having them bond ahead of dropping a bombshell like that seemed smart.

Inside, Alicia mixed lemon and lime cordial, Stacey's favourite, and she told Stacey to go show Kate the slide out back.

"Out back" was a garden, compact but much larger than the front of the house suggested, with enough room for a four-chair patio set, a barbecue, and a toddler's swing-and-slide combo. When Stacey was older, she might need more room, but for now she loved the swing and slide. In time, Alicia might dig out a border and plant some flowers, but the low-maintenance space was plenty.

"This is the slide." Stacey climbed the five-foot ladder and sat on top. "Here's where I sit first, and…" She pushed off and whooshed down with a "Wheee!" Then she ran around and, as she was climbing, revealed her next plan. "I can go on my tummy as well. Watch."

Sure enough, Stacey flew down head-first. Kate clapped and cheered.

Standing and moving around to the swing, Stacey sat on the seat, hands held at shoulder height. "And I can do this myself too."

It had taken a lot of patience to get her to try moving under her own steam, but now she demonstrated, kicking out and leaning back, bending her legs and shifting her weight forward, and pretty soon she was going. "See? Do you see?"

Kate again applauded.

"How about we let Kate sit down for a minute?" Alicia called.

Stacey shrugged and Kate came for a drink.

"How are you feeling?" Alicia asked. "Is this too much?"

"No, it's fine." Kate held herself with her elbows pinned in, the way junkies sometimes did. She was no drug abuser, though; part of her treatment was regular tests for alcohol and narcotics. She looked healthy, like a full-fledged *woman* now, not a girl growing up.

"It's nice." Kate referenced the drink, but was looking around the space. "All of it. It's nice." She remained uptight; still nervous.

"Take her a drink," Alicia suggested.

Kate paused, then selected the glass with the twirly straw and headed over to Stacey, who beamed back and accepted it, explaining how the liquid moved all around the shaped object due to her "suckage."

Alicia simply watched for the next ten minutes as Kate's elbows emerged from her waist and her shoulders loosened up, and the forced smile reached her eyes.

Five years ago, she had been taken by a kidnapper who only selected knockouts in the looks department. Brunettes. Big, beautiful eyes. Bodies that would not look out of place in a swimsuit-focused magazine. Looks had mattered to that killer. Maybe it was why Alicia focused on Kate's appearance so much.

After her father's actions in trying to get to the kidnapper ahead of the police had revealed him to be a man with an evil past, Kate had fluctuated between overeating and binge-drinking as a coping mechanism, which meant she piled on weight, to eating virtually nothing when the pain of her trauma closed off her appetite for anything but booze and hallucinogenic drugs. She wasted away to skin and bone—a clear-cut case of post-traumatic stress disorder, or PTSD.

That wild swing meant she'd never again be the beauty she once was; she'd aged faster than most, and the yo-yoing of her muscle mass meant her body would never know when to store fat and when to burn it, leaving her with a skinny torso and pear-shaped bottom. If she ever grew self-conscious about her looks, there'd be ways through diet and exercise to regain a firm set of buttocks and thighs, and maybe give her an athletic upper body, but she had bigger concerns now. The priority had to be her mind, her actions, her ability to live independently without the need for medication.

Primarily, though, assessing Kate physically gave Alicia an indication of her mental state. It was one reason Alicia went so deep into it. Her current appearance was exactly where it should be after what she went through. She'd started exercising again, something that helps with most mental health issues, but had yet to return to the level she had been at when she'd played rugby and run half-marathons.

Alicia planned to invite her to try kickboxing. But not yet.

After half an hour of play, Stacey yawned three times in a minute, and it was time for bed. The little girl protested, and so did Kate, pretending to be on her half-sister's side, which earned her a big, tight hug before evil-Alicia dragged Stacey away.

Their usual bedtime routine was the simple but effective bath-book-bed. Since it was after eight, Alicia skipped the bath. A quick change into jammies, brushing teeth, and washing her face, then checking to see if there was a wee hiding somewhere (there was, much to Stacey's surprise) and possibly the millionth reading of *The Gruffalo*. Then Stacey slipped under her covers and closed her eyes. Alicia kissed her daughter's forehead, and sensed the girl was asleep before she even reached the door. She left it ajar anyway, just as Stacey liked.

In the garden, Kate sat at the patio table, sipping her lemon and lime juice. The street was elevated at the north end of the suburb of Chapel Allerton, and over the fence, between two larger houses out the back, it was possible to see three or four miles toward the city centre. This was where Kate's eyes fell, lost in a minuscule view of a larger world.

"I'd like to have this someday," Kate said.

Alicia sat beside her and selected a glass of her own. "This?"

"Contentment."

"You will. Just don't rush it."

"Think I'll ever trust a guy?"

"In time."

The muscles in Kate's face contracted and the grip on her glass visibly tightened. She found something inside herself that relaxed everything. A breath, eyelids closed, and she returned to the contentment-seeking young woman she'd been moments earlier. Her gaze fell lower, though, no longer on the view.

"Everything is 'in time' or 'eventually' these days. Or 'with hard work.' My manager said that. At the coffee place I work. 'With hard work,' and 'in time,' I could be an assistant manager, and 'eventually' a manager of my own shop. He says that to a couple of us."

"Because you *are* working hard, Kate." Alicia detected her therapist voice leeching out, a voice she practiced but never employed professionally. "And *because* you are working hard, and *because* you are being patient, you're where you need to be right now. And where you'll need to be tomorrow. *Improving.*"

"But not 'normal' yet. Not *myself.*"

Kate plainly yearned to be the vivacious, spirited girl she'd been before the kidnapping. Before her world collapsed. Alicia had heard that directly from her. She shared some notes with Dr Rasmus, those Kate gave permission to discuss. She'd wanted Alicia to be there for her, to conduct her therapy after she voluntarily admitted herself to a mental health facility, but Alicia cited both the fact she had never practiced medically, and—more importantly—a conflict of interest.

*Family shouldn't treat family.*

"I'm not the same person either," Alicia said. "And I don't mean to compare myself to you. But I admit I'm harder than I was. Find trust almost impossible." This talk would have been easier two days ago, before *the Night of Iothor.* "It's not impossible to build it back up. With the right people."

"Think I'll ever get a great guy like you did?"

Alicia genuinely had to think for a moment about how to verbalise her response. "The guy I was with the other night? I'm not even sure that's going anywhere."

"You don't want it to?"

"I want it to, but this isn't about men, Kate. It's not about boyfriends. It's about finding a way to settle you in a place where you can have friends. Just friends at first. You want romance? Then…" Alicia almost said *it'll come eventually,* or *with time,* or that Kate should *be patient.* "You'll get there, Kate."

Kate nodded rapidly. "If I'd met someone. A friend. A boy or a girl, I mean. No one special, just … someone I want to trust … would you meet them for me too?"

Alicia didn't want to make a promise she couldn't keep, so she hedged her bets. "Let's take it a step at a time. *Is* there someone you like? Someone you'd like to trust, but having trouble?"

"Someone at work. She invites me to hang out, but … I'm always on shift alone with her. She's so nice to me. Chatty. Listens to me talking about my TV shows and rugby games I've watched. She watches some of the same ones."

"Are you asking me to vet someone? To check them out first? Because, that's kind of a step backward. I'm not sure I—"

"Nothing like that," Kate said hurriedly. "I wouldn't ask you to do that. No, I just … I want you to check that she's…" A tear breached and rolled down Kate's cheek. She wiped it away. "I'd like someone to check that she's *real.*"

Alicia's heart sank—a stone dropped into a lake, plunging into the muddy depths and dislodging the muck into a thick fog. She didn't know how to respond. A call to Dr Rasmus beckoned, but right now she had to assuage Kate's fear of slipping back into some hallucinatory realm.

"Kate … three years ago, the person you thought was talking to you when I found you in your old house—that was a product of your *condition*. Your illness. Combined with the alcohol and drugs, and the poor diet … it'd have been weird if you *didn't* hear voices."

"I didn't just hear them." Kate now sat up straighter. She relinquished the glass and folded her hands in her lap, a picture of grace and poise. Straightforward, no-nonsense words. Almost neutral. "I *saw* him. A man, a skinny man, with bony fingers. Eyes sunken, like a skull with just skin on it. I saw him as clearly as I see you. But I know he *couldn't* have been real." A momentary glance away indicated a degree of shame, but her steely return to Alicia meant she was at peace with this notion. "The police tested the house, and only found my DNA. No evidence of anyone else. He told me to make the best of things, and carry on my father's work. I … refused, and he was nice to me. I thought he'd get angry, and that's why…" Her poise faltered.

Although Alicia knew the story as surely as she knew *The Gruffalo* by heart, it was something Kate needed to speak aloud occasionally; an affirmation of sorts.

"That's why I came back to Leeds," Kate continued without emotion. "That's why I hid myself away. Then you found me. And I started my treatment." She swallowed, her lips pinched. "And I need to be sure anyone helping me, anyone being nice to me, is real. You understand?"

Alicia did understand, and told Kate so as she reached for her hand. She understood that indulging Kate's paranoia would set her back, but assuaging the fear would help her move on. Perhaps she could turn up to the coffee shop and specifically engage with both Kate and the other person on duty, just to show her it wasn't a hallucination.

Was that bad too?

She'd consult with Dr Rasmus to decide on an approach. Kate was his patient. It'd be his call.

Alicia was sure the Skinny Man did not exist, though. A murder aping the style of Richard Hague had emerged in Wolverhampton three years ago, near Kate's former residence. It had been staged in a far more gruesome tableau than Richard ever constructed, the only thing linking it to Kate being the vicinity to her home and her father's trademark single wound to the heart. The coroner's verdict remained open; the eye-watering volume of barbiturates in the victim's system would likely have killed the woman anyway, but they could equally have given her the strength, numbness, and mania to throw herself upon the sword puncturing her heart.

Kate had been captured on multiple cameras in Leeds in the days leading up to the woman's disappearance, and none found her in Wolverhampton, or any other place. Alicia had located her in her childhood home, having experienced a psychotic break— which had led to her her hiding herself away in an attempt to block out or chase away the hallucinations.

She gave no indication of a violent bloodlust.

Still, no arrests had been made regarding the death, no one even questioned except in the capacity of witnesses.

"The Skinny Man told me what to do," Kate said. "What to eat, how best to take the medicine ... the drugs, I mean. But I must have got them myself from somewhere. And now I don't have anyone telling me what to do. I have to make those decisions myself."

Alicia saw where she was going with this. "Your father."

Kate nodded, and the neutral tone of her words cracked back into something more human. "I don't want him to die. But it seems so cruel keeping him alive. It's like if I turn him off, it'll mean I start over. A reboot. But if I fail, if I'm the same the next day... it'll be like I let him die for no reason." She twisted in her seat to face Alicia, and Alicia saw the pain plaguing her. "Is it the right thing to do?"

Alicia experienced a momentary flutter in her throat. Nothing to do with Kate's situation, but the quiet yet definite filtering of information from her subconscious—from her computer's calculations that would not reveal themselves just yet —into semi-conscious understanding.

"A need to be led," Alicia said. "It takes away a person's responsibility."

Kate frowned. "Pardon?"

"Oh, not you." Alicia pulled away, reached for her glass of juice. "I mean, yes, you too. You want someone else to make the decision for you so if it's the wrong one, you can disassociate from it." She shouldn't be talking this way to Kate, filling her with blame, with responsibility she clearly wasn't ready for, but Alicia had to work it out for her own sanity. "Killers tend to be solitary figures, only bringing others in when their ego demands it. But in pairs, there is always a leader and a follower. When the leader quits, or can't carry on, the follower either takes on the mantle or goes into hibernation."

She was on a roll, and didn't want to stop.

"You're not talking about me anymore," Kate said.

"No. I'm talking about the fact someone was leading others a long time ago. A leader who quit, either forcibly or by choice, like your dad did. But there was more than one person involved. And that's the answer. Stop looking for the leader, and find the follower." Alicia beamed at Kate, took both her hands. "Thank you. You might just have helped me solve this."

# CHAPTER THIRTY-FOUR

THE FOLLOWING MORNING, Alicia spent some time sending official reports to Dr Rasmus, her engagement with his patient overstepping a line that she was uncomfortable keeping to herself. She departed late to drop off Stacey and make the journey to Moleford Bridge.

At least she'd had time for breakfast with her daughter today. The only downer was the Dot-Bot's frown and passive-aggressive grumble about how Alicia's job neglected her family time. Alicia would deal with that later.

On the way, DS Ball filled her in by phone regarding the information she'd requested, and used several colourful phrases to garnish the facts with as much personality as he could get away with.

His research showed James Grantham dwelled in an assisted living facility just shy of an all-out hospital. It was privately funded, but he qualified as an NHS resident, so the taxpayer contributed of an undisclosed amount to his costs. A complex of ten bungalows, it was technically a hospice as well as a private residence, specialising in end-of-life care to patients who wished to retain a measure of independence right up to the end.

Grantham's diabetes and emphysema suggested he'd be dead six months ago, which was what caused the local NHS trust to cave in to his niece's fervent and repeated demands three months before that.

Alicia wasn't sure if the niece's bid was to find the best care or to push the "old bastard," as the lady referred to her uncle in official correspondence, into a facility that would take responsibility for him. She knew for certain she had no desire to meet the niece, but would not mind ending up in a Rain-Or-Shine bungalow when she was too old and infirm to look after herself.

The complex was technically a gated community, but remained open with a single orderly posted on a security guard-style box. This was part of their duty of care to deter patients with a penchant for wandering back to homes that no longer existed from exploring the outside world. Others, like James Grantham, were permitted to come and go as they pleased, as long as they were in good health and took all precautions demanded by the doctors—in his case, the electric wheelchair/scooter, his oxygen tank, and big-button mobile phone with a speed dial to the office should he become stranded.

Alicia was worried she and Ball might have a hard time getting access, but James had free visitor access; this wasn't a hospital, after all, nor a prison. The orderly on the gate gave them directions through the holiday camp-style bungalows, his only warning being for them to not aggravate the man; he could be cantankerous, apparently.

"Didn't fancy bringing the boy wonder?" Ball said.

"You did the work on this," Alicia replied.

"Nothing to do with this guy's… what shall we call them? Political views?"

"I don't want to talk about politics anymore. We already lost focus on what's important, balancing our ethics with our investigation. I just want to figure out exactly who might have done those murders way back when, and who we can eliminate."

"And the two this week?"

"If we can eliminate ours, that narrows the field, right? And I think this guy could do with a bit of old school coppering."

They found James's house and rang the bell.

The door opened to James Grantham in a robe, using a walking stick. He wore thick glasses and his skin seemed to sag more heavily from his head than it had when he'd been seated and angry. Now he just looked sullen.

"Yeah," he said. "You're not the doctor."

Both presented ID.

"We met in the Strangers' Club," Alicia said.

"Right, yeah, we did. Rude coppers."

"May we come in for a quick word, Mr Grantham? Or do you prefer Jimmy?"

"I…" James appeared to struggle for breath. "I can spare some time. If it gets you off my friends' backs."

The pair entered as James stood aside.

"Thanks, Jimmy," Ball said.

The door closed, locking them into the musty space and the odour of eau-de-elderly.

As James hobbled to the mechanised chair that rose and fell to aid his standing and sitting, he said, "And let's stick with… Mr Grantham, eh? I pay your wages, after all."

He positioned himself at the chair and it automatically lowered him into position. Alicia and Ball remained standing.

Alicia rushed through the preliminary background, calling him "Mister" at every opportunity, even when it wasn't strictly necessary. She explained how they were looking into the historical murders as well as the recent ones, and James gave the rote response that no one he knew of did anything, and the current murders were probably honour killings or someone trying to pin them on patriots.

"We keep coming back to the Vanguard," Alicia said. "I know people like to think there are nefarious goings-on, that we're dumb coppers flailing around. But usually, our first suspect is the correct suspect. So when I ask about someone who was alive during the seventies killings, who might want to resurrect their hobby, it's not idle chit-chat. There was a weak follower and a strong leader back then—maybe more than one weak partner."

James took a hit from an oxygen tank beside his chair, the mask perched on the arm in a bracket. "You think I had something to do with it? Led a bunch of impressionable kids into the killing fields?"

"No," Alicia said. "I think you were a weak one. A follower."

James glared now, a hint of his former strength breaking through. "Get fu—"

The word cut off, a cough rising and multiplying. He reached for a container on a chair beside a coffee cup. The size of a whiskey tumbler, it had a funnel built into the top. James coughed harder, hacking at the air that wheezed into his lungs.

After thirty seconds or so he spat something into the beaker, wiped his lips, and placed it down. "I was *never* a follower. I built the Vanguard with Remy. He was smarter with words and shit, but I did the heavy lifting."

"The bodies of murder victims?" Alicia asked, keen to gauge his reaction.

"Bodies?" Another cough hit him, but did not require the expulsion of whatever that beaker contained.

"You know what I mean. You and your friends, the group-think exercise of hatred, spawning a murder spree. We have nearly all the pieces, we're just waiting for the first person to realise they have nowhere left to go. Even after all this time."

James's coughing got worse, but it was dry. *Fake.*

"Alicia," Ball said.

"No." Alicia was on a roll here, saw the cracks in James Grantham. "The first to come clean gets the easiest time of it."

James's face went red with the effort.

Ball tapped Alicia's arm subtly, keeping things formal in front of the suspect. "Ma'am, maybe we should have a quick word. Outside?"

But Alicia had heard the wet cough twice now, and this wasn't one of those. She sidestepped Ball and crouched at James's eye level. Far enough away to avoid any flying sputum. "*Talk* to me, Jimmy."

The dry hacking eased up, restarted with a minor burst, then was replaced by the sort of chuckle old friends use when reminiscing.

"Good times." James breathed deeply, as if about to fake another spell, but apparently thought better of it. "Proper free speech back then. No one pretended bad people were good people just to earn a vote or… get brownie points from the hippies." Now another hit of oxygen. "Just go, get out." His hand rose, limply aimed at his door. "Stop stirring up the past. Even if Remy did some stuff that weren't exactly on the level, law-wise, it doesn't matter. No one cares about a handful of dead niggers from the sixties."

Alicia whirred inside, excitement building. For once, she didn't need to interrogate her computer's conclusions. She snatched at James's answer. "Oh, ho-ho, Jimmy boy! You said the sixties. That's so cool!"

James held very still. "Yeah. I said that. Why?"

Alicia paced, forcing a sense of anticipation down. Second guessing herself, double-checking she had it right. She'd hoped to push him and have him angrily blurt out that it was all Remy, or someone else—an act of self-preservation. Her excitement at what might have been a far juicer slip of the tongue than she'd expected meant she could not stay still a moment longer. "The *sixties*, Jimmy."

"Mr Grantham, if you don't mind."

"Sure, okay. *Mizzz*-ter Grantham. You want to know the cool part?"

"What's that?"

"We've only identified bodies from the 1970s so far. They're the oldest. And a couple in the eighties. Why'd you say sixties?"

James looked at DS Ball as if for help, but the rotund detective responded with a nonplussed pursing of his lips, as if about to whistle a tune.

"I'm old," James said. "I get mixed up sometimes. The sixties, the seventies, who the hell cares? Hang on."

He summoned a rattling breath from his lungs. Three, four times. He exhaled in loud, shallow efforts, until his airways gripped something and brought it up. Then James hocked a massive ball of green-brown gloop onto the carpet at Alicia's feet. If she hadn't hopped back, it would have soiled her shoes.

"Nice," Ball said.

"Oops." James patted both arms of his chair, laughing. "Like I said, I get confused. I even forgot I had my spit-beaker to hand." The laughter caused him to draw the oxygen to his face again.

Alicia chased away the grossness of James's petulance, unwilling to give up so quickly. "Was it Remy? Was Bertie part of it? Did Audrey Phillips know?"

Each question drew deeper laughter from James.

"Jimmy—Mr Grantham—if you help us, we can help you. But if it comes out you were a part of it, and you didn't come clean, you'll spend what's left of your life somewhere a lot less pleasant than this."

James relinquished his canister and snorted. "I'm six months past due a clean death. You can't threaten me with anything. Arrest me, I don't care. I'll be dead before I see a courtroom. Anything we did, anything we didn't serve time for, *we got away with it*." His sneer built into a grin. "Accept it, honey. Let us die in our crippled bodies, or with our brains leaking out of our ears. None of us are worth punishing."

Alicia wrestled with whether to push him more, to try and

taunt a full confession out of him. Or take him down to Halifax or up to the command centre for a formal interview.

A brief would have him out of there on health grounds in half an hour, though. For now, she'd settle for simply knowing who killed those people fifty years earlier.

Whether or not she could prove it.

Yet.

# CHAPTER THIRTY-FIVE

IN THE MOBILE LAB, Malcolm Knowles had the pleasure of trawling Ryan Mohammad Najafi's electronic trail while Cross headed up an effort to spread a wide surveillance net, attempting to cover every angle of every suspect, be it the Vanguard, the families of the victims, or the girl who'd been seemingly stalking him for the past week. That particular social media account was the one to focus on, because it had been wiped from the net hours before Ryan's body was reported up on Stoodley Pike. Identify the device and use either cell towers or GPS to pinpoint as many historical locations as possible, and they might just get lucky—if not a precise address, then maybe, if it pinged in a populated area, a CCTV image would be forthcoming.

Unfortunately, social media companies and other internet-based entities were hard to serve warrants on, hiding behind foreign countries and data protection rules. Unless a crime was committed directly *through* that medium—such as hate speech or death threats—the mere suspicion of wrongdoing wasn't sufficient. It had to be severe enough to embarrass the company into giving up its data.

Massive overreaction and social outrage had their place occasionally.

Knowles couldn't help being distracted by the presence of the bodies, preserved in drawers, their possessions lined up and tagged, referenced back to the crimes of fifty and hundred years ago. Those remains brought out of the ground yesterday had been matched to some already-disturbed bodies, the potential high number of thirty-one whittled down to a grand total of twenty-seven.

*Twenty-seven murders.*

Undetected.

Disappearances not investigated. Not properly.

New killings. Inspired by older ones, or modelled after them so easily because it was the same people?

Whatever the answers, it was happening all over again. The dead shoved aside due to budget issues. It wouldn't be long before Alicia was called back to Leeds, and the only person who seemed to care about them was here, shuffling digital papers in an attempt to cross-match social media accounts to weed out a chain of connections, just in case the warrant applications failed.

With the new bones, the new flesh, the new possessions and items of clothing, there were new leads. He'd have to work them off-book, away from the Amina and Ryan killings, but he could do it.

Knowles's phone rang. He checked the caller ID and answered. "Hi, Alicia."

"Hi, yourself." She was on speakerphone, travelling. "You still working on figuring out who those people are?"

Knowles glanced around, searching for surveillance cameras.

Wasn't he just thinking about that? And if Alicia had cameras here, could they see into his head?

"Hello?" Alicia called. "Are you there? Have I lost him?"

"Can't tell." came a man's voice. DS Ball.

"I'm here," Knowles said.

"I'm guessing DNA is taking an age, and official ageing tests are going to be longer," Alicia said.

"We can subcontract the university, but that's expensive—"

"Do it. The ageing side, anyway. Pick some of the older ones you haven't IDed yet and see if any of them go back to the 1960s, not just the seventies."

"Why?"

"Because someone slipped up. I want to see if it's a muddled brain or a guy accidentally confessing to a fuller picture. I'll clear it with Cross myself."

"Okay, I can do that. Are you coming here?"

"Nah. I need to pay another visit. Let me know how it goes."

She hung up and Knowles smiled for the first time that day. He wasn't the only one who cared. And he wished he could be with Alicia, wherever she was going to end up.

"That's the cut and thrust of it." Alicia was sat in the day room of Daisyville Retirement Home with Audrey in her scrubs and Remy staring blankly at the outside world. "We estimated the bones at 1970s, and the oldest ones we IDed were that era. But when the results come back, we'll confirm Jimmy Grantham's slip means he knew something. I'd like to know what that is."

"How would I know?" Audrey said. "James and Remy were thick as thieves with Dan and a couple of others too, but…" She appraised Remy Duval with the kind of simpering look a mother offers a child who may or may not have told a lie. "I only knew they'd been in fights when I had to patch Remy up. Usually on football days. He'd be all bloody and proud, smiling like he'd just won major battle in some important war. I'd do the necessary and he'd insist on… well, he'd insist on celebrating. Just the two of us."

Ball had declined to come into the home, preferring to hang around outside and let Alicia work. There was no danger here, so

Alicia hadn't questioned it beyond a friendly prompt about why. He'd offered no explanation beyond "can't stand those places." Maybe she'd probe him a bit on it later, having detected a genuine phobia behind his words.

"Just the two of you." Alicia understood what that meant; another one of those saucy hints which she plainly thought were charming. "You know, when a football hooligan has been involved in a major incident, where people are injured or even killed, the thugs involved lay low. They have to."

Audrey frowned, faintly amused.

"I mean," Alicia said, "they can't go out celebrating with bruised knuckles and cuts and bruises elsewhere. The cops would pick them up. I'm going to go out on a limb and say these 'celebrations' were always at your place, not his. Am I right?"

Audrey straightened in her chair beside Remy. "Well, my place was always nicer."

"And you never married."

"No, I—"

"He never let you go out with him and the boys."

"No, he didn't think it was my scene. So rowdy."

"Do you know what police intelligence is?"

Audrey shook her head, the furrow of her brow deepening. "An oxymoron?"

"Good one." Alicia gave a sarcastic laugh. "When it came to hooliganism, back then and now, police would go undercover in known hangouts, peg the leaders, and then head outside into an unmarked vehicle and take photos as those leaders left. If a court case came up, the crews—and make no mistake, the Yorkshire Vanguard started as a crew of football hooligans, not 'patriots'— they got wind of these techniques. Now, it's all tapping mobile phones and monitoring hashtags, but back then they had to get creative."

Audrey twisted her body only a fraction, but it moved away

from Remy. A subconscious act of shame, of disappointment toward him. She knew where this was going.

"Having a bolthole where they could rest up was standard practice," Alicia said. "Somewhere the cops wouldn't have known about. A place even their mates didn't see."

"I knew his friends," Audrey said.

"When? Parties? Weddings maybe? Big groups of people where a girlfriend can get lost?"

Audrey couldn't look at Remy or Alicia. "Why are you saying these things? You think I deserve to get hurt now?"

"Because a wife always knows," Alicia said firmly. "Maybe you didn't realise at the time just how bad Jimmy and Remy and Bertie and whoever else were being. But you knew they were up to no good."

"Boys being boys." Audrey shook her head. "They get in fights, they... need someone to care for them. But it doesn't mean they did what you say." She faced Alicia square-on. "I'd like you to leave."

No one heard Audrey's request, so Alicia pretended she didn't hear either. "Who was the apprentice, Audrey? Who was young enough to be grooming his own apprentice now?"

"Why would they need an apprentice? This isn't a *garage*."

"Passing on knowledge to the next generation of Vanguard, perhaps? To carry on the fight?"

"Oh, pfft." Audrey threw her hands up and let them slap down to her thighs.

"It takes two people, *at least*, just to get the body up to Stoodley Pike, then the arrangement of it would be a whole other story. A leader, with knowledge of the older killings, and a follower, keen to learn. Maybe more than one follower."

"Same old story." Again, Audrey flapped her hands and let them drop back to her thighs. "Black and white motives. Good versus evil. And these boys, they have to be evil. I don't know why it's so hard for you to understand, but that nonsense is all behind us. Remy is a good man, and from what I read in the papers, the group he built has evolved. But none of that matters." She rose creakily to her feet and stood ramrod straight. "Now, it really is time to go."

Alicia glanced around, found a male nurse or orderly paying attention to them. She took a chance and addressed Remington Duval directly, concentrated on being herself, *the real Alicia.* "Hey, handsome, check me out." She tugged at her hair, presenting it simply rather than in a seductive manner. "Blonde hair, blue eyes, a proper Aryan princess, right?"

"Ex*cuse* me." Audrey said.

Chirpy, happy, big smile. "It's okay, Remy, you can tell me. Who else joined you in killing those people? What else did you do? Was it just the ones up the Beacon, or were there more before?" She knelt before him, trying to catch his eye.

"Detective, this is not acceptable!"

Audrey's raised voice attracted the male attendant now, prompting him to tidy up the dribbling mouth of the lady he was tending to, obviously ready to support the woman he must have worked with daily.

Alicia whispered, "Who was it, Remy?" She narrowed her eyes, etched out a shy smile. "Who did you use?"

The low tone did its job. What was left of Remy's instincts prompted him to lean closer by inches. It wasn't a lot, but it told Alicia he acknowledged her presence. His mouth worked silently.

"That's my boy, Remy," Alicia said. "Give it to me straight. Who did you train to follow in your footsteps? I wanna shake their hand and tell the world what you achieved."

A noise grated in Remy's throat.

"Detective, you're agitating him," Audrey said.

"I won't manhandle you out, miss." The male nurse had now crossed the space to intervene. "But I will ask you very politely to exit the building. If you don't leave, I will be making a formal complaint. Am I understood?"

Alicia kept it chirpy. "Of course, no problem at all." She held on to Remy, urging him silently to speak, to say anything, even another outburst, something to show she'd reached him.

"Now, please," Audrey said.

Alicia pushed to her feet and stared down at the man lolling his head to one side. "I guess this is goodbye."

She held out little hope of interviewing him formally, but Audrey was another matter. Even if she had been sidelined—a little wifey patching up her man and cooking and shagging, and whatever else a smitten girl got up to back then—she had more to offer. James, too, and maybe Bertie, and any number of people with whom Remington Duval interacted. But it'd be hard without the man himself to confirm her suspicions.

"I would have known," Audrey said firmly. "And I saw nothing but a roguish man making a few bad choices." She tilted her head toward the door. "Last chance, or I call your superiors."

Defeated, Alicia stepped away.

But then, quick as a snake, Remy's hand darted out and gripped Alicia's forearm.

Audrey gasped.

Remy's fingers were so thin that Alicia could detect the bones beneath. But while the curled digits appeared tight and talon-like, it was more like a loose belt around her. His tremble suggested those bones would snap if he pressed any tighter.

She expected a parting shot from him, a final word, either confession or denial. All she got, though, was a slow, steady turn of his head, a sneer aimed her way, almost identical to *Mr* Grantham's. He emitted a groan that she interpreted as mocking her.

The closest the man could get to laughing in her face.

# CHAPTER THIRTY-SIX

SCARLETT AUSTIN WASN'T A MUG, and she didn't like being taken for one. It was early evening, and Glenn had shagged her brains out already. She wasn't objecting to that. It had been her idea, after all, and he did a wonderful job—more aggressive than usual, as she had demanded. But the poor guy seemed cowed afterward, as if following her instructions for harder and faster somehow reduced his manliness. She didn't feel it reduced him in any way, but getting into a mood afterward surely did.

He dressed with a grunt and barely responded to her questions about where he was going.

"Out," was his one-word answer.

"Where?"

"Away from here. Just for a bit."

This had happened more than once recently—him screwing her, getting his jollies, and then leaving.

Scarlett saw her man's old habits resurfacing, the ones she had managed to eradicate after they'd declared love for each other and agreed to monogamy. Step by step, she'd got him to stop leaving clothes all over the place—both hers and his—and when they moved in together, he even washed up more than once a day.

Little things like the toilet seat, like asking about *her* day as well as telling her about his. And big things followed. Big things like showing her respect in public, avoiding pointless physical altercations "for a laugh," and not overtly eyeing up other women—although side-glances were unavoidable in a real man, so she never got upset about that.

The biggest thing she squeezed out of him, though, was treating sex like a squash game, like exercise. Sex was a two-way street, and she did not want to become a cum-bucket like the skanks he'd been with in the past, and which his friends still seemed to favour—girls who'd stay up until midnight just in case their guy was drunk and horny after a night out. These low-self-esteem slags even said outright they'd dump their guys if they weren't afraid of the consequences, and could find someone better.

It was truly sad.

As for Glenn jumping her bones and then buggering off, that wasn't something she'd stand for. Never. He needed to know where he stood.

Dayapreet Virk was aware of what people thought of him. Even the double takes and whispers he detected in the mezzanine bar area of the Golden Kasbar carried an almost mocking leer.

Moleford's newest upmarket ethnic dining experience was Lebanese, and Dayapreet had never experienced such food before. Watching over the chrome fittings, down into the dark, intimate lounge, he still felt like strangers were judging him as they passed behind: a hanger-on, a wannabe, a shadow to Abhu's shining light.

Because Dayapreet didn't cut a dashing figure, couldn't turn a phrase around to stun a debate opponent, nor take a subject and speak about it for whatever volume of time he had to fill, nor... anything, really, that involved being a public figure. But he wanted to serve his community, just as his cousin did. It wasn't a cling-on job, any more than it was for the famous kingmakers: the Alistair Campbells, the Karl Roves, the David Camerons—that latter going on to carve out his own career at the very pinnacle of politics.

Dayapreet would never achieve that, though. He didn't want to. He'd leave that to Abhu, and be satisfied he played his part.

For now, photographing and blogging, journaling and booking logistics were all important. He was Abhu's shadow, but not in the way his family viewed it.

He trailed the man.

He kept him on message.

He held him back from stretching too far.

Ambition was good, but too much would lead to burn out.

Like when Abhu allied himself with those Yorkshire Vanguard pricks. He'd done that without consulting Dayapreet or the other two strategists who worked, unpaid, on Abhu's career. Dayapreet rescued the bad publicity and converted it into something positive, bringing two groups together, to show one that brown people were proud to be British too, and to show the other that people like the Vanguard were not two-dimensional thugs who struggled to count to twelve without removing their socks.

It took a lot of thought to handle Abhu. Not that Dayapreet would ever call what he did "handling," not to Abhu's face. The councillor was impulsive, reckless, and spoke whatever came into his head. Yet, when it mattered, in public, he usually said the right thing. Usually *did* the right thing, in the end, even if it took someone with Dayapreet's attention to detail, with his forethought, to plan the moves properly. And during this difficult time in Moleford Bridge, Dayapreet had needed to cajole him plenty.

Abhu shouldn't have gone to the police; it was a clear attempt to appear better informed than others around him. He shouldn't have approached Tariq at the college the way he did; that was an obvious play at being seen as a friend to the imam, of harvesting political capital out of a tragedy. But he was right to go to the Vanguard.

*This time.*

He was right to unite Bertie Bradshaw and Tariq Bashir in staying the hell away from the police investigation. It was what a real public servant did, acting in the best interests of all concerned without demanding recognition.

Of course, Dayapreet would ensure Abhu got plenty of recognition, but not in a sleazy way; a leak here, a word in the right ear there, and his peace-making would seep into the public sphere. A trump card they could play when the time was right.

That was why Dayapreet was worried.

Five minutes ago, as Dayapreet started his second beer, Abhu cancelled their meet-up by text, but Dayapreet was not going to leave behind a five-quid beer.

Abhu rarely cancelled. It meant he was up to something. With someone else, more than likely. Dayapreet could only hope it wasn't something stupid.

He finished his beer, paid his bill, and asked for a takeout menu.


Lucy Viera prayed in the cool evening alongside Detective Inspector Cross. Outside the newly-blasted entrance to the gap in the earth where someone had deposited the remains of so many people, she and Bea Cross had reflected on death and what happens after, how prayers were being said across the town, the region, the country, for those killed this week. Yet these victims were all but viewed as a tantalising slice of horror fiction made real—the impact dulled through time passing.

The detective was a member of Lucy's congregation at the older of two local churches, even though it was farther from her house than the more modern one, and Lucy was pleased to see her showing true respect to the victims of such crimes. Too many people attended services as a means to hedge their bets, and rarely spoke to God or even about Him, yet when Lucy suggested a prayer, Beatrice Cross had bowed her head and clasped her hands together, and fell silent.

The suggestion, frankly, was an attempt to get Bea to leave Lucy alone. It usually worked.

Lucy was no fake, either, though, and took her duty seriously. Despite her advancing years, she saw the community as a charge, her responsibility toward it absolute. Although she did not originally trek to the mouth of this house of death to pray, she did not pass up the chance.

As well as fake parishioners, Lucy had encountered fake priests in her time, those who could be described as agnostic at best. Who saw events in the Bible as neat allegories, teaching tools thought up by wise churchmen in the Middle Ages, and adapted to more modern times. It was only in recent centuries, when the preservation of Bibles became sturdier, that manipulation of the book ceased, leaving the stories from those days—not Christ's—to remain mostly intact.

Although she never took the Bible literally, Lucy had a different interpretation than those trendy agnostic vicars and priests. She thought of the base stories as true, altered only slightly, and retconned to fit with the sensibilities of the age. The King James Bible might not be a hundred percent accurate, but there was more truth in there than seen on most news programmes or coming from the mouths of those charged with the welfare of the country's citizens.

There was no morality. Until you invoked the Bible.

Whether it was acknowledged as Jesus's example or God's word, most western laws came not from people but from the spiritual, and even basic morals originated between the pages of the hallowed book.

"Amen," Beatrice murmured.

Lucy also opened her eyes and found that Bea's drawn face had regained some of the stern tautness she was used to seeing.

"Will you be staying long?" Bea asked.

Lucy stared at the gaping hole in the hillside beyond the police cordon, fenced off by fluttering tape and two burly constables. "May I venture inside?"

Bea considered it for only two breaths. "No, I'm sorry, not just yet. When we've cleared it."

"You expect to find something? After all this time?"

"No, not *expect*. But we have to do it all thoroughly. Defence briefs are notorious for tying juries in knots when procedure isn't followed."

Lucy felt her eyebrows knit together. She loosened them before asking, "A jury, really? You think… someone might be arrested over this?"

"If they were young enough…" Bea trailed off, hands in her trouser pockets, hiking up her big coat to stuff them in there. She wouldn't look at Lucy. "I can't say much. You understand."

Lucy wasn't sure she did, but nodded anyway. There was something more to Bea's change of attitude. To her reluctance to be forthcoming. She'd never been that way with Lucy. "Is there something you'd like to ask?"

"No." Bea scuffed her feet on the hardscrabble ground.

"Nothing?"

The detective finally focussed on Lucy. "You were around at the time, weren't you?"

"And that's why you're worried? You suspect me?"

Bea gave a forced laugh. "Not *suspect*, no. But… if you knew anything—if you'd noticed disappearances, or something like that —you'd tell me, wouldn't you?"

Lucy stroked Bea's arm. "Of course. And you know, from your records, people did vanish. They turned up later, or they didn't. It wasn't like today where everyone can be tracked by their phone or a thousand CCTV cameras every square mile."

"So it was normal?"

"None of my parishioners were affected. We never had concerns. And there were only very occasional manhunts in Britain. So I'm sorry. Yes, I'm the right age, but I know very little."

Bea appeared to accept it, and after a little more small talk about how the next service would honour those found and say extensive prayers, the detective ducked inside, and Lucy was left to wander outside the cordon.

Since there was little point staying, she made a single back-and-forth circuit, then bade the constables on duty goodnight.

She took the longer, easier-on-the-knees path up to the top, to the Church on the Hill. In no rush to meet her Lord, she kept herself as fit as she could, but the twenty-minute trek took so much more out of her than the same route would have even ten years ago. With the sun a fine line on the horizon, Lucy wiped away a light sweat as she passed into the ruins. The place she'd met the other detective and the woman she wished so dearly she could have helped—Maisie Jackson.

Tragic woman.

She found no comfort in God, nor any spiritual outlet. She just shut herself away—cultivated a garden, as if bringing life from the soil would help her cope.

The moon was not quite full, but it had risen hours before the sun set and, combined with the final rays of sunlight, gave her more than enough illumination by which to see.

Lucy made her way over the uneven ground to the spot where the little detective had interrupted her prayers. Her bag was still here. She'd packed it with everything she thought she'd need, as much as she could possibly carry, including a torch and a headlamp.

She was more than excited.

Perhaps it was the anticipation, or maybe fooling everyone

into believing she was only here on God's business, or simply the fact that she knew things others did not.

That last facet worried her, thinking it might be sinful. Falling afoul of the adage that *knowledge is power* might lead to darker things.

Tonight, she felt rather powerful indeed.

Beside the altar, she fitted the lamp on her head, placed the torch in her pocket along with a stick of chalk, and flicked on the light. She pressed herself against the thick western wall, and shone the light across its surface, along to where the corner cut in for two feet, forming a shape like a chimney.

No one, not even Lucy or the church scholars, suspected anything amiss upon first viewing. The shape looked like an affectation, albeit not one you normally found in a church.

She again pressed one cheek to the stone and swept her light across the brickwork, locating the discrepancy she needed— around seven feet off the ground, high enough to avoid accidental discovery, and low enough for a man to reach.

After jumping to highlight the spot with the chalk, she returned to her bag for the rubber mallet. She'd brought a heavier one too, but didn't want to make much noise. It would carry for miles up here.

The brick she'd marked stuck out a couple of millimetres and was angled in a way that looked like an accidental flaw in the wall's construction. After heaving a large rock over, Lucy didn't have to stretch too far to touch the mark, where she traced the outline with her finger.

A tingle built through her hand, up her arm, and into her shoulders.

She tapped the block with the mallet. No need to chip away the mortar as she'd thought she might have to. Instead, the brick moved.

Lucy pushed it hard and it jiggled inward, then stopped.

She took the mallet, rested the rubber head against the brick, and added all the pressure she could summon. It grated as it slid inward, where it rested.

And nothing happened.

One last shove with the mallet, and a click sounded.

But not in the wall, as Lucy had expected. No secret door swinging open, gaping like a mouth to the underworld. This noise came from beneath her feet.

The flagstones were overgrown with weeds, but one appeared to be cleaner than the others. Less ridden with plants and a hundred years of dirt.

Ever the prepared vicar, she'd brought a crowbar too, which she now retrieved and jimmied into the stone that appeared to have cracked away from its neighbour.

It shifted.

Oh, the anticipation. The excitement.

She pushed it away, reminding herself of her solemn duty, not only to the people of her parish, but the Lord they all served.

This was God's work. Hopefully, those on this plane of existence would forgive her as He must surely do.

The flagstone came away, but she could not place it aside quietly. Instead she allowed it to bang down, and it echoed across the ruin, and most likely beyond.

"Oops."

She said a brief prayer that the sound wouldn't alert the police, and shone her larger torch into the hole.

Her grin spread all the way to her ears.

The ladder was plainly old, but the wrought iron rungs embedded in the funnel looked strong, and felt solid as she tested them with her feet, arms braced across the entrance in case something crumbled.

It held.

At sixty-eight years old, this was far and away the best thing she'd ever done. It would be the most important, too.

She descended as fast as she dared, a mere eight or ten feet, coming to a floor deliberately constructed and flattened, although the walls and roof were rough—a dome within the ground formed by God's hand or by the natural forces He created. A smell pervaded, which made her freeze.

She had to be mistaken.

But as she ventured deeper, the light on her head caught an object dead ahead of her. Sweeping the bigger torch all around, seeking out the corners, she established that the natural space got bigger. The roof was higher, the walls wider, forming a circle coming off this vestibule.

*No, not a circle.*

No wonder Father Pickersgill believed he was chosen.

But there was no time to savour her conclusion. At the centre of the wider section stood a solid rectangular cuboid, with a person lying on top. The two lights converged to reveal that the person was not moving. Blood ran down the sides of the … what was it? An altar? A sacrificial platform?

She traced the path of the man's blood, a gutter around the base acting as a sluice with a drain hole leading who-knew-where. Locating his face, she recognised the man: that annoyingly enthusiastic councillor, Abhu Noon.

He was open-eyed and wide-mouthed, his long hair freed from its turban. His throat had been cut from carotid to carotid and, in the beams of light, Lucy now saw that the altar was angled up at the feet, and his ankles were bound to prevent him slipping. His arms lay by his side, still attached, while his stomach had been splayed open.

Her first thought was of a butcher's block, but she quickly adjusted that thought; the body was more like a rodent caught by a cat, not for food but for sport.

And that smell … it wasn't the blood, but—

Flame flickered to life to her right. A hooded figure wielded a pole upon which a wrap of soaked rags burned. With the hood concealing their face, the person placed the pole in a wall bracket, a similar device to ones Lucy had seen adorning medieval castles, used for lighting before the advent of electricity. It carried the odour she'd picked up: flame, and camphor set alight.

"Hello, Lucy," the man said.

Lucy didn't know what else to say. "Hello."

The figure moved to the next old-world-style lamp and brought it to life with a disposable lighter. He then turned to her, and took down his hood. "You're late."

# CHAPTER THIRTY-SEVEN

IT WAS a night interrupted by too many thoughts and odd dreams. After a long day of requisitioning ancient intelligence reports from task forces assigned to 1970s football crews, specifically coverage of Remington Duval and James Grantham, Alicia had returned to her home hopeful of solving the murders, but despondent at the prospect of having no one to convict. It took hours for the civilian investigators to dig out the archives, and even then it would take a day or so to get the information over to her. She asked them to check one thing before shipping it all out, and she came away with what she needed.

The next morning, expecting a long day, Alicia arranged another sleepover at her mum's for Stacey, much to the Dot-Bot's pretend enthusiasm, then booked a hotel for the night, triggering Murphy's annoyed grumble—as her line manager, he got copied in on the email. So he rang her.

"I was expecting you back at Sheerton," he said in a voice usually reserved for DS Ball after an off-colour joke or for a detective who'd let something slip away because they didn't think procedure applied to them. "You're there to advise, for two to three days. Which means you're already overdue. *And* you took Ball with you."

"Two more days, Murphy, please." Alicia didn't want to annoy him too much. She was still his friend, and had promised when he took her on as a "proper copper" that she wouldn't undermine him. Sensing the disappointment in his nasal sigh, she added, "Hasn't Watson sent you backfill?"

"Yes, but…" Murphy moved around, presumably closing his door. "I don't have backfill for DS Ball. That's a favour to you. And the guy DCI Watson sent, he's decent. Solid enough. But he's obviously treading water, passing the time. I want you back. ASAP."

She said nothing.

"One more day," Murphy said. "And I'll be putting that in writing to Watson's chief super. Clear?"

"Clear."

It was more than he had to give her, and as she arrived late at the library situation room, she gave Watson, Knowles, and Cross the same information. Ball, again having arrived before her, asked about himself; Alicia said she assumed they were a package deal.

"Well, you've done good groundwork," Watson said. "For your last day, I want you to tie off everything you've got so far."

"I need another run at Remington Duval," Alicia said. "And—"

"No. You leave that senile twat alone."

"I have *proof.*"

That silenced them.

She said, "The files are on their way over, but I'll be able to match them the way I matched my random test case."

"Test case?" Watson said.

"The Vanguard was a football crew before it was a straight-up hate group. The police kept tabs on them, logging the leaders' movements, and the leaders knew it. They had to get creative to slip away. I checked against the disappearance date for one of our victims—Dana Reynolds, 5th March, 1978. The cops lost track of Remington Duval, James Grantham, and Danny Pryor. From March fourth to March sixth, they didn't show up at their usual haunts. Then all resurfaced the same day, the seventh."

Watson thought it through. "Proves nothin'."

"No, but when I show that they ditched their tails on days when each of our identified remains also vanished, that will be enough to see off reasonable doubt. Three or four, maybe not. But over twenty?"

Watson again shook his head. "The intelligence units wouldn't have been on the crews every second. Not even the leaders."

"But they'll have been on them a lot. It'll be enough. If it isn't, I'll … I don't know, I'll do a little dance for you at the Christmas party. Something involving balloons."

Watson laughed. "Might be worth taking that bet. Okay, then. We'll do some checking."

"So I can head back up to Daisyville Retirement Home?"

"Absolutely not." Watson stuffed his hands in his pockets. "I already had a pissed-off assistant manager chewing my ear off about you. Just finish up. Give us details of everyone involved, these intelligence reports, every suspect, every witness. Including that weirdo you've spent a bunch of taxpayer cash on. You've done all y'can. Thank you. Now go away." Watson faced Cross and Knowles. "Any word?"

"Word on what?" Alicia asked, not used to being sidelined.

Watson reacted like he'd been poked in the back, calming immediately, but plainly annoyed.

"Abhu Noon," Knowles said. "He's been reported missing."

DI Cross didn't seem happy, leaning on a wall with her arms folded and one foot placed over the other. "We have to move quick. There's rain on the way tonight. Just the tail end of what they're having down south, but it'll make any searches harder."

"And forensics," Ball said. "If he's dead."

"We lock this damn place down." Watson leaned on the table using his fists to support himself. "The whole town. Should've done it sooner."

Cross bobbed her head—not in agreement, but something else.

"I *know*, Bea," Watson said. "And you were right. *Damn.*"

Alicia had not been privy to nearly as much as she needed. She'd been pushed aside, the academic brought in to dot every "i" and cross every "t." Watson had never really wanted her on board, and had kept her in the quagmire of the past. This was why she was only just piecing together the clear conflict between Watson and Cross.

"So," Alicia said pleasantly. "The inspector wanted to go all out, bring in a ton of extra manpower to patrol, and maybe surveil, but the chief said no. Budgets? Or did you just worry about looking heavy-handed?"

Watson glowered her way.

"A bit of both," Cross said.

"Don't sweat it," Alicia said. "For what it's worth, you couldn't have predicted this."

Watson's glower deepened. "And what, exactly, would *you* know about it?"

"Everything I've seen of DI Cross's case shows it was designed to take Ryan away from busy areas. You know that, of course. But I'm guessing he wasn't the only one with a mysterious admirer."

Knowles took his cue. "There were others, yes." A pointed look at Watson.

The DCI swivelled his eyes at the ceiling, took a loud, cleansing breath, and pulled his jacket straight. "I can see I'm no longer needed. Congrats." He slapped Knowles on the shoulder. "You get t' be DCI today." He pointed at Alicia. "Your turn tomorrow, hun. 'Kay? That work for you both?"

Knowles clearly knew better than to speak.

"I'm cool with that," Alicia said. "Presumably I need to lose all sense of imagination, allow no hunches or theorising, no brainstorming—"

"I got plenty of imaginative thoughts right now." Watson's face had reddened. Not a furious bright red, but a tint. Enough to warn off others. "Y'understand, I got an imam stoking the embers of a community ready t' explode. I got his new best mate missing. I got a chief super who's bollocking me fer expending any resources on cold cases with no way t' solve 'em. Oh, and there's a frigging raincloud racing up ma' arse from the south, not t' mention bodies popping out a' the ground faster than a George A. Romero movie. And don't get me started on the press."

Alicia had avoided all news for the past three days, but she'd caught the occasional headline in petrol stations and when browsing her phone. They were going heavy in on the "dumb police do nothing" angle, with speculation rife about honour killings, race-hate crimes, and conspiracies involving the Freemasons.

"How many other guys were propositioned?" Alicia asked.

"I found three," Knowles replied. A glance at Watson. "It was a hunch, sir, based on the facts to hand. I had to follow it." With his boss appeased, if only minutely, he returned to Alicia. "I saw where Ryan was taken, how they had tempted him out there, how close—time-wise—it was to the previous killing, and … I didn't think they would be so specific. I thought they'd cast a wider net. See who bit."

"Makes sense. You said three?"

"Two more Muslims and a Jew. Similar stuff. All young men. All non-practicing of their religion. Approached online by some sexy young woman wanting to meet up."

"But most people are wise to that stuff now," Cross said.

"Yes," Knowles confirmed. "They all liked it at first, but details didn't wash, and all three assumed it was a catfishing expedition, or fraud, or whatever. Not genuine."

"But Ryan?" Alicia said.

"He didn't either," Cross said. "According to his mates, the stalker was so persistent he went along in person to confront whoever it was, and... well, you know the rest."

"The online traces?"

"Plenty of info, but it's just ghosts," Knowles said. "Nothing left to follow. As soon as Ryan was taken, the other accounts from the same IP as his stalker went dark. Devices disposed of."

"Meaning they'd exhausted that avenue," Alicia said.

"Meaning they knew we'd be onto them," Watson said. "Which is *why* it's a dead end for now."

Alicia wandered to the opposite side of the desk to Watson, bypassing Ball to look out the window at the town. It was a minor miracle that their location hadn't leaked out and drawn a campsite of media to the street outside, especially with Lauren and Costas telling anyone who asked that the police were "only interested in background."

Knowles stood at her shoulder. "What does it mean? That they went catfishing?"

"Are you testing me, Detective Constable?" Alicia's reply came out a little coy, almost flirtatious, but she hadn't meant it that way.

"A little," Knowles said.

"Stop pissing about, and talk," Watson said.

"Fine." Alicia turned to them. "The person who took Ryan is tech-savvy enough to set up fake accounts and target specific types of people online. That makes them younger than the likes of James Grantham. But old enough to not understand how aware people are of fake identities being set up to defraud others. Very few people Ryan's age would fall for it. That leaves the current crop of Vanguard, a ton of Tariq Bashir's followers, and Bertie Bradshaw stays in the frame, too, since we're not going to assume an older guy can't get up to speed on this kind of thing."

"Or...!" A finger poked the air as Watson made an exaggerated face of shock. "Maybe it's some random nutter!"

Alicia stayed silent, waiting for nobody to laugh, which took the wind out of Watson's sails. Once he deflated a tad, she said, "The killer is highly organised with a warped view of reality. In day-to-day life, he—*they*, actually—will appear normal, at least on the surface. A team. A leader, a follower—maybe more than one."

"Thank you, Professor Psychic." Watson's tone dripped with sarcasm and impatience. "We have done this job before. Perhaps y'd like to hear my profile of a multiple murderer."

Alicia was always happy to listen to other theories, right before punching someone in the face with her superior brilliance. Usually. "Go ahead."

By the window, Ball and Knowles both murmured something that sounded like, "Guv?"

"In a sec." Watson ticked off the items. "A serial killer is bloody mental."

Alicia conceded the point. "Often, someone will have experienced a psychotic break that activates their violence. A trigger. Yes."

"One who gets away with it for ages is going t' know all about police procedure and investigative techniques."

Again, she couldn't fault him. "They do read a lot of true crime books, and non-fiction by former detectives."

The third finger: "They like t' insert themselves into an investigation."

"Yes, sometimes. They'll join searches for disappeared people, suspected victims, hoping to glean a little info. Might even attempt to befriend the police detectives." She shuddered at the thought of how friendly she and Richard Hague had gotten. "Not as many cases see that now, though, what with twenty-four-hour news and the internet."

"Boss," Knowles said. "You should know about this—"

"You're the psychologist." Watson kept his attention on Alicia and dropped his hand to his side. "Who d' we know, close t' this investigation, who is intimately familiar with police methods? Hmm? Who inserted themselves by coming forward with information? Who offered you, DI Friend, a key in case you needed somewhere t' lay your pretty little head at night?" Watson adopted a sarcastic "thinking" face. "Someone with a past trauma likely t' be triggered by a shitload of water pouring into her town?"

Alicia let the annoyance simmer. She wasn't an angry person, not in these situations. Human, sure, vulnerable to sadness and tempers, but in these conversations, she was happy, full of herself in many ways. But based on experience, she was usually right. "You mean Maisie Jackson."

Cross tutted and moved away to her laptop, leaving the DCI to it.

Watson smiled. "Bingo."

"What trauma?" Alicia asked. "What could trigger her to get involved with us?"

"You didn't know?" The thinking face turned quizzical. "Oh, dear me. Y'didn't review the background check we had t' perform before contracting her? Hmm, right. Then maybe you should ask her."

"Or…" Alicia remembered herself, remembered how she wanted to behave, but summoning a smile or a lighter tone proved hard. "You could just grow up and tell me."

Watson grew serious. No sarcasm, no humour. "She and her husband were driving in some place abroad. Four, five years ago. Big adventure. She was at the wheel. Avoiding a sheep, or somethin'. She took the car through a fence, rolled it down a bank, and landed roof-first in a river." He gave Alicia a moment, then solemnly delivered the punchline. "Her children were in the back. Boy and a girl, I forget their names." He now looked ashamed, presumably at having used Alicia's lack of knowledge as a source of humour, now that the events dawned on him as *real*, as affecting a *real* human. "She stayed with 'em until she drowned too. Trying t' get 'em free. Her husband was thrown clear. He went back, though. Grabbed her, and the children. He revived her, but it was too late for the kids."

Alicia let the shock and sadness wash over her. But she was certain of one thing: "It's not her."

"You can't know that for sure." Watson coughed to return to his usual gruff manner. "Point is, y're not looking beyond the theories on the table. Have you even checked this Jackson woman's alibis?"

"Maybe... maybe I should have been more thorough, but... this needed knowledge of the original crime. It needed something driving the hatred. It needs a follower *and* a leader, minimum. Maisie is a loner. Perhaps crippled by grief, or just shutting it out, along with everyone else, but she wouldn't follow someone, and surely couldn't lead someone to murder. And if Abhu Noon is gone—"

"Sikh," Cross reminded everyone, "not a Muslim."

"But an enemy to the right person. And don't pretend any of you aren't thinking this. Abhu wants to be front and centre. A man like that doesn't just disappear. So unless—"

"Hey!" It was DS Ball.

They all turned to him.

"DC Knowles has been trying to get you to look at this," he said, "but you're all a bit busy scoring points off each other. If that takes precedence over a significant development in proceedings, go ahead. Otherwise, listen to the lad."

Cross spoke first. "Go head, Malcolm. What is it?"

Knowles stood aside and pointed at the window. "Umm, the forecast was wrong. It's raining again. Already. And those clouds coming this way look pretty hairy."

# PART V

# CHAPTER THIRTY-EIGHT

AND SO THE rain fell across Yorkshire for the second time in a month. The revised forecast blamed a weak jet stream for failing to buffer the weather system and restrict it to the southern part of Europe. The heavy clouds floated north, pushed by high pressure around the Balearics.

Storm Donald made landfall early in the southeast and leapt north as if a drop in the jet stream's pressure had burst a dam. It set the eye of the storm over Cornwall, and the thick banks of moisture-heavy cloud swelled.

"Cornwall." Maisie turned down the radio in her kitchen as the BBC Radio 4 weather presenter explained his and his colleagues' misstep. "We used to camp there. Have you been?"

"A while ago. It's a long journey." Alicia sipped her green tea, preferable to the nut milk alternative in regular tea.

"Britain's prettiest county, I think." Maisie had opted for green tea too, her usual mid-morning pick-me-up. "I never liked it as a child, travelling to the far southeast of the country in a clapped-out Rover towing a caravan." Her light American lilt sounded incongruous here, using British slang like *clapped-out,* speaking of a British childhood despite her parents not being raised here. "Those narrow lanes are not built for caravans. But Cornwall has the best beaches, safe campsites, lots of sun. When Peter and Joanne came along, Cuthbert and I rented a cottage there for holidays. When they were older we camped in a tent. They loved it. We loved it. The kids ran free on the campsite— went to the shops alone, fed chickens, gathered eggs from the farm next door. Then when they were a bit older, ten and eight, we ventured farther afield."

"Now you're alone," Alicia said. "Divorced."

"Separated. Cuthbert keeps asking me to pop down. He's the deputy chief constable, a real bigwig. Says he wants an outside consultant to come in on some cases, the ones that need a little out-of-the-box thinking."

"The detectives in Cornwall can't cope?"

Maisie smiled into her cup. "They cope fine. But there are bigger issues than single crimes to solve. Organised crime is big— drugs, that sort of thing. If they can clear up the regular one-off stuff faster, and I *can* solve those things quickly, then the detectives are freed up for the major crimes. But... I can't go."

Just the two of them in the room, while Knowles waited outside. Alicia noted Maisie was gazing at the two empty chairs as she spoke. "Because of your children?"

"Yes. Because of my children."

"They keep you company?"

Maisie nodded. "They're dead, Alicia. I know that. Understand it. I even accept it. They're not ghosts, either."

"But you see them."

Maisie closed her eyes and lowered her chin to her chest. "Please, give me a minute."

"Take what you need."

"I wasn't talking to you."

"They're here now?"

Maisie opened her eyes, red with the effort of restraining her tears. She addressed a chair directly. "Yes, Joanne. I have explained this many times already, but you keep forgetting." To the other chair: "You both died. I tried to save you, I did, but I wasn't... I wasn't strong enough."

"Maisie..." Alicia started, but she had no words for her.

"I'm sorry, Peter; your father and I... we couldn't go on living together. He moved to that lovely county, Cornwall. Look... why don't you two go play in the living room, or out in the garden. And don't bother the other policeman."

Maisie's eyes traced her children out of the room, so convincing that Alicia half-expected the chairs to move or a door to open and close. When they were apparently gone, Maisie's lips were thin and she swallowed, curled her fingers around her cup and met Alicia's look with one of defiance.

"I know they aren't real," she said. "Joanne is fourteen, now. Peter, twelve."

"They age?" Alicia said.

"Of course they do. Children age."

Alicia had encountered delusional behaviour before, where a person had convinced themselves that a fantasy had come to life. Maisie was different.

"You don't fight the hallucinations," Alicia said.

"Why would I fight something I created?"

Alicia sipped the tea, as much to think about this as warm herself inside. "Did your husband know?"

"I asked him to leave so I could be free to do as I pleased." Matter-of-fact, neither proud nor ashamed. "After the funeral, I couldn't function. I was medicated, of course, drinking on top of that. But in the end, even when I sobered up, a marriage can rarely survive in the shadow of a dead child, let alone two."

"You moved out here?"

"Cuthbert wanted a fresh start, so he picked the place we were happiest. But the place I was happiest wasn't a place. It was a moment in time."

"You recreated your children... intentionally?"

Maisie nodded. "It was heartbreaking at first, but as I started getting this house the way I wanted, I constructed them the ability to age. Like real kids. The more real they became, the easier I found it. I'll struggle soon, but I'll find mental barriers to block out those issues."

"What issues?"

"Teenagers rarely hang out with their parents. When they can't bring friends home, it'll be odd, and when they ask me why they can't go out to the cinema with other kids, I'll have to find a reason. Maybe I'll be honest with them."

Alicia tried to get into the mindset of the woman before her, a woman Alicia thought of as possessing a fiercely intelligent mind, a strong person of clear thought, yet who'd created a fantasy world in order to stave off grief. "And being honest with yourself?"

Maisie sat straighter. "How, exactly, am I not being honest with myself?"

"Convincing yourself you can have a life here with your late children. Ageing them in your mind, creating scenarios that fit as they grow. Will you imagine them going out to school, and coming home? Will you drop them at the gates?"

"Probably homeschool them."

"What happens when they're old enough to leave home? Will they come back to visit?"

"Yes." She said that as if it was the most obvious thing in the world. "They'll live with me a little longer than my generation did, then they'll go out and live the lives they would've had if I hadn't been *stupid* enough to argue with my husband over the radio station while driving. They'll worry about me as *I* age. They'll spend birthdays with me, Mother's Day brunch, eating Christmas dinner around this very table, and eventually they'll bring their spouses and children too. Which I will design just right for them.

My children will age as I do, and when I'm too infirm to move, they'll keep me company. They'll hold my hand on my deathbed, and they will live on until I am finally snatched into the void."

Alicia couldn't focus. It was stunning to see the woman defend clinging to a delusion. Only, it wasn't a delusion, not really. It was like a child taking comfort in an imaginary friend, playing with fairies in the garden, or speaking to a teddy bear to glean comfort from monsters under the bed.

"You can't live a life like that," Alicia said. "You must know this."

"Logically, yes. But it is the only thing that has kept me sane the past four years. If I can't live with my children, I won't live without them either."

Alicia didn't voice the obvious—that her statement made no sense—instead segueing to the usual refrain. "Perhaps you should talk to someone."

"I'm talking to you. When you're not here, I talk to them."

"I mean—"

"I know what you mean. And the answer is no."

"If the illusion shatters, or becomes unviable…"

"I'll deal with that if it happens."

"When it happens, it could be devastating. It could send you into a dissociative state where reality—"

"Crashes down around me, and the only way to cope is to disappear into my mental cage. I know. I wrote the damn chapter." Maisie stood abruptly and whipped away Alicia's half-cup of green tea, placed the two cups in the sink, and hunched over it, staring out the window at the steadily strengthening rain. "You promise me something here and now."

"What's that?"

"You will not return with social workers, mental health professionals, or literature detailing where I can get help. I will reject it out of hand. I'll lie convincingly to any professional, and they'll chalk it up to eccentricity. You'll be wasting your time, and theirs."

"But, Maisie—"

"Concentrate on something you *can* affect instead." She turned, her back to the sink and whatever she was seeing in her garden. "On something you have a faint chance of accomplishing. Like who might be responsible for those bodies that floated out of the ground, or who might be directing the current spate."

Alicia saw she wouldn't get anywhere with her, but made no promises about not returning to the subject. "Okay."

"Could Remy Duval be faking his dementia?" Maisie asked.

"Not unless he missed his calling as a method actor."

"What about James Grantham? Could he be passing on his knowledge?"

"He's a disgusting mess. His personality suggests an impotence to his life. I think that'd make him a follower, if he was involved at all. He'd want to *feel* powerful, he'd fantasise about it, but lacks drive."

"Life washes over him instead of him doing something about it?"

Alicia understood the woman's firm tone.

"Bertie?" Maisie suggested. "From follower in his youth to leader with experience?"

"We've floated the idea more than once," Alicia said. "It bears scrutiny."

"But of the current group, Glenn Bishop is a clear leader, isn't he?"

"Coming in from nowhere. Displacing the old guard." Alicia had thought of Glenn, attempting to mould the world to a certain image. "He even replaced the person who was expected to take over, and is doing a good job of making them appear respectable. Making them money. If anyone is acting independently, it's him."

"And you haven't eliminated him yet?"

"No."

Maisie gestured to the window. As if on cue, a gust slapped the glass with rain. "Then you'd better get a move on, young lady. Instead of drilling me about my coping mechanisms, maybe you should be kicking down a few doors, before Mother Nature washes everything away."

# CHAPTER THIRTY-NINE

THE RAIN CONTINUED TO FALL—STEADILY, but unceasing, growing in strength and volume as the morning wore on.

Throughout the hills of Calderdale, on already sodden ground, the water obeyed gravity without question, travelling ever downward. It sought out holes, access to the down-below, and poured into caves unseen, sometimes hidden for centuries, sometimes never viewed. And in the middle of all this stood the town of Moleford Bridge.

Within four hours, the hard, unploughed farmers' fields and the rocky, saturated terrain could no longer direct every drop of rain out to caves and uninhabited valleys, and a portion of that which fell on high ground discovered gravity worked just as well on tarmac as it did on mud and stone.

The steep roads saw kerbs swamped and drains unable to cope. This time, though, the humans who inhabited this place were prepared.

Some stacked sandbags, issued weeks earlier, along every low gap—doorsteps, windows, garages—and moved furniture and electricals upstairs. Then people had choices to make. For non-residents, it was simple to leave. The deluge did not prevent travel just yet—people who lived here could attempt to continue at their jobs, or accept the inevitable and just try to mitigate the damage; they could concentrate on themselves, or they could take in a wider picture.

One resident, Beatrice Cross, chose to relinquish her official duties as a police detective, and from a mobile lab on a hill she coordinated with officials around the town. While one of the council members was still missing, it was left to those remaining to make a decision. Pushed by the detective, they called in the army, who'd been on standby since the weather rumbled over this stricken land. The councillors could only hope things wouldn't be as bad as the previous flood.

Another detective, a pair, Alicia Friend and Malcolm Knowles, didn't know about the plans for the town. They were outsiders, and saw the incoming rain, the increased flow in the streets and all around, more as an inconvenience to their jobs than as a threat to homes or livelihoods. They saw the sweeping away of evidence, of stalled investigations.

To avoid that scenario they sped to the outskirts, to a house full of elderly people, one of whom was too ill to ever stand trial, but who seemed to be yearning to speak. To reveal things. Alicia's plan was to explain the legal implications—that he would never see jail, even if he confessed in full.

However, the property in which this man lived, Daisyville Retirement Home, was included in the town's plan. When Alicia and Malcolm arrived, a small army unit was already here, evacuating the residents, taking them to a temporary barracks where volunteers and professionals were already preparing meals, beds, and ablution facilities. Elderly people were strapped to gurneys and wheelchairs, rushed through the downpour, and secured in two covered trucks.

When the female detective, Alicia, spotted a nurse she knew amid the to-and-fro of the operation, she asked for time with Remington Duval. The nurse grew angry, gesticulating to the activity all around. When Alicia suggested it might be overkill, another official from the home explained that the basement had already started to flood. Last time, it got to waist deep. If it filled and made its way into the home, many of the people who lived here might fall ill with the damp, and pass away months or even years too early.

Surrounding this picturesque location, hills rose, and the road up which Alicia and Malcolm drove was indeed steep, and wound higher than the Daisyville Retirement Home. Up here, the land was almost flat, angled shallowly away from the road itself. Owned by a husband and wife, sheep still roamed upon it because it kept the land viable, made it seem useful. Atop limestone deposits, though, it was good for little except grazing, or staring down at a large house being evacuated by the army. It held moisture well, until the rain became a downpour.

Over in the suburb of Lainworth, the rain fell just as heavily, but without the ferocious runoff of the main bulk of Moleford. Not yet.

Soon, though.

A religious leader, a respected figure in the community named Tariq Bashir, reminded people of this at a public meeting. There were too many to fit inside the mosque, having been called here via social media to hear why they should leave their homes. He emphasised the need for personal vigilance, to ensure no one moved around alone, for there was still a killer at large. Help one another, he urged. All knew the worst affected; people should go to them first, then move on to their own properties. The mosque had not flooded the last time, so they would offer shelter to those in need. *All* those in need.

But Lainworth was not the only place threatened. Tariq Bashir suggested people move on, seek out others who could do with an extra pair of hands, extra muscle.

Returning to Moleford Bridge, thinking they could get ahead of the worsening weather and maybe, just maybe, cram in a little more information, Alicia and Malcolm found many of the men and women they deemed "scum" rallying around. This group, the Yorkshire Vanguard, had split into teams of four. They aided in the sandbagging of elderly and disabled persons' homes, while relatives and other workers took the residents to safety. With the waterway already less than a foot from breaking its banks, the Vanguard helped shore up the businesses nearest the river; they hoped to at least *divert* the overflow.

The Vanguard had come under much criticism throughout its existence, but today the members felt true pride. And its leadership, those officially in charge and those who led by example—people like Bertie Bradshaw—hoped folk would see this and soften their harsh opinions. Unlikely. But that wasn't why Bertie insisted the group get out there and be seen; protecting their community was always the objective. And this counted.

As he shifted his own sandbags and barked orders at Sean and Russel, he saw the two detectives approaching him. His heart sank. Even amid this chaos, where more important things needed tending to, there would be no reprieve from their accusations.

Malcolm Knowles hated the rain. His police-issue raincoat was great, but it didn't cover his legs, which were soaked within seconds of him and Alicia hopping out of the car and bounding over toward what appeared to be the coordination point for the arseholes pretending to give a shit about other people. He did not relish spending another moment in their presence. Yet he would never back away from this, never let anyone see how much their blind hatred, and the way it was growing across his country, frightened him.

Rain patted on their hoods, meaning they all had to raise their voices some.

"Hi, Bertie!" Alicia chirped as they came within a few feet.

The tone of Alicia's greeting suggested the greeting of a

nephew she hadn't seen since Christmas. Knowles understood it was her way of disarming people, of making them underestimate her, but it stung to see her being so nice to a man like Bertie Bradshaw.

"We're busy." Bertie swept an arm toward the line of sandbags growing out of the road like a countryside stone wall. The Vanguard guys hefted the "bricks" out of a van, passing them down a short chain to the barrier. "It'll be enough to see off a rise spilling onto the street, but doubt it'll hold back a surge. If you're here to help, great. If not, it can wait. We aren't going anywhere."

"Go for it, Malcolm," Alicia said.

Because she'd cast a glance at a couple of CCTV masts, Knowles twigged to her point: two cops doing nothing while racists pitched in to help the community. As he joined the short line of men receiving sandbags, he wondered if this image might do more harm: a black cop joining forces with white supremacists.

Would it serve him well, or badly?

He pulled his peaked hood farther over his head, and didn't look up as he received the first heavy sack.

"You know more than you let on," Alicia said.

"I really don't," Bertie answered.

"You knew James Grantham and Remington Duval. You knew Pryor senior, and the Grantham brother. You were part of these guys' activities. You'd have been a prime candidate for brainwashing."

Knowles paused and twisted momentarily, watching as Bertie shook his head—not in denial, more as if he couldn't fathom where this silly girl got her ideas.

"But I think you want to help us, Bertie," Alicia went on. "I think you want us to know who's taken up this mantle of executioner."

She was using big, bold words, like a speech from a historical or fantasy novel. Drawing out the megalomaniac in Bertie.

They'd planned it on the way over, and Alicia had asked Knowles not to interfere.

To watch. To observe. To *learn*.

Mentoring him, as she had the last time they'd worked together.

"What's it to be, Bertie? You were the passive follower, the innocent kid, corrupted by these guys who everyone feared. Only to a boy it'd have looked like respect—"

"*Oh, for crying out loud!*" The shout, the loss of temper from Bertie, hollered over the rain battering the waterproofs.

Alicia took a step back. Knowles rose to his full height and the four apes alongside him froze, bags in hand, unsure if they were needed. The biggest one, the fat guy—Russel Davy, Knowles remembered—placed his soggy brick in the right spot and gave the exchange his attention.

Bertie's hands found his hips, head bowed. "You really aren't going to let it lie, are you?"

"We can't," Knowles said.

Russel now joined in, his feet still planted in place. "Just piss off. At least we're *doing* something."

Unclear whether the idiot meant doing something about today's rain or about the country which they all called home, Knowles said, "Everything points at you. At people *like* you. The profiles of the victims, the need for action, the local knowledge. It might not be Remy Duval, or you, but there are too many things to be coincidences. So screw it if you feel like victims. You made victims of everyone who doesn't fit your vision of being British enough, so screw you too. Stop being such a bloody snowflake and give us something that'll *make* us piss off somewhere else."

The rainfall seemed to increase in volume. On the street, on the sandbags, on the hood above Knowles's brow. It dripped from the stiff peak and a gust blew a drop onto his chin.

"Okay," Bertie said, loud enough for all to hear. "Russel, take over. I'll be fifteen minutes with these fine defenders of the innocent."

Bertie travelled in the back of Alicia's car. Knowles worried they'd get stuck but Alicia said all she was concerned about was how these short journeys up and down the hilly town were playing havoc with her average miles per gallon.

"Silly, really," she said. "The guy who sold me the hybrid said I'd become obsessed with MPG, but I didn't believe him."

"I was the same way," Bertie said.

Knowles half-turned to him. "*You* have a hybrid car?"

"Outlander." Bertie gave a wry smile and stared out the window. "What, you think racist thugs don't care about the environment?"

He directed them to a narrow two-bed townhouse halfway up a hill leading to the church where Lucy Viera plied her trade.

There was another name that kept cropping up. Although she possessed an exotic surname, she had no accent, their background check showed she held a British passport, and her skin was technically Caucasian, tanned just a shade more than the average Vanguard member. Could she have been involved? She certainly had the knowledge.

Inside Bertie's townhouse, Knowles asked why Bertie didn't live in the flat over the Strangers' Club.

"I do, usually," Bertie said. "But I own this too. Me mam's."

*Me mam's.*

An infantile phrase coming from a seventy-something guy with a granite face and the ropy muscles of a life spent working physical jobs. But very northern-England. Knowles hadn't heard someone's mother referred to as "mam" for years, and that was usually in jest.

The house was tight, cramped, and boasted only the most basic of facilities: white goods such as a washing machine in the box kitchen with a bathroom to one end. The lounge had a hard-looking couch, two walnut bookcases against walls, and a cathode-ray TV—the sort of heavy cuboid Knowles had watched as a child. Also in this room were stacks of plastic and cardboard boxes, and some bulkier items that plainly didn't belong in a lounge: a bedside table, a woman's bicycle with a basket and a dry, semi-rusted chain, and another bookshelf—this one white MDF, half-empty, and positioned in the middle of the floor.

"Stuff from the cellar." Bertie entered and shimmied between the white bookcase and bike to a stack of seven boxes, three on top of four. He removed one and picked up another from the bottom row. "I shifted it up here after the club flooded. Just in case."

"You don't rent it out?" Knowles asked. "Didn't want to sell?"

Bertie placed the box on the couch and kept his eye on it, as if something might break out any moment. "She only died last year. Ninety-six."

Knowles made a mental calculation. If Bertie was in his seventies, that made his mother—

"A young mum," Alicia said.

"Yep."

"Alone?"

"Yes." Bertie produced a bunch of keys and flicked out a half-inch blade from a keyring.

"Tough back then," Knowles said.

"Not that tough." Bertie cut through the packing tape, although much of it fell away, dried out through age. He opened the flap. Photograph albums. "We lived in a place full of tolerant, nice people. A real sense of community." He rummaged, angling aside certain albums, plainly looking for something specific. "The Bible-bashers and sanctimonious upper-class twits gave us a bit of grief, a lot of sideways stink-eyes, but where we lived most of the time, it was... nice."

He pulled out a thick tome with a flowery hardback cover.

The white parts had yellowed and the colours faded, but as he opened the leaf it was obvious the photos within were well cared for.

"If the lads saw these, I'd never live it down." Bertie tapped one brittle, yellowed photograph three pages in.

A blonde woman in a flouncy dress wore a tiara made of flowers. In her early twenties, she gave a simpering gaze toward the photographer. Behind her, more people frolicked in a wooded area, all dressed in hemp or adorned in flowers or leaves, most with both.

*Hippies.*

"Me mam." Bertie used the phrase without humour or irony. It really was how he referred to her. "Doreen Bradshaw."

"Your father?" Knowles said.

"Dunno." Bertie shrugged, staring at the photo. "She always deflected that. Said it didn't matter. Never even hinted who it might be. Here."

Knowles noted the man handed the photo to Alicia, not him. Significant? Or just seniority coming into play?

Alicia turned another couple of pages. More photos from what looked like the same event, whatever it was. She paused on one snap of Doreen with a young boy, a mop-haired kid of around eight, grinning with a couple of teeth missing.

"You?" Alicia asked.

"Yeah," Bertie replied with a toneless detachment.

Later, the boy grew into a teenager, the woman still happy and smiley.

"No cameraphones, of course," Bertie said. "Film was expensive, so you saved photos for things you wanted to remember. No snapping pics of your dinner. So we're always happy on these."

"You weren't always?" Knowles asked.

"Of course not. We were a single-parent family in the sixties. Maybe early seventies here. She bought into the hippie stuff early on, happy when all these artists started showing up, actively promoting pleasure without judgement. Summer of love and all that. I was a teenager then."

"And you didn't go in for it?" Alicia asked. "Teen rebellion?"

"Oh, I loved it. I saw me mam on protests all over. *She* was the rebel. When I was old enough, we rebelled together. Promoting peace and demanding our government send the war-mongering Americans home from Menworth Hill. I wondered how anyone could be so brave. She faced down a police officer once. He was in full riot gear with pepper spray aimed right at her. She held out her arms like she was expecting a warm shower. Some people got a bit rowdy then, and the cop got trigger happy, and me mam got a faceful of pain."

Rain lashed the window. All three stared at a twenty-some-thing-year-old Bertie in a tie-dyed tee-shirt.

"She was my hero." Bertie gave a long laugh as he wiped his eyes.

"What happened?" Knowles asked. "Why..." He didn't know how to phrase *why are you now a racist prick?* politely.

Bertie coughed the memories away. "Mam got beaten up by a black immigrant when she brought him home from some party, but changed her mind and refused to sleep with him. Only avoided getting raped because it was here, in our house. I was twenty-four, still a happy hippie, but I woke up and came down-stairs, and seeing this monster hurting me mam... I lost it. Kicked the shit out of him. Mam didn't report it, and begged me to keep it quiet. Said people would blame his skin colour, not the nasty person inside. I denied it for years, of course. Let me mam's attitude about all people being good to brainwash me into thinking the same. I obeyed because I didn't think she'd lie to me. I didn't think she could be so naive. But in the end, the crime-wave of blacks and Irish, the dirty Indians and Pakistanis..." He gave the sort of shrug that suggested his explanation was final. "By the time I was in my thirties, I'd moved out, got away from her influence, and made up my own mind. Figured my happy youth was lost, and Britain could never be like that again, not when the face of it kept getting darker."

Bertie looked at Knowles.

"No offence meant," he said. "I know it's not all blacks, but… everywhere black folk go, crime follows. Everywhere Muslims congregate, hatred spews out of them. Making their women dress in sacks, forcing them to marry cousins, slaughtering animals in the most painful way—"

"Did your *mam* find out about your change of heart?" Alicia asked.

Bertie bowed his head. "She didn't speak to me for the last forty years of her life. She had no son. But when she died, I found all these." He closed the album and rested a hand on the back cover. "She kept all of them."

Alicia said nothing. A glance at Knowles.

"You didn't quit the Vanguard leadership because of the trouble," Knowles said. "That was a coincidence. You quit when you knew your mother was dying."

Bertie nodded. "I told her I quit the whole thing, opened a bar. And I haven't officially been a member since then."

"But your hate sticks with you."

"It's not hate." Bertie squeezed his eyes shut tight, and thin lines of tears traced down his cheeks. "It's love. Love of what I had, of my country. I just wanted the happiness back. The joy. It was all snatched away. By the government. By immigrants. By do-gooders wishing we could all live together like a big happy tribe. But reality comes along and smacks that in the teeth. Truth is, we can't get it back. We can just slow the creep for future generations. We're helpless to stop it."

Alicia reached out a hand, but withdrew it. The instinct to give comfort was so strong, but knowing who this man was, what he believed in the core of his being, stopped her short.

"Who I was doesn't matter," Bertie said. "All that matters is what I am now."

Alicia turned slowly away. Halted near the bookcase. "What's this?"

Bertie snapped out of his reverie and replied, "Oh, my books from the club. I had a few lying around, some duplicate copies, so I moved them here."

Alicia plucked one from the shelf, something about steam trains. Turned to the first page. "It's a library book."

"Oh yeah." Bertie received Alicia of it and placed it back. "I've been meaning to return them for years. Lauren and the guy, what's his name? Costas? They must have a list of missing books a mile long."

Alicia crouched before the shelves. "Are these all library books?"

"Some. Look, it was a time when they were young. The lads in the Vanguard. Russel started it, bringing gifts like a cat dropping off a bird at the bottom of the bed. They shoplifted a bit from Waterstones and Borders back when that was around, but the library was easier. Became a bit of a running joke. Birthdays, Christmas, that kind of thing. Bunch of them'd bring me a new book, the more obscure the better. Even Glenn joined in a few times, but he obviously thought it was stupid."

Knowles had been scanning the titles since Alicia pointed them out. He selected one, a thin volume with a shoddy cover in library plastic backing. "Isn't this the vicar?"

The book was titled *The Priest on the Hill: A History*, by Lucy Viera. The 1870s murders, with sketches laid out in brutal detail.

"Yeah, that was one of Glenn's," Bertie said. "Brought it to the club when he first got in with Russel and Sean, before he met Scarlett. It's about some murders, like... oh, Christ. I forgot all about it. Just local myths. But... wait a minute. You don't think—"

Alicia held up a finger to cut him off. "Hush please. Processing here."

Sure enough, Alicia had reverted to a look of pure concentration. Her brain practically hummed, but the lashes of rain outside, its ferocity increasing, drowned out any cogs turning.

"Where is Glenn?" Alicia asked.

"I don't know," Bertie replied. "Didn't show up after I sent out the round robin text message."

"But everyone else did?" Knowles said.

"Yeah. Glenn's probably off figuring out how to flog YV pin badges to people trying to dry out their houses. Maybe he thinks Facebook and Twitter will stop the water rising."

"Have you seen Lucy?" Alicia asked.

"The vicar? No, why should I?"

"Was she part of the movement in the olden days? Either your anti-immigration stuff or the hippies? Anything?"

"I don't remember her, no."

Alicia snapped her fingers. "Abhu Noon, missing. Glenn, a no-show. Scarlett, presumably with Glenn? Lucy Viera, present at every event we've witnessed to date, but nowhere to be found right now."

"Periodically inserting herself into the investigation," Knowles said. "She was here in the seventies, but before Bertie involved himself in the Nazi business."

"We're not Nazis," Bertie said.

Knowles ignored him, his own mind twisting and turning in an approximation of a storm. "Intimate knowledge of the subject, plus a drive to change the world one step at a time. Hearts and minds."

"My brain is burning," Alicia said. "Are you in the same place as me?"

"That Glenn could have found out about a former, reformed member of the Vanguard and persuaded her back to his cause?"

"That she is old enough to be part of this the first time around? In the 1970s, giving them the ideas for disposal, for humiliating their victims more than just killing them?"

"Like Bertie said before," Knowles added, recalling the line verbatim. "*If they didn't have birds egging 'em on, no way they'd have the balls to come home at night with bruised knuckles or missing teeth.*"

"Charismatic young buck. Someone to pass the mantle to. He comes along with a proposal to someone living a lie. Looking for redemption behind a dog collar. But she still needs the outlet."

Knowles grinned. "I think we're in the same place."

"Let's go see the vicar."

# CHAPTER FORTY

AFTER DROPPING Bertie back on the high street, now an inch deep in running water, Alicia drove at speed to the church of St. Mary's, built over a century ago, too high and too sturdy to fall victim to such flooding. The hotel Alicia booked was also high up, but on a different ridge line. Hopefully, she'd have somewhere to stay tonight, or Maisie Jackson and her imaginary children might be putting up a houseguest after all.

The church was locked up tight, and a handful of people milled around outside under umbrellas, many carrying bags and waterproof cases. Alicia expected the building to be open, ready to take in people who might suffer in this weather. She asked the first person she found, a man in his sixties, what was happening.

The man said, "Lucy isn't here. It's odd, and really quite disappointing. She would normally be ready and willing to go, but…" He shrugged, barely disguising his annoyance.

"You think she'll show?" Alicia asked, a hot swell in her gut.

"We've tried her mobile, and the phone in the vicarage just rings out. Giving her another ten minutes then we'll head to All Saints, see if they're better organised."

Knowles checked around the corner to the residence as the man indicated. "Is that where she lives, sir?"

"Yes. But she's not in."

Alicia marched toward the house, Knowles splashing along the path beside her.

"What are we doing?" he asked.

"Breaking in."

"We can't. We don't have—"

Alicia's sweet smile popped into being. "A member of the public informed us a missing person usually opens up for serious events. Said missing person is not answering her mobile phone. Hasn't informed anyone of her whereabouts. The landline rings out. Is that out of character enough to qualify as 'potentially in danger'?"

"Understood." Knowles sped up, only a couple of feet ahead, but it was enough. He launched a kick at the door, but it held tight. "Ow."

"Window," Alicia said. "Are you armed?"

From under his jacket, Knowles produced a telescopic baton and flicked it open, the heavy metal end extended. He swung it at the window in the middle of the door. It shattered and he cleared the frame of its glass teeth. Any burglar knows that people often keep their spare keys near the door, but as Knowles fished around inside, Lucy clearly wasn't one of those people.

"Lucy?" Knowles called through. "Lucy, it's the police. If you're in there, open up!"

"You know you already broke the window, right?"

He pulled back and tried to kick again. This time it shifted. A minor splintering of wood.

"I got the Yale lock off," Knowles said. "Just the big mortice one to go." He kicked again. Another shift of wood.

The heat Alicia felt earlier curdled into a nervous soup, expecting either a dead body or the place empty. They were either completely wrong about Lucy or bang on the money. Whichever way it panned out, they wouldn't get to press Lucy on her former involvement with the Vanguard, and more specifically with James Grantham and the like.

Was she directly involved or a willing patsy? Or just a cheerleader? An alibi in waiting? Or a witness who knew too much?

Knowles's next boot to the door flung it open and he stalked in first, baton readied to strike. He called to identify them as police once again, then shouted a warning for anyone inside to make themselves known. His third shout highlighted his willingness to use force to defend himself if necessary.

No reply.

Alicia found that three of the people from out front—the man she had spoken with before, and two women accompanying him—had ventured here to investigate the commotion. She flashed her ID through the rain and told them loudly, "We don't know what's happened to Lucy. Might be nothing, but we have to investigate. Please wait outside. If there is evidence of foul play, we'll need to treat this as a crime scene."

licia noted the panic and worry in their faces. It was a little cruel, but true. They might also find something else. Something she and Knowles needed to analyse in private.

They swept the small apartment. Nothing out of place. Nothing to suggest a struggle.

But out on her dining table, pages of old writing had been scattered. No, not scattered; *arranged*. Modern books, cracked and aged ledgers, loose-leafs of varying ages, the older ones inside plastic sleeves.

Knowles circled the table. "What is this?"

"Sorted in terms of contemporary accounts and historical." When Alicia saw that he didn't understand, she pointed out the system. "Items from the *time* of the Priest on the Hill killings, mostly pages from the journal of the man himself, I think." She meant the mottled pages laminated in clear plastic. "At least, they match the scans Maisie Jackson sent me. But she said Lucy only had a couple. There's lots more here." Alicia lost herself for a moment.

*One of them lied. But was it Maisie or Lucy?*

"Then papers written in the years after Father Pickersgill was exposed and executed." Ledgers and reprints in bindings similar to library books. "Newer versions of the story, from the twenties, the thirties." She moved the papers and ledgers with a pen rather than her hands, having arrived without gloves like an amateur.

Poking at the oldest section, she sifted the pages of a hand-written journal, up to twenty documents. Near the bottom was a larger parchment. Something different to the paper used for journalling. Thicker. No plastic sleeve, but it lay on a cotton sheet.

"Is that animal hide?" Knowles asked.

"Possibly." Alicia risked touching it with the back of her finger, feeling its leathery surface. "Definitely something like that." She lifted the item with the pen but it was browned and too old to identify with any certainty. "I've seen this sort of thing before. Treated and hardened. Usually more flexible."

Knowles had dug out a pair of gloves and donned them, picking up the thick parchment at the edges to avoid smudging any incriminating prints. Tilted it to the light. Stared across the surface. "It's like a schematic. Plans to something."

Alicia got close, spied the indentation and recognised the layout. "It's the church I saw yesterday. Where Lucy was hanging out. Above the big cavern with the bodies."

"But why put it on a piece of leather?" Knowles asked.

"Place it on the table and I'll tell you something that'll blow your mind."

Knowles gave her a quizzical frown, and he held it at a different angle. "Why on the table?"

"Because people tend to freak out when they find out they're holding human skin."

Knowles's mouth turned down and his eyes widened. He positioned to do what Alicia feared.

"Gently, please," she said. "Don't toss it away. It's no more toxic than it was a second ago."

As Knowles placed it back on the desk, Alicia rummaged through what looked like the most up to date jottings and sketches, settling on a pencil drawing of the church. It resembled the near-illegible lines on the skin parchment, copied from the original.

"If she has human skin in her home—"

"She may not have known it was human," Alicia said.

"How could she not?"

"*You* didn't."

Knowles reassessed. Changed tack. "Do you think Maisie knew? About the additional evidence here?"

"I couldn't say." Alicia allowed the idea to percolate, processing it objectively. "I doubt it, though. Would she risk us discovering this on our own if she wanted to be dishonest for whatever reason?"

"You said she's crazy."

"I'm not sure she is."

"She chats to dead children."

Alicia arranged four pencil drawings beside one another, different angles, different amounts of detail, each version improving on the last. All focussed on the end wall where Lucy was praying when Alicia had found her. Where Lucy had led her away from, to show her the sealed up hole down which Pickersgill supposedly threw the body parts.

"But Maisie's not delusional about it," Alicia said, half explaining, half concentrating on what she was seeing. "She knows they're not real, but wants to continue the fantasy."

"Yeah, that's totally sane." Knowles sounded as distracted as Alicia felt, speaking about Maisie Jackson but curious at linking the sketches to the skin.

"Whoever drew this—let's assume Lucy Viera for now—has explored that plan." Alicia referenced the skin again. "She's been up at the ruin of that church a while, and—" The reason two of the drawings looked different was that the wall was wider on one of them. "No way."

Alicia rummaged in her bag and withdrew the copy of Lucy's book on the Priest on the Hill, which Bertie had willingly signed over. It wasn't evidence as such, so no need to handle with care, avoiding prints. She flipped through the hundred-or-so pages to locate the section on theories. She'd memorised the contents page, and one heading sprang out at her.

More specifically, the subheading.

"Lucy left a section on myths and theories to the end." Alicia checked out the one that intrigued her. She read briefly, grinning at the very rough diagram on the next page, a primitive version of the detailed papers on the table. "One states the 'passage to hell' that was sealed by the Catholic Church was not the main entrance to Pickersgill's underworld. He had a crude room secretly built, accessible only if you triggered the mechanism correctly."

Knowles looked sceptical. "Are you serious?"

"It's not me who has to be serious. It's Lucy. And I think she absolutely believes it." Alicia tapped the page. "Lucy was looking for a secret room. And I'm going to bet she found it."

"I take it we're going out in the rain again."

"Call for backup, Malcolm. And dig out your wellies. This is gonna be rough."

# CHAPTER FORTY-ONE

WHILE DI CROSS advised Alicia against her proposed exploration, she was busy with the flooding operation, so didn't have much time to argue, emphasising only for Alicia to take no unnecessary risks. The lives of herself and the detectives under her were priority. Plus, the only backup to be spared was the one detective who'd been dismissed for the day and was heading out the door, returning to Leeds as ordered by his DCI.

Alicia found it odd that Detective Sergeant Ball didn't moan or bitch at being asked to accompany her and Knowles into the wild—indeed, he seemed positively giddy at delivering the news that forecasters now expected more rain to fall in twenty-four hours than had soaked the region earlier this month over a five-day period. Flash floods were expected, and the water level could rise even higher.

"Thunder and lightning too!" Ball said.

They met on the road closest to the Church on the Hill, which now trailed twin streams, one down each edge. Alicia checked the two men over, ensuring proper footwear and that the coats and over-trousers were waterproof. Wearing her detective inspector role seriously, she insisted on stab vests all round, along with pepper spray and truncheons. If she'd had time, she might have authorised firearms use, but they'd have had to trail all the way to Halifax. They had no evidence that anything but blades had been employed to date, so she expected the spray, vests, and batons should suffice.

"If it's too dangerous, we back off," Alicia said as they set out on the steepest path to the ruin. "Besides, aren't the army nearby?"

"Pretty sure they're not allowed to fire on civilians," Ball said. "Even psycho killers."

The three tramped over the path. Its edges were not secure, crumbling slightly whenever they got too close, but held together by the rocky undersoil. As they went on, the sky darkened, the rain grew heavier, and lightning flashed beyond the hills. Thunder rumbled seconds later.

"Ooh, this is going to be a good one," Ball said.

"Good?" Knowles said.

"Yeah, don't you just love this stuff?" Ball held his arms out toward the lightning flash. "The majesty of Mother Nature!"

Alicia would never have guessed those words would emerge from DS Ball, not if you'd given her a thousand guesses. She said, "Some people are just weird."

By the time they crested the peak and the church ruins came into view, all three were dripping wet, coats and trousers holding up well, while water streamed down their faces. Alicia checked that the sketch she had sealed in a clear evidence bag was still secure in her pocket, and led the way.

The ground was damper up here on the flatter land and the wind was more severe. Puddles sucked at Alicia's boots halfway up her shin, and the boys fared about the same. It was just standing water; the mud didn't extend into holes, so they were able to progress. They soon lost track of the path, though, arrowing directly for their destination.

Lightning flashed again, behind them, elongating their

shadows and illuminating the church ahead. Another rumble chased close behind.

When they reached the building, the wind was dying, but still rain poured.

Alicia checked the diagram and pointed. "There!"

All three headed for the wall and huddled around the paper. Alicia struggled to clear the drops from the plastic surface, but squinted through. "Can you see that?"

Knowles abandoned the paper and Alicia started to regret coming out here. But a man was missing, presumed dead, and they had their first real suspect to hand.

Lightning again. Double flash. Knowles lit up like a statue as he stared at the wall. "Anyone got a torch?"

Alicia and Ball carried torches, not yet necessary outdoors, but the clouds now blotted out the sun so much it was like twilight.

"The book talked about a brick that acts as a switch," Alicia said. "You see anything?"

"Not a thing," Knowles answered bluntly. "Hence, 'anyone got a torch?'"

"No one likes a defeatist," Ball said.

"Especially a cocky one," Alicia added pressing herself against the brickwork, searching out lines, imperfections. "Oh, that's neat."

Ball and Knowles simultaneously wiped hands over their faces and said, "What?"

Alicia hopped over to the rock, one she was sure hadn't been here the day before. "How tall is Lucy?"

Knowles hovered a hand over Alicia's head, then added four or five inches. "About there."

"Okay, keep that in mind." She got onto the rock and reached up. "Now add that much to my fingers."

Knowles stood up on the rock next to Alicia and added the four inches, holding his fingers on a brick.

"Around there," Alicia said. "Start pressing."

Lightning. Thunder.

Ball grinned. "It's almost on top of us."

"Just get us inside," Alicia said.

"Right you are, guv."

The two men gave each brick in the radius indicated a good shove, to no avail.

"Harder," Alicia said. "It's very old. And it'll need to be stiff so people don't stumble on it accidentally."

Ball took out his baton and Knowles followed suit. Keeping them housed in the hilts, they took turns giving the bricks a firm thump. Knowles got through three, and Ball two, before Ball's third elicited a hollow noise.

It was hard to be sure beneath the sound of the downpour, but when he hit it again, it was clear: the brick had moved.

The two men pushed with their batons, progressing another inch, until the rectangle halted and a click sounded. Then a clunk from nearby.

Nothing else happened.

Alicia put her hands on her hips, splashing water from her elbows. "Is anyone else disappointed the wall didn't spring open to reveal a huge demon statue blowing fire out of its nose?"

"Is that what you expected to find?" Knowles asked.

"No, but it'd have been cool. So what *did* we open?"

Much searching followed. It took Ball over a minute to trip over a dislodged paving slab. He crouched, listened.

"Drainage," he said. "The rain is falling through here."

Alicia attempted to get her fingers in, but she couldn't. With Knowles coming along to help, Ball edged her politely out of the way. He said, "Men's work."

"Remind me to write you up a report on sexist commentary," Alicia said.

"If you want to do this instead of me…" Ball half-stood from his lifting crouch.

"It's okay, sergeant, I'll overlook it this time."

The pair shifted the slab and they peered inside, down what genuinely resembled a drain, steel rungs embedded in the stone tube dropping ten feet.

"Okay, *now* we need a torch," Ball said.

"I don't think so." Alicia sat on her bum, feeling the wetness through her waterproof trousers. "I'm going down."

"Are you crazy?" Knowles said. "You don't have any idea what's in there."

"There's nothing down there. Everything was locked up tight. They reset the mechanism. The only thing likely to be down here is a kidnapped or dead councillor. And whatever the flickering light is."

The two men leaned in, finding the glow Alicia spotted beyond the hole.

"Okay," Ball said. "Off you go."

Alicia set off, carefully testing each metal bracket before adding her weight to it.

What if she was wrong? About the place being abandoned? What if there was more than one way in? Or if the mechanics could be operated from a second point, allowing egress if someone were trapped?

Just above the point where her feet would be visible to anyone waiting, she halted.

Anyone hiding here would know someone opened the hatch, and would likely be waiting. She couldn't risk sneaking out slowly.

Above her, the rain slowed, blocked somewhat by Knowles who had entered the pipe. He descended faster than she had, and she didn't want call out, alerting the person she imagined waiting for her.

Instead, she let go with one hand, took out her baton, focused on how she'd recently learned to kick someone really hard, and dropped.

The element of surprise was all she had going for her.

That, and almost six feet of youthful copper bringing up the rear.

*Yeah, let's do it.*

Alicia flicked out her baton to its full length, positioned her torch in the same hand, and darted forward, ready to dazzle anyone lying in wait.

Detective Sergeant Ball suddenly whipped his head around, then did a full turn. Déjà vu closed in from all sides, although this wasn't quite the same as last time.

He didn't think this serial killer, should he sneak up on a police officer, would possess a code of ethics that forbade killing cops. Unlike Richard Hague, who had beat Ball unconscious while he checked out a property in search of the missing Alicia Friend.

The other thing that was different here was Alicia descending voluntarily into a deep place. And it wasn't freezing bloody cold. It was a summer storm, the kind that always thrilled him for some reason, even when out in the middle of it.

Lightning illuminated the land again, confirming that Ball was, indeed, still alone.

There'd be no clunk on the back of the head this time. No weeks off work. No months of counselling in an attempt to stave off the constant fear that haunted him whenever he acted as backup for a colleague.

Not that he'd ever admit to the latter.

Still, he had it under control. It was just the circumstances that kept it on the periphery of his consciousness: Alicia, in the dark lair of a potential killer; Ball, up top, trying to keep her safe.

"You need me down there?" he called into the hole.

"No," Alicia replied sounding breathless.

"We need to call this in," Knowles added.

And just like that, DS Ball wished he was down in that hole with them.

Alicia was still frozen, seconds after her full frontal assault on... nothing. Well, no *one*. Even the torch wasn't needed. She and Knowles took it in: the cavern glowed with flame, old-style torches like she'd seen in a dozen movies about knights and swashbucklers roaming castles and ancient homes. In the middle rose a large block, and the comparison that sprang to mind— again, from what she'd seen in movies—was a sacrificial altar.

She couldn't yet make out if the smears upon it were blood or something else, but she expected them to be blood.

They had found the true church of the Priest on the Hill.

Alicia explored deeper. "We definitely need to call this in."

Knowles gripped her sleeve to halt her. "Alicia, someone left these on."

"Someone left these on for us to *find*."

"Or we interrupted them and they're hiding right now."

Alicia hefted her baton. "There's that. But there might also be someone in danger."

"Abhu Noon."

"Or Lucy Viera."

"Don't we think she's in on it?"

Alicia jiggled her arm so Knowles let go. She moved forward. "I think she was keeping it to herself because she wanted to see Father Pickersgill's secrets before anyone else. She'd been working on it for years and the new bodies meant someone might beat her to it. Plus, the church covered it up once..."

"She wants to record it."

Alicia pressed on, Knowles beside her, until she reached the altar—which did indeed appear stained with blood, a deep purple-brown in the firelight.

"Fresh." She noted the glisten of moisture upon the splashes and smears.

"This is a natural cave."

"And its shape." Again, Alicia made a full rotation, picturing how this cavern might look from above. "It's a crucifix."

"Made naturally?"

"Approximate shapes do happen. If an already deranged priest found this, carved out of the land by God Himself, how do you think he'd react?"

"It'd be a sign." Knowles bobbed his head in agreement. "Confirmation that God approved of the man's work."

"And granted him access to the underworld."

A mound stood at the head of the crucifix shape, round with a hole at the top, like a well.

"I'm betting this falls into the cave we found," Alicia said.

"Shit."

Alicia wasn't used to hearing Knowles swear, so she turned to him straight away, and saw what had given him cause for such language.

The thing she saw was Lucy's head. Lying in a nook, or the start of a passage, just off this top end of the cavern. Then as Alicia's eyes adjusted to the dark of the unlit corridor, Lucy's body became apparent.

Her disconnected legs lay where her arms should have been, arms in place of the legs. Her head had rolled out of position.

They were too late.

The vicar's passion for this story had killed her.

"The limbs are whole." Alicia pushed down the horrific image, forcing herself to be clinical. No time for introspection. "Not cut in two pieces. No real care taken with the arrangement. They were in a hurry. Meaning?"

Knowles stared, but Alicia could tell the younger man's mind was working. "Lucy wasn't an intended victim. She stumbled across this place and interrupted them." He lowered his head. "We're not going to find Abhu Noon, are we?"

## CHAPTER FORTY-TWO

SOME SAY the soul leaves the body upon death. Others believe the very concept of a soul demonstrates man's hubris, that the notion humans are somehow special in the circle of life is an act of denial or supreme ego.

How could these humans, these creatures of flesh and bone, be special? Why would God wait so long to imbue one of His creations with a soul?

After all, even the earliest human ancestors existed a mere eyeblink ago when compared to the limestone and soil of the land of Yorkshire—dubbed "God's Own Country" by the humans who inhabited it. But *man* invented *God,* not the other way around.

Or did he?

Perhaps humans *are* special. Their influence on the landscape overwhelms that of all other animals combined, paling only in the face of nature's most powerful wrath; volcanoes, earthquakes, tsunamis.

Could it be that something ethereal exists within all humans? Some spirit able to linger over the flesh when the heart stops beating, when the brain no longer fires? If such a thing as the human soul exists, the trauma of being ripped violently from its earthly vessel might cause it to linger, to explore, attempting to make sense of death.

If this were true of humans, then surely Abhu Noon's soul looked down aghast at the man's corpse floating through freshly unblocked caverns. Lashed to a raft constructed from a wooden door, the body was not cut up like the other victims enveloped in the land in recent times—recent from the *land's* perspective, of course. The route Abhu now embarked upon was an underground river, one known by many inhabitants, etched on maps and explored for sport.

But not today.

Today, it was too dangerous, and as its volume increased, it carried Abhu along its length, and out of one of several exit points.

Perhaps the man's soul sat on the corpse's chest, riding it like a sailboat, bemused as to what he was doing here, why he hadn't ascended to whatever holy place in which this particular human mind believed.

Would he know anything about his bodily destination? Would he be surprised at emerging into the open after hours floating in darkness?

Not that the outside was much brighter.

The storm, dubbed "Donald" by humans, raged at the land. It *fed* the land. It struck the land with electricity, and rumbled an angry war cry.

Outside now, Abhu Noon travelled along what was usually a small river, a tributary feeding a larger body, and now crossed land assigned to a farmer called Basil Warner.

The man himself, the farmer, had other things on his mind. He owned cattle and sheep, and he knew each one by sight. As he'd gathered them to shelter them from Storm Donald, one was missing. So he had come out to the grazing land, a crime scene released by the police to fulfil nature's function, searching for the sheep in the hope he could bring her home.

His clothes failed to keep out the rain, and the wind slapped his face and every inch of exposed skin. Once the cold and wet had penetrated, it was pointless trying to keep out more. So he pressed on, toward the odd shape cascading down the river that ran across his land.

Had anyone else been around, they would have heard Basil Warner mutter a prayer that the unusually large floating object would not turn out to be his missing animal. He pressed on to intercept regardless. He might have sought to save it, or to give it a ceremonial burial, simply to prevent its decaying flesh from corrupting the waterway farther down.

But his old bones refused to transport him there in time. They ached and his muscles reacted too slowly to his brain's commands, and the object passed him by.

It was not a sheep.

It was a man, a body, slashed from neck to groin, and then across his chest just below his pectoral muscles, then splayed open and the innards scooped out. The shape might have reminded some observers of the Christian symbol, upon which a man died over two thousand years ago. Some parts of the mortal man's flesh, including a strong rope of intestinal tract, trailed behind, while the remaining cavity had filled with water.

If it existed, what would the soul make of this? Watching on as the farmer ran as fast as his ageing legs would carry him, using his phone to call others who might send help.

Soon, the raft and its cargo drifted beyond the farmer's land, joining the main body of water and barrelling onward to the human settlement called Moleford Bridge. The river did not cut directly through homes, but it did draw people's attention—those observing the rising waters, those seeking to stem its destruction of their property.

People called out.

Shouted for the police to come. But none came straight away.

The corpse, observed now by more than just a man's soul, arrived at the town's lower points, flowing past pubs, past men creating walls of sand, observed, pointed at, before finally coming to a halt at a bridge.

With the water so high, the raft was too large to pass beneath. It stuck there on its arch, inches beneath the freshly restored coat of arms, battered by the flow behind.

Surely it would break in time. But for now, it served as a barrier. A plug.

And the water rose so much faster than before, creating panic in the builders.

This town was already being evacuated by the army. And in a couple of hours, even if the earthly remains of Abhu Noon were removed, this whole settlement would soon be underwater.

# CHAPTER FORTY-THREE

THE THREE DETECTIVES couldn't stay on the scene, despite procedure—and basic human decency—demanding they seal it off, preserve the evidence, and treat Lucy's body with respect. Unfortunately, given the situation with the weather and the activities around town, Alicia decided that staying in this location served no purpose. Instead, after ascertaining the body held no additional evidence, she photographed the scene in case things changed in the interim, then retreated back up top with Knowles. She ordered the boys to replace the flagstone and ensure the brick remained hidden—direct orders so no blame would fall on them if someone needed disciplining—and they retraced their steps to the road in silence. Even the lightning and thunder elicited no comment from DS Ball.

Ball's car was an unmarked police issue and Alicia's was her own, so they stashed their stab vests in Ball's boot and flopped into his seats—Alicia and Ball in front, Knowles in the back. Dripping wet, they made noises of relief as they wiped their faces and shook themselves off like dogs. Then they pulled their phones out from under the waterproofs—an instinct after being out of touch for so long—and learned about Abhu Noon's corpse arriving in Moleford Bridge and intensifying the community's efforts to hold off the inevitable.

"I think I have a plan," Alicia said.

"All ears," Ball said.

"We wait until there's only one person left alive, and arrest them."

The guys neither laughed nor frowned. With all that had gone on, Alicia hadn't thought herself capable of a joke, no matter how lame. But a certain gallows humour was almost necessary at this stage.

She went over once more how she'd read the scene—that Lucy was killed not out of glee or to make a point, but to silence her. The dismemberment appeared half-hearted at best, and the body had been stuffed in a passage that led close to the sealed-off hole which Lucy showed Alicia yesterday. It was probably the original entrance to this place, hidden by an intentional cave-in, inaccessible in times past without explosives.

"Who do we like for it?" Ball asked.

"Bertie gets a pass for now," Alicia said.

Knowles shook his head. "You ever sit with an ex-smoker near someone sparking up?"

"Self-righteous?" Ball said. "The zeal of the newly converted."

Alicia considered it, but things didn't work that way. "You mean he's a convert from kumbaya hippie-dom? Making him more fervent in his new beliefs than people already sold on it? No. Not to this degree. You need to start with a sociopathic mind, someone who feels nothing. Bertie feels. He feels too much, just lacks critical thinking. You need someone cold, who wants to influence the people around him, the world at large."

"Glenn." Knowles spoke with confidence and a firm nod.

"That's my feeling. Think about the books, the method, the timing. We're on the right track with the cult thing. But not like an ooga-booga supernatural conspiracy. It's simpler than that."

"He knows the books, knows the history," Knowles said.

"Glamorises violence," Ball added.

Alicia agreed with all that. "*And* he has always been wearing a mask."

The patter of rain eased somewhat, the wind now more audible.

"Businessman." Knowles seemed to be speaking as much to himself as the others in the damp car. "Pretending to be appeased in the community, lowering himself to team up with an Asian councillor. To drink tea with Muslims."

"Presenting a respectable image because he knows that's what's expected."

"Classic psychopath," Ball said.

"He's probably hiding something from those he's closest to."

"That they're disposable to him?" Knowles suggested.

"The girl," Ball said.

"Or Sean, who seems to hang on his every word. But a lover makes more sense. And if it's her, she's definitely in danger now."

"We're closing in." Knowles reached for the door handle. "He needs to cut his losses."

"She knows too much about him." Alicia grabbed her own handle and pulled, cracking the door and letting a fine spray in. "They spend so much time together. In the same way I think Audrey now knows Remy was a seriously sick bastard, Audrey must have suspected something at the time too. Maybe not this, but she knew something. The girl… *Scarlett*. If it's Glenn who's leading and not one of the others, then if Scarlett isn't dead already, she will be soon."

They called DI Cross, who seemed disgruntled at being called away from spinning her dozens of plates. She started to say as much on the speakerphone, but Knowles cut her off with a firm, "Ma'am, please just listen."

Alicia admired the lad's confidence, which she'd seen grow

each day as he got more involved in the case. Far more than earlier in the summer.

And Cross did listen.

They opened with the secret room, then worked back to how they'd found it, then fast-forwarded to the theories of who was responsible. A long silence on her end indicated that either she was thinking about another plate that needed spinning or she'd been cut off.

"Ma'am?" Knowles said.

"I'm here." Another pause from Cross, this one much briefer. "Okay, so Alicia—serial killer lore one-oh-one. I can't remember all the stages. Coveting, exploring, first steps, all that, but I remember the final stage."

"The spree stage," Alicia said. "Not all killers go through this, but some, when they feel they're about to be caught and prevented from doing it anymore, they'll try to cram in as many as possible."

"Could we be entering this stage?"

"More likely cleaning house," Ball said.

"That's a deep voice you've got, Alicia." Cross's disdain was uncalled for, but no one said anything. "Alicia, is it possible?"

"It's possible." Alicia glanced at Ball. "But the detective sergeant may be correct. Abhu was part of his target group: westernised minorities who appear to assimilate but are really—in Glenn's mind—a trojan horse trying to gain our trust. Lucy wasn't, despite her surname. Her body in the altar room, and the fact that he left the lights burning, suggests speed is of the essence. He abandoned that room. No intention of returning. That's the impression I get." That damn computer, spitting out conclusions without showing its workings. But it felt solid to Alicia. "He's done with the rituals. If he has a point to make, he'll make it."

"Clearing house." Ball sounded smug, and looked smug too.

Alicia couldn't blame him, frankly. "If it's Glenn, he has other enemies. And an accomplice to dispose of."

"And if it's not Glenn," Cross said, "then Glenn is the enemy, and possibly the next victim."

All paused to ingest this possibility.

Alicia spoke first. "Bottom line is, we need to find Glenn Bishop, Scarlett Austin, and anyone this killer—Glenn or A. N. Other—thinks is against him."

"Us?" Knowles said.

"Remy, James, Bertie—they could be all be witnesses," Ball said. "Sean and Russel too. That's a lot to round up."

Alicia grew cold, a wave of fear fingering icily through her. "And Maisie Jackson." She grabbed her own phone, scrolling for Maisie's number. "She researched them. They verbally abused her because they all think of her as an enemy. A hippie chick determined to fight against their cause."

"Elevate that to serial killer levels of paranoia…" Cross didn't need to finish.

Alicia dialled.

Maisie's phone rang. Then went to voicemail.

"No." Alicia dialled again.

They all waited, and the call again went to voicemail.

Alicia checked the time. Despite the twilight feel, it was barely six. "Could be out sorting her garden."

"You really believe that?" Cross asked.

"No," Alicia said. "I'm sending DS Ball back your way. You guys secure everyone else on our list. Me and Malcolm are going to check on Maisie."

# CHAPTER FORTY-FOUR

MAISIE HAD A HEADACHE. She didn't like headaches. They occurred most often when she was struggling to remember what age Joanne and Peter were at. In those cases she'd drink some lemon-ginger tea and a glass of water, and spend time in her garden with a herbal cigarette.

Some might call her state of mind meditation, or the modern fad of "mindfulness." When she investigated what this term meant, she had chuckled to herself because it was something she'd practiced her whole life. It helped when considering a tricky proposition, either when working as a consultant, or personally with a puzzle book open. So she practiced it now, without the benefit of herbal tea—or a herbal cigarette, for that matter.

A *home-grown* herbal cigarette.

She wouldn't say no to one of those right now, but she didn't have one to hand. For that matter, she wasn't exactly sure where she was.

"Peter? Joanne?"

No reply.

She returned to her mindful state, this time probing her body as well as her surroundings. The trickle of water had been the only sound, and she gradually became aware of the cold on her back. Then the hardness of the surface. A pinch to the skin on her wrists and ankles.

"Who's there?" she asked. "And why am I tied up?"

A man's voice answered, deep, no form revealed in the dark. "You should never have poked your nose into places that don't concern you."

"Oh, do spare me the thug-life language, son. I've heard it all before. And I hate clichés."

A light flickered on. Electrical. Maisie could move her head, and found the bulb hanging from one wall: a caged light with an orange flex connected to the plug by the top of a doorframe—a portable device like a builder might use to examine a crawlspace.

A man in a hooded robe stood before it, his face in shadow.

"That's…" Maisie struggled to find a descriptive phrase suitable for the sight. "That's really dumb."

"We'll see."

The robe was right out of an old Hammer Horror flick, from before such imagery descended into pastiche. The embroidered crucifixes around the hood and hems of the sleeves were a nice touch, though.

"No, I see fine right now," Maisie said. "Someone who's watched too many movies, read too many comic books. You think this is how serial killers look? How the leader of some religious or social movement instils fear in his enemies? *You look like a knobhead*. A cheap Halloween costume draped around a delusional twit."

The figure—shin-deep in water, with black Wellington boots visible as his robe swished on the surface—raised his hands and took down the hood. His wry smile and raised eyebrows suggested Maisie should be shocked at the reveal.

But she wasn't in the least bit surprised, and just sighed with the confirmation.

She was about to speak his name, humanise him as much as

possible, become his friend in the slim chance she might talk her way out of him killing her. But then he paced aside, wading easily, and what was revealed shot a bolt of panic through Maisie.

Peter and Joanne cowered in one corner, crouched and huddled together in a foot of water. Joanne hugged her brother tightly; his eyes were shut tight, Joanne's as wide as saucers.

"Mum," Joanne said. "Where are we?"

Maisie jerked against her bindings, anger surging.

"It'll do no good," her captor said. "They're secure."

Maisie managed to calm herself enough to see she was on a table, like cheap dining room furniture, through which hoops had been screwed into the corners and leather straps attached to hold her in place.

An improvised altar.

She moaned. Faced her children. Inside, the yearning to act as if they were real tore at her. If they were real she would have pleaded for their lives, begged her captor to let them go. She'd have lied about holding more evidence to reveal the man's identity should she disappear or die, but she'd give it to him if he would just

let

her

children

*live.*

If they lived, and she died, she would go quietly. She would not fight.

But this instinct ebbed away. Because she was going to die here regardless. The whole point of constructing a reality in which to live, one where Peter and Joanne existed, had been to keep them with her. Just because no one else could see the pair didn't mean Maisie had to surrender them.

*Again.*

No, she would cling to her kids to the end this time. She would be their mother until her heart ceased beating.

"It's okay," she said. "I'm here. No one can hurt you."

"I know." Her hooded man sounded confused. "But I can easily hurt you. And the cops can't ever touch me."

Maisie moved her head side-to-side, her mouth poised like the mother she was, delivering bad news. But she was not addressing her own child. "Son, DI Friend has worked it out already. She's probably on her way here with the cavalry right now."

The man barked a single laugh, eyeing someone behind Maisie, someone who moved only minutely. "Oh, no, you sympathetic bitch. She isn't. They can't catch me now. *Or* my girl."

# PART VI

# CHAPTER FORTY-FIVE

LED BY DI BEA CROSS, and circumventing the rising floodwaters, four police officers in all-weather gear arrived at the Strangers' Club an hour after Abhu Noon's raft blocked a major outgoing artery to accelerate the rising water. With another ten minutes—or so the lads had posted on Twitter—their improvised bank could've redirected the swell. Maybe if the cops hadn't been hassling a decent bloke doing his bit for the town, as someone commented, that extra pair of hands could've made up for those ten lost minutes and averted the swamping of a hairdresser, pub, and a coffeeshop.

There was only a quick mention on their feed that a man was dead—mutilated and sent riding down a river. Not blocking the outlet by design, Cross suspected, but intended to shock, to horrify.

The Tweeters also helpfully posted their location, the Strangers' Club, where they would wait out the storm.

All the gaps in the Strangers' Club's doors and windows were now shored up with sandbags, inside and out; placed as it was on a hill, most runoff should flow around it anyway. *If* they'd set it up right.

But DI Cross had to get in. She needed to ascertain the whereabouts of key suspects in the murders of Amina Shah, Ryan Mohammad, Lucy Viera, and Abhu Noon, and the disappearance of Maisie Jackson, whom Alicia and Knowles were unable to locate. Not answering her phone, nor available at her property; her door was locked, and there were signs of a struggle.

Bertie came to meet Cross's hammering, water now more than ankle deep across the pavement, deeper at the edges along the buildings. Officers waited with Cross, one as far back as the entrance to the rear yard in case anyone made a run for it.

"Not now," Bertie called. "Can't you just go do your jobs?"

"Mr Bradshaw." Water ran over Cross's hood and sprayed her face. "Let us in or we will have to break down the door."

"Where's your warrant?"

"Suspects are on your property; we don't need a warrant. And you are obstructing police officers from carrying out their duty, which is a crime. Since that's a crime, I need to question you about it … you see where my logic is going, Bertie."

"I'll open up round back. Come up the fire exit or my water defences—"

"We'll do our best to keep things clean, but if you don't open this door, we'll be forced to break it." Cross checked the water level. It was up to the sandbags on the front door, which was perpendicular to the flow from up the street. "Ten seconds."

Bertie's voice could be heard saying, "Bastards," and Cross felt torn. As a police officer she should be neutral, but couldn't help taking a little pleasure that her official duties, the procedure she had to follow, was discomforting to a guy like Bertie Bradshaw.

The locked clunked. The handle turned. The door opened.

"Thank you." Cross stepped inside as the first two sandbags against the door fell in and the small stream engulfed them, swamping the floor and creeping across the interior of the Strangers' Club. "That wasn't so bad, was it?"

Two officers joined her, leaving two for any runners, and

while he cursed out the worst words in the English language, Bertie and two lads Cross couldn't name replaced the sandbags and closed the door. About the equivalent of a standard bucketful had spread inside.

Everyone was on their feet, most people wet, towels allocated along with booze. Six men, two women, plus Bertie. Rough as badger balls.

"Sean Pryor." Cross faced the group as if they were an audience. "Russel Davy. Glenn Bishop." She scanned the small crowd. None of the principal suspects were present. "I need their whereabouts."

One of the women spat on the floor.

Cross twitched her head toward it, smiling at Bertie. "Hope you'll get her to clean that up." To the group: "I know at least one of you can tell us where these people are. Please cooperate, and you can get back to your party."

Silence.

Then Bertie said, "When the river went bonkers, Russ and Sean took off. Didn't wanna come here. Said they had other things to take care of. I swear they didn't say where they were going."

For some reason, Cross believed him. Like he'd lost the will to lie about his boys; no piss or vinegar left to spray.

"Have you tried his mobile?" some guy asked, to chuckles from his mates.

They had, of course, tried the suspects' mobiles. Traces took time, although warrants for electronic surveillance were on their way.

"Glenn Bishop?" Cross said.

"Never showed, never replied to our messages." Bertie's head cowed, his shoulders down. "Scarlett was ready, but she got a call and said she had to go. I guessed it was Glenn chickening out."

Cross stared him down. "That's all?"

"I don't care anymore." Partly addressing the group gathered on his damp floor, partly Cross, Bertie threw up his hands. "It's all bullshit. All of it. All of this. Patriotism. Community. Brotherhood. Not when the whole of rest of society is against us. Why not just hand each other over? And I would. I'd happily deep-fry Glenn *bloody* Bishop and serve him up with chips and mushy peas. But he ain't here." Hands on his hips. "In fact, screw the warrant. Search the place. All of it. In back, upstairs, the cellar that's probably six foot deep now. Go for it. You have my permission, if it gets you out of here quicker."

DI Cross did not expect to locate anyone or uncover anything, but she got him to repeat his permission, recording it on her phone, while the people in the bar stared on, not quite believing their eyes or ears but not voicing objection either. A round of drinks on the house appeased them at least temporarily.

Yet, as the constables she'd brought along carried out the search, DI Cross mused that she would not be surprised to see a *For Sale* sign outside the property within a month.

She called DCI Watson. "That unit we have on standby? We need them. Armed, sir. Yes, I know it's tough, but I think there may be another civilian in danger, possibly two. Maisie Jackson and Scarlett Austin are both missing. It may be a hostage situation, so I'll get Alicia to head up the op."

*A wife always knows.*

# CHAPTER FORTY-SIX

ALICIA HAD CHANGED into her only spare clothes—the sports tee-shirt and shorts she used for kickboxing class and the tracksuit she wore for warmups when the air-conditioned hall was especially cold—and picked up more police waterproofs. Knowles was waiting back at Maisie's to process the scene and to hope she came home after nipping out for a carton of hemp milk or whatever, while Alicia came to monitor the situation with Scarlett.

Alicia was licensed in firearms, but she hadn't been present to sign out a gun in Halifax. She could accompany the armed response unit, but would have to keep her soggy stab vest on, and hang back while the leader of the eight-strong squad—helicoptered in on Cross's request—approached Scarlett Austin's flat. They now readied to breach the outer building.

On the face of it, the residential block, constructed from the famous dark brick quarried locally, resembled the business it had once been—a foundry—but in the nineties it had been converted into executive apartments. Years later, the bursting of worldwide economic bubbles led to plenty of high-end landlords jumping ship and selling up, leaving the apartments to middle-income professionals.

Rain fell on Alicia and the firearms team as they chose to break in rather than risk alerting the residents. It was slow work, removing locks, cracking hinges off rather than smashing in the door.

If they were too noisy, and Glenn was hiding here with Scarlett, it might end badly. Worse, if Maisie wasn't already dead. But they had to risk coming here; they had to know what they were dealing with before they could consider mounting a proper search for Maisie Jackson—in this weather, it was all but impossible. But also, if Scarlett was helping Glenn...

"She's an accomplice," Alicia had reiterated at the briefing before deploying the ARU. "A follower. She'll probably break under basic questioning, and he'll know that. He'll kill her if we're too close."

"She might attack us to defend him." A statement, not a question, from the grizzled veteran team leader, an ex-soldier named Carter.

"She might." Alicia hoped Scarlett was helping Glenn or staying quiet out of fear rather than because she had fallen rapt under his spell. "I don't need to recite your rules of engagement. You do all you need to." She had no authority to override their op, but it was worth highlighting that she understood their position.

And now, here they were, about to breach. About to enter a situation where there was no direct intelligence, acting on calculated guesswork. It might pay off, or it might be nothing. They would know soon enough.

Scarlett had always liked the punk rock movement more than the music; the anarchy of the politics, the don't-give-a-crapness of the fans, and the musicians themselves. That's why she kept a rare, framed Sex Pistols poster near the front door of her flat.

And it was most definitely *her* flat. Something Glenn had never liked, but she wasn't ready to hand over joint ownership. Sure, he could have his name on the Sky TV and the Netflix account; if he moved out she could just cancel all that without a penalty to herself. But she never trusted that he wouldn't just up and move out with a floozy he found at one of his meetings, or some slag who turned his head.

It had been two years since he had first moved in, and she still didn't fully trust him.

*Does that say more about me than him?*

Her dad didn't like Glenn particularly, nor did her mum, but neither of them actively loathed him. They knew of his activities with the Vanguard, and Scarlett's association too, but she convinced them the same way Glenn had convinced that councillor, Abhu Noon. He was taking a bunch of supremacist morons and teaching them the difference between a fascist religious extremist and a genuine refugee.

He was doing a good thing.

They weren't fully convinced, but with their daughter insisting it was true, they had no choice but to begrudgingly accept his presence in their lives. There was just one thing niggling at Scarlett.

She *really* didn't trust Glenn Bishop.

At first, it was the sex that meant she couldn't get enough of him. Lots of it. And the laughter and the good times, and the fun, and a bit of cash coming in. Glenn was so focused on merchandising and drumming up support on social media and with the press, Scarlett sometimes wondered if he even cared about fixing the country as a whole, or if he saw it more as an entrepreneurial venture. Certainly, he was often out at all hours, claiming to be "on business."

Just lately, though, he'd ceased making excuses. As much as

she spoke in glowing terms about the guy, and about how she wore the trousers in the relationship, more and more he'd been shagging her and then buggering off. He was distracted at other times, too, keeping her at arm's length, chatting less and less.

It was for this reason that Scarlett decided to spend a rain-soaked day rifling through his things.

She'd come home early when he called, expecting a nice surprise. But when she turned up, he was already on the way out, apologising, explaining he had somewhere to be. He'd be back. He swore he would. And soon.

Meaning there was something more important to do. Something more important than her. That was why, a couple of hours ago, she searched every inch of the apartment.

It was how she'd found the journals.

At the back of his part of the closet, in a shoebox brittle with age. Five books. Hand-written, leather-bound volumes encompassing a period of time long before either of them was born: 1973 to 1977. Each was a different brand, a different manufacturer, suggesting it was the content that mattered.

Like a sweet teenage diary, each had a little lock, and also like those diaries they were easily accessed. *Un*like such diaries, however, the contents shocked her.

Shocked her so much she could not stop reading.

Glenn had hidden them from her. *Why?*

Scarlett didn't care about Glenn knowing she'd snooped; his attitude toward her recently did not warrant him getting upset. Him flitting out, using her, being a dick. No, she was in the right here.

She returned to the first of the journals to refresh her thoughts about Glenn, to calculate how they could help her get him back in her good graces. She read the first page again:

> **These accounts are to explain why we did what we did. If cornered, we will never be taken alive, so we wished to explain exactly, without the bias of the modern world.**

*Modern world.* In 1973. Right.

But what the hell was her man doing with such literature? *Why* would he have it?

The words trailed on:

> **People will not understand if we do not chronicle our mission. It is extreme, but it is necessary. And our mitigating circumstances are simple: our country is being stolen by outsiders, and those at the top of the heap don't care, because it does not affect them. We will evict the interlopers, and—**

A knock sounded at her door.

*The door.*

Inside the building, not the intercom outside. Meaning whoever it was had gained access without her buzzing them in.

Her parents had keys, Glenn had a key, her friend Mary had a just-in-case key.

She closed the journal and stood to check who was in the hall.

Three armed officers stood on one side of the door to Scarlett Austin's flat and three on the other, plus two crouched before the doorway at narrower angles, semi-autos aimed. Alicia wanted to be the one who spoke first, her voice familiar but also female and therefore less threatening. The team leader, Carter, had fought her on it, but in the end she got her way.

Simple risk.

An unknown male voice demanding to be let in would be more likely to spook those inside. The two worst case scenarios involved being shot through the door or the hostage being killed, and Alicia convinced her colleague she was best placed to avoid both.

Still, she pressed herself against the wall, a solid brick internal divide that no standard bullet could penetrate.

Alicia knocked again, recoiling to her safe spot, and called, "Hi, it's me, Alicia. You know, your friendly neighbourhood detective inspector. With the police."

No response.

A question flared in Carter's eyes: *What now?*

Alicia held up a finger: *One more try.*

Carter nodded and held up a finger, emphasising the *one*.

Alicia knocked.


Scarlett reached the door. The knock again. She frowned, reluctant to use the peep hole in case whoever was outside spotted the change in light.

Another knock.

Scarlett felt on the sideboard by the Sex Pistols poster and located a vase. She didn't know why the knock spooked her so much, but it might have something to do with Glenn's frequent disappearing acts lately.

With the vase in one hand, she whipped open the door.


With no reply, Carter ordered the breach. The hand-held ram

came into play, making light work of the interior door. The lock splintered on the first blow and slammed the door open.

Alicia watched from the back as the men rushed in, guns raised, announcing they were armed police and for anyone present to make themselves known. Leaving two posted on the door, she noted the Sex Pistols poster over the side board, a bunch of dead flowers in a vase—roses, she thought—and the smell of old greasy food, reminiscent of when she'd found Kate hiding out in her old, boarded up home earlier this year.

"They're not here," Alicia said.


Standing in the doorway, dripping wet and holding a bunch of roses, Glenn said, "I'm sorry. Didn't mean to scare you, hon. I've been a dick lately. I wanted to explain why."

"Why didn't you let yourself in?" Scarlett asked him.

"I wanted you to open the door and see me like this."

His big, damp smile made Scarlett feel like it was the first time they met, like he was making a goofy effort to impress her with his faux-geek credentials. She melted, and threw him a huge smile, standing aside to let him in.

"Did you hear about Basil Warner's farm?" He placed the flowers in the vase she had placed back on the sideboard.

"No, what happened?"

"Those two bodies they found, disturbed by the floods? Well, now there's more of them. And I think I know where they're from."

## CHAPTER FORTY-SEVEN

**THREE WEEKS AGO**

SCARLETT FROWNED. "You think you know where the bodies are from?"

"It's why I've been so focused on other things lately." Glenn led her by the hand toward the bedroom where Scarlett had spread the journals out on the bed. She held him back and he turned patiently to her. "I need to tell you something. A few things. I was given some journals recently. And I think they're the real deal. And they might mean trouble. For the Vanguard."

"Then I have something to tell you too," Scarlett said.

**NOW**

The apartment had been abandoned for at least a couple of days. The first sprouts of mould formed on plates stacked in the kitchen. The washing-up bowl was full and had a greasy film. Either the pair lived like slobs or they'd vacated the place with no plans on returning anytime soon.

Time to search.

She kept two cops with her, hands sheathed in rubber gloves, going through everything in a methodical manner. The kitchen, bathroom, lounge, and the spare bedroom. They'd found a couple of nasty looking weapons, legal to own but not carry on the street; enough weed for personal use, and several impressive sex toys.

*Kids.*

Finally, Alicia and one other officer—disgruntled at being reduced to standard duties until directly needed—searched the bedroom. They found nothing of interest except one item: a hardback, A5 book, a generic brand available from most stationers. It was tied shut with string and stuck with velcro to the underside of the bottom drawer of a chest of six.

Something not meant to be discovered.

Alicia opened it and found a diary of sorts. No dates, but it had clearly been written recently. Neat, deliberate cursive, joined up, unhurried and plain.

Alicia sat down to read it.

She read the opening passages—Scarlett's suspicions about Glenn cheating on her, the constant aloofness, and how she'd found the journals which described several murders committed in the 1970s. She commented how getting it all out in the open eased things in the relationship, but discussions over what to do regarding the books put strain on them, especially as more remains surfaced over time.

*It's been two weeks since the body parts showed up across Calderdale. When the news broke, Glenn acted positively giddy, like it was "seriously cool, man." He talked about the owner of the journals, how he respected that forebear of the Vanguard for entrusting him—us— with this secret. We both marvelled at how long they'd gotten away with it.*

*I'm glad everything is out in the open now. Glad that Glenn's suspicious behaviour stopped. Now I know where he was sneaking off to, it makes sense. Visiting this person regularly. I even thought it was cool of him when I found out.*

*Thing is, weird thing, I still sense a storm cloud. Like it's closing in on the owner of the journals.*

Without dates, it would be difficult to cement this as firm evidence, so Alicia couldn't simply skip to the bit where Scarlett explained what happened to the written accounts of the murders the police were supposed to be solving. She needed to read it all, pinpoint specific events.

*A new detective showed up, a black man. Smooth and cool, as well-dressed black men always seem to be. I'd never admit this to anyone around here (and PLEASE keep this to yourself, even if you're a burglar or a cop reading it after I'm dead or missing) but I've always wanted to sleep with one, a black man, just to see what it's like.*

*I always thought it'd stay a fantasy, unless something drastic changed between Glenn and me, but when we saw the guy on TV, I wondered if I should get "close" to him.*

*(You know what I mean by "close" right? Like ... intimate ... oh, yeah, I'd make that sacrifice)*

*I ran the suggestion by Glenn. He said it was a decent idea, but knowing I'd been ruined by a guy like that, he wouldn't ever be able to touch me again. Instead, I met with the person who gave us the journals, and you know what?*

*Didn't like 'em that much.*

*I never went back, although Glenn did. He came home from there one night, worried. Said if the police ever started connecting the deaths out there to decent people, the journals had to be burned.*

Uh-oh. Alicia had a feeling she wouldn't like what came next.

*The female detective, who is definitely shagging the black one in their downtime (or if she isn't she's a fool), did make a connection.*

*I tried to calm Glenn and told him it was all a fishing expedition. But Glenn did the maths and said it was feasible that a person killing in the seventies could still be alive right now. He said we needed to deflect attention from the real killers.*

Alicia frowned at that. She tried to remember if she'd stated the theory in earshot of anyone who might have relayed it to someone like Scarlett. But she just wasn't sure.

Still, if Alicia could think of that, and Malcolm picked up on the possibility even before her, there was no reason others wouldn't come up with it too. Heck, she might even have skim-read that same question in the press about the culprit still being with us today.

The fact Scarlett and Glenn knew who wrote the journals, knew who murdered the people uncovered by the previous flooding, pointed to one simple conclusion: if they wanted to deflect attention, then the culprits really were elderly, incapable of committing the modern murders.

*That blonde bitch has been spraying accusations around like confetti. Glenn's all in a tizzy and he's saying he needs to act. Do something.*

*So we've had a bonfire tonight. Taken the journals, burned them, scattered the ashes. No one will find them now.*

*The only problem is that there are more. We only got the ones from a five-year period.*

*We don't know where the others are, but we need to find out. Can't allow the cops to get their hands on them.*

Alicia formed a fist and swore under her breath. She would have shouted or punched something but didn't want to alert the two incredibly bored ARU officers waiting on her. Best thing she could do was press ahead.

*Glenn's ranting now. About the cops wanting to pin those old killings on a great man like Remy. He's manic. He's scaring me. He's going through his old stash of gear, he stuff he says was just to scare people back in the day.*

*I never liked him having all those things, the blades and stuff.*

*He said if he ever killed or even hurt someone with them, he'd have gotten rid of it. But he said it with a wink and a smirk, and I wasn't sure what he meant.*

*He's out of the flat now. I don't know what he took with him, but the rucksack looked light, with something straight and hard inside.*

*He owns a lot of blades in sheaths. I couldn't say for sure, but the shape of the bulge … I just hope he isn't going to do anything stupid. The last thing we need is a dead cop or something.*

The writing was more erratic here. Seemed like she was nervous. Next page:

*I wasn't going to update anything today, but I had to. Glenn came home late and I've no idea where he's been. He changed his clothes while he was out last night, and refused to tell me where he was.*

*Better I didn't know or something. Just that I had to give him a convincing alibi or everything we have will be gone.*

*I'm not sure what he meant by that. I mean, I own this place. Or my dad does. Glenn hasn't got any claim on it, and I don't rely on him for money, so screw him if he's gone and done something he might get in trouble over.*

Still no dates. The scribblings of a person needing to sort out her own thoughts, her own worries.

*I think he killed the pakki girl. The Muslim. I think her name is Amima or Amina. She was one of these who wore a sack on her head, like, "by choice" her family says, but we all know what a "choice" is for a Muslim woman.*

*Obey, or die.*

*I just don't understand why they hate themselves so much. Even them who stick to our laws and don't want to blow stuff up, they need a good slap. Need to be set free.*

*Any girl who demeans herself that way deserves vaginal mutilation. Not long now, I'm sure, until we'll have to accept that as "cultural differences" along with veils and beards and suicide vests.*

*I feel sorry for the girl, I do. Really. I know people think we hate all Muslims, but we don't. Personally, I'd like to help them, help pull them out of the dark ages.*

*But feeling sorry for her doesn't mean I'm not concerned with Glenn.*

*When he woke up he shagged the hell out of me. I wasn't complaining at the time, although it was rougher than usual. He went for it twice before going out—late—to work. He was in a mood when he did leave, and I was sore (in a good way).*

*And then I saw the news.*

*He's missing the weird machete he picked up in Scunthorpe last year. The one with the grip handle and the squared-off end and the serrated bit at the back. I wondered how the hell it would work in practical terms, but he said he was sure the people who made it had a use in mind.*

*I'm sure he didn't sell it or get rid of it. And it was the right size for the bag.*

Alicia photographed each page, sending them to Cross, Knowles, and Ball as she processed the contents in her own mind. Stored it all. Ignored the return text messages, choosing to read them later if they became a point of discussion rather than someone telling her to stop bloody texting them.

She needed to concentrate. Because something was percolating again.

Something was shaking loose within her.

*He's out again. Told me not to worry, that he'd be back whenever. Business.*

*No.*

*He's been using a phone I've never seen before, telling me he got it on trial. He's had it days, bringing it out occasionally, but it never really bothered me. He's had new phones to try out before. Sometimes, you don't want Vanguard business on your personal equipment.*

*But after getting a message on this new phone, he shot out the door with another bag.*

*I know it—I know he's not going out at eight p.m. on business.*

*He's either with his mates or seeing someone else, or he's trying to protect me from what he's doing. While I can't quite believe he'd actually kill someone, I can't shake the feeling that he might have. He was so worried about Remy being fingered in the older murders, I don't know what to think. Not really.*

*I mean, I do know what I think. What I suspect.*

*I'm so confused.*

Alicia knew exactly what to think too. She flipped the page to confirm.

*I only went and followed him. And I was right. So right to do it. He behaved like he knew what he was doing. Like some spy.*

*He was in this place, a doorway to some closed-down discount shop, and I hid in a bus shelter. Not a great place, but I was a long way away and pretended to be some dickhead sleeping off a booze session. I was dressed like a bloke, so from a distance he wouldn't have seen me.*

*I watched, though. I watched the pakki lad show up, all annoyed-looking, and I watched him look all shocked and pull something out of his neck. Then I watched Glenn just glide up as the guy dropped to the pavement, scooped him up, and carried the guy over his shoulder to some car.*

*No idea where he got the car from. None. We only have one between us. But he'd stashed this other one near the flat, so I'd been able to tail him.*

*Speaking of which, I didn't risk parking near where Glenn dropped this stolen car but I knew where it was so I could get there ahead of him.*

*It took ages to get out to the moors. That bloody church he'd been banging on about for weeks. Some ruin.*

*And I couldn't follow him secretly out there. I had to wait 'til he lugged the guy away, then run on. I had no idea what I'd say when I saw him, but I wanted to wait until he couldn't deny what he was doing, couldn't lie about "just scaring the guy" or some excuse like that.*

*I knew.*

*And I wanted to talk him out of it.*

*When he was trying to go down, into some hole in the ruins floor, Glenn saw me.*

*I'd been so wrong about him. He wasn't the man I thought,*

*not the man I hoped for. And if I didn't help him, if I didn't pretend to obey him, do everything he said, then I would be next.*

Alicia was now sure of her niggle. Sure she understood why her brain was throwing out conclusions she couldn't possibly prove. Something to do with timing.

*Glenn seems to trust me. I need evidence before I can go to the police, though. I wonder if he'll confide in someone else. Sean, maybe. Not fat-bastard-Russel. Not Bertie. There are others he might bring into this. Like proper psychos. Everyone knows Pingu killed a bloke last year after a Terriers away game, but no one talks about it directly. He just punched this Coventry fan a bunch of times and he stopped moving. Papers said he was dead. The only acknowledgment they gave Pingu was a round of applause when he walked in the Strangers' next.*

Pingu? That was a child's TV show, one Stacey loved.

Alicia shuddered. She'd be making a note of that, unable to see if it was an actual nickname or a code for Scarlett's journal.

*Sean and Russel did something dumb. I don't know why they'd screw with a copper like that, but Glenn is pissed. He told me he knew who the next victims would be, but I persuaded him to hold off on doing anything to them.*

*What if we could take the pressure off another way? What if we could point a finger at someone who was old enough to be around back then? Someone like Bertie? He'd need an accomplice to get the pakki up Stoodley Pike.*

*I know, because trailing his cut-up parts was a strain even for me and Glenn, not to mention the gear we had to take.*

*I'm still aching.*

*Glenn likes the idea of setting up other people. Bertie and Russel are perfect. Jilted in the leadership, desperate to do something the Vanguard is seen as condoning, and a pain in both our arses taken care of: 1) Glenn and Remy are out of the frame and 2) I get to keep my man out of jail because he won't need to kill anyone else.*

*Least of all me.*

*God, I sound like one of them, don't I? A Muslim woman.*

*But I'm not. I'll work it out. I'll be fine. I just need to keep Glenn sweet until it's all over. If I can please him, and help him pull off the frame-up, he'll be back to his old self.*

*I'll be able to live again.*

*It's risky, but we have to try.*

Alicia closed the journal. Lay back on the bed. Staring at the ceiling, she sent that final page to her trio of readers, knowing they probably weren't going through it as finely as she was.

She had to take the conclusion she reached, work into it. Use her conscious mind to spot the evidence her computerised subconscious had revealed.

Within three minutes, Knowles called. She answered.

"Alicia, those pages," he said.

"Yeah." Alicia was still distracted.

"They seem … odd. Am I reading too much into it?"

Alicia sat bolt upright. "You saw it too?"

"I'm not sure what I saw. But … I can't shake it. Like…"

"Like the journal is staged?"

"Yes." He sounded relieved.

"It's the timing, isn't it?"

"Timing?"

"Coincidence. She starts journaling just before Glenn

commits the first murder. The penmanship—it's all so even, so similar, except in a couple of places."

"What are we saying?" Knowles asked.

"We're saying it's all a fake." Alicia's heartbeat slowed now that she accepted someone else saw the flaws. "Everything in this book is fake. *Scarlett* is the alpha. Not Glenn. *She's* the one running this show."

# CHAPTER FORTY-EIGHT

MAISIE STARED AT THE CEILING. "My, Scarlett, you have come a long way."

The girl had stepped out from behind Maisie's loosely bound head, on the opposite side of the table to Glenn. Shadows of the furniture reflected back out of the water and shimmered over them both.

"Whose idea was all this?" Maisie asked.

Scarlett stared down at Maisie, face creased in remorse. "You don't think *I'm* capable of this, do you?"

Maisie was tied up like a sacrifice, yet still alive. She took in both the man with the stupid cloak over his regular clothes and Wellington boots, and the girl in the denim waistcoat, low-cut top, and hotpants, fisherman's waders to complete the ensemble.

Maisie still had no memory of how she got here. One minute she had been re-reading the literature Lucy Viera gave her, the next she was gradually waking.

They must have drugged her. No headache except the dull throb she associated with being a bit thirsty.

The water level had also risen while Glenn talked, as Scarlett hung back. Glenn delivered the standard speech of the racist, that "racism" is just an insult hurled at a patriot when they defend their shores, that liberals want to destroy the country by stealthily delivering death to the populace in the form of a birthrate genocide. As usual he never stopped to ask *why* a liberal might want to destroy a country, or even *if* a liberal might have other motivations for allowing more people of colour to live here than a racist deemed tolerable.

The fact he kept glancing over Maisie's head, and now seeing the way Scarlett was dressed…

"My dear," Maisie said. "Yes. You *are* perfectly capable of all this."

Scarlett placed a hand on her chest and looked aghast.

"He dresses up like the fantasy vision of what a cult messiah should look like," Maisie went on. "The fifty-year gaps between major killers was a nice touch. I understand why you thought such an absurd notion would work. A couple who live in a state of non-reality. You're convinced there's a bigger conspiracy out there haunting your lives. Whether it's the biased 'liberal media' or 'government elites' who don't see the damage they do to regular folk, or even that evil spectre of people who pray to a different imaginary friend than your parents did, coming along and living the life you wished you had. Of course you're going to come up with something absurd, which *you* would have believed if you weren't acting it out. But just because you're gullible to the news you wish was true, it doesn't mean we all are. I'm sorry, kids…" Maisie glanced to the side, seeing Peter and Joanne, no longer huddled in fear but standing in the water, now up to their thighs, holding hands and watching. "I'm sorry, Scarlett, but the police know it isn't some supernatural event. No intergenerational passing of the torch. It's two sick people, replaying history to their own tune."

Scarlett pulled her shoulders back and let her jaw hang open, working as if she didn't know what to say. She said, "Fine," and placed a hand on her belly.

"Your pet boy is already dressed like the hokey vision of a satanic priest, so why don't you bestow me with another cliché?"

"Which one?"

Maisie cast her eyes over her own body. "You've tied me up. I'm inevitably going to die. How about you lay out your plan in detail and give me the code to the self-destruct sequence?"

Glenn chuckled. "Stop going on about clichés, you dumb bitch. I know it seems stupid, but this all serves a bigger purpose."

"Why? What else can this be but a pair of fantasists playing dress-up?"

"Branding," Scarlett said. "A man in a hood cutting up invaders and traitors might not fool the intellectual elite, but bear something in mind." She continued to hold her hand over the gentle swell of her stomach. "How stupid is the average person in this country? Think on that, then remember that half the country is even dumber."

She was paraphrasing someone famous, but Maisie couldn't remember whom. The young woman was also correct. Maisie understood. "And going the other way, there are many more *almost* as dumb as the average."

"And we're not average," Glenn said.

"Meaning you can set this up, project the image of the cult rising every so often to punish the biggest danger to society— transients and outsiders, Jews, blacks, now Muslims—and enough people will believe it to make it true."

"We aren't a part of a bigger tradition going backward," Scarlett said. "But we can pretend we are, and start it for real going forward."

Maisie's gaze found the hand on Scarlett's belly, which she let drop. She appeared uncomfortable for the first time.

"You're pregnant," Maisie said.

Glenn snapped his head to his girlfriend. "What?"

"Hey!" Scarlett layered in on Maisie. "*I* wanted to be the one to tell him." Then she softened, returning to Glenn. "I'm sorry, babe. I would have told you sooner, but we had work to do."

Glenn's smile widened, a look of wonder spreading. "I'm gonna be a dad!"

"And we'll pass on our legacy," Scarlett said. "Doesn't have to be every fifty years, either. Make it every twenty. Who knows who we'll be defending ourselves against by then."

Glenn came around to her, staring at her stomach. She lifted her top and he lay his hand on her skin.

"Two months," she said. "Just a little swell. Boobs are a bit bigger."

The pair looked like any happy couple receiving the news, the way Maisie and Cuthbert had acted when the test came back positive. So full of hope for the future, anticipating happiness and laughter forever.

Off to the side, Peter and Joanne watched on. Hands by their sides, water crept up to their fingers, faces numb and expressionless.

"No," Maisie said. "It's not time."

"It *is* time." Scarlett shooed Glenn away. "It is time for people like us to make ourselves known." She pointed farther into the gloom.

Maisie strained against her bindings but made out a camera on a tripod, no red light to indicate it was running. "Ah, the internet. So helpful."

"Maybe, by the time we rise again—with luck—the Jews will have been sacrificed, consumed by the Muslims, which will lead to a race war that eradicates *them*. Blacks will have learned their place, and women like me will rule the world."

"Thought you people didn't like feminism."

"Oh, we love it," Glenn said. "Just interpret it different to progressives and liberals."

Maisie could only watch Peter and Joanne. "This isn't something you need to see."

"I'll be watching it all," Scarlett said.

Peter and Joanne turned their backs.

"Good," Maisie said. "Go peacefully. Don't see me like this."

Scarlett frowned.

To Scarlett and Glenn, Maisie said, "Your vision is warped. You can't just make a video and expect people to fall in line. And this certainly won't make women rulers of the world."

"We'll see." Scarlett now came in close. "So-called *feminists* say they don't want superiority. That they don't want to keep men down. They just want equality. But there is no equality. It's time the world came around to the fact that we *are* superior to men. Don't you understand? We bear life. We arrange their lives. Men need the release of sex and the knowledge they've landed a woman who *chooses* them. That's the male ego. They couldn't get by without us. So when I choose Glenn, he should be grateful. He *is* grateful. Our superiority means there's no need to close some imaginary wage gap. Women shouldn't *have* to work. We should be worshipped, and—"

"Oh, shut up, you stupid, vacuous bint," Maisie said. She checked all she could see. The children were gone. Only the three adults remained. "I think I've had enough of this tied-up-listening-to-the-plan nonsense. Let's get down to it."

Scarlett rose back upright. Glenn pulled up his hood.

"As you wish," Scarlett said.

# CHAPTER FORTY-NINE

ALICIA BELIEVED the aftermath of the second flood in a month would not reflect well on the West Yorkshire Police. They had an armed response unit present, four detectives, and a handful of constables and forensic techs. But DCI Watson had recalled a number of them to Halifax and returned the smattering they had borrowed to Huddersfield. If Moleford was flooding, other areas would too. That was the correct decision.

It was also a good decision by the council, urged by DI Cross, to have the army units set up shelters in a rehearsal of refugee centres. Up on the land surrounding the mobile lab, a small tent village had sprung up, along with food and hot drinks. Cots lined bigger tents where displaced people could sleep. A few dozen troops and their commanding officers would benefit from this real-world exercise.

But Alicia understood the property damage, the deaths of Lucy Viera and Abhu Noon, and the escape of Glenn Bishop and Scarlett Austin, might, in retrospect, be attributed to the police not moving quickly enough. If they'd pulled the pair in, they could have focused their attention and resources on teaming with the Vanguard and the army, and a respected member of the community wouldn't be missing. All they'd succeeded in doing since raiding the Strangers' Club was locating Sean Pryor and Russel Davy, ensconced in James Grantham's unaffected house, playing computer games. They were now under arrest, held in the refugee rehearsal camp, waiting for someone to question them.

With Alicia ordered by Watson to leave the investigation, it still wasn't clear whether Maisie was dead or alive.

When Alicia returned to her hotel, she found the ground floor flooded. She had thought it would be high enough to escape the worst, but a freshly built wall at the bottom end of the car park hadn't afforded sufficient drainage, backed up as it was from the saturation farther down, so the rains pooled, the run off added to it, and she was locked out due to safety fears.

That was how she ended up at Maisie's house. It was cordoned off, Knowles having headed to Cross's side, ready to deploy if needed. Alicia told the police officer on sentry duty, armed only with an umbrella, that she needed to look around and had a key. He checked her ID and let her through.

Inside, Alicia turned on the lights. It was a little messy from the search, but they'd taken nothing.

She removed her coat and wellies, checked she wasn't filthy or damp anywhere else, and flopped onto the couch. It was harder than a modern sofa but not uncomfortable. As she reclined sideways, the fabric sucked her in. Her eyes grew heavy.

*I haven't called Stacey.*

She sat up in panic, searching for her phone. Saw it was eight thirty.

Two text messages had landed from her mum, the first asking if Alicia was planning on saying goodnight to her daughter, then another saying not to worry, as Stacey was now in bed. The second one was signed off with yet another passive-aggressive comment:

*At least it'll be back to normal soon :-0*

The Dot-Bot's way of saying she didn't want to continue like this much longer. That was fine; neither did Alicia.

She shouldn't have gotten so engrossed in Moleford Bridge. Should have given her input then returned to Leeds like Murphy wanted. She needed to concentrate on things with Iothor, on helping Kate come to terms with her life, and making things up with Stacey.

Swimming.

That was the next thing she'd do. Stacey loved it, and it'd be a great place to bring Iothor. If he was still interested in her.

She hadn't called him, and had only replied to his text messages with perfunctory comments about seeing him soon and being really busy and sorry she couldn't talk.

The sleep that had threatened moments earlier evaporated, and Alicia paced the room.

She'd calm back down in a moment, maybe make a cup of herbal tea. For now, she busied herself near the coffee table, checking the stack of papers and books that Maisie used during her research. There didn't seem to be anything new.

Next to the papers, a photograph of two children stared back at Alicia—Peter and Joanne, perhaps eight and ten years old. Must have been taken just before their final family holiday.

Alicia couldn't imagine the pain.

She sometimes pictured how she'd react if she lost Stacey. Each image ended with DCI Murphy discovering her passed out, curled up on the girl's grave having consumed a bottle of whiskey, the words, "Not again," escaping Murphy's lips as he peeled her off the ground.

Morbid, but true.

How do you get over such an awful event? How does anyone?

When Alicia had discovered Maisie's coping mechanism, she believed she'd have to address it, to help cure the woman of the figments of her imagination. The psychologist in her knew it was unhealthy, but the mother in her chided her for judging. She had no right to take away Maisie's sliver of denial if it salved the hurt inside. Even if it was only temporary.

Maisie could guide the children through life and pass on her knowledge, raise them as all parents wished to raise their young. To see them thrive and—

Alicia dismissed her text messages and dialled Knowles, unsure what her brain was telling her.

He picked up. "We're a bit busy. Can it wait?"

She said, "What if Glenn and Scarlett are such acolytes that they really were communicating with Remy somehow? What if there's more to their relationship?"

"The visitor log showed the name Sean Pryor a lot. But I suppose that could have been faked. We can check the cameras there in the morning."

"The home." Alicia pondered the real reason she'd snagged on Daisyville. "It's empty."

"Yeah, the residents are up here in their own tent. Pretty calm, considering."

"It's empty, Malcolm. And if Glenn paid regular visits up there, he knows the evac plan. He knows the layout, the building."

A pause on Knowles's end. "A possible hiding place."

"Get over here," Alicia said. "And be careful."

# CHAPTER FIFTY

THE ARMY HAD BUILT their tent village on the flattest part of moorland they could find, where they linked up with DI Cross, whom they called a civilian organiser. DS Ball was assigned to watch Russel Davy and Sean Pryor like a glorified duty sergeant while the junior detective, Knowles, got to hobnob inside the nearby mobile lab, a portion of which now served as an operations centre, since the library could be two feet deep by now.

Ball was more experienced than Knowles, though. Outranked him. Yet, here he was guarding a police van, albeit under an awning that meant he didn't need to prance about with an umbrella; a chunky jacket and waterproof trousers sufficed. The outer doors of the van hung open but the cage remained locked. Inside, the prisoners' hands had been freed so they could eat, and they sat there fuming at their treatment. Each had been allowed a bathroom break, and both denied any wrongdoing.

They were a part of a core group of people who the police suspected were party to the three murders. The journal Alicia had texted them—which she proclaimed was "mostly fake"—mentioned other materials donated by Remy Duval. Someone like Sean, who had visited Remy often, was the obvious source for this.

As Ball considered Sean Pryor's visits to the home, a place that freaked Ball out more than he would ever let on, he planned to grill the lad as soon as they could establish somewhere to conduct an interview. Maybe that big mobile-lab-cum-operations-centre.

Ball was about to call in to suggest it, when the door to the lab opened. Knowles and Cross emerged, engaged in what appeared to be a heated debate. They were immediately approached by two men. The detectives tried to wave the men off as they walked away from the lab, holding hoods over their faces, a sidewind lashing them with rain. They were coming this way.

Closer, the two men harrying the detectives were clearly Tariq Bashir and Dayapreet Virk, and their voices grew audible. Words like "doing nothing" and "murdered" and "sue you people" carryied over the weather. They were definitely coming this way.

"This is my home too," Cross called, close enough now for Ball to listen in. "I need to catch this person, but there are other lives in danger right now."

"Get the information from these two." Tariq stabbed a finger toward Ball.

Okay, the finger was actually aimed at the van with Sean Pryor and Russel Davy inside.

"We will," Cross assured them. "But we have other priorities." She looked sharply at Ball. "I'm sure if there's some legal way to extract information in the meantime, we'll do so." Turning her attention back to the two angry men, Cross beckoned them to follow her.

Ball watched them go, Cross returning the interlopers to the care of two soldiers who were establishing a cordon. He had no idea how they'd got that close anyway. Maybe Cross had let them through as an act of goodwill or as witnesses. Didn't matter.

What mattered was Cross's telling hint.

*Some legal way to extract information…*

Ball hadn't been sidelined for no reason. It was *because* he outranked Knowles. *Because* he was more experienced.

He grinned. Faced the prisoners.

The little man and the fat man sat on opposite sides of the van, hands clasped as if still cuffed.

Ball said, "Pryor. Cool name."

"What do you mean by that?" Sean asked.

"Doesn't matter."

The rain sounded louder now that Ball stopped talking, beating out a rhythm on the van roof, on the canvas awning, as musical as a child's first xylophone. Annoying too. But Ball just rocked on his feet, waiting.

"What do you want?" Russel asked.

"Just wondering a few things." Again, Ball didn't go on, just waited for a voice to interrupt the *pitter-patter-bing-bang-pitter.*

Sean cracked first. "What things?"

Ball adopted an expression he thought of as 'genuinely baffled.' "What it's like growing up as a virulent racist with the name of one of the most famous *black* comedians of all time."

Sean shrugged. Swallowed. Eyes found the floor.

Russel kept his face as neutral as he could, which wasn't particularly neutral; his brow appeared to extend outward as his head dipped, which Ball had only witnessed happening on the dumbest, most Neanderthal-like people, an attempt to appear nonplussed.

Ball addressed Russel. "Not heard of Richard Pryor? I used to do a great impression of him. Not allowed now, of course. White guy trying to sound like a dead black man who suffered addiction." He rolled his eyes and gave a laugh. "*Suffered addiction.* Do you like that? It's the modern way of calling someone a smack-head. A drug addict. I'm guessing you guys aren't fans of political correctness."

Both shook their heads and smirked.

*Getting them to agree with you. First step. Now to cement that.*

Ball turned side-on, and leaned in. "Wanna hear my impression?"

The pair glanced at one another.

Sean shrugged once again.

Russel said, "Sure. Why not."

Oddly, Ball genuinely did do a good Richard Pryor. He possessed a gift for mimicking loud, brash American celebs—but not British ones for some reason. No idea where it came from. As a teen, he'd started with Peewee Herman and later copied a gloriously sweary Eddie Murphy routine, and even some Weird Al Yankovic. So when he worked his jaw, constricted his throat just so, and forced part of his voice through his nose, he was able to recite a couple of jokes from Pryor's *Live and Smokin'* stand-up routine, Ball's favourite of the late genius—avoiding any racial slurs, naturally.

The two thugs in the van/cell gave smiles, although Russel's was plainly forced, having never heard of Richard Pryor, but Ball took what he could get. He pressed a *shhhh* finger to his lips and allowed a conspiratorial wink. "Don't tell anyone, okay?"

"Nothing racist about that, man," Russel said. "Bloody elite."

Two things Ball noted. First, Russel offered support to Ball—not that anyone had banned him from doing Richard Pryor impressions; as long as he steered clear of Pryor's use of the N-word, he'd be fine both in and outside of work—and second, Russel referred to the "elite."

"Hate those guys," Ball replied. "The elite. Telling us what to say and think—"

"It's just like Glenn said," Sean interrupted.

That threw Ball a tad.

Sean's grin spread. "Gain our trust, make us like you. Agree with us. Then offer a way out of our situation. Copping to something or giving up a mate. Because we trust the pig, we turn on our own."

Russel's brow jutted more, hooding his eyes. "That true?"

Ball hadn't pegged Sean for a smart guy, and he let his surprise show, allowing the *pitter-ping-bing* play out.

"Glenn, hmm?" Ball said. "Glenn Bishop. The guy you gave Remy's stuff to."

"I didn't give him anything," Sean said. "And I don't have to talk to you."

The lad had been coached by a smarter person, a couple of tips on coppers' tricks made known to him and therefore ineffective. However, Ball had been around the block more times than he let on.

"We'll figure it out. We know you're the one who visited Remy a lot, and we know you all liked to deliver books as an offering to the boss. Mostly Bertie. But when it shifted to Glenn, maybe someone like you, Sean, figured you'd carry it on."

Sean continued to stare blankly at the floor, while Russel's lack of understanding manifested in his jaw tensing and trying to extend as far as his brow.

"You visited Remy Duval a few times. What was he like? Did he need drugs to be able to talk properly? Or was it his nurse who helped you out with the journals?"

"Don't know," Sean said. "No comment."

"Oh, we're going that route." Ball paced, a low chuckle, as if Sean's tactic was ridiculous. "The person who has those journals —the ones detailing what Remy did before his brain turned into mushy peas—that person is the prime suspect in four gruesome murders. So if we can't actually find the books themselves, but we know they exist, because *others* exist for different years, the only person we can blame is the person who we know came into possession of them. And that's you, Sean."

Sean's lips pinched and he blew air through them. "No comment."

"Yup, it's a toughie. Unless you testify that you received the books and passed them to Glenn, and unless you can show you absolutely did not team up with him…"

Ball stopped. He wasn't getting anywhere. The kid had more to offer—it was a gut feeling rather than "reading" him or piecing together obscure, disparate pieces of evidence. He needed a different approach. Gaining their trust didn't work. Time for the opposite.

"Forget it," Ball said. "It's your name on the visitor log. It's you who has no alibi. It's you who publicly used racist slurs against a woman in front of a detective. Means, motive, and opportunity. It's all we need for a conviction."

A lie, but it sounded convincing. And it *looked* convincing, judging by the paling of Sean's skin.

"You cover for Glenn, that's great," Ball said. "Serve a couple of years, you get out, you're a legend. But you're not getting out. Glenn's sat at home, loving that you're taking the fall, and—"

"No comment," Sean said.

"Why?" Russel asked.

Sean's head jerked and his glare landed on Russel. "What?"

"Why protect him? He's a knobhead. Making money while we get nothing. If he killed those people, he's a bigger knob than I thought. If he didn't, he's got nowt to worry about."

"Shut up, Russel. Glenn said they'd try to divide us."

"He's just telling the truth." Russel gestured to Ball. "While this piggie was doing all that funny black man stuff, I figured out exactly what Glenn was doing. He's using you, always has been."

Ball didn't let the warm smile inside himself reach his mouth. It was exactly what he had hoped for: the guy who hated Glenn given an excuse to grass him to the filth.

"What do you need to tell me, Russel?" Ball asked. "Help me help your mate."

Russel sighed, said sorry to Sean, then answered, "Sean never went up to the old folks' home, except one time with the rest of us."

"Shut up!" Sean said.

"He let Glenn use his bank card as ID. They don't need photos, just something with your name on. But it was always Glenn."

"They'll have cameras," Ball said.

"Yeah, but Glenn said it didn't matter. You need a warrant to get the pictures, and since he wasn't doing anything wrong, you wouldn't be able to get one."

"Why fake his ID, then?"

Russel shrugged. "Glenn's trying to modernise us. Doesn't want to be linked with the old boys. The ones who actually got out there and *did* something about our problems."

"He went up there a lot?"

"Loved that old man," Sean finally said. He still didn't look up. "Even went out of hours sometimes. Bribed some orderly and got a key made that let him in the front gate. Clever, like that. The bitch nurse would sometimes try to freeze Glenn out, but he got a lot of tips. Lots more understanding about what we need to do to fight back. Against the invaders. The elite."

Ball turned and stepped away. Tried to call Alicia. Straight to voicemail—she must be out of range, or near one of the cell towers that were down. "Damn."

He'd need a radio to reach her, but with the hills he didn't think it'd have the range.

Stepping out into the rain, it felt lighter now, and he was going to take a huge risk.

He jogged to the main cordon and found a single bobby, put him on guard duty back at the van. Then he ran to the car park, but there were no police vehicles left. Up to the lab-slash-command-centre, where could not find Cross or Knowles.

But Cross's hint was there to make sure Alicia was okay. That they located Glenn Bishop. And Ball could only think of one person nearby who might go against all good sense and help him.

# CHAPTER FIFTY-ONE

DAISYVILLE RETIREMENT HOME APPEARED DEAD. Alicia didn't enjoy taking dumb risks, despite her history to the contrary, but since her mobile had died shortly after she'd called Knowles, all they had was the police radio, a torch each, one miniature crowbar, and a hunch that Scarlett and Glenn couldn't venture too far. With the Church on the Hill being monitored by the army—on DI Cross's instruction—that was a bolthole they couldn't use.

This was one they could.

But it wasn't a slam-dunk. Alicia had to bear in mind that this was a purely long-shot exploratory expedition.

*Recon.*

Halfway up a steep hill, water flowed around, mostly down roads and along gullies designed to sluice it away. But like the rest of the area, saturated land sent the run-off downward. The natural and manmade channels could not cope, leaving random washes to spill over the land.

A minor inconvenience such as a building or motor vehicle wouldn't deter the power of Mother Nature.

They'd made three diversions to get here and had to walk the final half-mile. The front parking lot beyond the gate lay under eight inches of water with a single car swamped as if were bobbing in a lake; the only reason the flood wasn't deeper was that it spilled over the end, draining away.

Having splashed through that natural moat, Knowles jimmied the front door and they entered slowly.

Inside, pressed against the walls, they paused and listened.

Other than the rain on the roof and windows, they could hear very little.

"Police!" Alicia called. "If anyone is in here, make yourself known."

Nothing.

Knowles flicked out his baton to its full length. "You sure you want to do this without backup?"

"You can handle yourself, can't you?" Alicia said.

"I … I don't know what I'm facing."

For the first time, Alicia picked up on the man's fear. She didn't want to push him on this. "We're in trouble regardless of whether this pans out or not. A result will help, but I can't make you do this."

It was cruel. Essentially telling him she wouldn't blame him for turning tail and running away. She also knew he wouldn't take the offer.

Knowles led, shining the torch down past the reception desk. Alicia walked alongside him, saving her battery.

"Maisie!" Alicia called. "Make a noise if you're here."


The basement was now three feet deep in water. Maisie heard them calling her name, muffled through the thick walls and concrete, but she did not respond.

Upon entering, the detectives tripped some remote device linked to Scarlett's phone, and the pair ceased the elaborate production straight away. Scarlett actually appeared pleased.

Glenn downed tools—dressed again like the hokey satanic priest, about to use an actual, honest-to-god *scythe* on her. Where he got such a thing, Maisie couldn't imagine, although the police could easily track such a rare purchase once anyone saw the video of her being killed and mutilated with it.

When someone entered upstairs, they'd conferred behind the battery-powered camera on its tripod, then Glenn returned in his dumb hood and told Maisie they needed to leave. They claimed killing her this way was better in a way, letting the camera watch her drown; the SD card in the recording slot would be undamaged, and as long as the wifi stayed active—and it appeared connected the home's generator—the camera would continue to transmit footage to the cloud. People would still see what they inflicted upon her, one way or another.

They could have cut her throat, and still had time to pull out a *few* organs. But they didn't.

Behind the camera, Glenn stripped off his robe and the pair ascended a ladder, pulling themselves and the ladder back out of the window through which the water poured.

They left her.

Alive.

The rising water was only inches from her back now, and the camera still filmed. It was now positioned in the far corner so it could take in both Maisie, tied to the table, and the locked steel door and the window high up near the ceiling—open, spilling the water in more rapidly.

Leaving Maisie alive, though, could serve only one purpose: it was a trap.

She was *supposed* to call out. Attract attention. It was in line with how the two thought, especially the girl.

Scarlett obviously thought her intelligence, her sheer *brilliance*, could predict any behaviour, when in reality she was a narcissist with some personality disorder linked to control. The ultimate control was in forcing people to do her bidding without explicit giving order—manipulating them, as she clearly was Glenn. A close second was predicting how situations would pan out. Overly elaborate setups and executions, believing she knew what would happen next.

A trap.

An illusion.

One that served only to satisfy the egos of the two killers who had constructed it.

"Mum?" Joanne said.

Maisie twisted to her right where her daughter stood chest deep alongside Peter. "Go. You can't be here."

"Call out," Peter said.

"No."

Joanne burst into tears. "Please, mum. Please call to them."

"I don't need to." Maisie twitched her immobile right hand, waggling her fingers on the end of her wrist cuff. "You're here."

Peter, also crying now, came forward and held her hand. Maisie felt its warmth as if it were right here—the real boy, so solid, so real in this, her final moments on earth.

Her final moments, because the freezing water now inched over her back, covering the table as she shivered in her bindings.

"I don't have long," she said.

Joanne rushed to her, a little fast for a child through water, but the ripples looked real, and the splash she made speckled Maisie's face. The girl's body was warm as she hugged Maisie, and her tears ran over Maisie's face.

"Please call out, mum," Joanne said.

"I wanted you at my deathbed," Maisie said. "This is it."

"No." Peter was sobbing now. His forehead on her arm. "Don't give up. They're police. Or army. They can handle it."

Maisie tried to stay calm. "What if they can't?"

"Then it's their job," Joanne said. "They should keep you safe. They know the risks."

Peter stepped up his tears, his moaning. "Don't be selfish, mum. We can't lose you. We can't live without you."

Which was true. If Maisie died, the children no longer existed. She'd take them with her into the void. "But you're a manifestation of my subconscious."

"If that's true," Joanne said, "then you know a part of you wants to shout for help."

"All of me wants to."

"Then do it," Peter said.

"No."

Peter wiped his face with the backs of his hands, tears smearing. "If you were really ready to die, mum, we wouldn't be begging you. We'd be lying next to you, hugging you. Just waiting for the water to rise."

A huge wave of sadness curled through Maisie, drawing tears of her own. "Or maybe I can't lose you that way again. Please go."

"No." Joanne looked furious. Stubborn to the end. "I won't let you. Now scream." She pinched Maisie's cheek.

"Ow! Don't do that."

Peter reached under the water and nipped the really painful part of the upper arm, the skin around the triceps.

Maisie yelped that time. *Stupid.* The pain wasn't real. Even though it felt absolutely real. "Stop it."

"You stop it." Joanne poked her mum in the eye. "You're making us do this. Making us hurt you so you have to make a noise. You're putting the responsibility on our shoulders instead of your own."

"I know." Maisie sobbed freely, seeing her own motives, using these figments to justify her action. "And I don't want to endanger anyone."

The water almost covered her body now. Only her face was free.

"But you also have knowledge," Peter said. "You can help catch the bad people. Testify at their trial."

413

"Offer clues," Joanne added. "Help stop them hurting anyone else."

It was the only thing that made sense to Maisie. The only thing that justified what she wanted to do so badly. She didn't want to die. But she needed a reason to live. And Joanne gave it to her.

Ready to stick with the living a while longer, Maisie opened her mouth and began to shout.

It took less than two minutes for Alicia to establish that the door to the basement would not open. Braced against a roomful of water, they could not enter that way. She relayed this through the door to a thankfully-still-alive Maisie Jackson.

"The window," came her muffled reply. "Outside." Her words were garbled, followed by a cough. "Car park—"

"She's drowning," Knowles said, sprinting back up the stairs.

"Careful." Alicia followed out of the staircase, running alongside him. "They could still be here. Stay alert."

Back outside, the rain was either easing up or they were used to it, since neither hesitated. They got their bearings and needed no discussion about the layout. Both rushed to the side parking lot; Alicia barely had time to appreciate the irony of the sign reading "Overflow Car Park."

Along the base of the building, rows of windows and vents led to the cellar rooms, where the gas and electrics and other services would be located. Only one window was open. Four feet square, like the others around it.

Propped open by a sandbag.

Alicia hesitated only to check her immediate surroundings, then slid on her butt to open the frame on its hinge and hang her head inside.

A video camera's light and a bare bulb on a builder's flex illuminated the scene, which consisted of Maisie Jackson lying close to the surface of what looked like a swimming pool, although she was all but submerged. Alicia wriggled though feet first and dropped into the water.

The cold shocked her, jolting through her like an all-over ice-cream headache. Being so short, she ducked under for a second—her feet expected solid ground, but it was farther away than anticipated. She could tiptoe and keep her face out of the water, but swam instead, kicking over the camera tripod as she went.

It tipped, fell under the surface, and fizzled out. The radio and phone in her pocket would have gone the same way.

She reached Maisie, who had pulled as far up from her bindings as she could. The water had reached her lips and she couldn't stop it from going down her throat.

A splash signalled Knowles's arrival, and his sharp intake of breath showed Alicia wasn't being a wimp about the cold. The problem was his additional mass made the water rise again.

"Help me!" Alicia said.

Maisie's eyes were closed, head thrashing, her whole body jerking.

Alicia felt around Maisie's neck, finding a strap like a leather belt. "She's pulling too hard. I can't unfasten it. Hold her down."

"She'll drown." Malcolm swam alongside.

"I'll be quick."

Maisie's gag reflex kicked in, choking water back out, but unable to stop it going in.

"*Now*, Malcolm."

Knowles stared just a second. "If she drowns when I'm holding her…"

"It won't matter. She'll be dead anyway."

Knowles sucked in a breath, then pressed on Maisie's chest, shoving her head all the way under. She thrashed harder.

Alicia ducked under. Forced her eyes open. She could only see shapes, but it was enough to guide her hands to the strap. She fiddled, holding her own breath as a measure of how long Maisie had left.

She found the end of the binding, the metal buckle…

The older woman's resistance weakened. Less force in her thrashes.

Alicia removed the end of the beltlike strap. Pulled it free of the prong, leaving the hole empty. She surfaced.

Knowles let go of the woman.

For a second, nothing happened. The body bobbed gently, face exposed.

Knowles leaned over Maisie. "Is she—"

Maisie burst to life, coughing and spluttering, her shoulders back into the dry air, still confused, hacking water from her throat. The panic soon receded.

Alicia felt for the other straps, Maisie's wrists first.

A bang sounded.

Maisie croaked and shifted as Alicia freed her right hand. "I'm sorry," she said. "I'm so sorry."

Alicia untied Maisie's left hand, then as Knowles worked the ankles, she turned to the point where they entered.

The window had slammed shut and a rattle sounded, followed by a clunk. Water still poured in around the edges.

Glenn's voice penetrated from outside. "Enjoy drowning, arseholes."

# CHAPTER FIFTY-TWO

TARIQ'S big red beast of a minibus handled the standing water with the ease of a Land Rover. Ball was impressed with it, happy to be in the vehicle, until he saw Alicia's Auris parked a half-mile from Daisyville Retirement Home. Then told the near-mute driver to step on it.

Ball had considered DI Cross's hint a while longer, and her actions to date—keeping this man close and treating him as an important cog in the community relations network. It was still good policing, even if Tariq didn't exactly epitomise Ball's own philosophies on life. Which was putting it mildly.

The road wound on and the reason for Alicia abandoning her vehicle grew plain: a puddle that would have swamped her engine at the next tight corner. No such trouble for Tariq's Islam-Mobile, which slowed but negotiated the pooled water with ease. It was only when they climbed higher, aquaplaning despite the rainfall having eased somewhat, that the fluttering in Ball's stomach kicked up its own storm.

*A large gate.*

*A short driveway.*

*Car park at the top.*

"Pull over just before the gate," Ball said.

"Sure." Tariq did as instructed, halting the vehicle without shutting it down. "What's next?"

*A large house where Alicia could've been hurt, or worse.*

*Unknown bad guys possibly present on the premises.*

"Detective?" Tariq said. "What do we do now?"

Ball couldn't take a civilian in there. "Keep going up the hill. Try and signal for help."

Tariq slapped the wheel. "No. And you can't make me go. If the people who killed Amina and Ryan are here, I owe it to the families to—"

"You owe it to them to see justice done, not get yourself killed. I assume you aren't a trained military grunt or secret law enforcement operative?"

A pause. "No."

"There are two officers in there—or we can assume they are, due to the car—not answering their radio. Bring backup if you can."

Tariq thought it through.

"Be smart," Ball said. "I can't take you in there, and I can't go in until I know you'll be safe. Now can I rely on you?"

"Who do I bring? Police?"

"Whoever you find first. If it's the army, just tell 'em it's looters who attacked you and a couple of cops. If it's police, tell them Alicia's in trouble, cornered by the serial killer they've been working on."

"Alicia? Not you?"

Ball waved him off. "Make it Alicia. She's the golden girl and everyone knows her."

Tariq nodded firmly. "I'll do as you say. But you *must* catch these people."

"I'll do my best."

Ball jumped out, and Tariq pulled onto the road, steaming upward to circle back to a second staging area that he said he'd seen cropping up earlier. It meant Ball was alone, with just a radio and a baton for company.

Sucking up his fear, unsure which creeped him out more—the nature of a home full of old people waiting to die, or the prospect of history repeating itself.

He might not dream about having been knocked out years earlier, but he certainly thought about it, his instinct firing the occasional bolt of anxiety through him.

Whichever it was, the prospect of losing a fellow officer over-rode all that, and Ball rushed in through the front door, which had been jimmied open.

*Great. That'll help the jitters.*

Wet footprints showed him the direction the pair had gone, but a scattering of them suggested they had returned outside.

"Hello?" he called. "Police!"

A faint scream sounded. Like a TV turned down low.

"Alicia?"

Again, the scream. This time followed by shouts.

Ball headed deeper into the institution. Emergency lighting meant he could see where he was going, but not much else.

He remained cautious around each corner, through each door. Alert for every noise, every movement, every light shift that didn't quite seem right.

He reached a "No Entry" door, where the noise sounded loudest. It was propped open with a fire extinguisher, a flight of stairs beyond, ending with a door. The stairwell was almost entirely flooded.

"Alicia?" Ball called down the stairs.

"Glenn?" came Alicia's shrill voice. "Glenn, I'm telling you, Scarlett is dangerous. She won't let you live after this. You're a *tool.*"

"That's putting it lightly," Ball replied. "But I'm not Glenn."

"Ball? What are you doing here?" She sounded worried.

"Rescuing you. Any other way in except this door?"

"Get out of here." Panic rose in her tone. "They're in the building. Glenn and Scarlett."

"It's all clear out here. Come on, I'll—"

The sound of something solid striking his skull was familiar. The sick feeling came back to him too, and that uncontrollable wobble in the legs sent him to his knees. As he keeled over sideways, unable to keep his eyes open, he thought, *Just bloody perfect,* and was suddenly more embarrassed than afraid.

Then the world turned black, the only sensation one of coldness, and that he was soaking wet all over.

# CHAPTER FIFTY-THREE

INSTEAD OF RISKING the use of Scarlett's waterlogged vehicle, which they had planned to ditch anyway, Scarlett and Glenn tossed the keys and fled across the field out back of the old folks' home. They traversed a concrete path out to what was billed as an orchard but had long since ceased producing edible apples.

Scarlett would have preferred to watch the cops die, but it wasn't that sort of an event. It wasn't the *goal* here. Heck, if they didn't die, they'd help spread the word. Cement the legend. Glenn and Scarlett were now home free.

Once Glenn had knocked that unexpected copper out and kicked him into the pool in the basement, Scarlett insisted they go in case more followed.

Neither of them had responded to the lady-detective's accusations, trying to turn Glenn against her, and the dash into the heavy drizzle felt like a celebration. Filming three people drowning, with a fourth as good as dead already, was exactly the foundation upon which they could build.

The ground was sodden, of course, but it didn't matter. They had the best all-weather clothing money could buy, and had changed into it just before that final copper arrived. With a backpack full of non-perishable meals, the plan was to run into the wild, trekking a route that would take them to safety before fleeing the country on passports procured two weeks ago.

Ironically, the counterfeit documents had come from a Muslim gang, of the type who smuggled terrorists-in-waiting (or "refugees" as they were sometimes known) *into* the country. Scarlett liked that they used the same sort of people they were fighting against to aid their cause. Keeping Scarlett and Glenn alive was certainly a means to the immigrants' own defeat.

Glenn had arranged it all. Scarlett was grateful to him, and he was proud to have pleased her.

They took a long, winding route. Dirt, but infused with stony ground, one of the few such paths to survive thanks to steep channels on either side where run-off from the highest ground would divert, leaving only the rain to batter it.

Already, powering on, they looked back down on the home where the police and that hippie bitch were either dead or dying.

It was all perfect. In theory.

The trouble was, now as in their domesticity, she didn't trust Glenn. She had taken a long, long time to reach the point where she knew he'd do anything for her, but she never fully accepted his strength as a given. He was good at planning, at working the image, presenting Scarlett as an obedient little woman, but he too often behaved like that in private too. She expected him to, one day, demand their relationship become what he wanted it to be around his mates.

She couldn't allow that.

Up one of her sleeves, she'd stashed a knife that Glenn had ordered over the net—a Ka-Bar military fighting knife. It was razor sharp and, once they reached level ground, out of sight of any road or private property, Scarlett would slip it out and slash the back of Glenn's legs. Let him bleed a bit, then plunge it into his belly.

*Not* a kill-shot.

One that would kill him eventually, sure, and hopefully he'd die up here. As she "escaped." She'd try to leave the country, but if caught, she'd insist she was fleeing the clutches of a manipulative psychopath.

Claiming Glenn threatened her, insisted his mates would violate her before he killed her … they'd believe her. She'd be a hero. The plucky heroine who survived.

*Even if Glenn lives, he'll be the one to take the fall.*

It was odd. She loved him, but his devotion to that old fool in the home made him weak, and sacrificing him felt satisfying. Her dad had once told her these people weren't really patriots, but nationalists. To be a patriot, you had to lose something—to sacrifice a part of yourself, be it internally or physically, to do what was right despite the cost to oneself.

Well, what was killing your boyfriend if not a patriotic sacrifice?

A picky person would say it wasn't a *real* sacrifice. That devotion to Remy Duval, to the Vanguard's legacy, made Glenn less useful. Needing to divert attention from Remy, needing to kill, needing to safeguard their reputation … Glenn was *needy-needy-needy*, and his plan was badly thought out. Scarlet had saved it, saved *him*, to a point he didn't deserve to see their baby.

She would raise the child the right way. Instil in it the true value of loyalty, of sacrifice, of doing what needed to be done.

They crested the hill, ready to turn back to appreciate all they were leaving behind, all they'd never see again. The level ground was a godsend. Scarlett was ready for a drink, ready to eat her final meal with Glenn.

But something wasn't right. Glenn had stopped dead in his tracks.

Scarlett saw why.

Beside a four-way signpost on the public trail, two people were waiting. The handsome black detective whom Scarlett really wanted to bone, and the little blonde bitch who'd beaten her to it.

"How…?" Scarlett began, but ran out of energy to speak.

"Hey there." The blonde waved, a cheery smile even as the wind took her hood down. "You guys are under arrest. Cool, huh?"

# CHAPTER FIFTY-FOUR

"IT'S HARDER to knock someone unconscious than telly makes out." Alicia dangled a pair of handcuffs from her fingers, trying hard not to shiver. And failing. She was frozen through to her bones, soaked and trembling. "Especially when the silly person doing the assault dumps the victim in a pool of cold water. All that does is revive them faster."

Everyone's hoods were down, all faces out in the open. Alicia had tied back her hair, as had Scarlett. The men didn't have to worry about wind, but the rain, mostly a light shower now, still sprayed them with every gust. And every gust pushed Alicia toward curling into a ball and demanding someone light a fire nearby. She wanted to strip naked and wrap herself in a duvet, then take a hot shower and sleep for a week.

But there was work to be done.

"So am I going to put these on you?" Alicia said. "Or do you fancy saving me the bother?"

Both killers glanced at the public footpath leading to the moorland, away from the main road. No one needed a degree to see what they were thinking.

"We have your general direction, if you run," Alicia said. "If you hadn't noticed, there are a few army guys around, and they're not bad at tracking hostile individuals across barren terrain. Soon as they get here, we give them your description and they're off looking for a woman with a backpack."

Glenn twitched slightly, as Alicia had hoped he would.

"Oh, she'll be alone," Alicia said. "Scarlett's going to kill you the first chance she gets."

It was Scarlett who spoke first. "How did you *find* us?"

"We escaped," Knowles replied. "Then used our eyes. Saw you heading this way."

"Yeah, you're not exactly covert," Alicia said.

"Maisie told us there was a path up here." Knowles extended his own cuffs, still more than ten feet away, equally wet and, presumably, equally cold. "We took the road up and thought we'd bring you these. They'll suit you."

It wasn't quite that simple, of course.

Ball had come around quickly and started shouting. It had taken a couple of minutes for him to get his bearings. He'd have a concussion for sure, and had even vomited twice, but with no way to get the door open, he was able to function enough to seek out their window.

By the time he smashed the padlock Glenn had added, all three were floating—all *five,* if you included the kids, whom Maisie spoke to occasionally—and once all were out of the basement, they needed to work out what to do next.

Through squinting eyes, Ball mentioned that Tariq was bringing help, but Alicia chose not to probe how that partnership arose, instead weighing the possibility of retreat against the practicality of pursuit.

Their quarry had left their car in the flooded lot, meaning they were either still on the premises or fleeing on foot.

Maisie was the one who had spotted them in the distance, taking a winding path up toward the moors, and directed Alicia and Knowles along the road.

Wrapped in blankets from the home, Maisie would keep an eye on Ball, and Ball would reciprocate, both having been hurt in their own ways. They'd wait inside, get dry, stay warm, while Alicia and Knowles—against all good sense—pushed on, also wrapped in blankets.

It was easier going on the tarmac, even with the run-off impeding progress. A signpost marked the next stage, which again they hiked to on foot. That the track from the road was in such good shape was a minor miracle in itself, although it was probably due to so much water running down the hillside—most of it into Daisyville Retirement Home's basement.

Now, Alicia faced the pair of killers.

Scarlett glared at her. "How…"

Alicia grinned back at her and gave a little wave. "Decision time."

"Easy choice," Scarlett said, and rushed at Alicia.


Knowles wasn't sure if he wanted to tackle the girl or the guy, but the moment Scarlett went for Alicia and Glenn barrelled his way over, the decision was out of his hands.

However much society wished for parity or "equality" between genders, it was always harder for a man to hit a woman. A decent man, anyway. And Knowles strived to be decent.

With Glenn, though, he could strike without guilt.

Knowles flicked out his baton and saw Alicia do the same. They each positioned their instrument on their shoulder, a hand outstretched. Both issued the instruction, "Halt or I *will* strike," and neither assailant listened.

As they continued forward, weapons flashed in their hands. A mean-looking knife for Scarlett, military possibly, and a club of some sort for Glenn. It was Glenn who made it to his opponent first.

Knowles swung his baton, connecting with Glenn's lower leg,

and made him stumble. But Glenn was ready for it. He rolled, sprang up, and hit Knowles's wrist, his baton flying aside.

The club was a rounders bat, like a miniature baseball bat.

Now Knowles had to face him without a weapon.

Alicia tossed the baton to her other hand, allowing her to swing it upward, disarming Scarlett as she stabbed forward in a rage.

The knife flew several yards, spinning end-over-end, before sticking in the ground blade-first.

Alicia then struck at the killer's knee, but pulled the power on the blow, reluctant to cripple someone, even Scarlett.

The woman dropped, but pushed off with her good leg, tackling Alicia as if in a game of rugby. The pair slapped to the ground, the rough, springy heather meaning they didn't get coated in mud. Scarlett delivered several blows to Alicia's midriff, then switched to her face.

The baton was useless this close, so Alicia discarded it. After a particularly hard punch to her cheekbone, she summoned all she'd learned the past year in her kickboxing class—namely the boxing side—and formed a tight fist. She drove it hard into Scarlett's side. Scarlett grunted in pain—an effective strike. Alicia hit her in the same place, and Scarlet reared up.

As Scarlett's assault eased momentarily, Alicia wrapped her legs around her enemy, and shifted her over. Both women rolled, Alicia shaking loose. They found their feet.

Then they came together again.

Alicia was at least six inches shorter than Scarlett, maybe eight or nine, and though she'd never progressed to the point where she could compete in the ring, Alicia was confident enough to kick out. She stunned Scarlett with a firm heel to the thigh—a dead leg—and brought her next kick to the woman's face. Following it with a knee to the rib cage—avoiding the stomach after what Maisie explained about the pregnancy. Alicia then ended the bout when Scarlett bent over, with a knee to the jaw.

She cuffed the unconscious woman and spun to see how Knowles was doing. It wasn't good.

Glenn had overcome the detective constable, battered him into submission. And now as Knowles lay in a heap, Glenn retrieved Scarlett's discarded knife, and was heading back that way. Even if Alicia could reach them in time, she couldn't do much against someone like Glenn.

That didn't mean she wouldn't try, though.


Glenn laughed at the little blonde strumpet. Stupid bitch. Almost ruined everything. Sure, the plan got out of hand, but he'd enjoyed the fistfight with the black cop. Glenn didn't get into much physical stuff anymore, what with surveillance ruining the football crews and making those outings for a proper ruck a rare treat.

Cops get trained in effective techniques, but they were limited. They had rules to follow. Glenn never did. Smashing a rival crew, or pummelling a copper—or just some mouthy prick who needed teaching a lesson—they were all fun to destroy.

In recent years, though, he had concentrated on the bigger picture, meaning he could perpetrate less violence than before.

Some days it was really hard. Long-term planning, convincing people he could not be jailed due to his thoughts and feelings, keeping his words and actions guarded in public—it all took a toll. As Scarlett's dad often lectured, where's the patriotism if there's no personal sacrifice? Well, Glenn had sacrificed plenty, in more ways than one.

Killing the Muslims and that councillor was fun, though. A release he had needed. But this—knuckle on skin, hard-toed boots seeking out the soft spots of a man, and a *black* man as a bonus—was what he lived for. You could go through all the self-defence classes in the world, but when it came down to proper street-level fighting, experience and strength won out every time.

*A baton strike to the thigh.*

Yeah, right. Like he hadn't shaken that off a dozen times before.

The number of marches Glenn had been on, even pepper spray had little more effect than a chicken vindaloo—which he only ever ate these days when he knew the meat wasn't halal.

So he'd gotten the upper hand. Even allowed the detective to get a few blows in. It was hardly a contest, though. His happiness shining through, Glenn hit the black man half a dozen times, pummelling him until he fell, then kicked him in all the places that his retracted elbows couldn't protect.

Now he had a knife. Not that he could remember where it came from originally. He was pretty sure this was one that could be traced, since he had purchased it online with his own credit card. It was why he decided to leave the weapon in the flat when they'd abandoned the place.

Why would Scarlett be carrying it?

For a split-second he considered the bimbo cop's assertion that Scarlett was planning on doing away with him once they were free and clear.

But no.

He had Scarlett where he wanted her. A compromise agreement in many ways, one she supported him in. Advised him. But *he* was in charge. *He* was running this show.

Wasn't he?

He gripped the knife.

Even Maisie tried to get in his head with that bullshit about Scarlett being the boss, wearing the trousers.

Glenn had predicted they'd try stuff like that, and Scarlett had come up with just this scenario—that they'd lie, tell Glenn that Scarlett was playing him, or that she would betray him. The couple agreed—whatever happened, neither would flip on the other. They would fight to the end. No jail time. If they couldn't live free, they'd die on their own terms.

Standing over the prone detective, it didn't seem like that would be an issue. Even as the blonde bitch ran at him, he laughed, knowing it was pointless. She couldn't reach them in time, and even if she did, what could she do? Tap him gently with the baton like her colleague?

The black man, bleeding from his brow and mouth, held out a hand. "No ... please..."

Glenn pulled back his hand for a stab to the gut, one he would angle upward so it punctured the heart.

An engine revved.

Louder than the pathetic war cry from the blonde bimbo cop.

Glenn first checked to his left—the bimbo's approach, almost slow motion in its pathetic effort.

Then right, where a vehicle hurtled toward him.

A bright red minibus, tore over sodden moorland, mud and mulch kicking up behind in the faint light.

The black detective somehow found the strength to dive away, while Glenn's feet would not move out of the vehicle's path.

White Arabic script blazing across the bonnet told Glenn who the owner was.

A wet thump and the world blurring meant only one thing: he'd been hit by the vehicle at speed.

Glenn sensed the rush of air behind him as the force flung him backward. His vision narrowed before he hit the ground, zeroing in on that Arabic writing.

His final vision in this world, in that half-second before the darkness consumed him entirely, was the phrase he had reviled all his life: *Allahu-Akbar.*

God is great.

Well, Glenn was about to find out for sure.

# CHAPTER FIFTY-FIVE

IT WASN'T A PLEASANT AFTERMATH.

In the days that followed, Knowles was placed on medical leave and his union was informed he would face an internal inquiry regarding his actions at the Daisyville Retirement Home —namely placing himself in danger. A bit of a downer.

Alicia tried to take responsibility, since she was the ranking officer at the time, but then DI Cross jumped in with the same objection; it was *her* responsibility, not Alicia's. Both were suspended from front line duty pending an investigation, meaning they were still active detectives but would take on no new cases.

DS Ball was the only one not raising his hand for a suspension, happy to take a couple of weeks off with his second concussion in the line of duty. Not as cool as getting stabbed, as Alicia had been a few years ago, but he'd ride this one a while longer.

When Tariq Bashir was arrested for the death of Glenn Bishop, protests arose. One involved a bit of a skirmish between constables and a few emotional advocates for Tariq's immediate release. DCI Watson attempted to calm things by issuing statements that were clearly meant to be *read-between-the-lines-you-*

*idiots*, telling the world that "a male was arrested on suspicion of causing death by dangerous driving, as the law requires a full investigation into every unnatural death. *However*, extenuating circumstances may be taken into account regarding whether charges are brought."

To Alicia, it seemed as clear as day that the police were unlikely to pursue a conviction, but some people just had to make out like they were victims right to the end.

A day after his arrest, Tariq Bashir was released on police bail. Five days after that, he was set free with no charges.

Alicia used her downtime to make up with Stacey and appease both mother and daughter. She spent more time with Iothor, and learned more about Vikings than she had ever thought she could, his enthusiasm for his heritage inspiring a brief dalliance with her own family tree. But then the inquiry got underway, quashing all that. She had to defend her actions, and help the Crown Prosecution Service prepare a case against Scarlett Austin.

So far, Scarlett was sticking to her guns in claiming she was *forced* to participate, or Glenn would have killed her. Amongst other violent threats, many sexual. Alicia knew this to be false, and there were plenty of flags pointing that way, but their case wasn't rock solid by any means.

One evening, two weeks after the floods subsided, Kate Hague showed up unannounced on Alicia's doorstep. She wore a nice skirt and a smart blouse, and her hair was tied up. She had a handbag on one shoulder and she looked inches taller in her heels. She said, "It's today."

Alicia held still in the doorway. Iothor was in the garden with Stacey. "What is?"

"My dad's going to die."

Alicia was at the point now where she trusted Iothor with Stacey, and he was comfortable enough to offer to watch her without being asked. All Alicia had to do was say, "I think I need to nip out," and gesture to Kate, whom she invited in to say hi.

Kate had come in a taxi. Her mental health issues and medication forbade a driving licence at the moment, so Alicia drove her in the courtesy car covered by the West Yorkshire Police's insurance while her own got repaired.

The chit-chat on the way over was banal stuff, confirming Kate was doing well, that she'd trusted the non-imaginary friend from the coffee shop to come over and they had done some Netflix box sets. She was also using a new therapist—in addition to Dr Rasmus, not instead of—to attempt some visualisation exercises. These had calmed Kate enough to understand the full implications of turning off her father's machines.

Progress.

So there was little in the way of tension as Alicia accompanied Kate into the private hospital. Dr Rasmus and a senior consultant were waiting, as was Barbara, a nurse with whom Kate had grown close over the years. Without words, they showed Kate into her father's room.

Stepping over the threshold, her grip tightened only slightly in Alicia's hand, but there was none of the hesitation of the previous visit. Alicia, though, could think of no place worse than this right now. She was only here for the closure, and to support Kate.

Richard was a flabby mess in the bed. They performed physiotherapy daily, turned him regularly to prevent sores, monitored his every signal and electrical pulse from his heart and brain. He was just flesh right now, as dead as any corpse Alicia had seen. Yet, because of that heartbeat—the blood flowing, the brief, sporadic spike of activity from that oxygen-starved brain—he was still a part of her life.

The consultant went through Kate's options again, the medical summary of Richard Hague's condition, confirmation that this man would never, *ever* wake up to become a functioning human. He emphasised there was a 0.1% chance of him opening his eyes and breathing on his own, but even if that miracle occurred, after almost five years in this state, he would never be conscious. A newborn brain, incapable of learning, fed through a tube forever.

Kate signed the consent forms.

This was not killing someone. It was withdrawing treatment. Treatment that was almost cruel in a sense, to both the man lying there and the people whose lives he'd shattered.

There was no ceremonial Big Button™ to press which commenced a long *beeeeeeep* of the heart monitor. It was the consultant and nurse powering down several machines, one at a time.

The final device to be turned off was the breathing apparatus. Barbara did the honours regarding the machine, and the consultant snapped the clasp off Richard's tracheotomy tube, removing the support altogether.

And Richard breathed.

"This is normal," the consultant said. "Whenever we remove a patient's breathing support, they can carry on for a while. Your father will fade away slowly now, probably within twenty-four hours. Maybe more, it's hard to tell. You're welcome to wait."

Kate watched her father for a good thirty seconds. Alicia read no remorse or regret. There was no hint she wanted to change her mind. It was the most peaceful she'd seen the girl in years.

"No thanks," Kate said. "Just let me know when it's done. I've found an undertaker and he'll make arrangements for disposal of the body."

The clinical language worried Alicia, but not too much. It was good that Kate was moving on. And although Alicia was tempted to stay, to watch the Century Killer take his final breath, she had other things to do.

Kate came for dinner with Iothor and Stacey, and although it wasn't time to reveal to Stacey who this mystery woman really was, the two laughed together and later played a memory game, turning over cards to match pairs of animals.

It felt like unorthodox yet genuine family time.

The only thing missing for Alicia was what she hoped to achieve the following day. Yes, Calderdale could handle it, but Alicia wanted to do it herself. It wasn't a new investigation, but a continuation, and would help cement the case against Scarlett and finalise the cold cases of Shona Maynard, Valerie Msuba, Virgil Baines, and twenty-eight other murder victims.

# CHAPTER FIFTY-SIX

ALICIA MET DI Cross at the Daisyville Retirement Home with two constables as backup, ready to serve the arrest warrants.

They had discussed the approach before entering, both concerned the full horror of Remy's actions would never be fully exposed. Alicia had no doubt there would be others, not just those buried beneath the Church on the Hill. No one is born with such skill, and no one perfects their art so quickly.

Strategy agreed, they served the warrant to the front desk and were shown to Remington Duval's room, where the man lay sleeping. His nurse sat beside him in a cushioned chair. No scrubs. In fact, she looked quite elegant in a fitted tweed jacket and a pencil skirt, with her hair tied up and wearing what appeared to be designer-framed glasses.

"Thought I'd make an effort," she said. "I assume you'll be photographing me before a formal interview."

"Stand up, please," Cross instructed, removing her handcuffs.

Audrey remained seated. "Is that necessary?"

Alicia gave Audrey her most special smile, the dimple-heavy one reserved for the conclusion of cases like this one, where the culprit thought they'd got away with it. She recited Bertie's words: "*If they didn't have birds egging 'em on, no way they'd have the balls to come home at night…*" Head tilt. Shrug. "It's true, in this case. Jimmy Grantham was the bitch here. Remy's easily-led mate. You know we found his body yesterday?"

"James?" Audrey's hand fluttered to her chest. "He's dead?"

"Overdose," Cross said.

"Interesting note, though," Alicia said. "He wrote, 'Ya nearly had me. I win.' Not exactly a confession but in the context of my conversation with him a couple of weeks ago, I'm taking it that way."

Cross had more to add. "After matching more than half the victims's dates of disappearance to times the police lost track of Remy and James, we'd applied for arrest warrants. Had to go through relatives and responsible persons. As you clearly know by now. Word must have got to James, as it clearly has you."

"I have nothing to hide," Audrey said.

"But you won't deny it." Alicia sat opposite Audrey, on a chair pulled away from the wall. "Remy was a killer. And you knew it."

"It's all in the past." Audrey shook her head. "He's no danger to anyone. Am I a danger, detectives?"

"You helped commit almost thirty murders."

Audrey smirked. "Thirty. Oh, dear, Remy really did do a wonderful job, didn't he?"

"It's more? How many more?"

Audrey nodded. "Probably around thirty in that church place we found. One of Remy's silly strumpet girls came up with the place. I don't know if she was in on the full plan, or if she ended up far below with the others. But he kept on coming back to me."

"Are you confessing, Mrs Phillips?" Cross asked.

"It's Ms Phillips, actually. And I believe I am helping you fill in the blanks."

Alicia kept them on track. "You loved him so much you forgave his infidelities?"

"Always. And it's not infidelity when you have permission. I enjoyed *making love* with Remy. Not the things he sometimes wanted. For that, I told him to pick up a negro or something. And he kind of liked that. A bit of rape. I mean, we never called it that, of course, but it would sort of turn me on, watching him work out his frustration with a coloured girl while James held her down." Her tone mimicked that of a lady reminiscing about an amusing boat trip or a faux-pas at some party. "After, he'd be so tender with me, so gentle. Worshiping my body. I could handle him defiling those people, but I got a bit miffed with the local girls."

"Did he rape them too?" Alicia asked.

"Of course not!" The elderly woman seemed offended by the suggestion. "But he was a charismatic man. He spoke well, attracted a lot of us, men and women, to his cause. It made him seem powerful. Even when he was in his thirties, he was attracting girls half his age. Can you blame him?"

Cross stared at the floor.

"It started as fun for the boys," Audrey said. "A bet that they wouldn't dare kill a black. But they did. Went off to Liverpool—I think that was their first. They were scared after, but I soon pulled them back together. Remy, anyway." Her eyebrows bobbed. "*He* sorted Jimmy out. Kept him scared."

"How many others?" Alicia asked again.

Audrey waved it off. "Oh, I don't know. A few went wrong, of course. I went along a couple of times. Sometimes they raped, sometimes they didn't. Sometimes torture, sometimes a clean one. We even popped up to Scotland."

"Were you there often?" Cross asked.

"No, less than half." Audrey raised a finger to make a point. "But I never laid a hand on anyone. I just watched."

"And provided alibis for the others." Cross turned partially away.

"Go on," Alicia said. "You say it's all in the past. That there's no danger."

Audrey placed a hand on Remy's and gave him a loving look. "He didn't understand about character, not the way I do. Not the way he finally did when he got to know Priti, his nurse."

"He got away with it," Cross said. "Isn't even burdened by guilt the way you are."

"I'm not sure it's guilt." Audrey kept her hand still on Remy's, moving to his wrist. "It's more ... regret that we made those mistakes."

"Because you didn't understand. You didn't get it."

Audrey smiled and released Remy. "Mistakes. Youthful mistakes."

"You're younger than both James and Remy. *You* won't be getting away with it. And at least Remy will be named."

Audrey stood. "My job is done. But is there really any justice in prosecuting him? Or even me? I have at most four months to go." She touched her stomach. "The cancer will take me long before a jail sentence."

Just like James Grantham, she expected an illness would help her evade answering for what she did.

Remy's chest rose and fell.

Alicia said, "It's out of our hands. For now, he'll remain here."

"Empty of the past and the future." Audrey held out her hands for the cuffs.

"Time for everyone to move on, right?" Cross said sarcastically. "Everyone gets away with it, including you?"

"Oh, I don't think justice will be served that way."

Alicia frowned, again processing. She then said a name, one that had popped up in the files of the intelligence officers concerning the Vanguard's hooliganism. Not something she'd connected because the name was different now, but that niggle, that one thing she was going to look deeper into. The one unanswered question. But now it made sense.

"That's right, my dear. What a clever little thing you are."

"Looks like we have one more stop to make," Alicia said.

"Remy's head was turned," Alicia told the gathering of people in a hushed tone. "By someone much younger than him. Someone clever. Someone we considered too young to be a part of it, being ten or twelve years old at the time of the first murder."

"I've changed," the prisoner replied.

"I know. But not that much. And it doesn't matter anyway. We knew Audrey was the mother figure, like Scarlett was for Glenn, deranged through whatever as-yet-undiagnosed condition led her to enjoy the sadism. But for the murders of a couple of weeks ago, it had to be more than Glenn and Scarlett. Someone had to be pushing from long before the remains emerged on Basil Warner's farm. A relationship formed some time ago. An intelligent person. A way with words. Access to volumes of older works. An enthusiasm for the history of the surrounding area. Someone who'd love to get books into the hands of people who don't normally take an interest."

"No." Costas shook his head, held back by one of the constables Alicia and Cross had brought to the library. "Is a mistake."

"It was odd to even suspect you, Lauren," Alicia said. "But going back through photos of marches, intelligence dossiers on the football hooligans and their bits on the side, there you were. After 1976, the eighteen-year-old beauty hanging on Remy's arm. Every step of the way. Then throughout the modern era, with Remy so close to death, arranging the current crop to go see him. To cement the legend of the man. Present his diaries to the new acolytes, and make them scared of being exposed. Scarlett or Glenn, it doesn't matter. You were desperate to keep Remy's reputation intact, so instructed Scarlett to push Glenn into killing the same way. Access to the books, to the people, to the history. It was all you in the background."

Even in a wheelchair, not resisting, not even shouting, Lauren needed to be cuffed. Procedure. She stared at her lap. "Even if that was true, that I helped do something worse than march with them, you'd never prove it."

"I think we have about four months' worth of witness accounts from a woman scorned to help us piece it together. Hearsay, but we'll head in the right direction. Apparently, Jimmy Grantham told Audrey it was you who persuaded him to stop. When Peter Sutcliffe, the Yorkshire Ripper got caught, he says you got scared. You and Remy lasted a bit longer, but he dumped you after he wrapped his car around a tree." Alicia gestured to the chair. "He literally walked away with cuts and bruises, leaving his injured passenger with her spine snapped."

"An evil man," Cross said, "who persuaded women he was in love with them, and manipulated them into his world. Made them think they were important. But really, he just held onto you until someone more useful, or less of a drag, came along."

A tear rolled down Lauren's cheek, but she said nothing as the constable rolled her out to the van.

And although Alicia was more concerned with the anguished cries from Costas, whose world was about to implode with the knowledge his wife was not only once a serial killer's lover, tempting the man away from his long-term girlfriend, but who somehow resurrected her urges to inspire a new generation of death.

Were her actions directed toward supremacy?

Or was it the thrill of the kill? Of controlling others so absolutely that they would murder at her urging?

Alicia leaned toward the latter.

Despite this terrible turn for the man, though, Alicia was finally satisfied at her case drawing to an end. Everyone who could be punished would be. And those who could not would simply rot away to nothing.

# CHAPTER FIFTY-SEVEN

AFTER BOOKING the remaining suspects in Halifax, Alicia detoured back and stopped at Maisie Jackson's house. She was harvesting the garden, baskets full of veg. When she spotted Alicia, she beamed brightly and stood to greet her.

"I won't come too close," she said. "I'm filthy."

Alicia gazed around at the empty trellises where peas and beans had once hung. "Tidying up?"

"Pulling in the summer stock. I'll sow the winter stuff in the greenhouse. Do you eat chillis?"

"Sometimes."

"I have some for you. I have far too many. They'll only go to waste. And…" Maisie paused cautiously. "I also have enough of my other herbs to see me through the winter. I could spare a little if you…" Again, she let the sentence trail off.

"I'm fine for … herbs," Alicia said. "But I'll take a couple of chillis."

"Splendid." Maisie, her faint US accent almost eradicated with that one word, led Alicia toward the greenhouse.

As they walked, Alicia filled her in on the arrests, how the men were all but dead, and the women had been apprehended.

"An odd balance," Maisie commented. "The evil men do, cleaned up by the women who loved them."

"Who *thought* they loved them. Really, though, it was all an act. A legacy of manipulation."

Inside the greenhouse, Maisie plucked several peppers, showing Alicia the red cayennes and the green jalapeños, explaining that her cayennes were hotter than usual, so to only use half what a recipe called for.

Alicia thanked her, but after looking around the greenhouse, she had a question. "Are you really planning on sowing winter vegetables?"

"Why do you ask?"

"I don't see any equipment."

The greenhouse was all but bare, except some tomato plants and the remaining chillis. Maisie's special herbs were gone, presumably drying somewhere, and the clearing of the garden appeared more methodical than taking the ripe plants down.

"I thought I might explore my husband's offer," Maisie said.

"The deputy chief constable?"

"Correct. Remember I told you he had a lot on with the drugs problems? I'm flying down tonight to see if I can advise on a rather odd case. Something to do with a murder on a *lifeboat*, of all things. His officers have several cases each and he'd like this one solved."

"Getting back into the world," Alicia said. "Using your brain for something useful. It's a good move."

"We'll see. I doubt it'll be long term, but who knows?"

"Any chance of a reconciliation?"

Maisie shook her head sadly. "I don't think that's possible." She looked down and to the side. "We've discussed this, and it's still no. Too much has happened. Now let me speak to the lady." Back to Alicia.

"Will Peter and Joanne be going with you?" Alicia asked.

Maisie considered the question, turning slowly and gazing

around her property as she did so. "If they want to come, they'll come."

"Good luck."

"Thank you. And goodbye, Alicia. It was lovely getting to know you."

There was no hug, no kiss on the cheek, just a little handshake. Alicia left her then, not satisfied with the outcome, but hopeful. Hopeful for a brighter future.

For all of them.

# EPILOGUE

KATE'S FATHER lasted almost a whole week.

The doctors had told her that he might now take longer than twenty-four hours to "fade away" but she hadn't expected this much longer. It was abnormal but not unheard of, or so they assured her.

After the first couple of days, Kate grew worried that the stress and anxiety might threaten her stability. She thought maybe it would be too much, that the waiting might overwhelm her already fragile grasp on reality. But it didn't. In fact, she hadn't felt this serene in years.

Since before.

Now, it was like she was waiting for a train, frustrated at the delay.

Her friend Rachel, whom she'd met at work, had stopped by the previous day. They sat and chatted about some of the regular customers, and a couple of theories on the box set of a TV show they'd gotten into.

Having a real friend was nice.

Kate really felt like she was getting better.

Tonight, she had popped by the hospital after work and

Barbara informed her that her father's breathing was shallow and laboured. The nurse said they thought he was about to pass away a couple of times, only for him to start up again. It wouldn't be long now.

Kate hadn't planned on being here. Originally, she expected to wake the following morning and be informed the body was ready for collection. She was going to burn it and scatter the ashes somewhere significant—hadn't decided where yet. Maybe she'd consult the relatives of some of his victims. Or just flush him down the loo.

The man no longer meant anything to her. She'd come to terms with the fact that the father she thought she knew had never existed. The man who'd committed those awful crimes was the real Richard Hague, and he'd died in a basement with a bullet in the neck. The thing that occupied a bed here was just meat.

And she slept soundly knowing this.

In fact, she'd even slept tonight. A power nap in the relatives' room, waking to several bangs and shouts. She returned to what seemed like a commotion outside her father's room.

The jolt woke her properly—a spike of panic and anticipation and fear and resolve, all churning at once.

Shouting.

Orders being barked.

A huge *crack* sounded.

Someone fell over.

Kate had heard something like that before. Like the crack.

Her father, shooting her kidnapper through his own body. Giving her and Alicia a chance of escape.

It was a gunshot.

As Kate rushed closer, she saw that the person who fell over hadn't toppled on their own. It was Barbara, the nurse who'd kept her informed, who'd been so nice, who never talked down to her.

There was a bloody hole in her chest.

She lay on the floor, splayed lifelessly. Another shot came from room 237, where Kate's father should have died days earlier.

To one side, two guards lay with similar wounds. Behind a desk two, more people cowered, eyes closed, visible only to Kate from this angle.

And then two figures emerged from the room, all in black. Ski masks, gloves, boots. They were pulling the bed in which her father was lying, and two more pushed from behind.

Kate stared, unable to move, as one of the men pulled a gun and aimed it her way.

Kate could only whimper. "No…"

"Not her," one of the men said, at the back, his gruff voice almost a growl.

"You said no witnesses," replied the one next to him—a rail-thin figure, tall, a nasal voice.

"Not her," the man repeated.

And they were off.

But recognition piqued inside Kate.

The voice.

The thin man's frame, his height.

His hollow eyes boring into her as he passed, with her father in the bed where he'd lived the past five years. Years Kate had suffered, years she had tried to piece her life back together.

The time during which a hallucination had spoken to her. Spoken with the same nasal voice she'd just heard, glared with the same eyes from behind the mask.

That man, armed with his friends, rushing her father to the exit while she crouched, frozen in terror.

*The Skinny Man was real.*

And he'd come back for her father.

Alicia Friend will return in 2019

To keep up to date, follow A. D. Davies on your preferred retailer, or look him up on BookBub.

Alternatively, for exclusive news and previews, and the occasional freebie, join the mailing list:

http://addavies.com/Newsletter

ALSO BY A. D, DAVIES

**Adam Park Thrillers:**

*The Dead and the Missing*

*A Desperate Paradise*

*The Shadows of Empty men*

*Night at the George Washington Diner*

*Master the Flame*

*Under the Long White Cloud*

**Alicia Friend Investigations:**

*His First His Second*

*In Black In White*

*With Courage With Fear*

*A Friend in Spirit*

*To Hide To Seek*

*A Flood of Bones*

**Standalone:**

*Three Years Dead*

*Rite to Justice*

*The Sublime Freedom*

**Lost Origins Novels (as Antony Davies):**

*Tomb of Aradia*

*The Reaper Seal*

**Co-Authored**

*Project Return Fire* – with Joe Dinicola

THREE YEARS DEAD

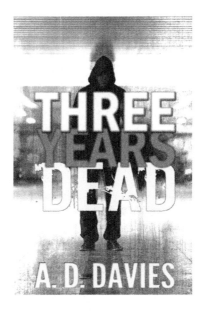

*When a good man . . . becomes a bad cop . . . but can't remember why.*

Detective Sergeant Martin Money wakes from a coma with no memory of the past three years. During those years, his reputation spiralled downwards, from decorated officer, through drug abuse, bribes, and multiple assaults on his wife, culminating in an attempt on his life, a crime nobody wants solving.

With only a junior detective willing to work with him, Martin investigates the disappearance of a sex worker, but to truly redeem himself, he must resist the temptations offered by that life, and work out why every single one of his former friends and colleagues seem to be lying to him.

# TOMB OF ARADIA

**The ancient world is not what we thought…**

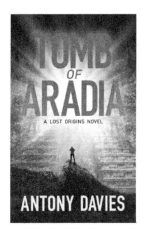

Freelance treasure hunter Jules has finally located the bangle stolen from his dying mother, an artifact that may unravel a centuries-old secret: the location of the Tomb of Aradia.

But when a reclusive billionaire beats him to the artifact, Jules has no choice but to join forces with an institute of unconventional archaeologists who reveal to him clues penned two thousand years ago, and who claim the bangle holds properties that science cannot explain. And Jules appears to be the only person who can activate them.

As both parties race to decipher the bangle's origins, they uncover a trail meant only for the holiest of men, leading to an apostle's manuscript, the hunt for a tomb alleged to conceal great power, and a breathless, globe-trotting adventure that threatens to destroy them all.

## THE DEAD AND THE MISSING

*A brutal international underworld. A lost girl. A PI who will burn it all.*

Adam Park is an ex-private investigator, now too wealthy to need a job. But when his old mentor's niece rips off a local criminal and flees the UK, Adam tracks the young woman and her violent, manipulative boyfriend through the Parisian underground. Here, and onward in Asia, he learns of a brutal criminal enterprise for whom people are just a business commodity.

To return the girl safely and protect the ones he loves, Adam will need to burn down his concepts of right and wrong, at any cost to his soul.

Printed in Great Britain
by Amazon